Accolades for Pamela Fagan

2014 USA Best Book Award Finalist
2014 Amazon Breakthrough Novel Award Quarter-finalist
2013 USA Best Book Award Finalist
2012 Winner of the Houston Writers Guild Ghost Story Contest
2012 USA Best Book Award Winner
2011 Winner of the Houston Writers Guild Novel Contest
2010 Winner of the Writers League of Texas Romance Contest

The Emily Series

"Grabs you by the throat from the get-go for a suspenseful, rollicking ride." — Ken Oder, author of *The Closing*

"Full of heart, humor, vivid characters, and suspense. Hutchins has done it again!" — Gay Yellen, author of *The Body Business*

"Hutchins is a master of tension." — R.L. Nolen, author of *Deadly Thyme*

"Intriguing mystery . . . captivating romance." — Patricia Flaherty Pagan, author of *Trail Ways Pilgrims*

"In my book . . . the makings of a great novel: cheating husbands, murder, and hot cowboys." — Melissa Algood, contributing author, *Eclectically Criminal*

The Michele Series

"Immediately hooked." — Terry Sykes-Bradshaw, author of *Sibling Revelry*

"Spellbinding." — Jo Bryan, Dry Creek Book Club

"Fast-paced mystery." ——Deb Krenzer, Book Reviewer

"Can't put it down." — Cathy Bader, Reader

"Full of real characters and powerful emotions." — Rhonda Erb, Editor

Heaven to Betsy

The Emily Series #1

By Pamela Fagan Hutchins

SkipJack Publishing books may be purchased for educational, business, or sales promotional use. For information, please write SkipJack Publishing.

First U.S. Edition
Pamela Fagan Hutchins

Heaven to Betsy/Pamela Fagan Hutchins
ISBN-13 978-1-939889-25-6 (SkipJack Publishing)

Dedication

To Eric, who I wish I knew then but am glad I know now.

Foreword

Heaven to Betsy is a work of fiction. Period. Any resemblance to actual persons, places, things, or events is just a lucky coincidence.

Table of Contents

Chapter One

I wedged myself up to the bar between an urban cowboy and a sequined octogenarian with a cigarette dangling from her lips. *Is that a gun in your holster or are you just glad to see me?* I shied away from Little Joe Cartwright or Brett Maverick or whoever the heck he thought he was while also trying to avoid the business end of Grandma's cancer stick. I looked up at myself in the mirror behind the premium liquor bottles, a head shorter than the cowboy and a head taller than the little old lady—and a damn sight more harried looking than either of them.

Why did everything have to be so hard? All I wanted was one teensy-tiny little drink. Well, that wasn't completely true. I also wanted as far away from my mother as I could get. Siberia-far, or maybe even Pluto-far. Oklahoma City-far would do in a pinch. Across the lobby from her in a hotel—which now called itself a Wyndham but which everyone in Amarillo would forever know as the Ambassador—wasn't nearly far enough. Especially since we were there for the wedding reception of my high school boyfriend, Scott, to his third wife—who was nineteen and pregnant.

I raised a finger and leaned across the wooden bar, trying to catch the attention of the bartender. Too late, I felt the wetness. I looked down. I'd plopped my breasts into someone else's spilled drink. Great. Just then, the bartender's blue-shadowed eyes swept over me.

"Virgin mojito, please," I said.

All I got was the back of her orange hair, teased so high it looked like cotton candy, Halloween-style. I grabbed a fistful of napkins from a dispenser and mopped up Lake Titicaca—the bar top and the underside of my rack. At least I'd worn a simple black dress tonight, so it wouldn't show. Much.

"Need some help, Blondie?" Little Joe asked. His voice had a rumbly drawl to it—not quite Texan but close—which I might have found pleasant if he hadn't called me by my hair color.

I studied him. He was tall, well over six feet—at least with his boots on—and a good ten years older than me, judging by his crow's feet. Age, or was it weathering? My eyes slipped down to his boots. The leather was worn, but cared-for, with a few dark lines of oil tracking scratch marks and scuffs. I flicked my eyes quickly back up, but not so fast that they didn't take in his narrow hips circled by a brown leather belt and his flat stomach behind the silver and turquoise buckle, the deep chest, and the wide set of his shoulders. His upper lip looked lighter than the rest of his face, like he normally wore a mustache and had just recently shaved it off, and whatever had weathered his face didn't hide his great cheekbones or the lone dimple to the left of his half-smiling mouth. Maybe Little Joe wasn't a city slicker after all.

Willie Nelson crooned in the background. He was a regular artist on the soundtrack to my life—my heroes have always been cowboys. Yeah, Willie, mine too, until they weren't. Back in another life, I'd had a weakness for Little Joe's type. I couldn't help it, really. I was the daughter of a steer-wrestling father. And now it wasn't just cowboys that had let me down, but the male species in general. So, did I need some help, from *this cowboy*?

"I don't think—"

"What're ya drinkin', sir?" the bartender asked.

Steam whistled from my ears like I was some fancy-schmancy espresso machine. Oh sure, ignore the woman and bring the guy another round. I wheeled toward the cowboy, ready to let fly a string of invectives about him and the barmaid and my whole miserable life in general, but I saw no drinks in front of him. Maybe it wasn't another round. I clamped down on my ire.

He looked me in the eye for a split second—long enough for an unwelcome frisson of pure animal response to unleash itself in my lady parts—then turned back to her.

"Bourbon neat. And a virgin mojito."

Spit in a well bucket, as my father used to say, before he left us for the circuit rodeos one year and never came back. Hell, maybe he was still saying it, somewhere else, wherever it was he'd gotten off to.

"That's really not necessary," I said.

Little Joe flexed his jaw and his lips twitched. "You looked like you had your hands full."

I wanted to tell him to keep his eyes further north, but thought better of it. Instead, I ignored his words and retrieved five dollars from my clutch. Holding one end of the bill, I wafted it toward him.

"Thank you for ordering my drink," I said in my most saccharine voice.

He nodded and took the money. As he straightened it and slid it into his battered, brown leather wallet, he said, "Name's Jack. Jack Holden."

"Emily Bernal." I scrubbed the dry bar with my pile of napkins until the bartender handed me my mojito. No fresh mint, so basically just a lemonade. I sighed. "Well, thanks again, and have a nice night."

He touched the brim of his gray felt cowboy hat.

Before I'd turned away from Jack, my mother's voice trilled in my ear like three-inch acrylic nails scratching across a chalkboard.

"There you are, Emily."

I tried to hide my shudder. "Yes, but I was just headed to the ladies' room."

She beamed at me, reflecting a vision of what I would look like in twenty-five years, if genetics trumped will: Indecently long legs made even longer by stilettos, better-than-medium height, round blue eyes, and dewy, Mary Kay-slathered skin going crepe-y at the edges. She'd fit her trim body—thicker through the middle—in a snug dress slightly less long than was proper for her age, and was wearing the best blonde that money could buy from the shelves of Walmart. Trailer park meets the Southern church lady—that was my mother.

She opened her mouth to torture me. "I was just telling Doug Munroe what a wonderful paralegal you are," she said, "and he wants to meet you. His law firm is really the best in town, and—"

"I'm not even sure if I'm staying," I said. "And I have a job." *And the beginnings of a killer headache*, I thought.

"A job in *Dallas*. If Rich isn't going to do conversion therapy, then you've really got to—"

I pushed back from the bar and flashed her a megawatt smile. Before I could answer, though, Jack's voice interrupted. "Agatha Phelps, always good to see you."

My mother took notice of Jack, tilting her head to the side, and shaking it.

"Oh my, if it isn't the infamous Jack Holden," she said. "What trouble are you causing tonight?"

He wiped a smile from his face. "I have a question for you."

She twinkled. "What is it?"

Jack's voice dropped lower, and Mother leaned in. I tried not to. "What's the difference between erotic and kinky?"

"I'm sure I don't know." She raised her brows. "And I can't think why any decent man should." She leaned closer, twinkled brighter.

"Erotic uses a feather and kinky uses the whole chicken." He smiled on the dimpled side of his face only. "And you know it's only part of my job."

My mother giggled like a tween girl. "That's the only reason I'll forgive your manners."

I shook my head. "I'll come find you later, Mother." They both looked at me, my mother's eyes wide like she'd forgotten I was there.

***

I studied my gap-toothed smile in the bathroom mirror, it and me in a gilded frame, and fluffed my bangs. They needed a spray of dry shampoo and blast of Aqua Net, neither of which I had with me. I turned to the side and smoothed my hand over my stomach. At least there was no baby bump, yet, and my dress was nearly dry. I lifted my chest and shoulders. "Put 'em on a shelf, ladies," my pageant coach used to remind us before we went onstage. That was more than twelve years ago, though, and my shelf was a little lower than it used to be.

A woman's voice from behind a stall door crowed, "Did you see Emily Phelps? I can't believe she showed her face tonight."

A second voice snarked from the stall next to her. "I hear she's not woman enough to keep her man."

They both laughed like she was Melissa-flippin'-McCarthy or something.

I picked my drink up from the counter and tossed it at the ground outside the two stalls. Overpriced lemonade splashed its target, eliciting a squeal.

"Woops," I said. "I guess I'm not woman enough to hold my drink either."

Damn, that felt good. I tucked my five-pound clutch under my arm, pushed out the door, and headed for the pool area as fast as I could wobble on my heels. I'd look for my mother later. For now, I just wanted to stand outside the fence around the little pool at the center of the atrium and imagine myself 3000 miles away from all of this pettiness. I wouldn't have a care in the world, and I'd gaze peacefully into the aquamarine ocean off of St. Marcos, the island home of my best friend, Katie. She used to be an attorney at Hailey & Hart, the law firm I probably still worked for in Dallas. Thinking of her in the same breath as I thought of my woes made me feel guilty, though. She'd emailed that morning asking if I'd heard from her husband, Nick, who hadn't come home last night. I hoped Nick was only a big douchebag like my husband, Rich, and not truly missing. I needed to call her. Well, why not now? Or when I got to the pool, anyway. It's not like I wanted to talk to anyone else.

But I had to make it past the happy couple's receiving line—which I'd already been through, thank you very much—before I could stare at the swimming pool. That is, I had to get through the throng of people who probably thought that I regretted giving Scott back his promise ring when I left for Texas Tech—a throng of very familiar faces, all of them reacting visibly at the sight of mine. A former neighbor, from back when we lived in town. A classmate I hadn't seen since graduation from AHS. Some kid I'd babysat when I was twelve. I fended off each greeting as I braved the gauntlet to the pool, repeating myself into a mantra.

"Oh my goodness!" Lean in, hug without touching bodies. One-handed shoulder-pat three times. "So great to see you. I'm meeting someone, can we catch up later?" Air kiss. "You, too. Bye-bye now!" Keep walking.

Was I as conspicuous as I felt? I tried not to imagine the inevitable whispers in my wake, because, sure as shooting, everyone here knew my business as well as if it had been front-page headline news—above the fold. I tested my face for the confident half-smile I was determined to wear and adjusted the corners of my mouth up ever so slightly.

The chlorine smell of the pool cut through to my cerebral cortex and I sharpened—in a good way. I placed my hands on the black metal top rail of the fence and looked over at the people gathered around the pool at patio tables. It wasn't as crowded as the bar area, but that wasn't saying much. My ex had married another local *and* they'd sprung for an open bar, so almost everyone in town had shown up. But I didn't care if I was alone in the crowd. I didn't care if I was standing in the stripper heels that I'd been forced to borrow from my mother who thought they were high-class. I didn't care if my life was in shambles and my marriage was history. I only cared about the next few good breaths. My eyes found the water, and I sucked in the chemically poisoned air like it was a magic potion. If I could just have about two minutes of this to shock my senses, I might survive the night.

Still breathing deeply, I pulled out my phone, scrolled through my favorites page, and pressed Katie's name. As it rang, I worried about the time difference. I could never remember which time of the year she was two hours later, versus the regular one hour later than me in Texas. Either way, it was only eight thirty here. It would be okay. After three rings, she picked up.

"Emily?"

"Katie! Has Nick shown up? I haven't heard from him at all."

"No, and his plane is missing and the police are no help." Her voice sounded brittle and shrill.

"Are you, um, holding up okay?" She used to have a problem with alcohol. I'd nearly added "sober," but she didn't sound drunk. Just scared.

"I'm not sure. But my in-laws are here—you remember Kurt and Julie?—and our nanny, Ruth. Kurt and I think Nick headed to the Dominican Republic on a case he's working. We're headed there in the morning."

Nick worked as a private investigator, so this didn't sound totally implausible. "I'm praying for you guys."

"Thank you. I was about to try to sleep, not that I'll be able to. How are things with you? Everything good?"

Now was not the time to weigh her down with my problems. I crossed my fingers. "Fine. I'm great, other than worried about you."

"Yeah, you and me both. Thanks for calling."

"I love you."

"I love you, too."

We hung up, and I stood staring at the water, my phone still in my hand. It sounded serious. Nick and Katie had twin baby girls and a preschool-age boy. I closed my eyes and said a short, silent prayer for Nick's safe return, then added, *And help me maintain just a little dignity as I go through all my . . . stuff. Amen.*

A throat cleared beside me, and I jumped.

"So, you're looking for a job?" a man's voice asked.

My eyes, the traitorous little magnets, tracked to the right, following the pull of the sound that I already knew was the voice of Jack, the man formerly known as Little Joe.

"You following me?" I asked.

The dimple twitched. "I do believe I staked my claim here first."

Oh. I didn't have a response to that. I just tried another breath of bleachy air.

"Agatha Phelps is your mother."

I pursed my lips, then answered. "I take it the two of you know each other."

"She roped me into teaching a class on Apache religion and its Mountain Spirits a few weeks ago in an 'Understanding our Neighbor' series on different religions at her church."

I snorted. "I didn't think the Panhandle Believers congregation was into comparative religions."

"Let's just say it felt more like they were gathering information to convert the last of the heathens."

"So why do you go there?"

"I don't." Jack raised an eyebrow at me—the one on the dimple side. "Your mother practically runs the place."

"Tell me about it."

"She talks about you."

The muscles around my eyes and across my forehead tightened up. Someday, I'd owe half my wrinkles to my mother and the other half to Rich. "That's great."

He cleared his throat. "I'm looking for a legal assistant at my law firm."

I reevaluated his cowboy authenticity again and decided he was still the real thing, just urbanized. I opened my mouth to say I wasn't looking for a job, but what came out was, "What type of law?"

His nice, rumbly voice said, "Criminal defense, mostly."

I shook my head. "No offense, but yuck. I do employment law."

The dimple again, but not so much that it pulled the side of his mouth up.

"Based on your taste in jokes, you'd probably enjoy the sexual harassment cases."

"My clients make your CEO harassment defendants look like they're still wearing training pants."

I remembered flipping through the paper that morning, over dry white bread and black coffee, because that's how we roll at my mother's house. What I recalled was a big criminal case, and quotes from the attorney. What was the name? Had it been Jack Holden? Yes. Yes it had.

"You're that attorney who got the super pimp acquitted last week, aren't you?" I said. "Whose client was the guy who ran the prostitution ring cleverly disguised as hot women delivering pizza in tap pants and bustiers? What do they call guys like him? Marketing geniuses? Or sleazeballs?"

He turned to me and dipped his head, speaking only after an uncomfortably intense and lengthy pause.

"You're that woman whose husband took all her money and left her for a man who pretends to be a woman, aren't you? What do they call that, experimentation? Or a fetish for transvestites?" He asked, sipping his Bourbon.

Boom! A sound like a cannon shook me to my pointy toes, followed by a nanosecond of stunned silence. A woman's scream pierced the air just as a loud, slapping sound reverberated from the surface of the pool. Water splashed up on my dress and I gasped. Jack pushed himself in front of me. There was another moment of profound silence, then noise exploded all around us. I was tucked behind Jack, his arms extended low behind him, on either side of me. I stepped around him to get a view of the pool. A cloud of red was growing in the water around what looked to be a man's torso.

"Well, that's something you don't see every day," Jack said.

I looked up from the grisly scene. The man had fallen from above the pool. My eyes climbed, searching each floor of balconies, moving like one of my grandmother's old Selectric typeballs across a blank page. There! I saw her, three floors up, a gun dangling in her two hands, her black hair pulled back, her white apron tied over her burgundy maid's dress. The shooter.

I leaned in toward Jack and pointed at the woman. "Better hurry, she looks like she needs a lawyer."

Chapter Two

The aroma of fresh-baked cookies and brewing coffee filled the air of the Panhandle Believers Church Sunday school wing the next morning. Watercolor renditions of Jesus with lambs, Jesus handing out loaves, and other well-known biblical scenes (featuring Jesus) adorned the pale blue walls. I walked down the hallway searching for Mother, trying to keep my footsteps quiet. Despite the fact that I was possibly the whitest girl in the Texas Panhandle, I liked to pretend I was an American Indian when I was a child, dressing up like one at Halloween, and hanging on Dad's every word as he taught me to move like an Indian scout. I tiptoed over linoleum floors like Sacajawea now, through unfamiliar territory.

I heard a female voice coming from the room ahead on my left. "Any prayer requests today?"

The respondent stopped me in my tracks. "You all know my daughter is home. Her husband has strayed, in a . . . most unnatural way. I need prayers for Jesus to heal his heart and convert him back to . . . relationships with women . . . with Emily."

The silence after her proclamation didn't last. I heard tsks and hmphs and oh mys.

I ground my teeth, but I didn't make a sound. Thank God I'd decided not to tell my mother my really big secret yet—that Rich had knocked me up before I'd found out about his other life. Never mind that it was practically the Immaculate Conception. Or maybe even a toilet seat conception. Our sex life had died off long before he'd met his boyfriend, except for an occasional drunken grope in the dark. But pregnant by your gay soon-to-be-ex-husband? Yeah, the Sunday school class would have had a field day with that little nugget of information.

"Thank you, Agatha. Anyone else?"

A different woman spoke. "My niece got married last night. Thank you all for coming."

A collective coo rippled through the room.

"Some Mexican woman murdered a man in the middle of the wedding. His body fell in the pool. Sue was standing there when it happened, and bloody water splashed on her shoes and dress."

The women in the room gasped, and the woman lowered her voice.

"She was so traumatized she went home with her mama and didn't leave for her honeymoon this morning. She thinks it's a sign that God doesn't favor her marriage. Please pray for Jesus to heal her heart and return her to her husband. And for that woman who ruined her wedding to be brought to justice."

Someone near the door spoke softly. "In Mexico."

And a voice near her said, "Uh huh."

Several more women asked for prayers for their ill family or relatives in the military, and a few others asked for praise for healing and babies and good fortune. The voice of the woman who had asked for the requests then led them in prayer. I turned to walk away before she got to me, and as I did so, I felt something catch on the floor. I looked down. The loose heel on my favorite brown leather riding boots had caught in a tear in the linoleum. I knew I should have glued it down this morning before I left Mother's house. It had ripped clean off.

"Great," I mumbled before I picked it up and stuffed it in my bulging handbag.

"Hi, Emily," said a male voice, grating and familiar.

I looked up into the face of my high school American history teacher. It was a good thing I'd recognized the voice, because I wouldn't have recognized him by sight. The formerly fastidious and slim man had tripled in size, and his hair had all fallen out on top, leaving a ring of muskrat brown on the sides and back.

"Hello, Mr. Walsh. You look well!" I ignored the fact that he had stopped walking, as if wanting to chat with me. "So sorry," I said. "I have to run."

I walked off, my gait uneven in my heel-less boot. I had to get out of here. This time I didn't employ stealth. I'd promised Mother when I dropped her off earlier that I'd join her for church after I finished my errands—I'd wanted to, even. The faith of my youth had deserted me in my twenties, and I yearned to return to it now that I was in crisis, to take sanctuary in it. To be the twelve-year-old who was baptized during vacation Bible school. The girl who felt real joy in her heart. But Mother had made me seem salacious to her friends here, and it didn't sit well with me. Their whole interaction didn't, really.

"Emily!"

I wasn't surprised to hear my mother's voice behind me. I waited for her to catch up. She had a bright smile on her face, but there was worry in her eyes.

"Yes?"

"Aren't you still joining me for church?"

I looked at the ceiling then back at her. "I don't think so."

"But I told all my friends—"

"Yes, I heard."

She lowered her voice and fussed with the lapel of her sunflower-yellow suit dress. "Where are you going?"

"I don't really know."

"What's wrong?" She grasped my wrist. "Emily, don't be ashamed because of what Rich has done. God loves you."

I pulled my wrist away. "Ashamed? Why would I be ashamed?"

Rich had cheated on me and humiliated me, but, when I got really quiet inside, I ached for the Rich I used to know. I hated that he felt he had to live a lie. Not bad enough that I forgave him for ruining my life, but still, it was sad that he'd spent years pretending. I didn't cause Rich to be Rich, and I sure didn't feel he could take a pill or go through "therapy" and be cured of being himself.

A sharp noise came from my throat. "It isn't God I have the problem with."

I pushed open the front door of the church and burst into the blinding sunlight. I turned back to look at the building. Brown brick. White trim and cross. Sprawling two-stories surrounded by black asphalt parking lots. It was a normal-enough-looking church. So what was wrong with it? As much as I needed solace right now, why couldn't I find it here? Was it the church, or was it me? The words of the women in the Sunday school room rang through my head again. If those were the people in a normal church, then maybe the congregation I was looking for wasn't normal at all. I headed for the car.

Five minutes later, I slipped into a booth at Whataburger with a copy of the Sunday paper and a small coffee. I took out my phone and pulled up my bank app to look at my account balances. I had seven hundred thirteen dollars in my checking account, down from the one thousand I'd had the last time I checked. Spit, I'd forgotten about using my debit card for my plane ticket here. This was all I had left from my last paycheck, and Rich had drained our joint accounts dry. I'd used up my paid time off with my law firm, and I wasn't sure how much more unpaid time they'd grant me. It was time to either find a job here or go back to Dallas—immediately.

I put my phone down and turned to the paper. A picture of the body in the pool last night filled the top half of the front page. Yellow crime scene tape circled the pool area. I flipped pages, barely reading the words. Sports section. No rodeo articles, but a picture of a small contingent of Kona Ironman Triathlon contestants from the area headed to Hawaii. I shook my head. Exercise for me was riding a horse, thank you very much. I'd leave the swimming, pedaling, and running to the masochists. I took a slug of lukewarm coffee. I took a bigger sip, then a gulp. I flipped more pages, reached the Classified Ads. One more sip of coffee in my cup. I raised it as I turned to the Jobs section, saw the ad for Litigation Paralegal Wanted, and stopped with my coffee cup halfway to my mouth.

***

Polk Street in downtown Amarillo on a Wednesday morning made a Sunday evening in the 'burbs of Dallas look gridlocked. Score one for West Texas. I'd spent many a Saturday night cruising Polk when I was in high school, and it didn't look markedly different than it had twelve plus years ago—except for the late model cars, and the Courtyard by Marriott in the old Fisk Building. Even the iconic art deco Paramount Theater façade and signage had been restored to its original glory. It was amazing how time seemed to stand still here. I turned down Fourth, parked, and walked the half-block back toward Polk.

I was heading to the Williams & Associates law firm, having responded to their ad for a litigation legal assistant in the paper and landing an interview. A few days ago, I would have sworn I'd be back in my Uptown condo in Dallas by now, handing divorce papers to Rich in person along with a piece of my mind. Something inside me, though, just couldn't return to the scene of his crime, and of my pain. Plus, my holdout in the condo would be short-lived. Rich and I hadn't saved much for rainy days. He had a premarital trust fund to turn to, thanks to his wealthy family, but I had no claim to it. I didn't have the money to pay for the place, not on my salary alone. Might as well let Rich move in Stormy—that was her name—or have the hassle of selling the place fall on his shoulders. So, here I was, interviewing for a job all the way up in Amarillo, while some anonymous process server was delivering my divorce petition in Dallas.

"Emily Phelps? Is that you?"

The heavy drawl stopped me as much as hearing my name did. I turned around. Melinda Stafford. My high school arch nemesis. She had teeth so white I wished I hadn't left my sunglasses in the car. Her helmet of chestnut hair gleamed above and around her face. As big as her hair was, her body was as tiny, compacted and sculpted like a yoga master. But instead of yoga pants, she had on a tailored brown jacket and a short, black pencil skirt with chunky leather pumps.

I feigned enthusiasm and choked some perky into my voice. People had plenty of reasons to talk about me without adding snob to the list.

"Hello, Melinda. How are you?"

She dug in the pricey red, orange, and pink Fossil purse hanging from her shoulder. No Target clothes or accessories for her—but then she always had been as shallow as a Texas river in August.

She said, "Fabulous. Just on my way in to work. I'm an ADA here. You know, Assistant District Attorney. Always lots to do."

Of course I knew what an ADA was—I didn't live in a shoebox. However, I hadn't heard she was one.

She pulled her hand out of her bag, producing a business card, which she extended toward me, then held onto it when I reached out and grasped it. She lowered her voice just enough to let me know we were girlfriends discussing something scandalous.

"My mom said she saw you at church yesterday. She's in your mother's Sunday school class, so I've heard all about what you've been up to, and I just can't wait to catch up over coffee. Call me." She released the card.

When Hell freezes over, I thought. I screwed my face up into its brightest smile. "Well, I won't keep you then," I said. "So nice to see you."

Off she went in one direction, and off I went in the other, seething. I should have been used to these excruciating reunions by now, but I wasn't. I needed to rise above them. That, or scat back to Dallas. Neither option set my wick afire, to be honest, but I'd just do the job interview, and later I could reevaluate my life for the millionth time.

It was only half a block to the Maxor Building, site of the Williams & Associates offices. The ten-story tan structure looked so native that it made me imagine it was once a Panhandle sandstorm that had blown itself out and stayed put. We had a lot of windstorms, but most of them blew through. The conditions in these parts were so rugged that many folks gave up and moved on like the storms. Only the toughest stuck around. The ones that left complained that all the cattle feedlots stunk—but that was just the smell of money, my dad had always said— and that the barren terrain was ugly. But not me. It was just different, in a vast way that was big on cloudless sky and Technicolor sunsets. It shouted of freedom and wide-open spaces. You could loosen your belt here, lean your head back, and draw a full breath. You could see a storm coming from a hundred miles away, and you could gallop a horse at full speed forever without stopping or turning unless you darn well wanted to. Those were the kinds of things you didn't realize you missed when beauty closed in on you. Or on me, rather. When it closed in on me, in Dallas. I'd only left this place all those years ago because it was time for me to go, not because I hated it.

I pushed the Maxor's glass doors open and walked to the elevators. I got off on the sixth floor and set my chin as I scanned the hallway for the Williams & Associates offices. I found them, just to my right. My appointment was at nine a.m., and it was five minutes till.

This was it. My first job interview in eight years. "You've got this," I whispered to myself. I ticked off my qualifications in my head. I'd worked as a legal assistant at a top-notch Dallas firm. The Texas Board of Legal Specialization had board-certified me as a paralegal in civil trial law. I had a magna cum laude degree in political science from Texas Tech that would have led to a law degree if I hadn't decided it was more important to marry my beautiful Colombian boyfriend. Ah, regrets. Well, despite my questionable personal choice, I was more than qualified for the job.

A text buzzed on my phone. I fumbled for it and read the message. It was from my friend Katie's brother, Collin: *Nick home safe. Katie asked me to let you know.*

I texted back quickly: *Thank God! Great news! How are you?*

I wanted to call Katie to tell her, too, but I held back. I didn't know where the heck Nick had been. And, if he'd done something bad, I didn't know what to say. I was partly responsible for getting the two of them together, and I didn't believe he had it in him to hurt her. But that's what I'd thought about Rich and me. I'd email her later, after I'd had more time to think about it.

Honestly, though, just seeing Collin's name pop up on my phone gave me a little buzz of excitement. Collin was a state cop in New Mexico, and he'd always had a crush on me, according to Katie. He was about as different from Rich as a man could be, which really appealed to me right now. I could do with someone who would make me feel good. Who was I kidding, though? Collin had *always* appealed to me. I just didn't meet him until after I married Rich. I waited a second to see if he'd text again, but then looked at my watch. Four minutes till nine. Time to get a move on.

I entered the offices and sat on a nubby tweed couch in a lobby that was empty except for a desk with nothing on it but a newspaper and a small handbell in the center. The newspaper sat face-up and fully assembled, like no one had read it. Of course, the top story was still the assisted topple of New Mexican Spike Howard into a hotel swimming pool, midwedding revelry, courtesy of the sexy señorita with the smoking gun.

I walked over to the desk and smoothed my hand over the picture of her standing on the balcony, then left the paper to peruse the rest of the lobby. Remington-like prints of cattle drives and buffalo hunts adorned the two full-sized walls, and a black iron, cursive Williams & Associates sculpture hung behind the desk. I listened carefully for a few moments, but only heard the ticking of a clock somewhere out of sight. My foot scrubbed against the Berber carpet. It was brand new, and very nice.

"Excuse me," I called out. "I'm Emily Bernal. Here to interview for the legal assistant position."

A clinking noise sounded from the interior of the offices, moving closer at a rapid clip. A tiny fluff of white dog bounded down the hall. Pomeranian. When it reached me, it stood on its hind legs and placed its front paws against my shins. It couldn't have weighed more than five pounds.

"Hello, you little sweetie pie. What's your name?" I set my handbag on the desk and reached down for the pink rhinestone collar and shuffled through the tags that had given away her approach. "Snowflake. That fits." I crouched down lower and massaged behind her ears. "Where's your owner, Snowflake? Or am I interviewing with you?"

"No, that would be my job," a familiar voice said.

"You're not Williams," I accused.

I tamped down the flicker of humiliation I felt at seeing Jack Holden and his damn dimple. This man knew all about my trials and tribulations and wasn't afraid to mention them in a less-than-complimentary way. Though maybe I'd deserved the way he'd said them to me. I wasn't at my best that night. I stood up, sucking in my stomach and straightening my posture until I reached my full height of five-foot-nine-and-five-eighths in my modest two-inch pumps.

"I'm 'and Associate.' Williams retired. I run the place for him."

I shook my head. "Did you do this on purpose?"

"Do what?"

"Lure me in here under false pretenses?"

His dimple puckered and the left side of his mouth rose. His jacket was gone, and so was his hat, revealing what appeared to be sun streaks in his dark hair. Otherwise, he looked about the same as he had on Saturday night. Pressed Wranglers, lived-in boots, and a vintage, red plaid Larry Mahan shirt.

"I'm pretty sure I placed an ad in the Sunday edition of the *Amarillo Globe News*. Not in a special message sent only to you."

I tapped the paper on the desk with my forefinger. "But the ad said litigation paralegal."

"Yes, we spend a lot of time in court."

"You left out the criminal part."

"Look, I didn't force you to come in today. If you don't want to interview, no hard feelings." He shrugged.

I realized I'd lost my manners, as my dear mother liked to say. "No, no, of course not. I'm glad to be here." I gestured toward the empty chair behind the desk. "I think I must have spoken with your secretary to set up this interview. Is she out or something?"

He nodded. "Yes."

The skin around my eyes tightened in confusion. Was that an answer to my question? It didn't feel like it.

He beckoned me with a wave of his hand. Snowflake fell in behind him and I followed the two of them down a long hall lined with wainscoting and more Western art. We passed a door on the right. He gestured toward it, turning and walking backwards for a few steps. "Kitchen. Bathrooms are back past the elevator." He reversed course again and we kept going, entering a door on the left. "Williams's old office. Mine now."

I drew in a ragged breath. The rectangular room we entered was easily a thousand square feet with windows all along the outside wall. The other walls were paneled, as were the floor and the ceiling. A picture gallery hung on the long interior wall beside me, with what looked shockingly like a real Remington in the center. Around it, lesser—but still magnificent—photographic pieces were carefully interspersed with framed diplomas and certificates. A large, arresting black and white of an old, abandoned mine stood out. Above the mine entrance, a lopsided sign read Sacramento Silver Mine. In the bottom right, the photographer had scrawled *Old Dreams at the Wrong Turn Ranch – Lena Holden*. A relative of Jack's? A framed photo of an old Indian hung there, too—one I couldn't fail to recognize, what with my Indian infatuation in my younger years: Geronimo. Below his picture was a quote of some kind, but I wasn't close enough to read the small print.

A round conference table with six cushioned leather chairs on casters stood in the near side of the room. In the center was a giant desk, and its natural wood beauty was marred only by a maelstrom of papers. Picture frames lined up on the near edge of the desk, their backs to the door. The far side of the room featured built-ins: cabinetry on the outside edges and shelving in the interior. Beautiful volumes of the South Western Reporter in tan, red, and black stood back to front to back along the shelves. A piece of fabric stuck out from the left side of the cabinets, like toilet paper on a shoe. Otherwise, the room was perfect.

"Have a seat at the table."

I lowered myself into the sumptuous dark brown leather and let my hand run across it. "Wow."

Jack sat in the chair across from me and Snowflake settled at his feet. "Williams spared no expense. I got it for pennies on the dollar. What he cared about most was that I carry on his legacy. He did a helluva job preserving human dignity and constitutional rights for decades, from right in this office."

"So his practice was . . ."

"Criminal law."

"Criminal defense?"

"Absolutely. Somebody has to make sure our rights are protected. Mr. Williams had a passion for due process—for privacy, for innocent until proven guilty, and for liberty."

A flicker of something patriotic stirred within me. When put like that, criminal defense sounded like a noble calling. "Is that why you do it?"

"I agree with him."

My flicker died in a wave of irritation. Jack had a way with not answering a question. Well, I wasn't going to beg for it. I pulled a pen from my handbag and a yellow pad from my briefcase.

"Can you tell me more about the job?" I asked.

"I have far too much work, and I need help, but help that doesn't require a law degree. We do a lot of legwork for our clients, and we've got a bunch of them." He chuckled. "Oh, and you were right about the woman in the hotel, by the way. Her name is Sofia Perez, and she did need a lawyer—the court-appointed one. Me."

I blushed. Ms. Diplomatic, that was me. But to think he now represented the killer I'd seen Saturday night, the perpetrator of the murder that was the talk of the town, was a little bit titillating, in a smarmy, reality-TV kind of way. And I wasn't above watching an occasional episode of *The Real Housewives of Orange County*.

"Holy cow, really?"

"Really. And she's an illegal immigrant, and the sole parent of a six-year-old girl no one can find. Sofia is a bit . . . distressed. Can't figure out heads from tails with her."

My heart lurched. I felt something in my gut and realized it was empathy. For the missing child, of course, but also for the killer, which surprised me. Maybe Jack was piping some brainwashing chemicals in through the vents. I tried to refocus on what he was saying.

"And besides all of our existing clients and their cases, we've got some high roller who wants to set me up on a retainer to defend his employees and associates. Could be a lot of work, because they're in a line of business that often puts them at risk for misunderstandings with the law."

"What, the mafia?"

"Night clubs and importing from Mexico. Anyway, I need help. I need it immediately. You told me everything I needed to know about you in the application you sent in with your resume. I assume that if I match your old salary at Hailey & Hart that would be sufficient? Plus, I have a little benefit program for my employees—standard stuff, medical, 401k, paid time off. I can give you a copy of all that paper-work."

Employees? What employees? I hadn't seen or heard a peep from anyone but him. The benefits and his offer didn't make sense, but it was far more generous than I'd expected in Amarillo where the cost of living was so much lower than in Dallas. And, boy, did I need the benefits, with a baby on the way.

"I'm, that's, I mean, thank you," I said. "That gives me a lot to think about."

He bounced his pen tip against the glass table and it made a sharp *clack* noise. "So that's a no?"

"It's a maybe. But I do have a question, if you don't mind."

"What's that?"

"Is Snowflake your dog?"

It had bugged me since I walked in. A big cowboy and a little white dog in a pink collar?

His face grew very still. "I'm responsible for her." He put down his pen and stood up, walking over to his desk.

Another non-answer. Had I touched a nerve? Ex-girlfriend? Ex-wife? Did Snowflake come with the office? God, this recalcitrant man was enough to drive a woman mad-cow crazy.

"Alrighty then." I stood up and wiped my sweaty hands on my skirt.

Jack returned and thrust a business card at me. I was accumulating quite a collection today.

"When can you give me an answer?" he asked.

I read the card. R. Jackson Holden. "Um, tomorrow morning?"

"How about by the end of today? I could really use your help with the Sofia Perez case tomorrow."

My throat felt constricted. The thought of working on Sofia's case excited me, but this was all really fast to make a decision so much bigger than he realized. I couldn't just say yes. A few things about Jack rang alarm bells with me. The office with no employees, the overly generous offer without asking me any questions. And the way he made my palms sweat. Especially that.

"I'll try."

I stuck my semi-dry hand out toward him. As his fingers touched mine, tiny shocks rocketed up my arm. We shook, his yellow topaz eyes boring into me as we did. I looked down at our clasped hands. No wedding ring.

***

The rest of my morning was busier than you'd expect for a woman with no life. I'd brought my walking clothes and made two laps around the minilakes of the Medi Park loop on the northwest side of town, enjoying the fall air and pondering my options. None of them seemed good, and my mind returned to Sofia's plight: a young mother far from home, facing possible life in prison, whose child had disappeared. I didn't know which was worse. And why had she shot that guy anyway? How could Sofia—or any mother—risk a life without her daughter unless she had no other choice? If she was here illegally, that probably meant she didn't have much support either.

I had always turned up my nose at criminal law, but this woman tugged at my heartstrings. Surely the police were looking for the little girl. I sighed. I really shouldn't let myself get caught up in this case when it was unlikely I'd take the job, but thinking about it calmed me in a strange way, in a "You think you've got it bad, Sister—what about her?" way. Because I didn't, even if I *was* about to become a single mom. Not compared to Sofia.

Or to my friend Katie, although at least Nick had returned home safely. Time to suck it up and write that email to her. I typed as I walked, my eyes darting back and forth from the path in front of me to my screen, like I was in REM sleep.

Katie – SOOOO happy to hear Nick is safe. When you have a chance, let me know what happened, and I'll fill you in on a few developments around here.

What I really wished was that I had the money to jet off to paradise to visit her. That I could cry on *her* shoulder for a change. Lord knew she owed me. She'd cried mine soggy for years before she and Nick got together, before she quit drinking. Looking back, it was an odd dynamic. She'd sort of been my boss, and was seven years older than me, but I'd been the one who was married and centered. Now the roles had reversed, only she didn't know it yet. I hit send.

When I'd finished walking the loops, I was queasy and craving veggie curry. Better than craving pickles or fried jalapeños, but it called for an emergency lunch stop at nearby My Thai. I hid in a corner in the back and ate quickly, hoping not to be recognized.

"Ma'am, are you ready for your check?"

I looked up at a waitress too old for her jet-black dyed hair and nose ring. She wasn't the waiter who'd taken care of me so far, but maybe they'd had a shift change. She wore a short-sleeved top, and her arms were covered in tattoos from wrist to elbow. Really, I thanked God regularly that I had resisted extra piercings and tattoos.

"Yes, thank you."

"I know you." She nodded and my shoulders stiffened. Not again. "You're the one who ran your car through the Taco Villa when we were in high school, right?"

I exhaled the tension away with breath I hadn't realized I'd held. "Guilty."

Her words took me back to my Oldsmobile Toronado, which I'd inherited when my father never came back to claim it. The thing was huge, truly defining the "full" in "full-sized," so I'd called it The Boat.

The Boat ejected oil like Spindletop and only turned to the left. What it lacked in drivability it made up for in space, though. One time I crammed eleven of my closest friends in it for the drive to Dick Bivins Stadium for the homecoming football game. Memories. And, yes, I had accidentally left it on and in drive when I dashed into the Taco Villa for a bean burrito (mild, extra sour cream) over lunch during school one day. It had ended up marooned on a pile of demolished bricks that used to be the front wall, engine revving.

"I was there. I'd just finished with a dentist's appointment and was ordering at the counter with my mom. Scared me to death."

"I'm so sorry."

"Oh no, it's okay. You got me out of fifth period."

We both laughed. I stuck out my hand. "I'm Emily."

We shook. "Nadine. I was a few years behind you at AHS."

"Well, it's been a pleasure running into you, Nadine."

"Do you live here?"

I paused. "Just moved back."

"Things are pretty much the same. If you ever need help settling in, though, I could reintroduce you to the Hummers crowd."

Hummers had been the hot hangout before I moved away, and still was.

I liked this woman, and not just because she didn't seem to know a thing about my recently sordid past.

"Thanks. That would be great," I said.

We traded phone numbers, then she held out the check, and I slipped in a twenty and handed it back to her. She smiled and moved on to another table.

My phone notified me of an incoming text. I didn't recognize the number. I opened it to find a picture of Stormy modeling one of my red silk nightgowns at my condo. And looking better than I did in it. My blood simmered. Another text followed it: *This is mine, too.* The simmer escalated to a rolling boil.

I attacked my iPhone with angry finger darts as I forwarded the photo to Rich and said: *Your boyfriend is a witch. While he's invading my privacy, tell him to make himself useful and box up my things and ship them to me.*

I stared at the phone, waiting. Seconds passed, minutes passed.

I felt Nadine's eyes on me and she mouthed, "Do you need anything?"

I pretended to smile, and shook my head no. I stared at my phone again. Still, no reply. Well, in the decision of whether to return to Dallas or stay here, this dropped a few lead weights on the staying here side of the scales. I'd liked my condo and job, but the only thing I'd truly miss in Dallas, besides anonymity, would be Goldie, the horse I rode a few weekends a month. She'd feel abandoned. Maybe someone could show her this picture of Stormy so she'd understand.

I saved the photo in case I needed it for the divorce, or as a reminder of why I was really, really pissed off at my soon-to-be-ex-husband.

Feeling like I deserved a good spoiling after that little nasty, I headed straight for a mani-pedi splurge at Top Ten Nails, which I put on my rapidly expanding credit card tab. I settled into the pedi chair with hot water bubbling over my feet and shoved my sunglasses on. I stuck my headphones in my phone jack and turned on some old No Doubt, then laid back and closed my eyes. One hour quieted the voices of the nosy noo-noos and their ilk in the bathroom at the wedding, and banished the memory of Stormy's picture—somewhat. When I was done, I left my sunglasses and headphones on while I made a trip to Natural Grocers for me, and the Walmart Supercenter for Mother. By the time I'd loaded the last of the bags in the car, I'd churned through my life and job options again and decided to hold out for a better fit on a job, with a less dangerous boss than the mysterious Jack. I just didn't need any more problems. Sofia's or his.

I pointed Mother's 2002 Honda Civic west on old Route 66—better known these days as I-40—and headed for home, passing the ten upended and graffiti-covered cars at the world-famous Cadillac Ranch. Technically, I'd grown up mostly in Bushland, a whopping fifteen miles from downtown Amarillo. Now it was barely on the outskirts of the city sprawl. Yes, at nearly 200,000 people, Amarillo was considered a city, thank you very much, but my dad had wanted a place for livestock. Our little white three-bedroom/two-bath house had fifteen acres and a barn, which he'd deemed just right. The barn had fallen into disrepair, after he left when I was sixteen, and the entire property screamed neglect. He'd taken the horses with him, and Mother had sold the three cows to a chop shop, one by one—much to my dismay—long ago, including even Sir Loin, whom I'd helped bottle-feed when he was an orphaned calf. Other houses, nicer houses, had sprung up around us.

I wished she'd let go and move closer to Panhandle Believers, where she worshiped and also worked as a church secretary, but she was stalwart. She had never divorced Dad, and she wasn't going to leave their home, either. She just lived her life here like it was Madame Tussauds and she was a wax figure, refusing to mention him. It killed me.

An ancient, multicolored Jeep Wrangler with a lift kit was parked in front when I got to the house. It was a vehicle I hadn't seen before. I loaded my arms with grocery bags and headed in. The sound of my mother's laughter from the den greeted me. She had Wednesdays off.

"Mother? I'm home. I have your groceries."

"Thanks, dear. When you're through, join us in the den."

Join us? Who was *us*? "Okay."

The inside of the house/Madame Tussauds had last been updated in my early teens. Red cedar paneling—Dad's stylistic input—made me feel like I was in a cheap ski lodge. The kitchen cabinets were also red cedar, clashing violently with busy floral wallpaper in blue and purple hues. Those had been Mother's contribution. All of this and gold Formica, too, which they'd chosen as a joint project. No wonder I had issues. I dropped the bags on the counter and made a second trip in from the car.

Mother's bright voice burbled one wall away, along with the occasional resonance of a deep male voice. A gentleman caller? When Hell froze over. Maybe it was church business. I put the groceries away, washed my hands, and went to the den. Mother sat on the red brick hearth with an array of photo albums at her feet. Beside her perched my omnipresent new friend Jack with one of the albums splayed across his knees. They both looked up when I came in.

I didn't bother to sit, just stood in the doorway. "What are you doing here?" I asked.

"Background check."

"I didn't say I'd take the job."

He shrugged. "Formalities."

"And you don't need to do it in person. With my mother." I glared at her, to make sure she knew this was not okay with me.

"Mother knows best," he said. Mine beamed. "Besides, when I saw you lived halfway to Heaven, I couldn't resist."

"Halfway to Heaven?"

"Nearer to the Land of Enchantment anyway."

I gaped, still uncomprehending.

"New Mexico," he continued. "My home state."

Heaven. Well, it kind of fit this place, in a completely opposite way.

He tapped his index finger against a page. "And look what I learned: Miss Rodeo Texas. I couldn't have gotten that by calling to verify your employment."

My jaw dropped.

"And you still have that cute little thing with your teeth." He pointed at his mouth, his lips curled back showing his teeth and altering his voice. Then he made an up and down motion above the crown of his head. "Your hair was even . . ." he trailed off, blinking, then said, "taller."

I stepped in front of him, hand out. "Give that to me."

My mother sighed and clasped her hands in front of her. "My baby girl has always been so beautiful."

An urge to throttle my mother came over me. I turned to face her, then stopped and sighed. It was undeniably my past.

"First runner-up," I corrected.

"Very impressive. It's sure to come in handy in our line of work."

I didn't want to imagine how. "Our?"

"I'm being optimistic."

"Sounds more like presumptuous."

He didn't comment, and flipped a page backward in time.

"Sit down, dear." Mother patted the hearth.

I lowered myself to the bricks. I hadn't looked at this album in years. I didn't want to now, with Jack, but I did want easy access to snatch the offending memory book away if necessary.

Jack held up a picture of a masked and caped woman riding a black horse around the track at Texas Tech's Jones Stadium in Lubbock, her long blonde hair trailing behind her in the wind. "What were you doing here?" he asked.

"I was the Masked Rider."

"Ah." His dimple appeared, digging deep in his cheek. "The Masked Rider of the Red Raiders. At New Mexico State we called you guys the Red Rodents."

I couldn't help laughing, a little.

My mother chirped in. "You should have seen her flying around that stadium, Jack. I was so proud of her."

He winked at Mother and flipped back another page. His face cracked into a lopsided smile. The page was filled with pictures of me riding an Appaloosa. Balancing my weight as she turned around a barrel, low over her neck with my hands on the reins as I yah'ed in her ear, rubbing her behind her ears with her nostrils wide as she heaved for air after a race. I wanted to trace my finger over every spot on her rump. I'd loved Flibbertigibbet, or Jib, as I'd called her, more than I'd loved any other horse, before or since. We were Southwest Region champs my senior year.

"You really did *do* rodeo," Jack said. "Not just the pageants, I mean."

"Scholarshipped and all."

He looked at me, past my mother. "Now I'm *really* impressed. Why barrel racing?"

I smiled wide. I loved it when I got this question. "Because girls weren't allowed to compete in bull riding. But I did goat tying, and I was a heeler and breakaway roper, too."

Mother grabbed my hand and squeezed it. "And she was a rodeo clown. You know, the ones who protect the riders from the bulls."

Gordon, one of the bull riders on the rodeo team at Tech—a guy who was a real mentor and friend to me—had been gored by a bull and died when I was a sophomore. It hit me harder than anything had in my life since my dad left. Gordon was the reason I had taken up rodeo clowning. But that was personal, so I kept quiet.

"That's something I never would have guessed." Jack made an exaggerated stretchy face with his eyebrows high, then nodded and flipped back a few more pages.

One photo took up the entire left-facing page. Me, with braces and two long braids tied off with little pink bows, only fourteen years old, holding an enormous trophy. Class IV All Around Champ, XIT Rodeo. Standing beside me, looking every inch the rodeo cowboy and proud papa, was my father. Incandescent in my eyes, at least back then. His big, scratchy hand had gripped my shoulder, and I could still remember its warmth through my pink snap-front Western shirt.

I reached past my mother, pulled the album to my knees, and shut it firmly. "Enough about me."

Mother put her hand on my arm. "We hadn't gotten to your kindergarten album yet."

Jack stood. "Another time, Agatha." I gave him a few Brownie points for letting the subject of my Wonder Years drop, for now at least. And then he said, "Emily, we have a meeting at the Potter County Detention Center at nine with Sofia. Can you be in the office by eight tomorrow so we can ride out there together?"

I shot a glance at the wall clock. It was four. Nearly end of the day. I pressed my palm against my abdomen, fingers splayed slightly over the cranberry bean-sized embryo inside. I'd told myself I wasn't going to work with Jack. I didn't like criminal law. But something about him knocked me off balance. And the thought of that woman and her child, the promise of getting out of my mother's cloying house each day, and the possibility of distracting myself from my messed up life? All good stuff, and I could keep looking and snag a more suitable job when it came along, if I wasn't so obviously pregnant by then that no one would hire me. Besides, beggars couldn't afford to be choosers and, as Jack had pointed out when we met, I was flat ass broke.

"See you then," I said.

Chapter Three

Snowflake greeted me as soon as I entered the office the next morning. I reached down to let her lick my hand and she jumped on her hind legs around me, dancing like a circus poodle.

"Good girl," I said. "Tomorrow I'll bring you a treat." My abdomen cramped and I pressed a hand into it, then stood back up. "Jack?"

I started walking down the hall toward his office. He appeared in the doorway, his dark brown hair wet, tucking a dress shirt into a pair of slacks. He held his hand up to stop me.

"Let's meet in the kitchen." He said. Then he disappeared.

I spoke under my breath and made a sharp right-hand turn. "Okay . . ."

Jack joined me moments later. We sat in hard-backed chairs at opposite sides of the rectangular wood-topped table. The smell of something cheesy and spicy hung in the air. Chorizo? I'd loved the Mexican sausage until I gave up meat five years earlier. My traitorous stomach growled, then lurched toward morning sickness. Clearly white toast with Mother wasn't going to cut it if I had to face the aroma of Jack's *desayuno* every morning.

Jack buttoned the cuffs on his shirt. "How was the drive in from Heaven?"

It took me only a split second to get his meaning. "It will be much nicer when I have my car here and don't have to ride with Mother."

"Ah, so it's like being dropped off in front of school."

"Yeah, pretty much." Only worse.

Jack tugged on his shirtfront with both hands then used them to smooth it. "So if you don't mind, I'm going to have you work at the desk out front. I set a computer up on it last night, and it's networked with my server."

I hadn't noticed. "And your secretary?"

"Works offsite."

"Uh huh." I wasn't in love with the idea, but this was basically a temp job. And it was better than officing in the kitchen, I supposed, since I hadn't noticed any other rooms in the office space.

"Also, when you come in each morning, if you could ring the bell on the front desk before you come down the hall, that would be great."

I stared at him a few beats then burst into laughter. Obviously he was kidding. I winked. "Okay."

"Thanks, and, really, do it any time you come down the hallway. Just give it a few good rings."

"You're serious? Why?"

"Why what?"

My mouth worked a little, but no words came out.

He threw his hands up. "I like my privacy. Just ring the bell, okay?"

I opened my eyes wide and raised my brows. "If you think that will be sufficient to save you from a sexual harassment lawsuit when you're back there doing," I waved my hand in the air, "you know, pervy stuff, it won't."

He rolled his eyes at me. "If that's all the commentary you have, it's time to leave for the jail."

He unfolded his long body, and I tried not to imagine the kinds of things I wasn't supposed to catch him doing in his office.

"I'll meet you at your desk in five," he said. "It's booted up. Username is Emily. Password is RodeoQueen, no space."

I performed the mother of all eye rolls back at him, but he'd already left.

***

The Potter County Detention Center was a twenty-minute drive from the office out to the middle of nowhere on Highway 60, past the International Airport, near the defunct Air Force Base, and halfway to the metropolis of Panhandle, as in the town of Panhandle, and not the general geographic area. Today was my first visit to the jail, despite my mother's warnings of delinquency and nights in the pokey when I'd come home tipsy three or four times in high school. A spooky, abandoned building loomed on the left side of the highway.

"That's the old jail," Jack said.

It looked like a set for *The Walking Dead*. Gunshots echoed, and I gripped the armrests as cramps hit me again.

Jack saw me tense up. "Shooting range."

We were passing a huge earthen berm. I relaxed, a little. How vulnerable Sofia must have felt on this long, scary drive. Not only was she caught dead-to-rights shooting some guy, but she wasn't even a citizen of this country. If I'd been her I'd have died of a coronary before ever reaching the jail.

Finally, on our right, we approached a large brown sheet-metal building that could have been a warehouse, or a furniture store, or a church—but was none of those. It was the jail. Jack pulled into the parking lot. The building was new-ish, and from the outside it looked like a giant cow poop had fallen from the sky and gone splat. Around it stood nothing but prairie, tumbleweeds, railroad tracks, boxcars, and cattle.

Jack led me through the glass doors into a foyer with linoleum tile squares, brown walls, and a plastic brown "rope" about eight feet long that separated a walkway along one side of the room from chairs on the other. At the end of the walkway was a brown-uniformed deputy behind glass. Jack moved to a line of tape on the floor in front of the deputy. Ahead of us was a sign on the glass that read "Wait behind the line until called."

I shivered and wrapped my arms around myself. The county was paying to keep this place subarctic, but they weren't wasting any money on air fresheners. It smelled like sweat, body odor, and overfull Pampers.

The deputy waved us forward. Jack put his driver's license in a drive-up bank teller drawer. I added mine, and the deputy slid them in.

Without looking up, she said, "What's the purpose of your visit?"

Jack cleared his throat and adjusted his tie, because that's what he had on. A tie. And a sports coat with his slacks. He still rocked his lived-in boots, but otherwise, he looked ready to go to church.

"I'm an attorney," he said, then pointed his thumb at me. "She's my paralegal, and we're here to see a client."

The woman squinted at him under her gray hair, so short it was practically a crew cut. Her eyes were lost in a maze of squinty wrinkles. She nodded. "Yeah, I recognize you. You represented me and my husband when they repo'd our mobile home."

This wasn't the reception I was used to getting when going to meet a client, after years in my shishi Dallas firm.

"Of course. I thought you looked familiar. How are you?" Gone was his almost-Texas accent, and in its place was a sho'nuff Amarillo drawl.

"Yeah, well, not so good. After you lost our case, my husband left me."

"I'm sorry to hear that."

She made a noise somewhere between a snort and a raspberry, picked up a pen, and looked down again. "Bar number?"

He leaned in and lowered his voice. "Double-oh-seven, 855198, license to litigate."

I held my breath for her response, cringing, but laughing on the inside. She looked up so slowly that I almost turned blue.

Her voice dripped acid as she said, "Client name?"

Jack gave it to her, and she typed a few keys before directing us to Attorney Room A3. We left the foyer and walked past some lockers and a bank of visitation phones where another deputy met us. Behind him yet another deputy escorted an officious-looking man with a clipboard. That deputy spoke into his radio, and, a few seconds later, there was a loud buzzing noise as the cage clanked open, literally shaking the floor and sending vibrations through my body. The deputy and clipboard guy entered the cage, and it clanked shut behind them. Another loud buzz sounded, followed by a clank of the interior door. More vibrations. They disappeared into the bowels of the prison, and the inner door clanked again, but not before a loud scream from within pierced my eardrums. More vibrations from the floor coursed through my body.

I started to sweat. All I had on under my jacket was a white tank that looked much more boobalicious than it had two months ago. I hadn't planned to take my jacket off, but the sudden surge of heat made it imperative. I slipped the jacket from my shoulders quickly and crossed my arms over my chest.

Our deputy, a heavyset fifty-something man with a gray buzz cut, introduced himself as Walker. He immediately noted what I was hiding behind my crossed arms with a nod and a smirk, and I scooched my arms further up. As he walked, his keys swung and jangled in counterpoint to his oddly graceful steps. He reached overhead to slap the hallway doorframe as we went through it—for God knew what reason—exposing the lower quarter of his gut, which wobbled like he was an overweight belly dancer. Or one of the hippos in Fantasia. I was transfixed.

"Emily." Jack spoke under his breath.

"What?"

"Keep your eyes in your head. He's married."

I sputtered.

He half-grinned.

The guard stopped at the first of two heavy blue doors that had A3 stenciled in white on them. "Here you go," he said. "The good room. You must be royalty or something."

"Thank you, Deputy Walker." Jack reached for the handle on the door nearest us, twisted it and opened the door. He gestured for me to enter first and whispered, "I think he likes you."

I accidentally whacked him with my handbag as I passed through.

Jack shut the door behind us, and we were alone. A single table dominated the attorney end of the room, running its full length from the doors on either side of it to the chain link fence separating us from the inmate area. There were two chairs on our side of the table, luckily, because I couldn't have gotten to the other side of it unless I went out and entered through the separate door.

"This is—"

"Twice as big as the other rooms," Jack said, interrupting my thought and turning it on its head. "It's bigger because it doubles as the Parole Hearing Room. In the other rooms, we're separated from the clients by plexiglass and have to talk with them on one of those visitation phones. It's a Hepatitis C nightmare waiting to happen."

"That's awful!"

Jack took the chair nearest the chain link barrier and I sat beside him, putting my yellow legal pad on the table in front of me, and my pen to its right.

"It has its upsides," Jack said. "The graffiti on the walls in there is pretty entertaining." He shook his head. "They call it an Attorney Room, but I can't imagine the attorneys are the ones writing 'Railroaded by dirty cop' on the walls."

"Yeah, they'd be more like '4th Amendment rocks,'" I said.

He laughed. "I called ahead to reserve this room so we could bond a little with Sofia. That's hard to do on one of those phones through plexiglass. We need her to open up to us. The only downside is that after we're done talking, she'll be strip-searched." He gestured at the chain link fence. "Since we could pass her a shank or drugs or anything we wanted to for that matter."

"How inhumane!"

"It's a jail, Emily."

"So Sofia will be searched . . . everywhere?"

"If by that you mean anal and vaginal, then yes, everywhere."

Poor Sofia! "And us?"

"Us, what?"

"Are we searched?"

He grinned. Before he could answer, a door opened in the area behind the chain link fence. Jack stood up and I followed suit. Deputy Walker led Sofia in. The tiny woman shuffled toward us in her leg shackles and enormous orange jumpsuit. Her wrists were handcuffed in front of her, and her heavy, dark hair was pulled into a low ponytail. A few wisps had fallen into her eyes and across her swollen, scabbed lips. She sat, eyes downcast, doing nothing about the strands of hair that would have driven me around the bend. She smelled like sweat and fear. The whole room did. I smiled at her, but she didn't so much as blink a bloodshot eye.

"I'll be right here if you need me. Knock twice," Deputy Walker said, pausing to demonstrate the rap-rap he was looking for, "when you're ready to leave or if she gets out of hand. You shouldn't have a problem with her, though." He winked at me, and my blood curdled. "She ain't but a little bitty ol' thing, and she's real quiet."

He exited and the door closed behind him with a heavy thud. We sat down.

Jack spoke first. "Hello again, Sofia. We met at your arraignment Monday. I'm your attorney, Jack Holden."

Her lips moved, and a whistley, Mexican-accented voice came out. "I remember you," she said. "Hello, Jack."

Her accent made the words sound like "Ell-oh, Jock."

"This is my assistant, Emily," Jack said.

"Mucho gusto, Sofia," I said. I'd minored in Spanish at Tech.

"Mucho gusto."

Jack put both his hands on the table in front of him. His thumbs did a quick dance on its surface. "So, Sofia, you understand you've been charged with the murder of Spike Howard, and that I entered a plea of not guilty on your behalf."

She nodded. "And you help me find my daughter."

A scream reverberated through our room. I jumped. It wasn't Sofia, but it sounded and felt like it was in there with us. What in God's name made someone scream like that?

Jack sucked his top lip in, and his forehead wrinkled. "Remember, we talked about that. Child Protective Services and the police are looking for her. Did CPS send an investigator out to meet with you yet?"

Her clasped hands writhed in their metal bracelets. "Si, yes, but they no find her."

"They're very good at what they do. I'm sure they'll find her soon."

"She's only six. We just move here, we have nobody," she said, her voice rising an octave across the words. "Please, you must help her." Her distress was so palpable that my own pulse sped up in response.

"My job is to help you. To defend you. If I am successful, we get you out of here, and you can take care of your daughter. That's what we need to talk about today."

"But I am guilty."

Clank. Buzz. Clank. The loud noises sounded like the ones I'd heard earlier when the door to the central prison was opened.

Jack pursed his lips. "What do you mean by that?"

"I pick up the gun from the table by the bed and I walk toward him, and I shoot him."

He shook his head, even though he said, "Right, you told me that before, but I need to know everything about what happened, so I can figure out how to defend you."

"What do you mean?"

"Well, we can say you were insane—crazy, loco en la cabeza—or temporarily insane." He drew the crazy circles in the air by his head.

"But I not crazy."

"I know you're not that kind of crazy, but the court says that if you don't know right from wrong, even just at that moment when you shot him, that's crazy."

She shook her head slowly as she spoke. "I know it is wrong to kill him, but I have no choice."

Clank. Buzz. Clank.

Jack drew a deep breath. "Why did you shoot him, Sofia? *Why* didn't you have a choice? Tell us that."

Sofia looked down and chewed her lip. We waited. She didn't answer.

"I can't defend you if you don't help me understand."

She looked up and I saw huge tears in the corners of her eyes threatening to spill into the tear tracks already cut through her cheeks. She shook her head, fast and hard this time, then stopped.

Jack glanced at me and gave the tiniest of nods. I shrugged my shoulders and lifted my eyebrows. He glared at me, his eyes throwing daggers. What did he want? I couldn't read his mind. He dug his boot heel into the bridge of my unbooted foot.

"Ow!" I snapped under my breath. Sofia looked at me. I looked at Jack.

Jack mouthed, "You talk to her."

We had a guilty murder defendant and Jack wanted me to take over the interview without any prep whatsoever on my first day of work ever as a criminal paralegal. This wasn't exactly how we did things at my firm in Dallas. Fine. I pushed one hand against my crampy abdomen as I gathered my thoughts. I spoke in my most gentle voice. "Sofia, what's wrong? What's making you quiet?"

She sniffed then wiped her nose with her forearm, causing her cuffs to rattle as she did, but she didn't answer.

If I were her, I would want to protect myself, unless I was protecting someone else. Like a child. "Tell me about your daughter."

She swallowed, hard. "She such a good girl."

Clank. Buzz. Clank. I felt my shoulders tense in response to the sounds.

"Does she go to school?"

Another scream, this one echoing in my cranium and vibrating through my body.

"No."

"What does she like to do?"

More screams. They were giving me a headache behind my right eye. I had to block them out.

A tear dripped down Sofia's cheek. "She color."

"Does she get that from you?"

Sofia shook her head. "When she scared, she sings." She smiled. "I teach her that."

"Does she have a favorite song?"

"'*Tengo una Muneca.*' It mean *I have . . .*"

"*A doll,*" I finished for her, then recited its lyrics, in English. "Dressed in blue with her little shirt and her lace shawl."

"Yes." Her smile widened. "She have a doll like that, too."

Her words reminded me of something I hadn't thought of in years. My mother, tucking my doll in with me, and singing "Hush Little Baby" to us both. Warmth spread through me.

"She must be wonderful," I said. "And you sound like a great mother. Does she look like you?"

She nodded and wiped her nose.

"What about her father? Could he have her?"

"No. We have no one. We are alone."

"Is he deceased? *Muerto?*"

Her head fell forward and she cast her eyes down. This time the tear fell on the surface of the table.

I leaned around Jack, toward her. "Sofia, what is it?"

Her head came back up, and both eyes bored into mine. "I am guilty. They will send me back to Mexico, no?"

Jack stepped back in. "If they find you guilty, yes. Or if you make a deal, probably."

"What is 'make a deal?'"

"Where the State of Texas offers you fewer years in jail if you plead guilty, and you agree. Then there's no trial."

She nodded, slowly, her eyes sharp and smart through her bruises.

He went on, taking his time. "The rule isn't one hundred percent clear, but the INS would hold a deportation hearing, and if they decide you committed a violent offense, and if you have been sentenced to a year or more of jail time, they usually send you back. Do you understand?"

Again, those intelligent eyes took it in, and she nodded.

"But if we get a not guilty verdict at a trial, then no deportation hearing. You stay."

"How long would that take, to be not guilty?

"We would have to go to trial, and that would be several months from now."

"And I stay in here?"

"Yes." Jack turned to me. "Her bail was set at one million dollars. The way it works is that the defendant or someone on her behalf has to come up with at least ten percent of that amount to meet bail. And they don't get it back. Sofia wasn't able to make bail. But if she had, they would have just transferred her to a federal facility to await a deportation hearing, so not ideal either way."

"Oh," I said to him—clank, buzz, clank—and then to Sofia, "*Lo siento.*"

"And my daughter? What about her?"

Jack stood up and leaned on the wall. "It all depends on what happens with you."

Their predicament made my mouth dry and I fought down nausea. I couldn't imagine how she felt. But then I couldn't imagine why she'd killed Spike Howard either, or why she was avoiding talking about her reasons with the only people who could help her.

Again, Sofia shook her head, even more violently this time. "I am guilty. I go back to Mexico. Soon is better than trial. Now. You tell the judge that."

The pregnancy hormones were wreaking havoc on my self-restraint, and I blurted out, "I don't understand. Why won't you let us help you?"

Sofia sat back in her chair. "It's for the best. You just help my daughter."

Jack said, "Sofia, if they deport you, they'll deport Valentina, too. Is that what you want?"

Sofia leaned forward and her voice grew strident. "Please help her. She is little. She is alone. You must find her. We have no family, not here, not in Mexico. She needs a family. She needs to stay here, in the U.S."

Clank. Buzz. Clank. Scream.

Jack stood up straight. "CPS is going to find her—the police will help them—and they will take care of her. She'll have her own attorney and the court will appoint someone special just to make sure she's doing okay. Our job is to help you. Do you really want to spend your life in a Mexican prison?"

Sofia looked at me. "Please, you must find my daughter. Protect her from the bad men. Please don't let them take her away."

Clank. Buzz. Clank. Scream.

Jack's eyes met mine, and both our brows rose. He didn't speak, so I answered her. "What bad men? Has someone tried to hurt her?"

Sofia started rubbing her fingers together and whispering in Spanish. I wasn't a Catholic, nor still fluent by any means, but I recognized Hail Marys when I heard them. She rocked back and forth, rubbing and touching her fingertips and continuing her frantic whispering. I heard a lot of *Dios*, and something about an "Elizabet" but that was all I could make out. She closed her eyes and prayed louder.

A sense of urgency was building in me, like a hot air balloon filling in my chest.

"What aren't you telling us?" I said. "You need to talk. Please, let us help you."

But Sofia didn't say another word.

***

My phone rang almost the second Sofia left. I looked at my screen. It was Rich.

"Do you mind if I take this real quick?" I asked Jack.

"No problem. You want me to wait outside?"

"If you don't mind."

Afraid that it would roll to voice mail because it was taking me so long to answer, I pressed to accept the call, but didn't say anything.

Jack grabbed his briefcase and sidled out the door.

From the phone I heard, "Hello? Is anyone there? This is Rich Bernal calling for Emily."

His Colombian English was stiff and formal, even after twelve years in the U.S.

I put the phone to my ear. "Hello, Rich Bernal, this is your green card speaking."

"Emily, please, you know that is not true." His Rs still rolled ever so slightly. His sexy voice was the second thing I'd noticed about him—after his mesmerizing eyes. Well, neither worked on me anymore.

"I wanted you to know that I received your text," he said, "and that I apologize on behalf of Stormy and myself."

"I've got a way you can make it all better."

"What is that?"

"I need my car, ASAP. Can you have someone deliver it to me?"

"Will you not be coming back to move your things?"

"You can throw stuff in the trunk—anything you haven't pawned or that Stormy hasn't already tried on, too, if you have time. I'll send a mover for the rest, later. Right now, I just need my wheels."

"That isn't fair, Emily. You must know I am no thief."

"Well, your boyfriend is."

He sat in silence for a long moment, and I could picture him pushing back the cuticles on his nails, or smoothing the hair back from his brow. "We must talk."

"About?"

"There are things you don't understand."

"Really? And here I thought you wanted to apologize."

"That, as well. But also how we manage the dissolution of our marriage. What we tell other people."

"I'm going with the truth. We can talk about the rest of it some other time. Right now, I need to get back to work."

"Emily, please wait."

I sighed. "What?"

"Truly, I care deeply about you, and the pain I have caused you pains me as well. I am sorry. You were not my green card. You are the finest woman I have ever met. I was raised under the expectation that I would marry and provide an heir for my father, as he did for his before me, and as my ancestors have done for hundreds of years."

"You know what?" I said. "I care about you, too, and I want you to be happy, despite your family. I just didn't want it to be at my expense. Goodbye, Rich."

I ended the call and set my phone down on the table—hard. My forehead followed it. It was a consolation of sorts that Rich would get more grief from his family than me, but one that made me feel strangely guilty. And I hadn't done a thing wrong. I wanted to hate Rich. I was certainly angry with him. He just wasn't very hateable. Visions of good times passed flitted through my head: breakfast in bed with crossword puzzles, Rich spooning chicken soup into my mouth while I was sick, seeing his car approach when I had a flat, his face in the crowd when I was racing through a rodeo arena. No, he wasn't hateable. And that made me even madder at him.

I couldn't keep Jack waiting. I gathered my things and went into the hall, where I almost didn't notice Deputy Walker escort us out. I loped to keep up with them, which wasn't easy because I really didn't feel so hot, even though I was relieved to discover that there was no strip search on our way out of the secured area.

My mind was spinning from the weird meeting. I still had no idea why Sofia had killed Spike. I had some guesses—maybe he'd attacked her in her hotel room. But she was the only one who could support that theory. And what about her daughter? Where was she? The practical side of me that had worked in law firms for eight years had other issues, too. Like a criminal attorney being so accommodating with advice on her non-criminal issues.

I exited into the parking lot, trailing behind my boss. Well, I couldn't get answers from Sofia, but I could try to get some from Jack.

"So, do you practice immigration and family law, too?" I asked.

"I grew up on the border. Practiced law there."

I felt too crappy to put up with more of his evasiveness, so I half-growled at him, "That's not an answer."

"Every lawyer on the border does a little immigration."

He walked to his side of the Jeep. I followed him. "And family law?" I asked.

"If I need to, yes." He opened his door and got in. I stood there. He lowered the window. "Are you coming?"

"So does the court pay you for all of that?" I asked.

His lips twitched and his eyes twinkled. "I hired a law practice manager, huh?"

I could play this game all day if he wanted to. I put a hand on my cocked hip and tapped my toe.

The stupid dimple appeared, but I refused to let it soften me. He said, "No, the court won't pay us for helping Sofia with her other problems. But she can't afford to pay for anyone else, and she needs help. So, I answer her questions."

"So her daughter? Can we help find her?"

"I answer her questions, but I don't take on free work. I'm not a private detective. The police are looking for the girl. CPS is looking for her. They'll find her. We can't lose focus. Sofia is a criminal defendant. She's our client—her daughter isn't."

His answer didn't sit well with me. I walked around to my side, trying to digest his words, and got in. As I did, a wave of nausea hit me. Ugh. I crossed my arms around my middle and leaned forward.

"You okay?" He braced his hand against my seat back and turned his head to look behind us, then started backing out of the parking space, old school.

"Uh huh. So what's next for her?"

I touched my forehead and felt a thin, cool layer of sweat. This felt like more than morning sickness. It felt like I'd eaten something spoiled, or had the stomach flu. I tightened my gut and stared out the front window.

Jack put the Jeep in drive and it lurched forward, which didn't help my situation.

"We've got to get her talking to us. Find out why she killed this guy and what kind of defense we can put on."

"But she said she wants to make a deal."

He turned on his blinker and the Jeep's engine raced as he transitioned from brake to gas pedal and rolled onto Highway 60. A metallic horn blared. Jack slammed on the brakes, and my body continued forward until it stopped with a painful jerk from the seat belt. I put my hand over my mouth to keep from throwing up and watched a little sky-blue Nissan LEAF drive away, the middle finger of its hunched male driver high in the air.

"Tree-hugging asshole," Jack yelled, saluting him back. He lowered his voice, and his hand. "Sorry. Those bastards make me sorry when I vote Democrat."

He pulled into our lane and accelerated hard.

"Yes," he said. "She says she wants a deal, and I'll make one for her—if she doesn't change her mind first. In the meantime, we need to see if we can find out anything about Sofia's life before last Saturday night, which is going to be hard. Most people who live in the U.S. illegally try not to leave tracks."

His last words hung in the air and chilled me. If Sofia was here illegally, so was Valentina. And, if what Jack said was true, how would anyone ever find that little girl?

Chapter Four

My nausea continued on and off that night and into the morning, but the cramps let up. I'd looked up nausea and cramps in first trimester online, and was relieved to learn it was normal. Just not fun. For about two seconds I considered calling in sick, but it was only my second day, and I'd woken up with an image in my mind of a black-haired waif with huge eyes that begged me to find her and keep her safe. I couldn't very well do that lying in bed. Besides, cowgirls aren't crybabies—that's what my dad had told me—and I had a feeling Jack ascribed to this point of view as well. It was Friday. I would call a doctor if I didn't feel better by lunch; I could lick my wounds over the weekend.

I crawled out of the twin bed I'd slept in for most of my childhood. It was lumpy, thin, and saggy. I also didn't love the western-themed matching bedspread and curtains as much as I had when mother had made them for me as an eleventh birthday present. I missed my California King back in Dallas, with the silver silk sheets and the black satin comforter. Come to think of it, though, I didn't love them all that much, either. They were Rich, through and through. My next bedroom would be all about me, the grown-up Emily—whenever I could figure her the heck out—and nobody else.

I stood at the closet door and surveyed my limited choices. I hadn't been thinking career wear when I'd bolted for home the day after Stormy had, well, stormed in on our romantic dinner—the one I'd made for Rich to celebrate sharing my great news with him. "The rabbit's died" took on a whole new meaning when Rich's scary secret lover showed up in our candlelit dining room, before I'd a chance to even tell him about the baby.

Also, because of that dead rabbit, my clothes would soon be snug. I'd have to get Rich to ship my things. And I'd need to shop . . . and tell Mother. The thought of admitting to her that I'd somehow gotten pregnant just before my husband revealed his double life as a cheating bisexual burned my biscuits. Almost as much as the dread of Rich learning about his baby, and the possibility of sharing custody with Rich and Stormy.

All kvetching about Stormy aside, it wasn't even that Rich preferred a man. It was just that I'd chosen heterosexual marriage, and I thought Rich had, too. If I'd been thrown over for a genetic female, I'd probably be as crazy mad as I was now. But it wouldn't be such a hot a topic of hometown gossip. So, yeah, fact: Stormy being a he who dressed as a she was probably never going to make my life easier. I put my palm over my abdomen. My little peanut and I would be delaying our announcement chat with Grandma as long as possible. Rich? Twice that long. I pulled out a stretchy navy pantsuit and held it in front of me. I would just wear this every day for the next two months and pretend I was stress-eating. Or not.

When I'd finished showering and dressing, I slipped into the kitchen to grab a quick breakfast. Not much appealed to me but, after dealing with the smell of Jack's food yesterday, I knew I had to have more than toast. I tiptoed to the refrigerator in the semi-darkness and opened the door and retrieved a plastic jug of OJ.

"I made coffee and toast," my mother said in her sparkly morning voice.

I startled, and the OJ jug hit the porcelain tile floor, cracking open. An orange lake formed in front of me and I jumped back. "Spit!"

"Sorry, dear."

Muttering under my breath, I crouched to the floor and started wiping up the mess.

"Good morning, Mother."

"How was your first day?"

Church activities the night before had kept Mother out late. I was asleep by the time she came home, so she hadn't had a chance to grill me about my job then.

"Peachy."

I threw the wet, orange paper towels in the trash under the sink.

"Did you enjoy working with Jack?" Mother asked. "He's such a gentleman, and so handsome."

Gentleman was not the word I'd have chosen to describe the man who told the chicken and the feather joke, but whatever.

"He was fine," I said.

I sat across from her at the ancient kitchen table. Art Deco green Formica on a round top perched on chrome legs. It went about as well as you'd expect with the rest of the kitchen.

"You know, you're thirty years old with only one Fallopian tube. If you're really splitting up with Rich, you could do worse than Jack."

She just had to bring up my Fallopian tube. Not what I wanted to talk about at breakfast. Part of me could understand—she'd yearned for grandkids since the day Rich and I got engaged. I reached over and squeezed her hand.

"It'll be okay, Mother. Really. Let's let that go for now."

She sat in silence for a moment. "Any interesting cases?"

I appreciated the change of subject. "Jack's representing the woman who killed the guy who fell into the pool at the wedding."

"No," my mother breathed.

Without her war paint, she looked closer to her age of fifty-five. Lines radiated from her mouth and eyes. Her white-blonde hair hung limp and thin. But her eyes flashed with interest.

"She's not even in this country legally," she said. "How can she afford Jack?"

I nibbled a corner of toast experimentally and swallowed. It went down okay, so I kept going, talking between bites.

"The court appointed the case to him. He has to take it. That's how it works."

She harrumphed. "So that woman doesn't pay a cent in taxes while the rest of us work to pay the bills for her defense when she murders a U.S. citizen in cold blood."

What she said was the truth, or at least part of it. I knew well how Mother felt about this issue. Things hadn't been easy for her, especially after Dad left, and she resented anyone she perceived as getting assistance that she didn't or couldn't get. It was harder for me to decide exactly where I stood on it. Especially after meeting Sofia yesterday.

"Well, she's our client, so you're going to have to make the best of it. Besides, her daughter is missing. She's only six."

She shook her head, pulling her pink, flowered housedress together at the collar. "What will my friends think when they hear you're working on her case?"

"Hear? Why would they even need to?"

"Well, you know. They're all very *interested* in what's going on with you."

I munched my toast and closed my eyes. I wondered if Jack would represent *me* pro bono if I accidentally committed a violent felony against my mother.

***

Right on time I walked through the door of the Williams & Associates offices. Snowflake was waiting for me. I hefted my purse onto the desk and pulled out a baggie. In it, I'd saved a toast crust for her.

"Sit." The dog sat her tiny bottom on the floor immediately. "Good girl." She took the snack I offered her and smacked it with gusto. "Where's the resident despot?" She swallowed but didn't answer.

As expected, the remaining odors of Jack's spicy breakfast lingered in the air. I activated my emergency plan, snatching a baggie of saltines from my purse and popping one in my mouth. I sucked lightly on it, absorbing the salt into my tongue and softening the cracker before chewing slowly. Ah.

I took a seat at my desk. The computer was already on and I wiggled the mouse to wake it up. Shaking my head, I typed in my username and the RodeoQueen password. The computer logged me in and pulled up my home screen. The background was rodeo me, in a crown and sash. I growled, long and low. Jack knew not what he was doing, messing with a pregnant woman first thing in the morning. I opened my settings and clicked through options until I was able to change the offending image. I replaced it with a nice, soothing beach scene and exhaled.

Time to beard the lion in his den. I rang the bell with vigor.

Silence.

Picking the bell up, I started walking down the hall, ringing it for all I was worth.

"Ready or not, here I come."

No answer.

From inside Jack's office, I heard a creak and a thump. Rustling and clacking noises. Then a smack. I made it to the doorway. I sucked in a breath for courage, and breached the ramparts.

Jack sat at his desk, laptop open in front of him. From this view, without his hat on, I could see gray woven into his hair.

He looked up. "Yes?"

I scanned the room suspiciously, looking for signs of the twenty or so people it would have taken to make all that racket. Or possibly a herd of runaway steers. The room was empty, though, except for him. Empty and normal looking. God knew what he'd been doing in here, and I sure as heck didn't want to know myself, but somehow I couldn't keep from asking anyway.

Walking to his desk, I said, "What was all that noise?"

"What noise?"

"It sounded like you were having a party. Or a bomb went off."

He shook his head. "I dropped some books."

"Huh." Maybe. "Well, whatever it was, I just wanted to tell you, you're a thief."

He raised one eyebrow, framing the amber eye below it perfectly. For a second, I stood there, mesmerized. My super-irritating boss really did have arrestingly beautiful eyes. I gave myself a mental slap. And *I* was pregnant and not-yet-officially divorced and *he* had posted my Miss Rodeo Amarillo picture on my computer.

"The picture of me? My computer background?"

"Ah, yes. No, not a thief."

I waited several long seconds for him to elaborate, but of course he didn't. I threw up my hands and let them fall back against my thighs. It was only 8:05 in the morning and already he had me discombobulated. I'd have to learn not to let this man get my goat.

"Well, I'm here. What would you like me to work on?"

He lifted a file from his desk into the air. "Here's Sofia's file. Find out everything there is to know about her."

"Not a problem. I've tracked down enough people in my years as a paralegal—if Sofia's information can be found, I'll find it."

I reached out for the file but he held onto it. I put my hand down.

"And call Judith," he said. "Tell her we'll be there by noon tomorrow and can meet with Paul Johnson after lunch. Ask her to make all the arrangements."

"Who's Judith?"

"My secretary."

Ah, the missing secretary. "Can I get a phone number?"

He offered the file and I grabbed it. He scribbled something on a piece of paper. I grabbed that, too, and read the number. The area code was 575. I held the paper up.

"Where's 575?"

"Tularosa."

"Tula-huh?"

He cocked his head at me. "New Mexico. Near Alamogordo."

I still drew a blank.

He shook his head. "Southwest of Ruidoso, Albuquerque, Santa Fe?"

"Oh. Never heard of it. Why do I call her there?"

"Because that's where she is."

My hand itched. Did I really want to slap my boss? I'd never been a violent person before my pregnancy. I clenched my fist and used my most patient voice: "Why is she there?"

"Because that's where my office is."

"I thought this was your office?"

"This is my office, too."

"You realize you're about as clear as a mud puddle right now, don't you?"

He spoke very slowly and distinctly. "I have offices in Amarillo *and* in Tularosa. We are going to New Mexico tomorrow. Do you hear me now?"

"We, Kemosabe? I don't recall you asking me if I could travel. And for how long?"

He raised his left brow, the dimple side. The man had a lot of left-centric talent, I'd give him that.

"You have other plans?" He asked, sounding shocked at the thought.

Forget slapping. I wanted to strangle him, which made him the second person I'd imagined inflicting injury upon in the span of an hour. Was it them or was it me?

Them. Definitely them.

***

By noon my nausea had abated enough that I decided I didn't need to see a doctor. There was almost nothing I hated more than doctors, even at the best of times. I'd been in Amarillo for two weeks now and *still* hadn't set up an appointment with an obstetrician. It was pretty much a guarantee that, once I did, my cat would be out of the bag. No point in rushing to get to someplace I wasn't ready to go. Plus, I'd seen a doc in Dallas after I'd first peed on a stick. He'd said everything looked fine. I wasn't the first pregnant woman in the history of the world, and I'd survive.

Working diligently through the morning, Snowflake and I learned all there was to learn about Sofia Cristiana Perez of Amarillo via Mexico: nada. As in not a darn thing. Although the file on Sofia that Jack had given me was anorexically thin, I already knew from it that she had no prior criminal record, or any other kind of official record for that matter. Still, I double-checked everything imaginable. I also knew most of the information she'd given us was bogus. She'd submitted the

Social Security number of a woman named Maria Delgado to her employers at the Wyndham/Ambassador. In fact, that's the name they knew her by. The phone number she'd given them was a throwaway. The address matched a mailbox storefront. When she was arrested, she'd given the police a different address, one for a very sketchy apartment complex that didn't have a name, in an even sketchier part of town. That's also when she'd told them about Valentina. The police and CPS had gone to pick the girl up, but she was gone.

That was about all we knew.

I sighed. What now? Snowflake sighed, circled three times, and curled up in a ball under my desk. I rubbed the little ball of fluff with my toes. Jack had left for the courthouse two hours ago, so I was on my own for additional ideas. I found a notepad in the desk drawer that said Williams & Associates at the top in the same stylized text as the wall hanging behind my desk. I co-opted it and started a list.

1. Call apartment's office.
2. Find the real Maria Delgado.
3. Call CPS to find out what they know from looking for Valentina.

I chewed on the capped end of my pen, then added

4. Find out more about Spike Howard.

No phone number was listed online for the nameless apartments. I pulled up the property records for their address. A Michael Q. Scott owned them, though what possible middle name started with a Q, I couldn't imagine. I did a white pages search. Found him and his phone number. Dialed it. When he answered, I explained why I was calling.

His voice was high-pitched, and very loud. "Lady, I don't give out no information on my renters without a court order. They got as much a right to privacy as anybody."

"But—"

"I already told the police and that CPS fairy. Ain't nobody named Sofia Perez rent from me. That apartment's rented by a totally different feller. He's all paid up through December. That's all I care about."

"Could you ask him to call me, Mr. Scott?"

"What, are you deaf? I don't give out no information on my renters."

I thought hard. What did I have left? An appeal to his humanity? "I'm not asking you to give me information, just to have him call me. A little girl's life could depend on it—a little girl that lived in that apartment."

"Yeah, well, I don't know no little girl that lives there neither. So bring me a court order or leave me alone."

He hung up.

Well, I knew more than I had before I'd called, but still nothing about Sofia. I would just have to visit the apartments on Monday. Not something to look forward to, so I prayed I'd find leads that would point me in a different direction. That meant back to my list. I put a star by the apartments' address and moved on to the next item. Find Maria Delgado. Nah. That one would be hard. I skipped to the third one. Call CPS. Much easier.

I dialed the number for the CPS investigator listed in the file: Wallace Gray. An automated voice answered and asked me to leave a message. I said my piece and ended the call. Crap. I looked at the fourth item. Find out who Spike Howard is. That was no easier than "find Maria Delgado," so I skipped back to item two.

I started by hunting for the Maria Delgado that matched the Social Security number Sofia had used for her job. I plugged the name and number into a couple of different databases. On the tenth one, PeopleFinders—voila—I found a phone number with an 806 area code. I dialed and someone picked up on the first ring.

"*Hola?*"

"Is this Maria Delgado?"

"*Yo soy* Maria."

I whipped out my stumbling college Spanish on her, and I managed to glean that a) she had no idea who Sofia Perez was, b) she had no idea how Sofia Perez had gotten her Social Security number, and c) she didn't know nothing 'bout nobody. Not that I believed her, I just had no leverage to get her to talk. I asked for her address, but she refused to give it to me.

That's okay. I had it from the Internet. I read it to her. "*Sí?*"

She hung up.

I put a big star by her address. More fun follow-up for Monday.

Spike Howard was next. According to the *Amarillo Globe News* articles about the shooting, he worked for an import business and was visiting Amarillo on behalf of his employer. I Googled him and found a mother lode of information. I clicked, shuddered, scrolled, grimaced, and printed screens. Mr. Howard was from Roswell, New Mexico. All I knew about Roswell was that some spaceship supposedly crashed there and was covered up by the feds. That, and it was the location for the supernatural show we in Lubbock followed with cult-like glee while I was in college, since Roswell was only about a few hours away.

But where Spike Howard lived wasn't the most interesting part of what I found—though maybe interesting was the wrong word for it. More like the most disturbing part. Spike boasted a criminal record with assault charges going back to his teens in Dona Ana County, which was pretty far south from Roswell. In fact, it was on the border. Those crimes were bad enough, but it got worse. He'd done time under the "sexual conduct with a minor" section of the New Mexico criminal statutes. My stomach roiled as I read an article from the *Roswell Daily Record* that said he and an accomplice—an Amarillo man named Harvey Dulles—had exposed themselves to the ten-year-old daughter of Howard's live-in girlfriend in Roswell, then had taken turns making her touch them down *there*.

"An Amarillo connection?" I breathed. Snowflake snorted and rolled over in her sleep. Yes, Spike's friend Harvey was from Amarillo.

My phone chimed, interrupting me, and I jumped a little, bouncing my chair and jarring Snowflake. She yipped and rearranged herself.

Collin: *Sorry slow response. Traveling. I'm good. How are you?*

I smiled. It's always nice to hear from good-looking men who like you. I couldn't revel in it long, though. I was onto something with my research, no matter how oogie it was.

Neither Spike nor Harvey spent more than five years inside prison, which shocked me. How could child molesters get out so fast? Wouldn't they be the same people with the same tendencies doing the same thing, just to new victims? God, I hoped Jack didn't represent *that* type of defendant. I wanted no part of defending child molesters.

I starting running Harvey Dulles through all my favorite databases. After his release, he'd returned to Amarillo—according to his voter's registration information—and he owned a house here, per the property records, which it appeared he'd inherited from his mother. Spike's connection to Harvey was too significant to ignore. Was Spike really in Amarillo on business, or was he hanging out with his old buddy? Or both? I printed out pictures of each man and put them in my file. Neither one was going to win any beauty contests, but Harvey was especially ugly with a smashed-in nose and shaved head.

A thought chilled me. What if Sofia had taken her daughter to work with her? What if this child molester, Spike, had exposed himself to Valentina, or worse? That would be enough to make a mother grab a gun and blow a man's head off.

My phone rang. Another number I didn't recognize. I answered. "Emily speaking."

The male voice that answered transported me back to Oak Lawn in Dallas. "This is Wallace Gray. I'm the CPS investigator working on the case of Valentina Perez. You called about her."

I straightened my posture. Excellent! "Hi, Wallace. Yes, I did. I'm Emily Bernal, the legal assistant for Jack Holden. He's representing Sofia Perez, Valentina's mother. We met with Sofia yesterday, and she was really worried about her daughter. I was hoping you had some good news about her that you could share with me."

"Nooooo, I wish I did." His voice dropped. "You're not tape recording me, are you?"

That got my attention. "No, why?"

"Because I am not granting permission to be recorded, and I don't want what I say on the news. So, this is all off the record."

"I'm not a reporter. I'm just a paralegal looking for our client's daughter."

"Good." Now he flat out whispered. "Then may I speak frankly?"

I tucked my phone tighter toward my shoulder and dropped my voice, too. "Yes, please." I almost laughed at myself. We were acting like two kids telling secrets on the playground.

"We can't find anyone that has ever seen or heard of Valentina."

I stood up, accidentally knocking my chair back, its rollers not responding on the carpeted floor. Snowflake raised her head. She looked like she was starting to get annoyed with me.

"No one?" I asked.

"No one. Not neighbors, not your client's co-workers. She's not enrolled in school or day care. The police haven't found anything, either." He pitched his voice even lower and softer.

I cupped my hand over my non-phone ear to block out other sounds as he spoke.

"Is it possible your client's, you know, nuts?" He asked.

Was it? I thought about the woman I'd talked to the day before. "Hmmm. I've only met her once. She didn't seem crazy."

Nausea came over me again, and I slipped the last saltine from my baggie and nibbled it silently. Snowflake smacked her lips. I fished some broken pieces out of the bag and tossed them to her. She licked them daintily, then swallowed them whole.

"There was no evidence whatsoever that a child lived in that apartment. None. Not clothes, a toothbrush, toys, nothing. Wait, I take that back. There was one picture on the refrigerator—an odd drawing of a brown person in a skirt. But that was it."

"That sounds promising, at least as evidence of a child. Did you get anything else from it?"

Snack completed, Snowflake stood up and stretched, then whined. I shot her a look. What did the whine mean?

"Yeah, it was interesting. The guy in the picture wore a skirt and no shirt, and he had a big thing on his head—feathers or horns or something. He was dancing or hopping, too. There were two letters in the bottom right corner, an E and a P."

"Where little artists usually sign their pictures. Those aren't her initials, though."

The P could be for Perez, but the E didn't fit Sofia or Valentina. Snowflake's whines had increased in the last minute and now she walked to the door and started howling.

"Nope. But it did look like it was drawn by a child, a young child, although I can't say whether it was a boy or a girl, if that would even mean anything. But there were no pictures of a girl in the apartment. The police said there were none in Sofia's purse or on her phone either."

I shook my head. "That's just odd. What kind of mother doesn't have pictures of her kid?"

"The kind that doesn't have one, maybe." He clucked.

Snowflake's howls changed to glass-shattering yips.

"What's that noise?"

"The office mascot, Jack's dog."

I decided Snowflake must be asking for a potty break, which wasn't a bad idea for me, either. Yesterday afternoon Jack had set me up to take her out every few hours. I snapped my fingers and she leapt over to me as I pulled her leash from my left hand drawer. I clipped it on, then grabbed a doody bag before returning to the subject at hand.

"But Sofia was genuinely upset, to the extent she wasn't acting in her own best interests. She seemed sincere to me."

I opened the door and Snowflake lunged against the leash like a five-pound sled dog.

"As she would, if she was delusional."

"She said she wasn't crazy. Of course, she could be delusional about being sane."

Delusions of sanity. I could relate to that. I pressed the elevator call button.

"Have you *ever* had a murder defendant that didn't want to claim they were crazy?" Wallace asked. "That's crazy right there, to say you're not crazy."

I laughed. "Would you believe this is my first murder defendant? My first criminal case, even. I just started yesterday. I've been a civil litigation paralegal for nearly ten years. In Dallas."

Ding. We entered the elevator and Snowflake paced and whined. I prayed the call wouldn't drop and that the dog could hold it until we got outside. The doors closed and we descended.

The connection held up, and Wallace continued. "So you don't know the first thing about anything, do you, girl? Of course not. You just moved to Amarillo. The real question is why do a damn fool thing like that?"

The elevator doors opened at the ground floor, and we exited—me calmly, and Snowflake like the place was on fire.

"I can't say I didn't know better. I grew up here." Snowflake all but came unhinged as we walked outside to the Maxor courtyard. A huge outdoor kitchen area on the far side of a stone patio dominated the space, but the whole square area was surrounded by grass and mature oak trees nestled against the building's L-shape. Outside a black metal fence, downtown buzzed by us on two sides.

Wallace laughed once, loud, like a bark. "I'm so sorry."

I unclipped Snowflake. Her tags jingled as she bounded into the grass and got down to her business. Atta girl. She looked at me with something like relief on her little features.

"Yeah, I know, but waddaya gonna do?"

"Tell me about it. I got transferred here from Houston. Well, I'd be happy to help you in any way I can. You just say the word and Wallace is on the way."

"I'll take you up on it, and soon. But let me just ask you: Are the police and CPS still actively looking for Valentina?"

His tone darkened. "Absolutely. This mama may be crazy as a June bug, but if there's even the slightest chance some little six-year-old girl is out there alone with all the predators there are in this world, I simply will not give up until I find her."

His words filled me like helium, and it was so real I imagined I'd sound like Minnie Mouse when I spoke. He was one of the *truly* good guys. I bagged up Snowflake's leave-behind and tossed it in the trash before we reentered the building. The dog pranced like she owned the place now.

"Good. Did Sofia tell you anything about bad men she was afraid of?" I asked. "Afraid would get Valentina? She hinted at this with us and then clammed up."

"Huh-uh," he said. "And that would be weird, since she told me she just let the girl stay at home with the door locked while she was at work."

That felt wrong. Sofia didn't seem like the kind of mother to leave her six-year-old at home alone, especially if she was scared of bad men. We hopped an elevator going up.

"Nothing about the father?" I asked.

"She said he was dead."

"Okay, she didn't give you much more than she gave us, then."

The doors parted at our floor. Snowflake lunged against the leash, panting and straining toward the office. I tugged her gently in the other direction and she looked up at me, confused.

"Well, your bad guy angle is new to me," Wallace said. "Listen, the police are still going door-to-door and talking to informants, checking in with homeless shelters, and rousting people in all the usual types of places kids go in that area. We'll keep looking for her. And you let me know if you guys learn anything, okay?"

I pushed the bathroom door open and let Snowflake walk in first.

"I will," I said.

Then I had a thought—I didn't want to go alone to the shady areas I'd have to visit as I searched for information on Sofia.

"I'm going to visit witnesses that may have information about Valentina on Monday," I said. "Some you may have already talked to, but sometimes people decide to open up when you circle back to them.

One of them you didn't mention, though. The woman whose identity Sofia used to get a job."

I'd positioned myself in a stall.

"Could you hang on a second?" I pressed mute.

"Sure."

Snowflake stood in front of me, staring. It gave me stage fright. I closed my eyes. Better.

When I was done, I ended mute and said, "I'm back. I was telling you about going to talk to witnesses. If you'd like to come with me, to any or all of them, you're welcome to. Strength in numbers."

"Would I ever. Who's driving?"

I washed my hands at the creamy tan marble sink. I wasn't sure when Rich would have my car delivered.

"I don't have a car here. Yet." Yeah, that made me sound like a loser. "I'm getting mine shipped to me soon," I added quickly.

I turned to look for a blower. None. I eyed the towel dispenser. Empty. Okay. I fanned my hands, which basically did nothing. I wiped them on my navy pants.

"How about I pick you up at nine thirty? If we have time, I can take you to lunch at the GoldenLight Café. Great burgers and, *Lord*, the Frito pie! You'll probably go into cardiac arrest after your first bite, but it'll be worth it."

I pulled the door open to Williams & Associates, unclipping Snowflake to let her run free. She sprinted back to Jack's office like white lightning. I decided not to tell Wallace that I was a vegetarian—yet. I lowered myself into my chair and leaned my head back.

"Perfect," I said, before giving him the address.

I ended the call smiling. Not that I wasn't going to worry about that little girl—whether she was real or not—but at least Wallace was on the case.

The door swung inward, and my boss followed. My heart did a little acrobatic number in my chest, which annoyed the pee-waddlin'-squat out of me. He had a longer list of bad qualities than Rich, and I went through them in my mind: eccentric, annoying, cryptic, and pushy.

Snowflake careened down the hall and launched herself at him full speed. He crouched and caught her in one arm, mid-flight. She set upon him with kisses and yips.

"Well? Did you break Sofia's case wide open yet?" Jack asked. He set the dog down and she ran circles around the office, jumping on and off the couch during each loop.

"I keep learning less instead of more," I said. "But the police and CPS think she's dreaming up the daughter. They're still looking, but—"

"What?"

He put one arm over his head and one at his waist and did a little mariachi dance. Snowflake stood on her hind legs in front of him then started hopping and spinning.

"We'll plead insanity," he said. "And the APD and CPS will testify on our behalf. That's the best news I've heard all day!"

I raised my brows as my mouth fell open. I didn't know about *Sofia's* mental health, but I was pretty sure my boss was nuts.

Chapter Five

When Jack told me we were going to New Mexico on Saturday, I assumed he meant on Southwest Airlines. I knew things were amiss when he directed me to meet him at the Tradewind Airport. I hadn't ever heard of it, and I was pretty sure that Southwest hadn't either. It turned out that the little airport was only ten minutes south of downtown. Emphasis on the *little* part. It had a convenient location going for it, but nothing else that I could see. Mother drove me, and she pulled into the tree-lined lot, right up behind Jack's car. He emerged from the driver's seat, and I waved at him. He waved back.

I got out and pulled my luggage from the backseat.

Jack, with Snowflake on a pink leash at his heels, came around to stand beside me, facing my mother and her open window.

"Agatha, I hope you're having a blessed Saturday," he said.

I heard the teasing note in his voice, but it didn't seem she did.

"You too, Jack."

Then she bit her lip and my heart sank to my stomach. *Here we go.*

"This trip doesn't have anything to do with that illegal alien client of yours, does it?" my mother asked.

I cringed. I could only thank God that she hadn't added "or her little brown girl" like she had with me last night, as she explained how messed up it was that not only were we paying for that woman's defense but for the girl's schooling and health care. Maybe she'd forgotten I'd married a brown man (notwithstanding that it didn't end well)? My God, if she was that upset about Valentina, I'd hate to see how she'd act if she learned I was pro-choice.

Jack ignored the implications of her comment. I realized I didn't know how he felt about these issues himself.

"No, nothing at all," he said. "We're on a different case entirely."

Which I wished we weren't. I had ended yesterday energized, engaged, and determined. I would have rather visited the witnesses in

Sofia's case today, and maybe I could have turned up some leads on Valentina's whereabouts. A cloudy vision of the little girl I'd never seen had haunted my dreams again last night. In them, we were at a rodeo. I had on my bright red-and-yellow clown uniform and was in the ring, protecting the cowboys when she ran in, a tiny wisp of girl in pink Barbie pajamas. A bull charged toward her and, before I could distract it, I woke up. I wasn't sure it was Valentina, but who else would it be after a day of researching her mother and her?

"Oh good. Well, take good care of Emily. She's been through a lot lately, what with—"

I stepped up to her window, blocking her access to Jack. I leaned in and kissed her cheek. "Goodbye, Mother."

She took the hint and rolled up her window. When I was sure I'd seen the last of her taillights, I turned and started wheeling my suitcase toward a pint-sized terminal. My little bag bounced and hopped across the pockmarked parking lot. It appeared it had last been resurfaced after the Second World War. Jack—and the ever-jingly Snowflake— caught up to me.

He tugged on the sleeve of my turquoise tunic and said, "This way."

He pointed toward a large sheet-metal hangar—not unlike the county jail where we'd met with Sofia—then took off at breakneck speed. Snowflake's legs churned to keep up with him. All she needed was a little buggy behind her and she'd look just like a thimble-sized harness racing horse.

After a few minutes, I'd fallen a hundred feet behind them. A white-hot feeling rose up in my insides and I thought about chucking a rock at him to remind him I was back here. Dear God, what was it with me and all of these felonious urges lately? I scowled, at myself and at my boss.

"'Scuse me, Jack, hold up."

Jack turned back. The morning sun made him look like a young John Wayne on the big screen. "Sorry."

He waited for me, then slowed down enough that I could trot beside him. That worked for about fifteen seconds. The weather was crisp and football-ready, but I was sweaty and lightheaded. I fell behind again, so I reached out to grasp his arm.

"Stop, please."

He did, turning quite abruptly, and my forward momentum plowed me (and my suitcase) into him. He caught me by an elbow on one side and my waist on the other. Even in his grasp I kept going until my face landed against his chest. Somehow, Jack managed to keep us both upright. The impact sent shockwaves of sex-starved pregnancy hormones rushing through my body. With only my knit tunic and leggings separating me from him and his cowboy wear, he felt good. Darn good. Snowflake yelped at our feet, but I tried to block her out and linger in the unexpectedly nice moment.

"Whoa, Bessie," Jack said in my ear.

I bristled. That solved my hormonal problem. "Are you calling me a bovine?"

I wrenched my arm away and stood back on my own two feet.

He squinted at me, looking a little spooked. Then his mouth made an O.

"Uh," he said, "just an expression."

Pausing for emphasis between the words, I said, "Jack. Ass."

His jaw fell. "What?"

"Just an expression."

I raked a murderous glare across his face, daring him to cross me, but instead he grinned ear to ear.

"Jack. Ass." He said it just like I had. "I like it."

"Argh!"

I didn't care that I was yelling as I started marching toward the hangar again, dragging my bag, which by now had a rock caught in one of its wheels, which stopped spinning. I hated that he'd driven me to cursing, and hated it even more that he liked it. He caught up easily and fell in stride with me.

Well, the horse was out of the barn, so I might as well ride it. "Do you mind telling me what the travel arrangements are, Mr. Ass?"

Was it my imagination, or was that a twinkle in the eyes that didn't meet mine? "Sure. I have a Cessna 172—er, Skyhawk. It's very comfortable. Snowflake rides shotgun, so you'll be in back. You can even nap. It'll take about three and a half hours to get there."

This didn't sound right. This sounded really quite wrong, in fact. I swallowed, hard.

"A Skyhawk? Is that a jet?"

He laughed, too loud. "No, it's, um, a single engine, and, uh, it has high wings and a propeller."

Suddenly I saw spots. I didn't look at him, just tried to breathe evenly and get through this spell of lightheadedness. As my vision cleared, I spied a totem-pole-like sign ahead. White arrows pointed from it in all directions. Big blue letters on each arrow identified different destinations and mileage to them from here. Albuquerque was about halfway down: 285.

I gulped a big breath and spoke in a rush: "You didn't think it might be worth mentioning to me that we're flying in a toy-sized airplane? And where's the pilot of this thing anyway?" My voice wobbled like I was singing opera.

He turned to me, and his whole body radiated his grin. "Emily, you aren't scared of small planes, are you?"

***

Four hours and three barf bags later, Jack hollered back to me that we were making our final descent. Snowflake peered out the side of her kennel from where it was buckled into the seatbelt in the front passenger seat.

I shot a feeble bird toward the front seat and muttered, "Not you, Snowflake."

I kept my head in bag number four, my body slumped against the side of the plane, and my head vibrating along with the frame. The engine, prop, and wind noises were unbelievably loud, and I was now attuned to every change in the sounds—and even more so to every bounce and wobble. I already knew we were going down. The only question was whether it was by design or not; I was past caring much.

I decided to sit back up. I loved Albuquerque, and if we were going to die, I wanted the last thing I saw to be the city and the Sandia Mountains, not the inside of the airplane. All I had left was the dry heaves, anyway. I couldn't believe how sick I'd been. I'd never gotten airsick before. It was probably my little bean. I kept the bag right where it was, just in case, and peered out the window.

What I saw cleared my head and dried my mouth instantly. No city. No mountains. Just desert right below, coming at us, fast.

"Jack, we're going to crash!" I screamed, lurching forward and dropping my barf bag to the floor.

I put my head between my knees and my hands over the back of my head. The barf bag had fallen on its side between my feet and the last of my stomach bile trickled out and pooled in a foamy mess that managed to reach both of my soles. At least I hadn't worn sandals.

No answer from Jack. Just then the plane hit the ground with a wrenching jolt. I tensed, ready for us to cartwheel into broken bits and flames. The plane roared, then slowed so fast it was like the wheels had hit a sandbar. My body weight strained forward against my seat belt, and my head bounced on my knees as we careened over rough earth.

And then the pressure eased and we slowed, almost to a stop, and made a tight left turn. The plane rolled forward almost casually, jostling me again, but more gently this time. Slowly, I sat up. No carnage. No inferno. We had landed, and I wasn't dead.

The plane was taxiing down what looked like a little dirt road to a tan metal barn with a silver roof. Beside it was a pole with an orange flag—no, an orange bag or sock of some kind—blowing horizontally in the strong wind. Next to it was some kind of big white tank on thin metal legs. I could now see mountains behind us to my left, which I was very glad I hadn't seen before landing. They were way too close. Where were we?

A vintage blue Suburban was parked near the barn. As I watched, a woman of medium height with long, dark gray hair got out of the driver's side. She was clad in blue jeans and a boxy shirt that, even from a distance, had a New Mexican vibe to it. Earthen colors. Something long hanging in the neck area. As we got closer, I could see that she wore moccasins on her feet, and that she had dark skin, sharp features, and broad cheekbones. She walked to the barn and raised its door. Jack pulled the plane to the entrance, turned it around facing back where we'd come from, then shut it off.

The instant quiet was deafening.

He opened his door and hopped out, then leaned back in, saying, "Welcome to New Mexico."

I thought very seriously for a moment about punching him in the throat. But he was the only criminal attorney I knew, and it was pretty clear I was going to need him to represent me sooner rather than later at the rate my hormones were going. I kept silent and gritted my teeth.

Jack moved his seat forward and stepped out of my line of vision. Outside, I heard the woman greeting him and his friendly reply. I had to pull myself together. I unbuckled my seat belt and carefully gathered up my three full puke bags. Stepping gingerly over the mess in the floorboard, I followed him out, then reached back in for bag four on the floor. I held them up to show Jack, cocked my head, and lifted my shoulders.

He pointed to a barrel inside the barn. "You okay? Need a bottle of water?"

I tilted my chin higher and nodded.

"There's a case of bottled water just on the other side of the hangar from the barrel."

"Thank you."

I disposed of my mess and grabbed a water, sucking saliva like mouthwash through the insides of my mouth to try to make it a little less vile. I uncapped the bottle, took a slug, swished and spit away from Jack and the woman, then greedily sucked down half the contents. Only then did I walk back toward them, smoothing my hair into place.

Jack put his hand on the woman's shoulder. "Judith, this is Emily. Emily, Judith."

His secretary. The one I'd talked to on the phone. I dipped my head. "Hello, Judith. Very nice to meet you. I'd shake your hand, but it was a rough flight and I'm . . ."

She nodded as I trailed off, but didn't say a word to me. To Jack she said, "I had Mickey drop me off, Boss. I thought I'd make sure everything here was all right and ride back to the office with you."

I wondered how much there really was to take care of here, in the middle of a pasture, but she went on.

"I mowed the runway and ran off some pronghorns," she said. "We've got some prairie dogs that have set up down near the end. I don't think they'll be a problem, but you might want to take a look."

Wow. If that was the kind of work his secretary did, I was really glad I was the paralegal.

Jack treated it like her mowing the runway was no big deal. "Thanks. Sounds good."

He got Snowflake out and grabbed our bags while I retrieved my purse. We took our things to the Suburban, and Snowflake and I got in, but Jack walked back to the plane with Judith. They positioned themselves on either side of the fuselage, leaning over at the waist and placing their hands on the struts. Together they rolled the plane a few feet to the tank I'd seen earlier. Jack lifted a nozzle and stuck it into the wing of the plane. Fuel, I surmised. While this was going on, Jack went into the barn and came out with a spray can of Lysol. He leaned into the backseat and appeared to spray it, for a very long time, then brought the bottle back and tossed it in the trash barrel. I burned with mortification. A few minutes later, he and Judith pushed the Skyhawk backwards into the barn. Then they came back out, Jack pulling the door down shut behind him. He fastened a padlock, then followed Judith to the Suburban. He clambered into the driver's seat and she went to the front passenger side.

"Next stop, the office," Jack said, starting the Suburban down a dirt road leading away from the barn and the runway.

The land was dotted with clusters of green yucca (with tall stalks of dried blossoms) and other high desert plants, like tufts of cascading bear grass. There were some whitish-pink and some bright yellow flowered shrubs, neither of which I recognized. The nearby foothills were treed, although we were too far away for me to tell with what. There were no trees out here on the desert plain. It looked so desolate, with no people or buildings in sight—save the hangar behind us. More desolate even than the Panhandle.

The Panhandle might not have trees, but it had grassland—not desert—and there weren't many spots that were as devoid of civilization as this. Heck, as devoid of all forms of life. I felt like I was on the surface of the moon, a million miles away from my own life. Not just from my life in Dallas, but from my reestablished life in Amarillo. From Sofia, who was doing God knew what in a prison, and from Valentina, the little girl I'd never seen but couldn't get out of my mind. I hoped they were all right. There was nothing I could do from here.

My phone chimed. "Sorry," I said. I turned off the ringer and read the text.

Collin: *Emily, you there?*

Me: *If by "there" you mean New Mexico, the answer is yes.*

I hit send. The answer came back immediately.

Collin: *No way! Where?*

Me: *Tularosa.*

I thought I was in Tularosa, anyway. I definitely wasn't in Albuquerque. We could have been anywhere, though.

Collin: *"So you're near Alamogordo?"*

I remembered Jack's explanation.

Me: *Yes.*

Collin: *That's where I am this weekend. How long are you there? Any chance of getting together?*

Collin lived in Taos and was based out of Santa Fe. What was he doing here? And wanting to get together, now, when I was pregnant? He didn't even know I was getting a divorce.

I typed: *I would love it. I'm here for work, just for the weekend. I'll let you know my plans as soon as I talk to my boss. So . . . maybe.*

We crossed a cattle guard and turned right onto a paved highway. I looked back at the entrance, marked with a metal sign suspended above the gate: Wrong Turn Ranch. Wind tossed it to and fro. The name sounded familiar.

"Where are we?" I asked.

Jack turned until I saw his profile and said, "Highway 70. Halfway between Bent and Tularosa. The Sacramento Mountains and Lincoln National Forest are behind us, the Sierra Blancas behind you to your right. We'll be at my office in about ten minutes."

I laid my head back against the seat and let my eyes close. It had been a rough few hours. Judith and Jack talked while I remembered Collin and his 501 jeans, looking as much like Tom Cruise in *Top Gun* as Tom Cruise ever had. I strolled into the dream as the Kelly McGillis character, the instructor in the leather jacket, only I had a baby bump, and Tom Cruise didn't give me a second glance.

I must have dozed off, because when the Suburban jolted to a stop (typical Jack), it woke me up abruptly. I looked around us. We were on a broad, small-town street in a residential neighborhood. Scrubby trees and patchy yards stretched in front of stucco houses—or adobe, I guess they called it here. Jack had parked in front of a small, red adobe house with a Columbia blue door and a metal Kokopelli bear totem painted in the same color hanging beside it. The front yard was grassless and covered in small, red landscaping rocks. An aged bronze sign hung like a flag off a pole. It read Law Office.

Jack put the Suburban in park and said, "Home sweet home."

Chapter Six

Judith ushered me inside. "Lobby," she said as we walked through what once was a den. It now housed an old leather couch and side chair, a coffee table with a Johnny Football-covered Sports Illustrated on top of a stack of magazines. A deer antler lamp sat on an end table between the couch and chair. Black and white photos of mountain and desert scenes adorned the walls.

"Kitchen." She pointed to her left as we walked down a central hall. The small room had white cabinets and appliances on three sides with a wooden table and chairs in the center.

She swung to the right. "Conference room." A large, weathered, round wooden table anchored the room. Burgundy leather rolling chairs surrounded it. A corner table held a phone. Again, landscape photography hung on the walls, these in color.

Judith took a few steps, then stopped and turned to me. "Here's the bathroom," she said, indicating the door on the right side of the hall. "Jack's office." The left. "Mine." The right again. "He had me set an extra desk up for you," she said. "You have your laptop?"

"Yes, I brought it." I patted my shoulder bag. I'd even stashed my clutch in it, since I'd prepped it for airport security. It was nearly two pounds lighter and a few inches slimmer than usual. I flashed her a big smile. Her face remained still. I noticed that, for a woman of her age in such a dry climate, she sure didn't have many smile wrinkles or laugh lines.

She stood in the doorway to her office and pointed at a bare table. "The network cable's underneath."

"Thanks."

She walked in soundlessly, not so much as flinching to show she'd heard me.

Jack came up behind me, his boots noisier than Judith's. "Everything good?"

I nodded. Judith's cold welcome wasn't something I would unload on him.

"What's our plan?" I asked.

"Judith ordered in lunch for our meeting with Paul Johnson. He'll be here at one. That's . . ." he glanced at his watch, "in half an hour."

I had time to brush my teeth and take a French shower, at least. "Is the car unlocked? I need to grab my overnight bag."

He tossed me the keys—a horrible throw—and my left hand shot up and caught them as they went past my ear.

"Why don't you come to my office when you're done and I'll bring you up to speed."

"Thanks. One more thing." I inhaled and my breath hit a wall, stopping shallow. "I have a friend in Alamogordo. Do we have time for me to go out for breakfast tomorrow?"

His eyes narrowed slightly. "We'll leave about ten a.m. Can you be back and ready by then?"

"Yes, thank you."

I rushed through my ablutions in the ancient bathroom. It was so small that my elbow hit the rubber ducky shower curtain while I washed my face. I rubbed my face with a tear away paper towel from a kitchen-style roll, then put on some nude lipstick and mascara. *Still too pale*, I thought. I swiped the lipstick over my cheekbones and lightly rubbed it in. Better. In the mirror, I saw a photograph behind me. The photographer had captured four Native American dancers with elaborate headdresses, their bare torsos painted with white symbols, skirts hanging almost to their knees over moccasin boots. I turned to study it. It was really beautiful. The photographer had signed it in the bottom right corner. I leaned in close to read the name: *Mountain Spirits. Lena Holden.*

I thought about the name for a moment. I recognized it—and not just because of the obvious last name—but I couldn't place it. Damn pregnancy hormones. Besides turning me into a rage monster, they'd siphoned off a fair portion of my brain function.

I took a moment to text Collin before I left the bathroom: *I can meet for an early breakfast if you can come up my way.*

I packed up my bathroom bag and returned it to the car, then went to Jack's office.

His Tularosa digs were nothing much compared to the ones in Amarillo, but it was still a nice, warm space. A rug that looked to be a Native design graced one wall, a bookcase covered another, and UNM Law and NMSU diplomas hung on either side of a large, bare window. The desk here looked much like the one in Amarillo: messy, with picture frames turned to face Jack. Two armchairs with cowhide upholstery sat in front of his desk; I took the one nearest the door. Jack had his back to me, a book in his lap. Snowflake snoozed in a bed by the door, looking awfully at home.

I cleared my throat.

Jack swiveled around and set the book on his desk and closed it. I read the title: *Spider Woman's Daughter.* Anne Hillerman.

"New client," he said. "Paul Johnson. Native New Mexican. Grew up in Las Cruces. Made his money in nightclubs, in New Mexico and West Texas. Started importing cheap art from Mexico. You know, like the metal chickens and geckos. Made more money. Has a ranch just east of here—gorgeous place, near Bent."

He said this like the location would mean something to me. It rang a little bell, but I couldn't place it.

"Not far from where we flew in this morning," he said.

Ah. The bell rang louder. "What are we doing for him?" I asked.

"Nothing yet. He asked me for this meeting so he could explain what he's looking for. He wants me on retainer."

"You mentioned that his employees tend to attract negative legal attention?"

"Yep," Jack said. "Bouncers. Truck drivers. Warehouse guards. Rough types."

"What do you want me to do during the meeting?" I asked.

"Listen. Ask questions. Then, next week, I want you to find out everything there is to know about him."

"That's all?"

"And eat. I have a feeling your stomach is kind of empty."

***

"Hello?" a girl's voice called from the front of the office.

Judith was in the kitchen working on lunch, so I walked out to the lobby. A tall, thin teenage girl in knee-high buckskin moccasins stood there. Freckles covered her cheeks and a large, distinctive nose, but elsewhere her skin was so white it was almost blue. It was her hair that captured my attention. Somehow she'd fashioned her kinky black hair into individual locks, almost like ringlets, except that it radiated from her head, no strand longer than what appeared to be shoulder length. It was part Afro, part dreadlocks, and part finger-in-a-light-socket. I couldn't have made a single hair on my head defy gravity like hers.

"Hell-*lo*." She snapped me out of my trance.

I adjusted my tunic, and cleared my throat. "How may I help you?"

"My father sent me in to find out if this is Jack Holden's office. He has a meeting with him." She dragged out the "fa" in father and dropped an octave on "ther." The girl didn't like her dad much.

"Yes, this is the place."

"He said to tell him he's on the phone and will be in as quickly as he can." She rolled her eyes ever so slightly. "That means don't hold your breath."

"Great. Thank you."

The girl made a show of giving the place a once-over, then walked out without another word on whisper-soft footsteps that put my scouting skills to shame.

Twenty minutes later, Paul Johnson joined us in the conference room. Jack and I made small talk with him as we got situated. He didn't look like any businessman I'd ever known. He looked like a bouncer gone to seed—with a grizzled chin and hooded eyes—who'd stolen himself some fancy cowboy clothes. He stood six foot six in his boots, and he had to be at least three hundred pounds. His buttocks and thighs strained against Cinch jeans, and his girth tested the snaps on his shirt. Despite all of that, he had a ready smile and booming laugh, so I ignored the seediness as best I could and concentrated on the fact that he wanted to bring a lot of business to the firm I worked for, however temporarily.

Judith rolled in a cart and arranged three place settings in front of us. Addressing Jack, she said, "It's from Casa de Suenos."

"Thanks. Good call. Best New Mexican food in Southern New Mexico." Jack smiled at her.

"In all of New Mexico." Paul reached for one of the two plates of enchiladas. There was red chili and green chili—he chose red.

I wondered if any of the entrees were meatless. "Thank you." I reached for a platter of fried things. Fried appetizers were usually veggie. And anything fried was my favorite food group these days. I pushed two onto my plate.

Judith nodded at me. "Avocados Borrachos. Beer battered fried avocados. They're good with that jalapeño ranch dressing."

This was as friendly as she'd been to me so far, and I was so shocked I couldn't think of a response before she turned and disappeared, leaving the door open.

I scooped some of the ranch onto my plate, then added generous helpings of rice and beans. I looked up at Jack, and he nodded at my plate and raised his left eyebrow. It rehabilitated some of the sexiness he'd lost by flying me in a small plane to a dirt runway in the middle of nowhere. I grabbed another avocado and wiggled my eyebrows back. He hadn't put a thing on his plate. I dipped the avocado in ranch, then bit into it. I groaned, and both men looked over at me.

"Excuse me." I coughed into my napkin. "Something stuck in my throat."

Jack's dimple appeared quick as a heartbeat and disappeared just as fast. "Are you okay?"

I felt my checks heat. "Yes, thank you."

Paul dug back into his food, but he was the next one to break the silence anyway, speaking through a big mouthful as he chewed. *Raised in a barn*, I thought.

"Thanks for having me over to talk, and for the lunch," Paul said. "I just bought some property on the south side of 70. I guess that makes us practically neighbors, Jack."

I caught a glimpse of a half-masticated bite of red enchilada in Paul's mouth. My gag response hovered near the surface these days, and that triggered it. I covered my mouth with my hand and pretended to cough again, averting my eyes. I saw the twinkle in Jack's.

"You said on the phone you wanted to talk to me about putting my firm on retainer to help you when there are criminal matters impacting your business dealings." Jack said, not acknowledging Paul's comment about neighbors.

Paul said, "That's right."

This time, he showed us green enchilada, but I was able to suppress my gag. I put my fork down.

"May I ask how you found us?"

Paul popped a whole fried avocado in his mouth and said, "I read about you in the Alamogordo paper, a few years back—when you were still with the DA's office. Then I heard on the news that you were representing that woman up in Amarillo, the one that murdered the Roswell guy, and that you had an office here, too. I said, 'That's the attorney I need to call.'"

Jack stuck to the subject, still talking over an empty plate. "You have employees that have been charged with murder?"

Paul shook his head and held up his hand, still chewing. Too much food crammed in his maw for even him to talk through it? That must be some mouthful. He opened his mouth and sprayed some rice on the table in front of him. I looked away.

"No," he said, "but assault and battery. New Mexico and West Texas. You never know when a man will have to defend himself with deadly force in the kinds of work I have them doing, though." He paused, looked at his food, then back up at Jack. "Is that what that woman in Amarillo was doing? Defending herself?"

I'd known Jack just long enough to see the change that came over him. His jaw flexed, barely perceptibly, and his pupils dilated. His nostrils flared ever so slightly. And he thumped his pen once, hard on the tabletop.

"Run me through your businesses and where you operate. Then we'll need to go over your past legal troubles, and what you're facing now. See if I can help, and how."

I pushed my sadly full plate back, opened my laptop, and started taking notes.

Chapter Seven

After our meeting concluded, I devoted the rest of the afternoon to researching the names of businesses Paul had given us. I wouldn't have thought it in the first ten minutes, but after spending two hours with Paul, I liked the guy. I think he'd even won Jack over. He had a self-deprecating sense of humor and told funny stories about the nightclub business and the escapades of drunken patrons.

As I worked, I kept flashing back on the signed photo of the Mountain Spirits in the bathroom. I went and studied it again and perused the other photos in the lobby. Lena Holden's name appeared in the bottom right corner of all of them. Who was she? I returned to my laptop and resumed work. Finally, I broke down.

"Judith?"

The woman hadn't said a word since I'd returned to our shared space after the meeting, hadn't even glanced my way. In a flat voice, she answered without looking away from her computer screen.

"Yes."

I rolled my chair in her direction—not too close, but close enough that I could talk in a voice that Jack couldn't hear. "The photographs in the office are so beautiful. They're signed by Lena Holden. Is she related to Jack?"

Two eyes sharp as flint slowly rose to meet mine. The hair I'd thought was gray earlier was really more salt-and-pepper. She wore it pulled back into one long braid, and the black strands running through it matched her eyes. Her nose dominated her face, but she was beautiful, nonetheless. Without changing expression, she stared at me until I almost said, "Never mind."

Then she looked back at her screen. "Jack's wife."

"Oh, okay. Thank you. I, um, didn't know her name," I lied, heart pounding.

Jack's wife. I rolled back to my desk, flummoxed. Well, he must have been one of those guys who didn't wear a wedding band. I should have guessed it, given that he never gave a straight answer to a question, but I couldn't help feeling misled.

It took all I had to focus on my work. I'd made it only about halfway through my list when Jack asked me to brief him on what I'd found so far. My research was as gappy as the hair on a mangy dog at that point, so I stalled him for ten more minutes and scurried to pull something together.

When I had myself somewhat organized, I joined him in his office. I gave him the quick run-down on Johnson, looking at my yellow pad instead of up at him. In a nutshell, it was too soon to tell much about his new client but, so far, I'd found nothing that contradicted what Johnson had told us.

"I'll finish the rest when we get back to Amarillo," I said. "Especially the stuff about Mr. Johnson, personally."

"Sounds good," Jack said. "I have a stack of other clients I need to get you started on soon, too."

That made me think about Sofia. And Valentina. "Have you heard anything about Sofia?" I asked.

I snuck a glance down at the phone in my lap to see if I had any notifications from Wallace, but I didn't. Other than him texting to confirm that he was picking me up at nine thirty on Monday, I hadn't heard from him, but it wasn't as if I'd expected to—it's just that I'd hoped for good news.

Jack looked at me funny, like *I* was funny. "The guards don't exactly call me with updates on my clients," he said.

"Yeah, well, I—never mind."

I wanted to pop off at him, but I was tired. Belatedly, I realized that, once again, he hadn't even answered what I'd asked.

From the lobby area of the office, Judith called out goodbye. The front door shut behind her and Jack and I were left alone.

"Time for us to pack up." He stood and grabbed his briefcase.

I stood, too, and asked, "Where am I staying?"

Tularosa didn't seem like it had a lot of hotels, and I had left everything up to Judith, at his request.

"The guest suite at Wrong Turn Ranch," he said as he closed his laptop and disconnected his power cord.

"Where we landed today?"

"Um hmm." He stuck his laptop in his bag. The Anne Hillerman book followed it.

I hadn't seen signs for a bed and breakfast at the entrance. Oh well. It must be a nice place, if it had a landing strip. I felt a flicker of hopeful excitement that sent tingles through my body, reenergizing me, enough that my bad mood started to fade away.

"Okay," I said.

I gathered all my things, then stopped. Even if this job with Jack was just short term, it didn't hurt to try to win Judith over. Plus, maybe I had unknowingly offended her somehow. She'd taken care of everything for me, after all, whether she'd wanted to or not. I would try harder. I jotted a quick thank-you note to her and left it in her chair.

Jack, Snowflake, and I got in the Suburban and drove out of town, toward the mountains. The setting sun cast a red glow across their slopes, and the desert in front of us looked almost golden in the evening light. A pronghorn antelope with large horns grazed off the highway to our right and, in the distance, the rugged desert topography morphed rapidly into foothills.

I snuck a glance at Jack's profile and asked, "Did you grow up here?"

He nodded—and kept nodding for a few seconds. "My dad bred race horses."

My jaw dropped. "You're kidding me. That's awesome!"

The last of my hurt feelings gave way. I could be upset later. This topic was too alluring to resist.

The way his face moved, I knew his left side was smiling and dimpled, even though the part I could see remained basically the same.

"Yeah, it wasn't bad. He and Mom retired to the RV touring life. They stop in a few times a year."

"What happened to the horses?"

"They're still around. There's a full staff and a ranch manager who profit-shares, so it runs like a top."

"I'd love to see it, if we have time."

He shot me a funny look. "I think we can fit it in."

He turned on his left blinker, and we turned into the Wrong Turn Ranch gate.

"That's a funny name," I said.

We drove fifteen feet further and Jack braked at a small sign. I read "If you're here, you've made a wrong turn. Highway 70 is behind you."

I laughed. "I love it."

He was looking at me, so I got an eyeful of the dimple and lopsided smile this time. His wife must love those. Irritation flickered in me, but it wasn't enough to overcome the good feelings that had taken over. Jack drove on, and the road split in two in front of us. The left fork was less traveled. He stayed to the right.

"Airstrip that way." He pointed left.

How convenient that the ranch had an airstrip on their property for visitors. I wondered how many people really flew themselves around, though. It made for a unique marketing angle for a remote B&B, I supposed. It could help to differentiate them for an upscale clientele. Maybe that's why they didn't have a sign for the B&B on the road. Privacy for the rich and famous. I hugged myself.

The road wound to the right, toward the mountains. "We came right over these mountains when we landed?" I asked.

"Yep."

I couldn't believe I'd been completely oblivious to them, but then I *had* been otherwise occupied. Ahead of us I saw the B&B. It was a large, two-story log house set against the foothills of the mountains. It had what looked like a guest house way off in the distance behind it, and multiple ranch-type outbuildings closer-in of various sizes in tan metal with silver roofs. The main house looked well-kept, but like it had seen a lot of history—the good kind.

I sighed. "It's beautiful."

"And really warm for this time of year. Some of the trees haven't even dropped their leaves yet." Jack said. He gestured toward the mountains, and I saw flashes of yellow and red in the treetops, deciduous outposts in a vast expanse of evergreen.

I turned my attention back toward the B&B. Beyond the buildings I saw something even better. I drew a reverent breath. Horses. *Lots* of horses. As we drew closer, I could see that they were quarter horses—really amazing ones—in blacks and rich browns. A truck pulled up to their gate and a black horse with one white sock ran toward it, tail and head both high in the air.

"They even have horses," I said. "What a great place."

"Yeah, I think it is."

Jack pulled to a stop in the circle in front of the house. I got out with my purse and laptop bag and went to the rear to get my suitcase. Jack set Snowflake on the ground and waved me off. I almost scampered up the steps to the front porch, my heart thumping with excitement. What a fantastic getaway this was turning out to be, small planes and barf bags aside. When I reached the door, I stopped. Snowflake sat and looked up at me questioningly. I wasn't sure of my B&B etiquette. Knock, or go on in?

Jack solved it for me. He shouted, "It should be unlocked."

I held my breath, pulled the lever on the front door, and pushed it open. The front entry opened onto a trussed great room. A stone chimney was centered on one wall, stretching to the high ceiling. The stones were enormous, some at least a few hundred pounds. Leather furniture and Southwestern rugs and blankets filled the space. My heart caught in my throat. Most women dreamed of mansions on grand estates or in exotic cities. Not me. I dreamed of a ranch house and horses and mountains and ... I faltered, the emotion of my true situation catching up with me: broke, almost single, pregnant, living with her mother in Amarillo, and about to be co-parenting with an ex and his cross-dressing lover. Well, this was still what I dreamed of, even if I only had it for tonight.

Jack set my bag down behind me. I turned to him, and I could barely contain myself.

"This place is perfect," I said. "Thank you so much!" And then I launched myself at him and hugged him so tight, I heard a little oomph as I squeezed the wind out of him. I let him go. "Oh God, I'm so sorry. I just, well, thank you. This is a real treat for me."

His eyes were wide, but he was laughing. "I'll show you to your room."

"Are you staying here, too?"

"Yes, I am. And if you hurry up and grab a jacket in case it cools off, I'll take you to see the horses."

I grabbed my suitcase and yelled, "Let's go!"

***

Ten minutes later, I was chewing Jack's already minimal posterior down to a nub.

"You could have just told me," I said. "You know, like used words, and said 'Emily, Wrong Turn Ranch is my place.' And then you could have given me a choice whether I was even comfortable staying at the house of my boss, whom I've known less than a week."

He listened attentively and calmly, not batting an eye. When I had finished my tirade, he pursed his lips.

"So you don't want to go for a ride?" he asked.

"ARGH!" I said, almost shouting. "I *do* want to go for a ride. But that's beside the point."

"Well, my point is that we're going to have to hurry." He lifted his head and slung it back toward the east. "Sun's setting."

"Fine."

He nodded. "Fine." He started walking toward the barn again.

"Howdy, Jack," a man's voice said as we approached the largest of the tan structures.

Sliding doors opened to a wide interior corridor. Ah, horse stable—not barn. A sacred place.

"Hey, Mickey. This is Emily, and we want to get in a quick ride before sunset. She's an old hand. Can I grab Jarhead for her?"

A large man with a low black ponytail fastened with a long silver-studded leather strap was halfway down a ladder extending up into a loft area. When he reached the ground, he dusted his hands on his loose jeans, then lifted off a straw cowboy hat and mopped his forehead with his arm. "Evening, Emily."

"Hello, Mickey."

He put his hands on the back of his hips and leaned back, stretching. "Jarhead's fine. He's at the end down there on the left. You want me to saddle him up?"

"No, but do you mind bringing a saddle to fit Emily? Sun's sinking. And how's the big boy?"

"Hopper's good. We brought him in this morning and got him ready for you."

Jack strode down the center corridor, and Mickey fell in beside him. Instead, I lingered at each stall. The horses stuck their heads out. They were beautiful quarter horses and my heart ached with memories and affection. A mare heavy with foal. A stallion, bellowing. A yearling with a bandage on its face. I loved the tough little quarter horses. They were the horses of my youth, bred for power and sturdy like a tank—the mount of choice for cowhands because their sprinting, spinning, stopping, and backing prowess make them ideal for working cattle. And for racing. In fact, quarter horses got their name because they are the fastest animals in the world at the quarter mile.

Then I came to a thoroughbred, which stopped me short.

"You raise thoroughbreds, too?" I asked.

Thoroughbreds are also racers, but over longer distances. They are taller and leaner than the muscle-bound quarter horses, and also more flighty. You don't often see them on ranches out West because they don't have the power, skills, durability, or temperament to make themselves valuable.

Both men turned to me where I was standing in front of the stall of a pawing, snorting black horse. He bobbed his head up and down, then reared on his hind legs. Jack walked back to stand with me and Mickey disappeared through a doorway.

"That's Hopper," Jack said.

The horse calmed down and stuck his head out of the stall like the others, reaching toward Jack, who moved forward and placed his hands on the sides of the animal's head and scratched in long strokes up to his ears and down to underneath his muzzle.

Puzzling. The name, the thoroughbred amongst all the quarter horses.

"He's yours then?" I asked.

"He's a jumper." Jack released the animal and walked to the end of the barn. "This is Jarhead. He's a retired racer."

I went over to say hello to the deep red horse. His hindquarters were massive, and, as he shifted his hooves in the stall, his muscles flexed and rippled.

"Hey, Jarhead," I said, holding my hand out for him to sniff.

Mickey returned with saddles, blankets, bridles, and brushes. "Here you go."

Jack slapped Mickey on the back and turned to me. "You good saddling him?"

I smiled and reached for a brush.

***

"We pasture the yearlings along here." Jack held his hand out, pointing, and swept it to his right, indicating several enclosures. Hopper pranced underneath him, moving forward in a sideways trot that was mostly in place. Jack swung around and indicated additional enclosures. "Mares and foals, newly pregnant mares, and those over there are some more retired racers."

"This is quite an operation."

Jack pushed Hopper into a canter, and Jarhead bounced under me, eager to catch him, but waiting, just barely, for my okay. I clucked and squeezed my heels in gently. The power as he surged forward sent adrenaline racing through my veins. Jib, my Tech barrel racer, had exploded like that at the start of a race. Well, almost. Jarhead was in a whole different class of racer. I reined him in.

"Settle down," I said. "We're just out for a Sunday drive, old boy."

The horse made impatient panting noises in rhythm with his steps. We pulled alongside Jack and Hopper.

"Jarhead placed in the All American Futurity ten years ago. He lives to sprint. Don't be afraid to remind him who's in charge."

At his words, I literally couldn't catch my breath for a few seconds. Jack had me on equine royalty. The world famous All American Futurity had a purse of over two million dollars. It was the richest horse race in the world, and I sat astride a horse who had come in second.

"Holy cow." A smile spread uncontrollably all across my face. "No worries, I'm good."

The left side of Jack's features crinkled and lifted.

We came to a corner in the fences. I recognized two side-by-side posts as a gate. Jack got down and handed me Hopper's reins. He walked to the two posts and pulled them closer together, slipping a wire loop off the top of one, and then lifting that post out of a wire loop near its base. He carried the post and short section of barbed wire fence forward, and I walked Jarhead through, leading Hopper as he danced with high knees like a show horse. Jack left the gate on the ground and remounted Hopper. The horses loped along, and I drank in the arid high country. Highway 70 sloped in front of us to the right, and across it was the entrance to another ranch.

I pointed. "What's over there?"

"Our new client."

Well, Paul hadn't been kidding when he said he and Jack were neighbors. Like, across the street.

We continued uphill and parallel to the road. When we got to the top of a treed rise, Jack pulled Hopper up. We let the horses walk and catch their breath.

Jack waved his hand at the crown of his head.

"What?"

"Your hair." He poofed his palm upward from his crown. "It's got that *Something About Mary* look to it."

I reached up, and, sure enough, my bangs stood spiky and pointed north. Aqua Net and wind weren't a great combination. I tried to smash them down and looked at Jack.

"Uh uh, not yet."

I pressed my palm down to hold them against my head and said, "You may just have to call me Cameron the rest of the night." Hand still holding my hair, I looked into the distance over to Johnson's place. I saw something tall and metallic sticking up in the air against a hillside. "That's a crane!"

"Lots of construction going on."

"Does he live out there?"

Jack pointed further to the east. "See the roofs?"

"Yes."

"That's his house, and headquarters." He turned Hopper back the way we'd come. "Sun's almost set. Time to get back. When we have more time, remind me to show you the cemetery, and the silver mine ruins."

He urged the thoroughbred into a full gallop, and I gave Jarhead a loud "yah" and let the racer feel the old thrill of leaving another horse behind to eat his dust.

Chapter Eight

Clods of dirt flew around me. I was standing in the middle of a rodeo ring. My scalp itched, and I reached up to scratch it under my fright wig, but I had no wig. I patted my head. Something sprouted from each side of the top. Hairy things. Wide at the base and tapering to a point. Hollow in the front. Were they ears? But I wasn't an animal. I brought my hand down, touching my face as I went, and bumped into some kind of mask over my nose. A protrusion. Hairy again, and ending in a smooth button.

Dust settled. I saw a little girl. Dark skinned. A short pink nightgown and fuzzy pink slippers. Long black hair in a ponytail. Her back was to me, and I looked beyond her, toward the chutes. I heard the snort of a bull, an unmistakable sound, a sound of pure testosterone and bad temper. The metal railings of the chute clanged as he threw his body against them, and dust filled my nostrils along with the musky odor of the bull. Metal crashed hard—so hard I could feel the vibrations in my feet—and then the enormous bull was out. Two thousand pounds of writhing, twisting, jumping, thrashing, stomping black fur on the hoof barreled at me, one sharp horn jutting from each side of his head. The little girl turned to me and screamed, catching the bull's attention. A cowboy still clung to the bull's back, one arm raised per the rules, but the bull pivoted his body as he jumped, literally bending his front half in the opposite direction midair, and the cowboy flew off, landing inches from the metal rails. The bull bucked wildly toward the girl.

It was my job to get between the bull and the other people in the ring, but how could I? I'd been out of position when he entered it. My heart hammered in my chest, and I lifted my arms to wave at him, ready to lure him away from her. He swung his muzzle around, slinging snot and saliva, and his eyes locked onto mine. He thundered past the girl and straight toward me.

I gasped and sat up. Heaving breaths, I placed a hand over my chest. My heart pounded inside like Jarhead's galloping hooves. It was just a dream, I told myself, as I sucked in air. Slowly, I became aware of my surroundings. Something smelled good. Bacon. How many years had it been since I'd had any? My hungry stomach lurched.

I flopped into the pillows and pulled the fluffy, white duvet back to my chin. Through half-closed eyes I took in the mountain springtime colors of the room and concentrated on breathing in slowly through my mouth. Bright lavender, yellow, and green accents made the room look like a field of wildflowers. Tall pine furniture brought in the high desert forest. It soothed me. And, truly, it even beat the honeymoon suite I'd shared with Rich in Belize for luxury.

Ugh, I didn't need my ex in my mind spoiling this for me. It made me remember that he still hadn't signed the divorce papers. I wanted them done before he found out about my pregnancy. I'd thought he'd have signed and returned them on the day he got them. What was he waiting for? He'd moved on to his new life already. It was time to let me move on to mine.

I tossed the covers to the foot of the bed and swung my feet over the side. My phone sat on the bedside table, and I snatched it up to see the time. I read the digital display, but in my mind I heard my father's version: The little hand is almost to the seven and the big hand is two freckles past a hair. Collin would arrive to pick me up any minute. I scrambled to the bathroom and broke my own personal record for speed showering and throwing on makeup—without even barfing. My abdomen cramped up a few times, but I told it to cut it out, and it seemed to listen. I gave my nails a once-over. They were rounded and smooth and the clear coat of polish would have to do. Pregnancy had strengthened them. I donned a clean pair of leggings and a red and black tunic with my boots, pulled my ponytail back in place, and dashed down the log-hewn staircase, only fifteen minutes late.

The stairs landed between the kitchen area and the great room. Along with the bacon smells I'd noticed earlier, several voices wafted toward me from the kitchen side on my left—male and female voices, chatting and laughing. In fact, it sounded like a party.

I burst into the slate gray and blue kitchen, but nobody even looked up to greet me.

Jack stood sideways at the stainless steel range, stirring something in a skillet and talking to a man and a woman who were seated in tall, wooden stools at the bar. Jack picked something from the skillet and tossed it downward.

He said, "There you go, girl."

Snowflake.

The vent pulled an aromatic cloud upwards, and its noise masked my arrival. The man seated on one of the stools was definitely Collin— from his dark blonde, military-style hair cut to his twinkling eyes and the permanent smirk that varied from unrestrained to its current, barely visible quotation marks on either side of his closed mouth. He turned and whispered to the woman seated next to him—a woman I didn't recognize. Jack's wife, maybe? She had straight brown hair, hanging shoulder length. In profile, her blue eyes looked enormous while her small nose tilted up just a smidge. She seemed tiny, but muscular, and her voice sounded rough, like a mini food processor.

I realized I was gaping, and I gave myself a mental smack. I was invited to this party, too. I walked up to Collin and said, "Hey, Stranger!"

He stood up and hugged me off my feet. "Hey, you!"

"I see you've already met my boss."

"Yeah, somebody slept in, and we've gotten a tour of the whole 1500 acres. Haven't seen you in over a year, but that's fine, Em, you go ahead and get your beauty rest."

"Hey now!" I socked him in his upper arm. Solid.

Collin didn't even pretend my punch had hurt. "Jack made us mimosas and Irish coffees, and we've decided this is the best breakfast spot in Otero County, so pull up a stool. I'm buying."

"And I'm Tamara." The beautiful little brunette dragged my attention away from Collin and stuck out her hand.

I shook it. "Emily."

Tamara? Not Lena, Jack's wife? So, was Tamara here to see Jack or was she with Collin? Was I supposed to recognize her name?

Jack waved a spatula to get my attention, interrupting my musings. I lifted my eyes to him. His hair looked damp at the ends, and longish. No hat. A white tee with his jeans.

"Want to set the table for me?" he asked.

"Sure."

I scrutinized my boss harder. Host and short-order cook. This I hadn't expected.

"Silverware in the drawer to the right of the dishwasher. Plates above to the left, glasses above to the right, napkins in the dispenser closest to the table."

I set to work on the silverware, counting to four each for spoons, forks, and knives.

"So, Collin, fill me in," I said. "What've you been up to?"

"Just got back from St. Marcos. And Puerto Rico. And the Dominican Republic."

"What?" I stopped halfway to the table, silverware in hand.

"Yeah, I joined on the hunt for Nick," he said. "Long story short: Bad guys sabotaged his plane and it crashed flying out of the DR. Tamara helped us figure out where he went down, and we—Katie, Nick's dad, and me—plucked him off a rock he'd drifted to west of Puerto Rico, then cruised back to St. Marcos on a luxury yacht where we ran into more bad guys and had a shoot-out in a south shore harbor." He took a sip of coffee. "All's well that ends well."

I set the silverware on the table with a thump. "Oh my God," I said. "I knew he was missing and that he'd made it home safely. That's it. I had no idea of the rest. No wonder Katie hasn't answered my email."

I went back for the plates.

Tamara leaned over and kissed Collin long and hard on the lips. "You try to get yourself shot up wherever you go."

I tried to keep my eyebrows from shooting up. Well, that answered the question of who Tamara had come with—and pretty much ruled out an admiring Collin rehabilitating my bruised ego.

"You're no slouch in that department, either." Collin cleared his throat, pressing the side of his closed fist against his mouth. "Tamara flies Black Hawks for the good old U.S. Army. Why she agreed to marry a lowly state cop, the world will never know."

Collin had proposed to a military pilot. It defied imagination. The fact that he was engaged was mindboggling, but to a military pilot? Times two. A stripper would have made more sense, given his past. Tamara held out her left hand, and a big, fat sparkler caught the light from the fixture above. Except the light wasn't even on. The square diamond sparkled all on its own.

I put the plates on the table and flashed a lot of teeth as I said, "Congratulations."

My words came out sort of squealy, and I realized I was a little jealous. I'd thought I was the only woman with class Collin had ever noticed. I looked up to find Jack's eyes on me. Collin's engagement was disappointing, but Jack being married, I realized, had hit me far harder. I looked away from my boss and lifted Tamara's hand to inspect the rock. Snowflake had joined me and gazed up as if to see it, too.

"Gorgeous," I said. "And shocking that a lunkhead like Collin could pick it out."

"Isn't it? And I had no idea he was going to propose, either, so I didn't have any input. But it's perfect. Makes up for most of his other faults."

I looked away from Tamara and the ring, up and across the kitchen island, and found Jack's eyes still on me, assessing me like I'd assessed the diamond.

A fifth voice, a male one, pulled me away from Jack's gaze. "Somebody making breakfast?"

We all turned and Snowflake sprinted across the room. I saw Mickey standing in the doorway, his long hair loose, his jeans clean and pressed. He leaned down and ruffled the little dog's fur.

"I am." Jack said as he turned off the gas under the skillet and pulled it away from the burner. "Everyone, this is Mickey, the pride of Mescalero, New Mexico, and the Wrong Turn Ranch Manager for the last ten years. We're both Aggies, but he got his degree from the Texas institution and played linebacker while doing it." Mickey held up a thumb, the gesture known throughout the Southwest as "Gig 'em," which told us that Mickey had gone to Texas A&M.

The words "Ranch Manager" sunk in. I didn't know why I had assumed Mickey was a stable hand. Heat crept over my face. I felt petty. I'd just been caught in the act of stereotyping, even if no one knew it but me.

Mickey introduced himself to Tamara and Collin then turned to me. "Morning, Emily. How was Jarhead?"

I rallied. "Amazing. I think he wants to move to Texas with me."

Mickey threw his head back and laughed. "Oh no. He's the one horse here we can't afford to let go. His stud fees keep this place running. But he loves attention and needs a lot of exercise, so come back and see him anytime."

"I will."

Jack broke in. "Grub's almost ready. You staying?"

"My wife made me one of those green smoothie things this morning." Everyone else groaned, but it sounded good to me. "But if there's enough, I can help you make sure nothing goes to waste, before we head out to church."

"More than enough."

"Okay, but it's got to be our little secret."

I grabbed one more plate and laid a setting of silverware on it before passing it to Mickey, who turned and put it on the table.

Collin stood up and stretched his arms over his head, exposing a little ab in the process. He'd bulked up some since I'd seen him a year ago. Like he'd worked out more, lifted more.

"Okay, Em," Collin said. "I spilled, now it's your turn. What have you been up to?"

Where to begin? I shot a quick glance at Jack, who stood frozen at the refrigerator door, his eyebrow in a high peak as he watched to see how I'd handle this one.

"Gee, let's see," I said. And without thinking it through, I blurted out, "Well, a lot, like at the romantic dinner I had staged to tell Rich we were having a baby, his lover, a cross-dressing man named Stormy, pulled a Glenn Close, so I moved back in with my mother in Amarillo—which Jack calls Heaven only it's anything but—where I listen to her go on and on about the sanctity of marriage and the wonderful results of conversion therapy. So I filed for a divorce, took a job with Jack, and here I am."

Too late, I remembered Jack hadn't known the baby part. I looked at my feet. Well, he was going to figure it out soon enough anyway.

"Holy shit." Collin sat back down.

"That's what I said. Sort of."

I leaned my weight on the countertop through my hands and babbled to fill the Grand Canyon-sized silence that had fallen over the room. I didn't dare look at Jack again.

"So Jack has me working on all kinds of great distracting stuff," I said. "Like trying to figure out why his undocumented client killed a Roswell man before our very eyes at my high school boyfriend's wedding and whether or not Jack's new across-the-highway neighbor is guilty of anything worse than horrible table manners."

"Nice summary," Jack said.

My eyes cut to Jack, but Mickey pulled them to him as he spoke. "Tell your mother, with all due respect, that Native American history does not shine a righteous light on reparative therapy. I can't condone cheating, but I have some empathy for your husband with the conversion issue." He pointed to his head of long hair. "Some Christians in the Americas thought our long hair made us heathens, once upon a time, and tried to force us to change who we were, culturally."

"I don't think modern medicine shines a righteous light on reparative therapy either," Jack added.

Collin said, "I think the military's version of it was 'beat that shit out of 'em.'"

"Which no one shines a righteous light on these days, even the military," his fiancée said.

"Well, my mother is nuts, and she doesn't listen anyway. I've decided to ignore her. I hope Rich does, too." I surveyed the room starting with Collin. "But, honestly, even with my, um, messy personal life, what's keeping me awake at night is a work thing. The six-year-old daughter of our client has gone missing, and Jack won't let me go find her."

Jack set a container of sour cream out on the island, then waggled his finger. "A girl who is not our client."

My shoulders bowed up. "But maybe if we found her we'd figure out why our client shot the guy, and we could defend her."

Jack grabbed a set of tall wooden salt and pepper shakers from the kitchen countertop and deposited them on the table.

"We can," he said, "when CPS or the police find her, because that's their job."

We glared at each other for a few seconds, until Mickey interrupted us.

"A missing little girl, huh?" Mickey cleared his throat. "You probably could tell by looking at me that I'm Native American. Apache. So is Jack, by the way, if he hasn't told you already, although only one quarter, courtesy of his grandmother, who is also mine, a fact he forgot to mention earlier. We're first cousins." He slapped Jack on the back, and Jack bowed his head and grinned. "So here's what the old ones taught us, and maybe this will help you sleep better, Emily."

He turned to the group, and his voice took on a storytelling tone, and I could picture him in front of a fire, the eager faces of young Apache kids gazing up at him.

"The Mountain Spirits ensure the well-being of the Apache people. From the earliest I can remember, we would gather to watch the dancers, who danced to summon the Mountain Spirits. One of the dancers was always dressed as a clown. The Clown was greatly feared by all of us children, because our parents told us that if we were bad, the Clown would take us away."

Collin pounded a fist on the counter. "I knew it. Those fuckers always terrified me."

Tamara hooted and Mickey and Jack hee-hawed. Not me. I remained silent, transfixed by Mickey's words. "Go on," I urged him, when the others had settled down.

Mickey went to the cabinet and retrieved a coffee mug. It had the Wrong Turn Ranch's WTR on it, as if it had been burned into the cream-colored mug with a red-hot branding iron.

Mickey poured coffee as he continued. "They did this to teach us discipline, to make us listen to the lessons of the Mountain Spirit Dancers, lessons that would teach us how to survive. As we grew older, we realized that the Clown was there as our teacher, to save us from the evil in the world. So, Emily, whenever I hear about a child that is lost, I think about the Mountain Spirit Dancers and especially the Clown, and I hope they taught their lessons well to her."

I had a troubling thought. "She's not Apache, though. She's Mexican."

He stirred milk into his coffee mug. "Geronimo is arguably the most famous Apache. Perhaps you've heard this quote from him? 'There is one God looking down on us all. We are all the children of one God.' Our God extends past the boundaries of a reservation, or a tribe, or a country. My personal belief tells me that you should have faith that spirits are working to cast out the evil, and you will find her."

Collin raised his mimosa. "That sounds good to me. Followed up with a little honest detective work and a can of whoop-ass."

Laughter rang in the kitchen again, echoing in my skull, rattling loose the dream I'd woken to that morning. Only now, in the dream, I was the clown fighting evil. Or at least a big, evil-looking bull.

Jack held a platter in each hand. Eggs and bacon on one, skillet potatoes and tortillas on the other. "Ghost stories over," he said. "Buffet style breakfast tacos. Grab a plate and get after it."

The others gathered to eat, but I sat lost in my thoughts.

***

Jack ferried Snowflake and me to the little airstrip in the Suburban.

I broke the silence first. "Thanks for that."

He drove with one hand on the wheel, the other hanging out the open window. "For what?" he asked.

"Breakfast. It was nice."

I looked out the side window. A black mare loped in the pasture to the right, tail high in the air. A glossy colt ran beside her on impossibly long legs.

"I was going to tell you about the baby thing," I said. "I hadn't found the right time."

He nodded. "Anything else you need to tell me?"

"Like what?"

"Like the story between you and your friend Collin?"

"No story. You now know all my dirty little secrets." Even the ones I didn't owe a married boss.

His face twitched in a way that told me his left side was smiling. "You do keep it interesting."

He parked the Suburban outside the hangar, and we both exited the vehicle. This time, I helped him pull the plane out. He used some kind of pusher-lever-thingamajiggy attached to the front wheel, and the whole operation was easier than it looked. I pulled the Suburban into the hangar for him and closed and locked the pull-down door.

I was a little nervous about getting sick again, but I tried to block it from my mind. Instead, I watched Jack's preflight ritual.

He noticed, and when we got in the plane he said, "You were kinda mad at me on the way here. I skipped my normal safety talk because you didn't seem in a receptive mood."

"That's an understatement."

He grinned. "Just remember it's highly preferable to enter and exit the cabin when the propeller isn't spinning. But even if it's off, always approach from the backside of the plane. It could get turned on suddenly. And stranger things have happened than propellers flying off or people tripping and falling into them. Just give them a wide berth, whether they're on or off, okay?"

"No problem." I didn't want to lose my head like Marie Antoinette.

He reached into a large case in between the front seats and pulled out a folded brown paper grocery sack. "I thought you might need this for the trip back."

He handed it to me. It was lined with a Hefty trash bag. Written in black Sharpie on the side were the words Emily's Barf Bag.

I took it from him. "Thanks, Jack Ass." And then I held it in front of my face so he couldn't see my huge grin.

Chapter Nine

Monday morning I arrived at Williams & Associates to see Snowflake's nose pressed against the glass panel to the side of the entry door. When she saw me, she started spinning and leaping. She looked especially feminine and shiny. And damp. Very, very damp. How could I not smile, seeing her? So I did, and then gave her the crusts I'd saved her from my breakfast toast.

The first thing I did upon entering was start ringing the bell. I put some elbow grease into it. Wallace would pick me up in forty-five minutes. I needed a tête-à-tête with the inscrutable one before I left.

He surprised me with an immediate response. "Come on back, Emily. I have someone I want you to meet."

I furrowed my brow. "Snowflake, what did you put in his breakfast taco this morning?" She followed me into Jack's office.

There I saw a sallow, wizened man. Strands of silvery hair swept across the crown of his head. His suit hung from his frame, three sizes too large, but it was dapper and immaculate. He was sitting behind Jack's desk like he owned the place. Jack sat in one of the chairs in front of it.

I felt like I needed to push my lower jaw back up. "Yes, boss?"

Jack stood and raised his voice, over-enunciating his words. "I want you to meet Clyde Williams, the name partner of Williams & Associates. We were just going over our files. Clyde, this is our new paralegal, Emily, the one I was telling you we stole from a top-notch Dallas firm."

I choked and covered it by clearing my throat. Stepping briskly forward, I leaned across the desk and extended my hand. Clyde took it and bowed his head to me. He kissed the top of my hand, and I nearly giggled. Old guys rule.

I emulated Jack's speaking voice. "An honor to meet you, sir." I gestured to my baggy jeans and sweater. "I apologize for my attire. I'm interviewing witnesses today, and they might find traditional office attire off-putting."

His voice rasped and broke as he spoke. "Not a problem, young lady. A treat to meet you. Welcome to my little firm. I've been under the weather of late and Jack has graciously stepped in to cover the caseload while I'm out. Good man, Jack. Glad we were able to trade favors in each of our times of need."

I shot Jack a look. What the heck did Clyde mean, and which man had told me the real story of their alliance? My money was on Clyde. I didn't dwell on it, though, not while Clyde was turning on the charm.

"Jack has told me we're very lucky to have you."

"Oh—"

Jack cut my moment short. "Emily is working primarily on the two new matters we discussed: Perez and Johnson. I'm integrating her into some of the other clients this week. I could really use her help on Freeman and Escalante. Freeman, you'll recall, is charged with a bogus resisting arrest and assault of a police officer, and Escalante with armed robbery when he turned the tables on a militant religious group that was harassing him. They're good cases."

I didn't want to work on anything but Valentina, but I kept my lips zipped.

Clyde clasped his hands together. His knobby knuckles dwarfed the rest of his fingers.

"I wish I could say I've recovered enough to dig in and help on the day-to-day caseload, but not yet. I'll just have to stick with an advice and counsel role until the quacks clear me for duty." He sighed. "Damn far sight from back when your dad and I fought in Korea together, son. Old age isn't for sissies."

He unclasped his hands and placed them on the arms of his chair. He pushed down and his rickety body slowly rose. I wanted to leap around the desk and help him, but Jack didn't move, so I held my breath and waited. Ten seconds later, Clyde stood to his full height— five feet, two inches, or thereabouts. He grabbed the cane he'd hooked over the chair arm and started toward the door.

The walk to the lobby took another five minutes.

I whispered to Jack as we trailed Clyde: "I'm following up in person with witnesses that may be able to shed some light on Sofia. The CPS investigator wants to tag along."

"Focus on Sofia, not Valentina," Jack hissed at me.

I hissed back, "I know. Anyway, the CPS guy is picking me up in half an hour. Unless you have something else for me, I plan to use any other time I have left today to work on the Johnson background information. Okay?"

He scowled. "I have an evidentiary hearing on Freeman, so I'll be in court this morning, and Johnson has already called twice today. My plate is full through Wednesday, so let's sit down soon and talk about the other cases I need you working on."

That sounded as close to a yes as I could expect him to choke out, having known him for a week. Well, I'd just have to find Valentina fast then.

"Okay," I said.

We reached the exit and Clyde turned. "Nice carpet, Jack. Is it new?"

Jack wiped the scowl from his face. "Yes, sir, it is." The left side of his face twitched up. "Steve Rogan couldn't pay his bill."

Clyde beamed. "Service in kind. Gives a man his dignity. Nicely done."

I felt like the only one in the room that spoke English. What the heck were they talking about?

Clyde reached for my hand again. "Young lady, you seem like a sensible sort."

If only he knew, but I wasn't going to burst his bubble.

"Take care of Jack," Clyde said. "He's one of the best, and he's had a rough go of it."

I wanted to pump Clyde for more information, but with Jack glowering at me, I refrained.

"Yes, sir. Absolutely."

Remembering what he'd said about his military service, I saluted, then felt silly, but he cackled and squeezed my arm.

He nodded at my stony boss, seemingly oblivious to Jack's ill humor. "She'll do."

***

Wallace had texted me to meet him at the curb, and our timing was perfect. He pulled up in a silver Nissan Altima, and I didn't even have to break stride as I exited the building. The car's shiny, spotless exterior shot an intense glare into my eyes, and I shielded them with my hand as I walked toward it.

I set my purse on a floor so clean that I almost lifted my feet. As I swung my eyes to the driver, I couldn't help but notice that the entire inside shone like the outside, without a scratch, stain, or other blight in sight. Wallace inspected me with neon blue eyes as he eased off the brake.

"I really hope you're Wallace." I said, smiling at him. He had a lovely cherub's face under a head of thick, sandy hair.

He nodded, then eased away from the curb so gently it felt like we were riding in a bubble. The car purred.

"I am. Nice to meet you, Miss Emily. Where are we headed?"

We passed between the two fiberglass quarter horse statues at Third and Polk. On the left, a buckskin painted with a mountain stream scene on one side. On the right, a palomino decorated with paintings of Marilyn Monroe. The quarter horse statues were all over the city, and I loved them.

"Fifteenth and Adams." I recited a street number.

His face spasmed, Jim Carrey style. "That's an ick part of town."

"Yeah. Maria Delgado isn't living the glamorous life."

Wallace shook his head. "One-third of the Hispanic population in Amarillo is living below poverty level," he said. "Poverty drives a lot of our removals, although I have to give props to the Rainbow Room. They help a lot of impoverished families keep their kids, by outfitting them with the basic necessities: car seats, clothing, diapers." He shook his head again. "But they can't help when the desperation of poverty leads to violence or substance abuse."

"How do you deal with all that? Worrying about Valentina alone is eating me up."

He tossed his head, sending his wavy, highlighted bangs back in place, and said, "Jäger shots and group sex." I must have gasped aloud because he laughed and added, "Just kidding. We're in Amarillo, remember? I work out like a fiend. Triathlon."

"You bicycle in the winds out here? That's impressive."

"Not all that impressive. I know someone who did the Kona Ironman this weekend. *That's* impressive."

I'd flipped through the coverage the night before and had quite a surprise. A woman I met when I went as Katie's plus-one to a Baylor Law School reunion was being interviewed on TV. Michele Lopez Hanson had done the Ironman as a tribute to her pro-triathlete husband, who'd been murdered a few months earlier. He'd been a great guy, and I felt tremendously sad for her—and a little in awe, as well. Another reminder that I didn't have a corner on the "going through tough stuff" market.

"I had a friend who did it, too," I said. "I need to find something to help me with the stress, but I don't think it'll be endurance athletics. Or Jäger shots and group sex."

He decelerated the Altima gently as we approached the dilapidated white box of a house that appeared to be our destination. The car stopped so gradually that I couldn't be sure when it happened. A text came in on my phone. I read it quickly, and my cheeks flamed.

Collin: *You look great, even knocked up.*

Collin was fun and funny and magnetic and easy on the eyes, but I wasn't sure how to take his text. He was engaged, and I liked Tamara. I knew how to respect commitments, even if Rich and Stormy didn't. Well, Collin had always been a kidder. He was probably playing with me now. I just wouldn't play back.

"Game plan?" Wallace asked.

I turned off my screen and put away my phone. "I'll ask her how Sofia got her information, and then maybe some follow-up questions. When I'm done, she's all yours."

"Got it."

We climbed out and picked our way through tufts of grass and broken glass in all different colors. A dark brown piece had a scrap of red and silver label on it and the letters *ECAT*. I steered clear of it. If there was a sidewalk, the yard had long since consumed it. The house sat on cinder blocks, and I saw yellow eyes peering at us from underneath it. I hesitated, but there was no growl, just a fetid odor, like something rotten. Or dead. I kept going, wobbling on the first wooden step, and Wallace grabbed my arm. He was several inches taller than me. Lean, but toned.

"Thanks," I said

"Can't have you getting injured before we even question a witness."

My eyes swept from his brown tasseled loafers and up over his long-legged khakis-with-a-white-button-down-shirt kind of outfit.

"A fashion conservative." I actually said that, didn't just think it. Spit.

"Camouflage." He looked at me seriously, eyes twinkling. "Sometimes I go crazy and wear a blue shirt, though."

I chuckled and knocked on the door. It felt insubstantial against my knuckles. I thought I heard movement inside the house, and I leaned close and listened. If there had been a noise, it had stopped. We stood and waited for another thirty seconds. I knocked again and walked over to the lone front window to the right of the door. The boards sagged under my weight. I stuck my nose close to the glass and framed my eyes with my hands. The dust on the window partially obscured my vision. I made out a couch, a TV with a protruding pre-LCD backside, and a low coffee table with a peeling wood-veneer surface.

I gave up. "I don't see anyone, but I could have sworn I heard people in the back of the house."

"We can come back later," Wallace said. "If we stand here much longer, we might get shot."

I clutched my handbag tighter. "That wouldn't be pleasant."

As we walked back toward the Altima, Wallace said, "So, you work for the infamous Jack Holden."

"I do. But why is he infamous?"

"Maybe more enigmatic than infamous. Nobody knows a thing about him other than that he's a great attorney. And hot. The cowboy thing really isn't in right now . . . but on him? It's classic."

I couldn't argue with any of that. I had a thought. "Have you ever seen his wife?"

"Nope. Didn't know he was married." Wallace unlocked the Altima with his clicker. "Check your shoes before you get in, please."

I twisted to see the heel of my kicked back foot. It looked good. I repeated it for the other and decided it needed a scraping to get the grass off, but there was no curb. I scrubbed the bottom of my foot against the asphalt street. That would have to do.

I lowered myself into the car beside Wallace. He pulled out a Handi Wipe and cleaned his hands before putting them on the steering wheel, then dropped it in a car-sized trash can on the back of my seat.

I suppressed a smile. "Can we try the hotel formerly known as the Ambassador next?"

"The hotel formerly known as the Ambassador. I like that. We could do a symbol for them, like Prince."

"A Ghostbusters type of thing, only with a dead body in the circle."

He laughed. "Let's head there now. What are you wanting to get out of it?"

"I'm hoping some of Sofia's coworkers can tell me about her. Something. Anything."

"Well, they didn't tell me diddly squat," Wallace said. "But maybe they'll like you better than me. Shucks, I already like you better than me."

I laughed. Wallace made a precise three-point turn, and we drove back to Adams and then south to I-40. He stayed on the access road until we approached the Ambassador, and he pulled in and parked.

"Since I talked to the manager once before, why don't you let me lead?" He asked. "He might be more cooperative with me than with someone from a defense law firm."

"Good idea."

Wallace hurried off. A text came in for me.

Mom: *I'll pick you up at 5:15, okay, honey?*

God, I wished Rich would hurry up with my car.

Me: *Yep. Thanks, Mother.*

The hotel formerly known as the Ambassador had a Monday morning busy-ness to it, but without the big crowd from Scott's wedding, or the black comedy vibe that Spike's tumble into the pool had given it. I wondered if the murder had helped or hurt their business. It wouldn't have made me want to stay here, but the marketing gurus always say that there's no such thing as bad press.

I walked over to the tables at the pool. Clear water rocked gently as a woman with a white swim cap breaststroked its length. She moved so slowly she nearly sank.

The steady thump-thump of footsteps alerted me to Wallace's approach. "We're in," he said. "Or, I am. I told him you were my colleague, so don't mention your law firm."

"Slick move," I said. I got up and followed him toward the managers' offices.

"He's going to bring them to us one by one, and the HR woman will sit in on the interviews. We're to check in with her first."

Wallace seemed to know his way around, and we ended up outside an office that said *Linda Grace* on a nameplate to the right of the door. He knocked on the wall beside it.

"Linda? CPS here for the follow-up interviews."

Industrial-grade neutral paint covered the bare walls—and it smelled fresh. The woman behind the modular, L-shaped desk pointed to the two chairs in front of it.

"Have a seat," she said.

Sitting in her own chair, she looked round, like a Weeble, with a very squat neck. And short like a Weeble, too. I wondered if her feet even reached the floor. She didn't help matters by wearing a red and purple horizontally striped dress. A silver-accented frame decorated with a cross showed Linda standing with an older man (whose stringy beard gave me the icks) and two children who seemed about six years old—a boy and a girl. From their size, they looked like they must be either twins or very close in age.

"This is my colleague Emily," Wallace said.

I smiled and said, "Nice to meet you, Linda."

She nodded and typed something at her keyboard.

We sat. Wallace leaned to me and whispered, "She's a real people person, puts the human in human resources."

I stifled the laugh that tried to sneak out.

Wallace shifted in his seat and leaned forward. The voice he used dripped honey. "Linda, we just have a few short questions for you before the first witness arrives."

Linda made a bitter beer face. "I already talked to the police."

"Yes, but we're trying to find Valentina, Sofia's daughter."

Without the facial contortions, Linda's features looked porcine. Her skin was pale, and she had dark circles under her eyes.

"We knew her as Maria." Linda said. She tilted her head as she studied me. "Say, don't I know you?"

I struggled to place her face. "I'm not sure. I grew up here. Went to Amarillo High. Graduated twelve years ago."

She crossed her arms. Her bosom created such a protrusion that it looked like she was dancing an Irish jig. "Yes, we're the same age," she said. "I went to Tascosa. I heard you just moved back to town."

This wasn't going anywhere good. "Yes, I did."

Her piggy eyes squinted, and, for the first time, she smiled. "You're the one whose husband—"

I broke in. "So about Maria." I felt Wallace's eyes boring into me, but I ignored him. "As we try to help her daughter, anything we can learn about her as a mother and who she associated with is incredibly helpful. We're trying to figure out how Sofia found the Maria Delgado identity. It's possible that whoever helped her get it has Valentina. Or maybe she wrote something on her application that would lead us to Valentina. I was hoping you'd let us look at her employee file, or, even better, give us a copy."

Pink spread across Linda's face. "Those are confidential employee documents."

"Of course," I said.

I licked my lips. Linda would feel defensive about being tricked by an applicant. She had to report new hires to the INS, and the hotel could get in a load of trouble if she'd half-assed the hiring process. I tried to sound empathetic.

"It must be very frustrating that she submitted fraudulent papers," I said. "But Sofia isn't still your employee, is she? If you'd like, we could get a waiver from her. It's just hard, since she's in prison, and it might take us a week." I pointed at her framed picture. "Meanwhile, there's a little girl, just about your daughter's age in that picture, missing. I can only imagine how frightened she must be. I hope Valentina can make it a week. I hope she's not being molested or tortured, that she has food—"

Linda held up her hand. "Stop. I know she's missing, but the police already have the documents."

Wallace broke in. "Nobody wants to find her more than CPS, not even the city police, and we're a *state* agency. Your cooperation would be much appreciated, and I wouldn't ask if we didn't believe it was the Christian thing to do, ma'am."

I wanted to applaud. Wallace might not be from around here, but he'd figured out how to work within the system. I gave him a silent *woot.*

Linda lumbered to her feet. She pushed her chair back with her body and headed for the door. As she walked, the heavy brush of her thighs against each other made a grating pantyhose sound. Wallace and I looked at each other and I slapped my hand over my mouth. He licked his index finger and tapped it in the air as if touching it to a hot stove. God would smite us for sure now. Wallace had used the Lord's name to pressure a witness, and then we'd been uncharitable toward the woman helping us. Her attitude sure made it hard to be nice, though. I resolved to try harder anyway.

Linda returned, panting. She handed me a stack of papers, without a word.

I thumbed through them. An application, the results of a background check, some new hire paperwork, and copies of Maria Delgado's Social Security card and green card.

"Thank you very much," I said.

Linda grunted.

Wallace perused the documents as I did, and I pointed to the list of references on her application, then at the emergency contact in her new hire papers. My hands felt tingly with excitement. Leads.

A stiff, male voice behind us interrupted my thoughts. "If you and your colleague would be so kind as to join us, Mr. Gray, I have arranged for the coworkers of the woman we knew as Ms. Delgado to take turns speaking to you. You, too, Linda."

By the time I'd hefted my handbag and turned around, all I saw was the retreating backside of an African American man. I moved quickly with Wallace behind me and Linda trailing us. The man stopped at a doorway and turned. He had incredibly good posture—God, how my pageant coach would have loved him—and hazel eyes that were almost green. He wore a white dress shirt with the Wyndham logo on the collar and a name badge above it that read Russell Grant.

"Thank you, sir."

Wallace echoed me. "Thank you, Mr. Grant."

We entered to find a white woman waiting for us in a room identical to Linda's office except that it held a round, faux cherry table with four chairs instead of a modular desk. There was nothing on the walls in there, either. Maybe the hotel just hadn't rehung the decorations yet after painting.

Wallace and I both greeted the woman and took our seats. Without lifting her eyes from the table, she mumbled a reply in the voice of a three-pack-a-day smoker. She wore a burgundy service dress and had mostly gray hair and a stocky frame. Linda joined us a minute later, moving in a side-to-side rocking motion and breathing harder than before. She was definitely on a path to cut to the front of the line on the heart transplant list.

The manager stepped inside. "You'll be speaking to Cindy here first," he said. "Then I'll bring Aracelli in fifteen minutes, and you'll finish up with Roberto in another fifteen. They're the only ones available."

He left, closing the door behind him.

The meeting with Cindy yielded nothing. She kept her eyes on the table and spoke in a detached voice. She knew "Maria" only at work, they didn't talk, she'd never seen her daughter, and she didn't know anyone who was friendly with her. Aracelli had nothing for us either, but her voice strained and cracked when she spoke—once I thought I even saw tears. But, no matter how hard I tried, I couldn't get her to talk about Sofia.

Roberto was a different story.

The slight man wore a male version of the same burgundy service clothes the women wore. He looked into my eyes as he talked, and his tone was urgent.

"I work in the big rooms, the ballrooms, and I fix little things in the guest rooms," he said. "Leaky sinks. Shower curtain rods. Things like that." He looked straight at Linda. "I been here six months, I work hard." He turned back to us. "Maria work hard, too. She very serious about work and about her daughter. Two times she bring a little girl here and hide her while she work." He looked down. "I sorry I no tell you, Mrs. Linda."

I kicked Wallace under the table. This contradicted what Roberto's coworkers had told both of us, so far, about Sofia.

Before Linda could speak, I asked him, "Valentina?"

"Yes, she call her Valentina. The girl pretty, like her mama. She don't talk. She just sleep and color pictures. She color pictures for me."

"Where did Valentina sleep and color pictures?"

"She little, and she ride on her mama's cart, hide behind the curtain."

"Did she ever go into the rooms?"

"Yes, I see her once."

Linda sniffed. "We can talk about this later, Roberto."

His voice came out very soft. "Yes, Mrs. Linda."

I wanted to whack Linda for casting a pall on our conversation, but I forged ahead.

"Roberto, this is very helpful. Just a few more questions. Did Sofia—Maria—tell you about any friends?"

"No one."

"Anybody Valentina stayed with?"

"No."

"A man, her husband, or Valentina's father, perhaps?"

"Never."

"Nothing about bad men, or men wanting to hurt or take her or Valentina?"

"No, Miss." Roberto's shoulders heaved and he put his face in both hands and rubbed it. When he looked back up and dropped his hands, he shook his head. "I wish she did. I wish I could help that little girl."

I started to thank him, but he sat up straight again and said, "Wait. You ask about bad men, and I saw a man that might do something maybe bad. He have a bald head, shaved"—he rubbed his scalp—"and he run out of the hotel that night. The night Maria, I mean Sofia, shoot that other man." He raised his hands palms up. "I think, why he in a hurry? But then I forget and never see him again."

I wanted to pound the table and shout, "Yes!" But I settled with asking him follow-ups. "Was he white?"

"Yes?"

"How old?"

"Not so young, not so old."

"Did he have anyone with him?"

"I don't think so." He shook his head. "No."

"Did you see where he went, or if he left in a vehicle?" I asked.

"No," he said. "Sorry."

I reached across the table and patted his hand. "Don't be sorry. This is great. Thank you, Roberto. Thank you."

"Is that all?"

"It is. Adios."

"Adios." He rose to leave and Linda went with him.

Valentina had been here, and Spike might have seen her. Remembering Spike's past and his connection to his old partner in crime—Harvey—here in Amarillo, it wasn't out of the question that Harvey had been here, too. If Harvey and Spike were together, they could have been up to their old tricks with Valentina. Sofia might have caught them in the act, and, as a mother, she would have had to stop them. They might be the "bad men" she told Jack and me about. Heck, Harvey might even be the guy Roberto had seen running from the hotel. His description fit. Too late, I realized I should have shown the picture of Harvey to Roberto.

It was possible. It was more than possible. I whispered a prayer that I was wrong, that a convicted child molester did not have Valentina, then turned to Wallace.

"I think I know where to find her. And we need to hurry."

Chapter Ten

Wallace punched it through the yellow light on the access road at Georgia Street.

"So you think this Harvey and Spike molested Valentina, and Harvey has her?" he said.

"Maybe," I said, "and it's terrifying."

"I need to call it in."

I ignored his comment, and he kept driving. Harvey's address was in the file I'd brought with me, and I entered it into the Maps app on my phone. He lived southeast of downtown, in the home he'd inherited from his mother before he'd done time. Siri called out the directions in her mezzo staccato voice: "Continue on Interstate 40 for 3.4 miles."

Wallace had the Altima up to ninety-five miles per hour. He whipped around slower traffic like Jeff Gordon as he continued to accelerate. Siri had us exit at Ross-Osage, and Wallace took the corner with wheels screeching. He made another hard right on Twenty-seventh.

"We're almost there," he said.

We came to an intersection. One of Stanley Marsh's many fake traffic signs throughout the city was planted in the yard of the house on the corner. This one read Undead End. Cryptic Texas kitsch, but this time it was eerie as well. We made our last left at the corner onto Olive Street and Wallace slowed down.

"It's up on the right, nearly to the end of the block." Wallace pointed. The street dead-ended a few hundred feet after Harvey's house.

"What is that, where the street ends? It looks like . . ."

"Llano Cemetery."

It was creepy—made creepier by the undead sign. Not that I believed in the undead; live people were way scarier than zombies anyway. Wallace executed a perfect U-turn again and parked facing Twenty-seventh across from the gloomy gray house belonging to Harvey. There were no other cars in front of it. It looked better than Maria Delgado's, but that wasn't saying much. It had a front sidewalk and a shuttered window left of the front door. A garage jutted off of the right front of the house in an L—an obvious afterthought added by someone with little or no construction skills. The yard was even worse than Delgado's, though, and the paint was cracked and peeling on the garage and window frames. Missing shingles on the roof formed a crazy quilt pattern.

I opened the car door and jumped out. My heart hammered harder than it had the time Jib had stumbled at full gallop and I'd watched, helpless, as the ground came at me in slow motion. Jib had rolled over me, but we'd both come out of it okay. I said a little prayer for Valentina, for Wallace, and for me—that we all would be okay now, too.

I spoke into the car: "Wallace, we need a plan."

"Yeah, here's a plan," he said. "We call my office and the cops. By the book."

"I can't stand the thought of leaving her in there another second," I said.

I pulled my hair off my face and behind my head in one hand. The wind had picked up quite a bit in the last two hours.

"If she's in there," Wallace said.

"And if she's not, we look like idiots for running off to the police and accusing this guy half-cocked," I said.

"There is that."

I made a decision. "I'm going in," I said.

"You're going to get me arrested," Wallace replied.

"Nah, it will be fine."

"I hope this means you thought of something."

It didn't. I refrained from saying so.

He climbed out and locked his car. "Fine," he said. "But I have 911 punched into my phone, and I'm dialing if we see any sign of her."

I ran to the front garage and peeked in through one of the dirty windows. No vehicles, but a tire sat in the middle of the floor beside a large oil stain. A rake and shovel hung on the wall.

"Come on." I motioned for Wallace to follow me around back.

"Don't you want to start with the doorbell?" he asked in a hiss louder than his speaking voice.

I ignored him. Moving quickly, I opened the side gate to the back yard and slipped through. The first window we came to had battered shades covering it from the inside. The next window was high, small, and opaque. I moved on and peered in the last side window. No lights. No people. A mattress on the floor. A bedroom?

I ran into the deserted, treeless back yard. It made the front look pampered. Someone had burned a pile of garbage on the concrete patio, leaving behind a can of Wolf Brand Chili with a half-burned label and a pile of ash. The wind sifted the ash and scattered some in our direction.

The window on the near side of the back door had a black trash bag over a missing pane with duct tape that was starting to lose its adhesive at the edges. This window looked in on the other side of the same empty bedroom I'd just seen.

On the opposite side of the back door, we found the window to the kitchen. Again, no people. A large cardboard box sat upturned in the tiny eating area. A rat was scavenging on a plate and fork sitting on the box. The sink below the window had another garbage bag in it, and roaches scurried in and out. The refrigerator door hung open.

I tried the back door and, to my surprise and horror, the handle turned. I pushed the door inward as softly as I could, and it swung open. I arrested its progress before it hit the cabinets inside and leaned in after it.

Wallace stumbled backward. "Oh no. No no no. No trespassing."

"But it's open," I said.

"It's still trespassing. I could get fired."

Would Jack fire me if I got arrested for trespassing? Probably not. And if he did, wasn't my job with him temporary anyway? I felt an odd pang in my chest at the thought, but I refused to consider what it meant. I didn't have time to get sappy. I lifted my chin and stepped over the threshold.

"Oh shit, Emily. Come on now, don't go in there."

"I'll be right back. You just keep a lookout."

I tiptoed into the kitchen. If Valentina was in here, she was leaving with me.

***

The stench in the house hit me with the force of a one-ton bull. Rotting garbage. Urine and feces. The rat looked up at me from its perch on the box, its front paws to its face, its tiny jaws working on its prize. The roaches ignored me. I pulled out my phone and activated a low-beam flashlight app, forcing myself to walk through the kitchen and the dark doorway beyond it.

The kitchen emptied into a den that had access to the front door. There was a bedroll on the carpet—carpet that crunched under my feet. Beside the bedroll was a backpack in a bluish color, flat and empty. A pair of men's tube socks partially inside out, bunched up in sweaty, dirt-caked folds hung from the backpack's open zipper. No people in here, at least not now. Because there obviously *was* a person living here—a gross person who preferred life in the dark away from prying eyes.

Another doorway on the far side of the room beckoned, darker than the one from the kitchen. Sweat trickled down my back and I stood frozen in place. Someone had to do this. Someone had to care about this little girl enough to do this; the only someone here was me. I crept across the living room. My mouth and eyes watered, and something large pushed my heartbeat up into the base of my throat, nearly gagging me. I stopped, swallowing over and over until the nausea passed and I could slink forward again.

The doorway entered a short hall with a bathroom in the middle and doorways to my right and left. I knew there was a bedroom to the left—I'd seen it through the window. It had looked empty, but what about the closets? Or what if the person living here had fled to this bedroom after I'd peeked in earlier? I couldn't skip it. I had to be thorough. So I stepped into the tiny room—it was empty, thank God— passed the mattress, and faced the closet. Its door was ajar. It was empty, too. I hadn't known I was holding my breath until I realized I was lightheaded; I exhaled in a gush, trying desperately to quiet my breath.

A text chimed. I froze. If someone was in here, they now knew for sure that I was, too. It could be Wallace warning me of something, so I glanced at it.

Rich: *When can we finish our talk?*

Sheesh. Ex-husband. If I ended up dead because that text alerted the boogie man, it would be his fault. It figured that he'd continue to mess things up for me. But no boogie man jumped out. I stayed motionless for several seconds, then moved on.

The bathroom was next. I poked my head out the bedroom door. The hall was still empty. Belatedly, it occurred to me that a weapon would have been a smart idea. I'd left my handbag in the car, though, so if I came upon someone who wasn't glad to see me, I'd get to practice my rusty self-defense skills. I rolled my neck, and it cracked. Thanks to years of goat tying and classes at the YMCA in Dallas, I'd learned that my strength was in getting an attacker flipped and on the ground. Then I could drive my palm up through the bridge of his nose or jab my fingers in his eyes. If I had to. I shuddered, swallowing down more nausea. For the first time since I'd entered the house, I remembered that I was pregnant. A pregnant woman had no business in here. But then, neither did Valentina.

I made my way silently into the bathroom. It was peppered with little spotlights from where the crushed blinds gapped. Dark stains streaked the sink and curtainless tub. The laminate had detached from the countertop and broken away in patches. But there was nothing and no one in the room.

Again, I leaned out slowly to check the hall before entering it. All clear. On to the last room. Its door was three-quarters of the way shut.

I didn't like that at all. I held my phone's flashlight in my left hand and pushed the door back until it met the wall with a thud. No doorstop. No sound in the room. A sharp pain ripped through my abdomen and I dropped to my knees in shock, a strangled cry escaping my lips before I could hold it in. My phone bounced once helplessly on the carpet, landing flashlight down.

"Emily!" Wallace's voice echoed through the silent house, and his footsteps followed it. In seconds he was on the ground behind me, his hands on my shoulders. "What happened? Are you okay?"

"I think . . . yeah, I'm fine. I don't know what happened. A cramp or something."

This baby seemed to want me to always know it was there. I didn't think this cramp was normal, though. When we finished today, I'd make a "first available" obstetrician appointment. I'd vomited up my news in New Mexico yesterday and lived through it. I'd survive the onslaught of Amarillo gossip that my condition would unleash, too.

Wallace slipped his arm under my shoulder and around my back. He hefted me up, grunting at first until I helped him.

"I'm sorry to scare you," I said. "Really, I'm fine. Thank you."

"I thought you'd been stabbed or something," he said.

It had felt like it. "Yeah, I overreacted." I took several deep breaths and waited for the pain. None came. "Just one more room and we're done."

Having Wallace with me gave me courage. I stepped into the room, avoiding another mattress and a pile of crap (literal crap, the origins of which I didn't want to consider) and faced the closed closet door. I yanked it open, and screamed my fool head off.

I wasn't the only one. The two teenagers huddled in the closet joined in with me. I backpedaled and fell onto the mattress. Wallace, who had remained in the doorway, leapt into the room, arms raised in a judo posture, knees flexed, on his toes.

The screaming stopped.

"Don't hurt us," one of the teenagers said in a high-pitched voice.

The other added in a slightly deeper one, "I know we're not supposed to be here. We'll move out, I swear."

"What in hell? How old are you?" Wallace reached a hand out and pulled me to my feet. "Emily, give me some light."

I pointed my phone at their torsos so as not to blind them. They were filthy. Two gangly waifs in blue jeans and sweatshirts, ridiculous, dark knit caps on their heads. Girls? I looked closer. One a girl, one a boy. The girl had one green eye and one brown eye, and the boy had a nasty scar on his neck—long since healed, but brutal looking.

The boy spoke. "Eighteen."

Wallace put his hands on his hips. "Don't try to bullshit me."

They looked at each other, and the girl whimpered softly.

The boy repeated, "Eighteen. So you can't call our parents."

Wallace shook his head. "Show me some ID."

The boy stood up and helped the girl stand, too. "We don't have to show you nothing. You're not the cops."

Wallace pulled out his wallet and flipped it open to an ID, which he pointed at them. "Better. Child Protective Services."

I put my hand on his arm. He looked at me, and I mouthed, "My turn, please?"

He swept his hand at me and gave a slight bow.

I turned to the kids. "We're looking for a man named Harvey Dulles. This is his house. Have you seen him?"

Two head shakes. Still, it was the boy who answered. "The skinhead that lived here left last week."

Last week? That was around the time Sofia killed Spike. "How do you know?"

The girl piped in. "Because we've been camping out in the cemetery for a while now, and we watch the neighborhood. He packed up his truck like he wasn't coming back. We waited a few days, and when nobody came, we moved in." She looked down. "It was starting to get cold at night."

"Have you seen a little Hispanic girl, about six years old?"

They both shook their heads. I wrestled with the information. So Harvey had moved out. Why would he abandon a home he owned free and clear? That was suspicious behavior. Irrational and suspicious. I wanted to cry, to flail, to scream. I didn't.

I turned to Wallace. "All yours."

His voice softened. "Here's the deal. I can't pretend I don't see two kids who are fifteen at the oldest standing in front of me without enough to eat, not going to school, and with no one to keep them safe. I promise I'm going to help you guys, but you're going to have to come with us."

The boy bristled. "Yeah, like CPS ever helped us before? That's why we're here. We got stuck in a house where we were raped and beaten. We made a run for it. Bet CPS doesn't even know we're gone and those foster assholes are still cashing the checks."

Wallace swallowed hard; I heard his throat catch. "It's not supposed to be like that. If I'd known that was happening, I'd have taken you away from them and turned them over to the cops. Which is what I'm going to do now." He pointed at the door. "Let's go."

They stood there.

"When was the last time you two ate?" Wallace asked. "I'm buying you a quick lunch before we do anything else."

The boy stepped forward, pulling the girl with him. They headed toward the door, and Wallace followed them out. I fell in behind them. When we reached the back door to the house, the boy suddenly pushed the girl through the door and pulled it shut behind him. The two teens sprinted across the yard, catapulting themselves up and over the fence around the cemetery. By the time Wallace wrestled the door open and the two of us were outside, they'd disappeared from sight, back into their secret world.

I thought back to the sign at the end of the block: *Undead End.* Well, yes, in a way it was undead. As in two real live kids living feral in a cemetery. It hurt to think about it.

"Dammit." Wallace snapped his head forward and then back, punctuating his frustration. He pulled out his cell phone and typed rapidly, then put the phone to his ear. "Marsha, hi, this is Wallace. I'm at Twenty-seventh and Olive, by Llano Cemetery. I saw two youth, a boy and a girl about fifteen years old, who came out of an abandoned house. They were filthy and malnourished. When I tried to talk to them, they claimed to have escaped an abusive foster home and bolted into the cemetery. I didn't get their names, but the boy had a big scar on his neck and the girl had different colored eyes. They were both white, I think." He paused. "Yes, thank you." He hung up and put his phone in his pocket.

I pressed my hand into my aching abdomen and said, "Wow."

"Yeah. It breaks my heart to see kids like that, to hear what they've been through."

"What do we do now?" I asked.

"Nothing we can do. The cops will try to pick them up for us, and we'll move them. I'll see if I can figure out who they are, what family they were placed with, and arrange for a little visit with the foster parents."

We walked back around to the front of the house. My thoughts ricocheted between the two waifs we'd just seen and Valentina, whose situation was even more dire.

"Do you see stuff like this a lot?" I asked.

"Too much. There are so many good foster parents, but there are some who are in it to milk the system, or to take advantage of the helpless. Sometimes I hate people."

I walked through the gate first, and he shut it behind us. I put my hand on his arm. "I had no idea it was so bad. I mean, you read about this stuff, but it's never touched my life before. What you do, well, Wallace, you're one of my heroes."

He started to smile and then his face collapsed into trembling lips and blinking eyes. He pulled me to him in a long hug.

"Thank you." He held me back out again. "What about you, Ms. Asskicker? Charging into that house alone with nothing but your good looks to protect you? You're *my* hero."

He slung an arm around my shoulder, and we walked back to the car together.

Chapter Eleven

It turned out that "quick" to Wallace did not mean eating in the car. But by now that didn't surprise me. Because we were running behind, we skipped the GoldenLight Restaurant in favor of a counter order at Wienerschnitzel. Wallace: chili cheese dogs. Me: two orders of large fries.

I got a text from Jack: *Back at office. Status?*

Had it only been that morning that I'd talked to Jack and met Clyde? I tried to remember if I'd told him when I'd return. I knew how badly he wanted me to move on to other clients. I glanced at my phone. One-thirty p.m. Well, Wallace and I only had one more stop. I could be in my chair and working on Johnson by three p.m., at the latest. How mad could Jack be? Pretty mad, probably. That called for emergency measures.

Me: *On the road to last witness. Stopping by office in 15.*

I added on two chili cheese dogs and a large fry for Jack.

"Wanna meet the hot enigma that is my boss before our next stop?" I asked.

Wallace wiggled his eyebrows. "Do bears wear fur?"

We planted ourselves in a yellow and red laminate booth where I scarfed down my fries as my stomach did happy cartwheels.

Wallace gave me the stink eye. "You don't do mystery meat?"

"I don't do meat at all."

He pulled his mouth into a moue. "Vegetarian?"

"Yep."

"Huh. And I thought it was hard to be gay in Amarillo."

I pulled a skinny, yellow highlighter from my handbag to mark the names of Sofia's references for her work persona: Sofia Perez—using herself as a reference for her fictitious work identity, that made me snort—and Liliana Diaz. Both numbers looked familiar, and I rifled through the big Redrope file I'd brought with me from the office, an almost-red accordion file that was simply known in legal circles as a Redrope. The phone number for "Sofia" matched the number of the phone the police found on her at the time of her arrest. Well, she was certain to get a good reference there. More interesting, the phone number given for Liliana Diaz turned out to be the number I'd called to speak to the real Maria Delgado on Friday.

I lifted my eyes from the page and grinned. "Like hell Maria knows nothing."

"Oh yeah." He shimmied his shoulders and torso in a chair dance as he bobbed his head. "She can run, but she can't hide."

I recalled that Sofia had given one more name in her paperwork. I'd seen it in there somewhere, earlier. I flipped past the application to the new hire paperwork. Bingo.

"Emergency contact: Victoria. No last name given," I said. "Wanna call it?"

"Sure."

Wallace punched in the digits as I read them aloud. He held the phone to his ear, eyebrows raised at me while he waited.

"What do you want to bet it's out of service?" He said. Then his expression changed. "Yes, hello, my name is Wallace Gray, and I'm calling about Maria Delgado—" His mouth dropped into an O. "Hello?" He shook his head at me as he lowered his phone. "A woman answered and then she hung up on me."

"Let me try." I dialed from my own phone. Three rings. Five. Ten. No answer, and no voice mail. "Well, that sucks." I stuck my wadded up napkin into my empty, nested fry holders and drained the last of my iced tea. "I'm ready when you are."

We threw away our trash and pushed the doors open into the bright midday sun. After we got back out to the Altima, Wallace handed me a Handi Wipe and we repeated our cleaning ritual like raccoons. We drove downtown with the bag of food for Jack after we had everything to Wallace's satisfaction.

When we reached the office, I rang the bell on my desk immediately.

Wallace dropped his head and looked at me under furrowed brows. "What in God's name are you doing?"

"Jack likes his privacy."

Wallace gasped, a hand over his chest. "OMG, he's naked back there, isn't he?"

"I sure as heck hope not." I rang again. "Jack, it's Emily. I have Wallace from CPS with me."

Heavy boot steps sounded in the hall. Wallace adjusted his posture. And damn me to Hades, I adjusted my girls, too. I would have been ashamed of us both, if I'd had time.

Jack sauntered into the lobby, his hand extended. "Wallace from CPS, nice to meet you. I'm Jack Holden."

Wallace's voice came out deeper than it had with me. "A pleasure. I've heard your name many times. And, of course, our interests overlap now with your client Sofia Perez, and CPS looking for her missing daughter, Valentina."

I held up the bag. "I brought you food. In case you hadn't eaten."

Jack shifted his eyes from my face to the bag and back again. "A peace offering? Do I even want to know why?"

Wallace busted out a gut laugh, and I hurried to speak before he finished. Jack didn't need to know *everything*.

"Just being considerate," I said. "Agatha's training."

Jack took the bag and rustled through it as he said, "My new paralegal is trying to expand her duties to law practice manager—not that I don't need the help—but she has her heart set on working the family law angle, Wallace. I keep trying to tell her that our focus is the criminal defendant, that we can count on CPS, the police, and the ad litem."

He snared a chili cheese dog, wrapped it in a napkin, and peeled back the paper wrapper.

"I can attest that she had a laser focus on Sofia today."

Jack took a bite and chewed, eyes twinkling in a way that said he wasn't convinced Wallace was telling the whole truth. He got a little chili on the left side of his mouth, so when he half-smiled around his mouthful, the chili rose toward the dimple. My stomach fluttered, and an urge to lick it off came out of nowhere. I never had thoughts like that, especially not about married men. It had to be the pregnancy hormones. It had to be. Well, surely it was okay just to *look*. I forced a dry-mouth swallow.

"Laser focus," I said.

Jack finished his bite. "When do you think you'll be finished with the interviews?"

"I should be back around two-thirty," I said. "Three at the latest."

"Okay, then," he said.

"Nice to meet you, Mr. Holden." Wallace nodded.

"Jack, please. You, too."

We exited the office, and, as we walked to the elevator, Wallace fanned his face with his hand. "The chili on his mouth," he said. "Oh, honey, to be that napkin."

"Tell me about it."

A few minutes later, we headed north toward Sofia's little, nameless apartment, which appeared to be three blocks west of Maria Delgado's place, according to Siri.

"This is it," Wallace said, as we approached a dumpy block of buildings. "Help me find the manager's office. Last time I was here, the guy was already at Sofia's place with the police."

"I've got my eyes peeled," I said.

Wallace drove slowly around the block. Two-story four-plexes with white siding squatted on scraggly turf, one after another. Gaps in the siding revealed black liner, making the complex look like a mouth full of bad teeth. There were no balconies or patios. No grassy lawns or playgrounds. No parking lots. A worried cat slunk between two of the buildings with an underfed dog hot on its tail. Cars in a rainbow of colors—but similar in their states of dilapidation—lined the streets.

"There it is." I pointed to a ground floor unit with a sign in its window that said Manager.

Unfortunately, there was no parking space near his unit, so we circled again and parked along the street on the opposite side of the complex.

"We're right by their apartment. I saw it last week. Want to go there first?"

I nodded. "Sure." I kept my Redrope and handbag under my arm and followed Wallace between the buildings, placing my feet carefully amidst piles of dog poop. "Nice place."

He snorted. "It's worse than you think. Most of these units house multiple families. It's like little Mexico City."

Residents had strung clotheslines from window to window between buildings and their clothes and linens waved like flags.

I pointed to them. "No laundry room."

"No nothing." Wallace stopped in front of unit 1C, an interior ground floor apartment. "This is where Sofia lived." He knocked. "I wouldn't be surprised if the manager has already moved in another family. It appears to be a high-turnover business."

There was no answer.

"Want to try some neighbors?" Wallace looked around at the nearest ground floor units.

I smiled and jiggled the doorknob. The lock felt flimsy, like interior doorknob locks. I used to unlock the door to my parents' bedroom when I was a kid, using just my mother's hairpins. I'd put my hair up over lunch, securing the runaway strands with bobby pins, so I pulled one out. I slipped it in the lock and wiggled it gently until I heard a click. I pushed the door open and walked in.

Wallace shook his head. "She graduates to breaking and entering."

"Does that mean you're the lookout again?"

He sighed and followed me, closing the door and relocking it behind him. "You're an incredibly bad influence."

"You should have known me in high school."

"Were you one of those wild Amarillo girls who drank Boone's Farm wine and snuck out to spy on the devil worshippers at the Marsh estate?"

I winked at him. "Don't make me lie to you." I walked into the kitchen. A crayon drawing hung from the refrigerator by a magnet. "Is this the drawing you told me about?"

"Yeah. I guess the cops didn't consider this evidence."

I snatched it down and slipped it in my file. "Good. I do."

"Lord, woman. Do all paralegals act like you?"

"It seems criminal law has already had an impact on me." I reached for a drawer.

Wallace stopped me. "At least use a towel to keep your fingerprints off stuff, okay?"

"Good idea." A dishrag hung over the kitchen faucet. I picked it up, then started opening drawers and cabinets with that hand. I found a few pieces of silverware, some plates with daisies in the center, and a stack of plastic tumblers. The only food to speak of was a bag of rice and one of beans.

"Not much here," I said.

Wallace shook his head, his face soft. "Yeah, a pretty meager existence."

I walked the confines of the apartment with Wallace watching me. I checked under the couch, between and behind cushions, in closets, cabinets, and every other nook and cranny. No jacks, candy, or colors. No nothing.

"You were right," I said. "No sign of a child living here, except for that drawing."

Still, though I didn't know how to explain it, I felt Valentina's presence. I sat down on the worn, silvery blue sofa, pulled the drawing back out, and studied it. A lone man stood in front of a hill. The man had on shorts, or maybe it was a short skirt. The artist had scribbled all over his brown body in white crayon. On his head were big ears, sort of like animal ears. His nose was big, too, but more like a snout. Brown scribble over the face. Black for the hair. The man smiled back at me, and in the crude drawing, I thought I saw affection on his face. The man wasn't scary, but he wasn't familiar either. I put the drawing away and stood up.

Wallace was sitting at the kitchen table checking his phone.

"Onward," I said.

He jumped to his feet. "Manager's office?"

I shook my head. "Let's chat with the neighbors while we're over here." I pried a space between the slats of the plastic white blinds. "Coast's clear."

I opened the door for Wallace and he exited. I relocked the doorknob and headed to unit 1B, adjacent to Sofia's place. I heard children's giggles and a happy squeal.

"*Niños, parada*," a woman said, which I translated automatically to "Children, stop" in my head. I knocked.

Silence.

I sensed a presence on the other side of the door. Possibly the woman who I had heard talking to the kids?

"Hello, ma'am. I'm from Sofia's attorney's office. She sent me to talk to you."

Silence.

Going on a hunch, I added, "Victoria, please?"

Silence.

I said all of it again, in Spanish. This time I heard the sound of a hand lock turning, and the door opened three inches. Narrowed black eyes regarded me from the slit behind a security chain.

I smiled. "*Tu hables ingles?*"

"*Si.* Yes."

"Good. Hello, Victoria. I'm from the office of Jack Holden. He is the attorney who represents Sofia. We're trying to help her. Could I talk to you for just a minute? Maybe we could walk outside, or my colleague Wallace—" I gestured back at him, "and I could come in for a minute?"

She stared at me.

I saw movement behind her, and one little hand appeared around her knee. Then a face. Then above it, another face. And by her waist, a third one. Three little girls.

"Not him. I talk to you *solamente*. Five minutes. You come in."

I turned to Wallace and whispered, "Maybe you could knock on a few more doors?"

He nodded and left.

I turned back to her. "Thank you."

She opened the door, revealing a small woman with long, dark hair in a low bun. She tugged at her purple velour shorts. Her T-shirt said Amarillo Sox on it.

"Beautiful little girls," I said.

I smiled at them, and the cuties giggled and ran to the couch—a threadbare number in a silvery blue, like Sofia's. The fibers were so synthetic looking that if I'd thrown a match on it I wasn't sure if it would melt or catch fire. Each of the girls held a doll, and the littlest girl's doll looked homemade, with long, brown yarn hair, a blue dress, and a piece of ivory-colored lace over her shoulders. I winked at her, and she held the doll up for me to see, grinning so wide my heart melted.

"Thank you," Victoria said.

She pointed at her wooden kitchen table, and we took seats adjacent to each other. My chair wobbled at its joints, so I held very still. There were no lights on in the apartment, and I struggled to adjust to the dim atmosphere.

"Victoria, what is your last name?"

She paused. "Jones."

I nearly laughed at the obvious lie, but instead I nodded with a serious expression on my face. I didn't want to spook her or insult her.

"Thank you, Ms. Jones," I said. "Now, you know that Sofia is in jail, for shooting a man, right?"

Victoria nodded, eyes steady and wide.

"Had you ever met the man she shot—Spike Howard?"

She shook her head no.

I grabbed the file and retrieved a picture of Spike. "But you've seen his picture in the paper and know who I'm talking about, right? This man?"

She nodded. "I never see him before."

"Did you see any other men around Sofia's place?"

"No."

I pulled out the picture I'd printed of Harvey. "How about him?"

She shook her head.

"Have you known Sofia long?"

She put her hands on either side of the seat of her chair, and slid them under her thighs. "Since she move in. One month, maybe two."

"How do you know her?"

"Her daughter play with mine."

"Ah, so you know Valentina."

The girls giggled again, and Victoria shushed them. "*Sí*, yes."

"Sofia is very worried about her. Have you seen Valentina since Sofia was arrested?"

Victoria's eyes shot over to the girls, then upwards, then down at her feet. "No."

"Do you ever babysit her, keep her when Sofia is at work?"

Victoria moved her hands and squeezed them between her knees. "No."

"Never? Not even when she goes to the grocery store?"

She studied the tabletop in front of her. "No. *Nunca.*"

Never. "Okay." I thought for a moment. "What about Maria Delgado?"

Victoria moved her head back and forth in tiny shakes. "I don't know her."

I leaned closer to whisper, "Did Sofia ever talk about where she came from or—"

"No." Victoria sat up in her chair, leaning against the backrest ramrod straight.

I continued: "Her husband—"

"No." She rocked back and forth just a little.

"Or why they came? Maybe some bad men?"

"No." She wrapped her arms around herself and continued the rocking.

"No?"

"*Nada,*" she whispered, still rocking.

Nothing. Which is what she had told me. Nothing. She was lying. I was sure of it. But why? What was she scared of? I needed time to think. I rummaged through the papers in my Redrope to buy myself time. An idea came to me, and I looked at the black-haired little girls again. All three had a high single ponytail and wore pink Barbie pj's. One appeared to be about five years old, and the others were maybe seven and eight. Close to Valentina's age.

"You were friends with Valentina, right?" I asked them.

Victoria jumped up, knocking into the table as she shushed the girls. "I answer your questions," she said. "You go now."

I nodded, and slowly put the pictures of Spike and Harvey back in my file.

I walked to the door, Victoria on my heels.

"Thank you, Victoria."

She was already closing the door behind me as I crossed its threshold. I heard her engage the doorknob lock and slide the security chain until it dropped into position with a tiny but final plink.

Chapter Twelve

Five minutes later, Wallace and I walked to the manager's office, comparing notes along the way. He hadn't been able to get anyone to open the door. I hadn't been able to get a straight answer out of Victoria. Together, we added up to a goose egg on our efforts.

"At least we figured out who the woman with the incredibly bad phone manners was," Wallace pointed out.

"It's the little things," I agreed. But even I realized that my voice sounded flat.

Wallace put his hand on my shoulder. "You know, most of the time the people here illegally are too scared to talk. If they get involved, they could be discovered, and that could lead to deportation. So don't feel bad that Victoria didn't open up to you. Remember, you got her to open that door, so now we know who she is. That really *is* something."

Wallace knocked on the door of the manager's unit, 8A. The door flew open and an emaciated white man wearing a wife-beater T-shirt stepped out, an army tattoo on his left arm and a challenging look on his face. His B.O. backed me up two steps, and I put a fist under my nose.

He trained his flashing eyes on Wallace. "You again."

Wallace cleared his throat. "This is Emily Bernal from the law firm representing Sofia—"

The man turned on me, blasting me with halitosis. "I already talked to you on the phone, lady."

He fished a pack of Camels and a lighter with a suggestive female silhouette on it from the rear pocket of his jeans.

Hello to you, too, Mr. Michael Q. Scott, I thought.

"I was hoping you might be able to tell me if you'd ever seen either of these men." I pulled out the photos of Spike and Harvey and splayed them in one hand in front of him.

Very deliberately, Scott picked a cigarette out of the pack, shoved it between his lips, returned the pack to his back pocket, clicked his lighter until it flamed, lit his cigarette, and puffed three times. He didn't so much as glance at the photos. "Nope."

My blood started simmering. "I assume that means no you *won't* since you didn't look. However, I am asking you, as nicely as I can, to just look at these photos one time. Have you ever seen either of these men?"

He sucked his cig and then blew out smoke. He shifted his eyes to the pictures and stuck the lighter in his pocket. "Yeah."

"Both of them?"

"Nah. I seen the dead one on the news. Never seen the other guy."

The simmer in my blood sped up. "Mr. Scott, Sofia is very worried about her daughter. Have you seen her anywhere?"

"God, lady, I already told you. I didn't even know she had a daughter."

I felt pressure building under the lid of my simmering pot. "Funny. Her next-door neighbor, Victoria, did. She said her three daughters used to play with Valentina."

He snorted. "You're lying."

I came to a full, rolling boil. "I most certainly am not."

"You want to know how I know you're lying?" He pointed his cigarette at me, and I fantasized briefly about smashing it back into his face. He continued: "Because Victoria Nunez in 1B only has two kids. She brings 'em with her everywhere."

I stood motionless. If she only had two daughters, why had she told me all three girls were hers?

But before I'd even finished the thought a woman's unearthly screams rent the air from the interior of the complex.

I turned and sprinted back to Victoria's apartment.

***

Cramps ripped through my abdomen as I rounded the last corner, panting and grimacing. I ignored the pain. Victoria and two of the little girls stood huddled and screaming outside their apartment. Victoria clutched the cloth doll I'd last seen in the arms of the smallest of the three girls. She wasn't there with them now.

I reached Victoria and leaned on my knees. Between ragged breaths I asked, "What is it? Are you okay?"

Victoria shook her head and her screams turned to sobs. "He took her. A bad man took her."

"Took who?"

"V-V-V-Valentina!"

Now I screamed. "No!"

I looked at the doll with new eyes and realized what a fool I'd been. The doll had a blue shirt with a lace shawl, just as Sofia had told me—a doll to match the lyrics of her daughter's favorite song.

Wallace arrived seconds after me. He grabbed Victoria by both arms. His voice was preternaturally calm. "Who took her, Victoria?"

"*No lo sé. Algún hombre la tomó de esa manera.*" She pointed through the building.

Wallace opened his mouth, then looked at me.

I translated. "She said, 'I don't know. Some man took her that way.' To the street."

I took off again, toward the street we'd parked on. Wallace's Altima stuck out from the clunkers lining the curb, but no cars were moving and there were no empty spaces. I ran to the right down the block, peering in windows, searching between cars. Nothing. I ran back, scanning the cars and the buildings across the street. I met Wallace where I'd started as he ran back from checking the street in the other direction.

"Did you see anything?" I asked him.

"Not a damn thing."

"We've got to talk to Victoria."

"First I have to call 911, and my office."

"But I have to talk to her first," I insisted.

"Then talk fast. I can lose my job—or get thrown in jail—if I don't follow protocol."

He pressed a button on his phone and put it to his ears, and I ran back to the apartment.

When I reached Victoria and her daughters, she'd gathered both girls into her arms where they cried together on the small scrap of concrete outside the door to their home.

"Victoria, I need you to talk to me. I need you to tell me everything. *Pronto.*"

"You not find her?"

I shook my head and pointed to her apartment. She set the girls down and headed inside, holding tight to two little hands. She sat at her kitchen table, and pulled her children up onto either side of her lap.

I didn't have time to be warm and fuzzy. The cops would be here soon, and I needed answers. "Start from the beginning, Victoria Nunez."

I pulled a yellow pad and pen from my Redrope.

Victoria wiped her eyes and nodded. "I keep Valentina while Sofia working. I watch TV and see news that the *policia* arrest Sofia. Sofia tell me that if anything happen to her, hide Valentina, so I-I-I . . ." She put both her hands over her face and sobbed momentarily, then gathered herself and continued. "So I tell people Valentina mine."

I nodded. "Good. Now, have you ever seen the men whose pictures I showed you, or any other men around here?"

"No, never, but Valentina talk about her papa. Say he tell her and her mama to come here on the train that goes underground. Only, when they get there, it's a bus with a dog on it. She say he's coming, that he come soon. That he stay and work so the mean cowboy who's scared of Indians can make pretty jewelry." She threw up her hands and shrugged. "I do not understand her, but she say it."

None of it made sense to me, either. I scribbled notes verbatim, frantically, and prayed I'd be able to decipher them later.

"Did she tell you where her father worked?" I asked.

Wallace walked in and took one of the seats.

"She say Mexico."

"What did Sofia say about him?"

"She never say nothing." Victoria nuzzled the side of the head of the sobbing older girl and squeezed her little one.

"What did Valentina have when the man took her? What was she wearing?"

"She still in Barbie clothes, pink, and the man have a gun. Valentina's brave, she grab her backpack and try to run away, but he catch her." Victoria choked on a sob, then spoke again. "She drop her doll. She love her doll."

"What did the backpack look like?"

"Pink Barbie. Valentina like everything pink Barbie."

"What did she have in it?"

Victoria's eyes widened. "She never lets anyone touch it. I don't know."

That was weird. I wasn't an expert on little girls, but from what I'd seen and what I remembered from my own childhood, a little girl showed off her treasures, got them out and took a loving daily inventory, caressed them and sang to them. I heard sirens outside, and my racing heart sped up even faster. I had to hurry.

"Tell me about the man who took her," I said. "What did he look like?"

"Big man, white, no hair on his head, and a tattoo here—" she pointed to the inside of her left upper arm, "that say E-S-L." She pronounced it Ay-Essay-Ellay. "But the E's funny."

I swung the paper around to her. "Can you draw it?"

She nodded, and did, drawing the Greek letter sigma: Σ.

I heard footsteps outside. "Do you have a picture of Valentina?"

Victoria reached in her pocket and got her phone, nodding. "I text you one, yes?"

"Yes." I said my number and she typed it and hit send.

A loud knock sounded at the door. "Police."

"We've gotta let them in," Wallace said under his breath.

I shoved the paper and pen into my folder. "Thank you, Victoria. You've helped Sofia and Valentina a lot. I will tell Sofia. The police will want to talk to you now."

I placed my hand on hers and gripped it. I squeezed, and she flipped hers and squeezed mine back.

Tears rolled down her cheeks again. She whispered, more to herself than to me, "*Lo siento. Lo siento.*"

Wallace opened the door and let the cops in.

Chapter Thirteen

A big-bellied, uni-browed police officer with basset-hound eyes and a bad attitude questioned both of us. Officer Samson. I made a mental note not to get in his way in the future, but he let Wallace and me go an hour after he arrived.

I'd texted Jack moments after the police got there: *Must talk ASAP. Where are you?*

I hoped he wasn't mad that three o'clock had long since passed. I kept sneaking peeks at my phone, but heard nothing until we were walking away to the car.

Jack: *Driving to PCCB.*

PCCB, PCCB, PCCB? I realized I had stopped and was tapping my foot. Relax girl, I told myself. I didn't do my best thinking when I let myself get all jacked up. I took several deep breaths and tried again. PCCB . . . Potter County Courts Building. I nodded.

I texted: *Meet you there.*

I climbed into the Altima. Wallace pulled four wipes out and handed me two. I sanitized like the Energizer Bunny, my adrenaline still pumping.

"Can you drop me at the Potter County Courts Building?" I asked. "I have to meet Jack." I dropped my wipes in the little trashcan and buckled in.

"On my way." He peeled rubber. "You're good at this, you know?"

I blew air through my pressed lips. "I don't know about that, but I really, really want to find this little girl."

He nodded. "Me, too. Hey, can I get a copy of your notes from your interviews with Victoria?"

"Absolutely. I'll scan them for you now. Just call or text later if you have questions."

I used Tiny Scan on my phone to text them to him while he drove, holding myself upright as he took all the corners too fast, like he'd done

on the way to Harvey's place. He had some legit driving skills. I hit
send on my text to him and looked up. He had pulled into the parking
lot behind a familiar building that looked a heck of a lot like *2001: A
Space Odyssey*'s version of a courthouse. I'd never had reason to go to
the PCCB in my youth, but I had been in the old art deco Potter
County Court*house*. The Courts Building was nothing like that one.

I turned to Wallace. "It's my first time here, and—"

He smiled and pointed. "Through the back door there. Security's
just inside it."

Security. "Oh no."

"Huh?"

"I forgot about going through a metal detector."

He frowned. "You're packing?"

"Yeah."

He guffawed and slapped his knee. "You really are an 'Amarilla'
girl, aren't you?" He said, aping the local accent like a native.

"Guilty. And yet I forgot my handbag in the car when we were at
Harvey's house. How smart was that?"

He opened his glove compartment. "Stash it in there, Annie Oak-
ley. They probably won't even make you go through the metal detec-
tors—I'll bet every attorney in that building's carrying—but better safe
than sorry. And you're going to have to come bail me out if I get
thrown in jail for possessing it without a license."

I put my treasured gun in the glove box and grinned. "Of course.
Thank you. For everything."

"You, too. We did good today."

"Yes, we did." I put my hand on the door handle and tucked the
Redrope folder and handbag under my arm, then stopped. "We're
going to find her, aren't we? I mean, she's got to be okay."

Wallace leaned toward me and snagged me in a hug. "I sure hope
so. I'll be on my knees praying we do, morning and night."

I twisted and put my arm around him, squeezing tight for a long
few seconds. I loved that Wallace was a man of faith. Did he manage to
find a church here where he felt at home? I made a mental note to ask

him later. Mother's church was a no-go, but I was pretty sure I'd go to Hell if I didn't expose my baby to religion, starting in utero. I almost laughed at the thought. This was more a sign I was an "Amarilla" girl than even my concealed handgun permit or the lessons at the shooting range along with the engraved baby Glock 26 (now in Wallace's glove box) that my father had given me on my fifteenth birthday. "Wrong girl," it said around the mouth of the barrel.

We released each other and I bounded out of the car.

"Wait," he hollered, and I stopped. "For your safety, take the ramp, on the left."

"What?"

He pointed toward the building. "When it's dry, always use the ramp. When it's wet, always use the stairs. It's maintained by the county." He rolled his eyes. "Just trust me."

I laughed and waved goodbye and took off for the courthouse. My feet pounded a quick drumbeat on the sidewalk. Jack had just reached the top of the ramp, so I called out to him. He looked my way, saw me, and waited. He didn't appear pissed, but he didn't look warm and fuzzy either.

I picked up my pace for the last few steps up the tiled incline and over an oddly painted metal bridge of some sort.

"Thanks," I said. "So glad I caught you."

"I'm in a hurry," he said. "We'll talk inside."

"Okay."

We entered, and he gestured toward the security station. The PCCB was shaped like an L inside from this direction, with security jammed into the corner at its base with a corridor to the right as its horizontal line, and a corridor in front of us as its vertical line.

"What is that odor?" I asked Jack. The whole place smelled musty and vaguely unhealthy.

"Vanity, plus precipitation."

"Jack, seriously, what is it?"

"This place leaks like a sieve."

"Ah."

I plopped my now-two-pounds-lighter handbag onto the conveyor belt and walked slowly through the scanner.

"Hello, Mr. Holden." The Potter County Deputy manning the scanner looked at Jack like a long-lost friend, his white teeth gleaming except for the missing left eyetooth.

"How's your sciatica?" Jack walked around the security station while he chatted.

"Pains me something fierce when it rains, but, other than that, I can't complain."

"Take care, Lucius."

"You too, Mr. Holden."

Lucius waved me through the metal detector, and I collected my handbag on the other side.

Just then, I heard a commotion. I turned to see a female deputy handcuffing the man behind me in the line. A Leatherman tool lay out on the conveyor belt, but that didn't seem to be the problem.

The woman—a dead ringer for my mother—held a baggie in front of the man's face and said, "Sir, you are under arrest for possession of an illegal controlled substance."

Jack pulled me along by my upper arm. "Happens all the time."

"What?"

"Some poor sap surrenders his knife only to have his dope fall out right in front of the deputies."

I laughed. "Another potential client."

"Somebody has to protect their rights, and it keeps me from digging ditches."

We headed to the elevators. There were two, but one had a piece of white copier paper taped to it. In large, black print it read OUT OF ODER. While I started telling Jack about the day's discoveries, Jack pressed the up button, then pulled a pen from his briefcase.

"I found out a lot more about Sofia, but something even bigger happened."

Jack drew an R below and between the O and D with an upward pointing arrow. Then he wrote (-1 Sp) at the top of the paper. The elevator doors opened, revealing a floor that looked like the top of a bunch of blue Legos and walls plastered with sheets of wood-grained paper. I stopped speaking. Two men in business suits stepped out, one looking like any ol' attorney in Dallas, and the other in boots, a felt Cowboy hat, and a Western-cut suit with snazzy lapel stitching. We got on, and before we turned around, I saw a flier for "Birthday Cake! Cheryl is turning the big 5-0! Join us in the District Clerk's Office for Cake and Fun!" taped to the back of the elevator. Jack pressed the button for the fifth floor.

"Go on," he said.

"We found Valentina. I mean, we found where she'd been staying."

He raised his eyebrows.

I took that as, "Great job. Please continue." So I did. "She was with the neighbor who babysat her, Victoria, who was also Sofia's emergency contact at work, but that's beside the point. Sofia had made Victoria promise to hide Valentina if anything ever happened to her. And, at first, Victoria lied to us and said she didn't know where Valentina was. But then the apartment manager said Victoria just had two daughters, and there were three girls there when I interviewed her. As we were talking to Mr. Slum Lord, Victoria and her girls started screaming their heads off, so we ran back." I stopped to breathe.

The elevator doors opened on the fifth floor. A woman with a cane and long silver hair got on before we could get off. Jack pressed the Open Doors button and we waited for her to situate herself.

"First floor, please," she said in a voice that didn't waver.

He pressed the 1 button, with his index finger this time, and we slipped out before the doors closed, in front of two soft drink machines covered in more fliers.

"Keep talking." He pointed to our right and we walked into a large foyer, then he turned left toward the doors of the DA's office.

"And one of the little girls was gone. A man had just kidnapped Valentina. We ran after him, but we didn't get a look at him."

"Did you see his car, get a license plate?"

"No, nothing."

"Jiminy Christmas."

He pulled open the door to the DA's office and I walked ahead of him into a very small foyer.

I lowered my voice. "I know. Then Wallace called 911, so I hurried in to talk to Victoria before the cops could get there. And that's when she told me everything, only it made no sense, and we still have no idea where Valentina is, or who took her. But Victoria sent me a picture."

I pulled it up and put my phone in front of his face. He stopped, gazing for a second with me at Sofia, sans bruises and swelling with her pink-clad little angel. Then he broke away and nodded to the large blonde woman who was looking at us from behind a glass panel. She was surrounded at her desk by framed inspirational religious quotes, pictures of horses (my kind of woman), and photos of her with two look-alike girls.

"Jack Holden. I have an appointment with ADA—"

The woman interrupted him, her voice thick with small-town Panhandle twang. "Oh yes. Just a moment. You can wait over in the lobby."

Jack's brows furrowed and we walked back into the small waiting area behind us. He lowered his voice, a little, and said, "I hate it when these prima donna ADAs make me wait. I never made a defense attorney sit out here like a kid outside the principal's office when I was an ADA."

Just as we were about to take seats, a new woman's voice said, "Jack." It was a voice that raised the hairs on the back of my neck.

Both of us whirled. It was Melinda, tucked into a black pencil skirt and starched, white, tailored blouse that fit like a leotard. I fought the urge to lick my thumb and scrub the dirty spots off my jeans from my earlier tumbles. Instead, I fluffed my bangs and smoothed the sides of my ponytail.

She did a double take. "Emily. What are you doing here?"

Before I could answer, Jack did. "Emily's my paralegal. I assume she's welcome at our meeting?"

"Um, yeah. Sure. Right this way."

Was it my imagination, or did her pressed lips mean my presence irritated her? Or maybe it disappointed her? She'd looked at Jack a moment ago like a red-tailed hawk I'd once seen lock eyes on a rabbit seconds before snatching it into the sky, twenty feet from where I sat daydreaming in summer grass. I'd had nightmares about hawks for a week after that. Oddly enough, I'd had nightmares about Melinda for twenty years.

The door past the receptionist's area buzzed, and we followed Melinda's sashaying hips through it and down a hall to an open door on our left. She gestured for us to go in.

Right before we entered what looked like a small conference room, I whispered to Jack. "I just don't know how we're going to tell Sofia."

He looked me in the eyes, and something in them caught me off guard and sent my heart lurching into my throat. I stopped, and he did, too. He smiled at me. Automatically, idiotically, I smiled back, and I felt myself go all gooey. He had the most amazing tawny eyes, especially when they looked at me like that.

Long seconds later, he finally turned to Melinda and said, "So, what's this emergency summons about anyway?"

We walked in and she shut the door with a heavy thud. I put my hands to my cheeks to see if they were as hot as they felt. They were. Melinda and I both took seats—her at the head of the table, and me on the far side—but Jack stood by the chair nearest the door. He'd missed a loop with his belt, and I found myself wanting to fix it for him, which was his wife's job. That made my cheeks even hotter. How was it that Jack could distract me like this when, seconds ago, I'd been so upset about Valentina's kidnapping?

Melinda clasped her hands in front of her on the table. "I wanted to tell you in person, before you heard about it on the news. There's been an incident at the jail."

Jack stopped short, his hand on the back of a chair. "What kind of incident?"

"The kind where your client Sofia Perez was killed, unfortunately."

It took a moment for the shock of her words to break through the haze Jack's eyes had put me in, and I gasped aloud. Sofia, dead? I'd only met her once, but my entire life had revolved around her and her daughter for the last week. Valentina, missing . . . and no longer with a mother, or even a father (that we knew about). Well, I guess we wouldn't have to worry about how to break the news to Sofia about Valentina after all.

To my horror, I burst into tears.

Chapter Fourteen

I paced in front of Jack's desk.

"But we could file a wrongful death suit on Valentina's behalf, as Sofia's survivor. Or on behalf of Sofia's estate. Or something!"

That last part came out a little louder than I'd intended. Too late, I realized it was probably bad form to yell at the top of your lungs at your boss of one week. But, really, Jack could drive anyone into a frenzy. The man was infuriating. One minute he was confusing me with inappropriate goo-goo eyes in the DA's office, and the next he was shutting me down about Valentina. When she needed my help more than ever.

Jack didn't yell back, but Snowflake shivered in her sheepskin doggy bed beside his desk. "It's called a survival action, but Valentina isn't our client."

"Sofia is."

"Emily, finding Valentina has nothing to do with filing a survival action."

"But our client was murdered in cold blood. Melinda may call it a gang fight, but that's a crock and you know it. How come Sofia was the only one hurt, much less killed? And on the same day Valentina gets snatched? Something more is going on here, Jack. Something much, much more. And the DA's office is covering it up. It's total bull honky!"

A big grin spread across his face ear to ear. "Bull what?"

I crossed my arms and glared at him. "You heard me."

Jack stood up and started pacing back and forth behind his desk, which made Snowflake sit up and whine.

"You're right," he said. "The circumstances suck, and a survival action isn't out of the question. But not until we're caught up on some other things. Then, and only then, I very well may support your request to expand the practice into civil litigation and ask you to help look into it. In the meantime, you did an amazing job today and really broke things open for the police. They're going to find Valentina, and you'll have made that possible. But, Emily, that's their job, not yours." His voice softened. "You certainly have a passion for managing my practice, and I'm not complaining about it. Passion is good."

I stared at the floor, thinking for a moment. "I haven't told you everything."

Jack leaned back against one of his tall cabinets. "Oh, shit."

"What? No, I didn't do anything. Well, I mean, I didn't get caught doing anything." I held up my hand as Jack started to interrupt. "Just listen. We know Sofia shot Spike, but she wouldn't say why. I looked into Spike's background, and he did time for molesting a child with another guy—a Harvey Dulles from Amarillo. I gave you a copy of my research, remember?"

"Right."

"Well, today I learned Sofia used to bring Valentina to work and hide her there, where she'd sleep or read or color or whatever."

"So?"

I crouched beside the shivering Snowflake and started massaging her neck. Poor girl didn't like high emotion. She still shook, but she seemed to relax some into my hand. "So, Spike has a record for doing bad stuff with kids. Sofia shot him. What if those two things are related? I got to thinking: what about the possibility that his old buddy Harvey was there, too? One of the hotel employees said he saw a man running away from the hotel the night Sofia shot Spike, a man that fits the description for Harvey. Harvey could be a witness for us. Or, he might even be the one who has Valentina."

Jack rubbed his jaw. "Okay. I'm still listening."

I stood back up and leaned my tush against the edge of Jack's desk, facing him. "Wallace and I went to Harvey's house before we went to see Victoria," I said. "Before I knew she had Valentina. Harvey wasn't there. Two homeless teenagers told us he moved out in a hurry last week. I haven't checked with his employer yet to see if he's still working, but he could have her, Jack."

He shook his head. "Did you tell the police about Harvey? Because Valentina—"

"I know. Isn't our client. And yes, I told the officer that questioned me at Victoria's my theory. I got a few nods, but he wasn't won over."

"Is that all?"

I thought about trespassing at Harvey's house and my B&E at Sofia's apartment.

"Yeah, that's all," I said. "I just wanted you to know everything, plus, it could be a lead for a survival suit."

"Which we aren't going to look into yet."

I crouched and resumed stroking Snowflake, as much to soothe myself now as her.

"I know, but just keep it in mind," I said. "We've got one known creep living in Amarillo, and his creepy buddy shows up here. Sofia kills the buddy, so isn't it possible creep number one knows people that know people in PCDC? He could be behind Sofia's death, too."

"Noted. For the future. For now, just finish Johnson. Then I need to unleash your passion and brilliance on my other cases."

I crossed my fingers behind my back and said, "No problem."

***

Mother picked me up at the curb forty-five minutes later for the ride back to Heaven. Suddenly, a heavy tiredness coursed through me so hard that I could barely lift my hand to open the door. I flopped into the seat like a lead weight.

"Hi, Mother," I said.

When she didn't reply, I turned to her. She was biting her lip—always a bad sign. Today had already been a long, hard day. I closed my eyes. *Lord, give me strength.*

I tried again. "What's wrong?"

She tilted her head back, the better to raise her nose in the air. "Imagine my disappointment to have to hear through the grapevine that my own daughter is having my first grandbaby, instead of hearing it from her."

Well, this wasn't good. Surely the news of my just-booked-half-an-hour-ago OB appointment for Wednesday hadn't spread that fast.

"Who told you that?"

"So you aren't denying it?" She braked at a green light and the car behind her honked. She pressed the accelerator.

I let my weary head fall back against the front seat cushion as we shot forward. "Um, congratulations, Grandmother."

She cleared her throat, then went silent.

"Mother, I'm only eight weeks along." Well, nearly nine, but who was counting? "I just found out myself. I had planned to tell you tonight anyway." I hoped the crossed fingers I'd used with Jack earlier had a lasting effect. "So, who told you?"

"Katie emailed me. One of those online cards from Jacquie Lawson." She sniffed. "It was just lovely. A little bear with balloons."

I choked back a groan. Collin. I hadn't mentioned "mum's the word" when I'd told my story in New Mexico. Especially in relation to *my* mum.

"How sweet of her," I said.

"She's very kind. And so I called Rich—"

"You *what*?!" I sat forward so hard and fast the seat belt pinched me. "No, Mother, no, tell me you didn't."

"What? He didn't pick up so I just left him a voice mail."

Oh God, oh no, oh, my mother. "WHAT DID YOU SAY?"

"Don't use that tone with me, young lady. I told him congratulations on the baby and how excited I was to be a grandmother."

I put my head in my hands and then a giggle started that seemed to ricochet back at me as it bounced off the insides of the car, escalating and multiplying until it was a symphony of inharmonious cackles. I giggled so hard I needed to change my panties. I laughed, literally, until I cried, and by the time it stopped, I was choking on little sobs.

"You called Rich instead of me."

Now it was her turn for the hot seat, and she squirmed.

"Well, I—your new job, and, because I just—so, yes, and I knew I'd see you soon anyway." She clamped her mouth shut.

I blubbered a little as I spoke. "Mother, that man's lover crashed my baby announcement dinner, and Rich chose *him* over me. So, guess what? I hadn't told him yet. He doesn't get to share this part. It was supposed to be my little secret. My baby. Mine. Not his, and not Stormy's."

"Emily Josephine Phelps Bernal, you cannot mean to tell me you aren't going back to Dallas to raise this child with him."

She put on her blinker and turned onto the I-40 access road.

"I most certainly can."

"You can't divorce Rich now. The baby is proof he's not gay."

I hooted. I couldn't help it. "Were you not listening to the part where he doesn't want to be married to me, the part where he chose Stormy, who is a man? I'm sorry, Mother, but the ability to make a baby does not determine your sexual orientation."

She huffed. "Still, I cannot for the life of me see how you, a girl whose own father left you, would deny your child a father?"

She accelerated up the entrance ramp and merged into what passed for rush hour traffic in Amarillo. My pulse accelerated with the car. I held my tongue, fuming, working it out in my mind. What was this about? How could she say these things to me? Dad left when I was nearly grown. And it *had* hurt. It *still* hurt. Yet I knew it probably hurt her more. Lord knows she was the one who had to face the humiliation when other people whispered. I was beginning to understand what that must have been like. Plus, for years he'd sent postcards and letters and gifts and checks to me. He'd called on my birthdays. He'd begged my forgiveness and tried to explain, in his own way, that he wasn't the kind of man to live in one place, with one woman, and that he couldn't come back anymore.

So, yeah, it had hurt, but I hadn't felt as "left" as she had. That was until I was a senior in college, anyway, when all his cards and letters just stopped, and he never called me again. I had Rich who told me he wanted to be my husband, so I didn't need a father, and I moved on, too. An arrow sliced through my heart and out my back. Now I'd moved on from being left by a father to being left by a husband.

I softened my tone. "Mother, it is in part because I had a father at home and lost him that I fully understand the difference between what I went through and what it means that my child's father won't ever live in our house. This baby will always have a father, but won't have to know the hurt of a father leaving."

"But what will I tell my friends?" she shrieked, turning to me, and swerving into the lane to our right.

A horn blared and Mother jumped in her seat, overcorrecting to her left, earning her another honk. She straightened her wheel and squeezed her lips together. I grabbed the armrest on the door. She wasn't going to have to worry about this if she killed us both. I bit my lip hard, holding it in. I'd grown up believing in honoring and respecting my parents. I didn't always practice it, but I tried. Right now, I tried really, really hard.

I turned the radio on as a distraction. "A murder suspect was killed today in a prison riot at the Potter County Detention Center—"

I snapped the dial off.

Mother made a *hrmph* sound. "At least the rest of us won't have to pay to keep another criminal fed and clothed for the rest of their life."

"Enough!" My yell was so loud and high-pitched it hurt my own ears, and Mother ducked. "Enough with your comments. If you so much as open your mouth the rest of the way home, I'll . . . I'll . . ." I stopped. I had no idea what I'd do, I just knew neither of us was going to like it. I exhaled and dialed down my volume. "Just enough, okay?"

She bit her lip, again. It was white, as were her knuckles. I felt a little bit guilty, but not so much that I wasn't able to appreciate the blessed silence on the rest of the drive.

Chapter Fifteen

I stalked from the elevator to the office the next morning an hour early in a hailstorm of text messages from my soon-to-be ex-husband. I hit the front door like a battering ram.

Rich: *Why didn't you tell me?*

Rich: *We must talk!*

Rich: *I deserve a reply!*

Those were the three latest I'd received. Oh, I had a reply for him. Boy, did I have a reply. I grabbed the door and threw my whole body into slamming it. The door swung closed on its hydraulic brake to a whispery soft landing behind me.

Snowflake met me, but she slunk away when she saw the mood I was in. No toast crusts for her today. I slammed my handbag down on my desk. I hadn't slept worth a dang last night. Dreams of Valentina tormented me, her screams, her sweet face and her adorable little Barbie pj's, a large bald tattooed man dragging her by the arm away from the rodeo arena while I watched, helpless, standing directly in the path of a charging bull. Hours later, I was struggling to keep my toast down and reeling from bickering with my mother the entire drive to work. Rich's text barrage was just piling on at this point.

A note lay on my chair. *Johnson and only Johnson until you're done.* Oh, not Jack, too. The yellow-bellied sapsucker didn't have the guts to tell me to my face. He had to leave me a little note. I wanted to scream at him. *I know, I know, already. I know what you are ordering me to do, to ignore an innocent little girl who needs someone to care what happens to her so that I can go to work for clients who have done bad things.*

The bell on my desk beckoned me, not to ring it, no, but rather to ignore it. It beckoned me down the hall on sneaky feet. It beckoned me to Jack's luxurious and oh-so-private office. So I led with my chin and sailed down the hall, holding the clacker of the bell still as I moved soundlessly toward my boss.

Once at the door to his office, I stopped at the precipice, teetering on a doubt. He had asked me to ring the bell to give him his privacy.

The devil on my shoulder whispered in my ear. *Well, wouldn't a little privacy be nice? You sure don't have any, though, so why should he?*

Nah, bell shmell. It was a stupid, chauvinistic rule, and it shouldn't be okay to hold me hostage in the lobby so he could hide behind his "privacy."

I took a deep breath and barged in, bell clanging. "Screw your bell rule, Mr. Holden, I'm not playing your little power game anymore."

The first words came out as a bellow, the last few words came out a whisper, as I took in what I saw.

Jack's tall built-in cabinet on the left side of the office was open, revealing an enormous photographic portrait of a family in what looked like hiking clothes, in a mountain setting with tall pine trees and a glistening stream. In the middle stood a striking woman with flawless skin the color of toasted caramel. Her long black hair was thick and lustrous, parted on the side and swept back as if with her fingers. The camera had caught her smile midlaugh. It lit her eyes like sparklers. She had one arm around two grinning kids: a little girl—maybe eight years old?—who was lucky enough to look just like her mother and a little boy who shared their looks and appeared to be slightly younger than his sister. On the other side of the boy, his arm around the two children, too, stood Jack. But that Jack had hair down to his shoulders and looked fifteen years younger than the short-haired man standing beside the portrait now, glaring at me like a bull does at the rodeo clown just before he tosses her over the rail.

"Is there a problem, Emily?" he said, nostrils flared, fists balled.

I now took in the easel and paper in front of him, and the unfinished charcoal drawing of the little girl from the portrait on a spotted pony. A hideaway bed extended from the left built-in cabinet, Snowflake huddled in terror on a pillow. I took in the man in his white tee and his jeans, a Fender shirt on a hanger looking ready for wear on the table. I smelled spices and cheese and, on his desk, I saw his breakfast taco.

Suddenly I knew the answer to all his mysterious morning noises, and, worse, knew what a horrible person I was.

I tried to answer him. "No." No sound except a wheezy crackling noise came out, and I repeated myself, louder. "No." I backed up, my hand behind me on the doorframe. "I'm sorry."

I fled back to the lobby and on to the bathroom down the hall, face in my hands, tears leaking through my fingers. What a dumbass I was. A total dumbass. A total clueless dumbass. I shook my head, cringing, as I remembered Jack's face, and the picture of his daughter that he'd drawn from that beautiful, beautiful portrait of his family. A total clueless, selfish dumbass.

I leaned against the closed door inside a bathroom stall. Still, what was he doing living on a pullout bed in his Amarillo office if he had a family like that somewhere? They sure weren't living at Wrong Turn Ranch in New Mexico either. And then it hit me. He wouldn't have a shrine like that to his family if they were still with him. So, had Jack's wife left him, and taken the kids? Was he in the middle of a divorce? It was possible, but it didn't change my invasion of his privacy, or how upset he was with me, or how upset I was with myself. It could mean he hadn't misled me about his marital status, and that my anger about it had been unjust, though.

Five snuffling minutes later, I washed my face and slunk to my desk. I booted up my laptop. Typing the words RodeoQueen somehow brought the rain down from my eyes again. I mopped them with my light peach sweater. Bangs and thuds resounded from Jack's office, and I flinched at each sound. I opened my Johnson file and tried to find my place.

Footsteps approached along with the tinkle of Snowflake's tags. I tensed, not ready to face him.

"Here are the other client files with instructions for your next few projects when you're done with Johnson. I'll be in court today." His voice sounded tight and echo-y.

I tried to make myself sound neutral, even though tears threatened to fall again. "Okay, thanks."

He opened the door and disappeared down the hall with Snowflake and me staring at the space he left behind.

***

I spent the morning on a variety of tasks, most of them not work related. Of course, there was my ongoing text war with Rich. Luckily, he'd disappeared about an hour ago. I needed the breather—from him and from a persistent ache in my abdomen, which I hoped was just stress.

I had emailed a few prospective employers about jobs I found in the *Globe News*. One as a legal secretary, another as a receptionist. Unfortunately, there weren't any ads for paralegals. I hated to take a job outside my field, especially for less money, but I'd blown it this morning, and I needed a backup plan—fast. I hoped Jack didn't fire me before I found something else. My heart lurched and made a liar out of me— it knew I hoped he didn't fire me at all.

I checked my personal email, something I only did every few days. In it was an email from Katie, dated yesterday.

Emily: Congratulations on the baby! Collin told me the fantastic news, and also a lot of other not-so-great things, but I want to hear it from you. Call me, and I promise I won't make it all about me for a change. <3 Tell your mother hello for me, and take your prenatal vitamins.

I would call her, for sure, but not when Jack could walk in. I flagged the message.

On a whim, I had texted Nadine, the waitress from My Thai: *It's Emily. We bonded the other day over my crash landing into Taco Villa back in the day, and we talked about getting together. Want to grab dinner?*

Despite all the nonwork stuff, I had uncovered a wealth of juicy nuggets for Jack on Paul Johnson, so I felt virtuous about that, at least. I eyed the new client files. My stomach growled. Which to deal with first? Neither.

I grabbed my phone and texted Wallace. Again: *Any news on Valentina? Do you know if the police found Maria Delgado or Harvey?*

When neither Wallace nor Nadine answered me, the new project work seemed to glow like a bright light, refusing to be ignored. I grabbed the first file.

My phone rang. Thank God. "Hello?"

Crackle. "—Ily Ber—" Crackle.

"Our reception is terrible. This is Emily Bernal speaking."

"I have your—" Crackle-crackle.

I stood up. "I can't hear you."

Crackle-crackle-crackle. "—car."

I climbed up on the couch, trying to get my phone higher, to reach better coverage. "Can you repeat that?"

The call dropped.

The door opened. Wallace stood in the doorway in pressed khakis, work boots, and some Paul Bunyan-like plaid shirt. His eyebrows shot up.

I tried for a graceful dismount. "Um, bad cell reception."

"That's what I'd say if I was caught doing a Tom Cruise on the couch."

I laughed and he held up a bag. 575 Pizzeria. "I got a red pie and a white one," he said. "Both meatless, since I learned you were a rebel yesterday. Hungry?"

My mouth watered. "You went all the way to 575 Pizzeria?"

"I'd have gone twice that far for their pizza."

We walked to the kitchen. Was my tongue hanging out like a dog's, or did it just feel like it? I grabbed plates and napkins and set them out while Wallace extracted the boxes from the bag. When he opened the first lid and that cheesy, doughy goodness wafted my way, I nearly cried.

"I've had a really bad day. Pizza is about the only thing in the world that could make it better. You're psychic."

He grinned, mouth full of a piece of the basil, garlic, and pine nuts red pie.

I put a piece of each pie on my plate. "And today? Let's just say today can bite me."

I chomped into the white pie and exhaled to cool the cheesy part that stuck to the roof of my mouth. It was wonderful, and I admired it in my hand, covered in stripes of white cheese and green chiles.

He laughed, half-choking. "You're not much of a cusser."

I brandished a slice. "I may not cuss tough, but I fight tough."

"I believe that after yesterday."

"Hey, you didn't happen to bring my gun with you, did you?"

"No way in hell I'm carrying that thing without a license," Wallace said. "Do you know what happens to men as gorgeous as me in the slammer? I like to choose my dates, thank you very much."

I snorted, then laughed. "Did you find those teenagers we saw yesterday?"

Wallace held a hand up until he finished chewing a bite. "The police did. The kids' names are Greg Easley and Farrah Farud. Their case worker—Byron, you'd like him, good guy—took them back to a group home until we investigate the abuse allegations."

"That's good, I guess."

He waggled his hand and nodded. "It's a start."

We ate in silence a few moments until I had enough food in me to return to my favorite topic. "You brought me an update on Valentina, didn't you?"

"Now who's psychic?" He grinned.

"Psycho, more like it."

A voice in the lobby interrupted. "Excuse me, anyone here?"

I took a gulp of my tea through a bite of red pie before saying, "Yes, just a moment!" I jumped to my feet, chewing frantically and mopping sauce from my face and hands.

"Expecting someone?"

I headed to the door, looking back at him. "Nope."

The man in the lobby/my office looked about my age, ordinary in a white skin, brown hair, brown eyes kind of way, in clean blue jeans and a long-sleeved blue tee with the words Professional Drivers, Inc. across the chest. He held a clipboard and a ring of keys. He had a pleasant smell that I couldn't place.

"Hello, may I help you?"

"I'm looking for Emily Bernal." His voice had a weary undertone to its friendliness.

"That's me."

He nodded. "I called earlier. I have your car for you. I'll just need a credit card and to take you downstairs so you can check it out and sign for it."

Rich had failed to mention when I should expect my car, since baby talk had dominated the last fifteen hours of our interactions. I took the bill and recoiled. Gas, delivery fee, and money for a taxi to the airport and a plane ticket back to Dallas. It was more than I had left in my checking account. I retrieved my Visa card and handed it to him.

"Thanks," I said.

He swiped the card in his phone reader and typed on his screen.

Wallace had joined us by now. "Looks like you can drive this afternoon," he said.

I scribbled my name with my fingertip on the phone extended toward me. "Where are we going this afternoon?" I asked Wallace.

"Well, no one's tracked down Maria Delgado yet. Obviously the job calls for our Scooby Doo investigator team skills."

I laughed again. Thank God Wallace had come. "A team on which I am clearly Velma. Can we look for Harvey when we've corralled Maria?"

"Yep. And then, later, you might want to play around on the Internet. With the name Antonio Rosa."

"Why's that?"

"The gay-hating manager of the apartments finally coughed up a name to the cops. Antonio is the guy who paid for Sofia and Valentina's apartment."

"Heck yeah." Before I could stop myself, I did a fist pump, and even went a little airborne. It wasn't pretty.

Wallace burst out laughing at my feeble curse and leap, and I laughed, too, loud and real, heart hammering. The bad morning receded a little. We were going to find Valentina—I just knew it.

The driver interrupted. I'd forgotten he was there. "If you don't mind, I've got a plane to catch."

"Of course," I said.

Wallace added, "Pick me up at my office."

Jack wasn't here to ask permission, so I pretended that if he had been, he would have said yes.

Chapter Sixteen

The light green Mustang I'd given myself as a landing-my-first-job reward eight years ago still ran like a top, but it was looking rode hard and put up wet. I didn't even think about cleaning it until two blocks from the CPS building when it hit me how far it was below Wallace's standards. The delivery driver had used paper mats, but those had only covered dirty mats and carpet underneath. Residue of lattes past clung to the drink holders. A gym bag with used clothing glared at me from \ behind the passenger seat. Trash of spurious origins littered the back floor mats. I searched the glove compartment and console at a red light. No Handi Wipes. No miniature trash can. Oh well. Too late to do anything about it.

Wallace stood on the sidewalk in front of a nondescript building (amongst other nondescript buildings and large surface parking lots) fiddling with his phone. I tapped my horn lightly, and he looked up. My car withered under his scrutiny, and he hadn't even gotten in yet.

He slammed the door and then gasped. "Emily. No."

"It's not like you're going to get Ebola from it or something."

Wallace cocked his head, eyebrows up but eyes soft. "I'm not so sure. That's why Uncle Wallace is going to treat you to the most divine car wash ever." I sputtered but he shook his head. "This little baby is borderline vintage, and she deserves preservation."

Wallace directed me to the The Works car wash, and, once there, paraded around like a VIP. Talk about a place where everybody knows your name. He must have practically lived there, or owned stock. The trip to The Works for auto detailing set us back forty-five minutes. I decided not to let it bother me that we'd spent the time on my car. I'd left Jack a note that I'd be back in by midafternoon, and we were just making one stop at Maria's. It shouldn't take that long, and even I had to admit that the Mustang looked fabulous, with a little prance in her step after the detailing. Just in time to hang out in a neighborhood where she would have blended better in her previous condition.

Wallace made no secret of studying me as we drove away from The Works. "Okay, so I've held back as long as I can. Who peed in your Post Toasties today?"

I shook my head. "Who didn't?" Then, because there was nothing else I could do, I laughed. "After the quality time we've spent together, I feel it's time to share."

"Sharing time, yes!"

I laughed harder, startled by his shout. "So, I'm back in Amarillo because a gay transgender man named Stormy who was dressed like a woman crashed my 'Surprise, honey, I'm pregnant' party to stake his claim to my husband, Rich, who had in the meantime drained our finances Sahara dry."

Wallace stared at me for a moment. I looked at his face. Expressionless. I was afraid I'd offended him somehow, but then he said, "Wow, that's some major-league sharing. I hope you don't expect me to top that."

I shook my head. "Oh, and that's not even all. My girlfriend Katie found out from her brother Collin that I was preggers, so she congratulated my mother, who ripped me a new one for keeping her in the dark and took it upon herself to inform my ex, whom I hadn't told yet either and who's basically been strafing me with text fire all day. Oh, and I got in a snit at Jack and barged in on him half-dressed and in the midst of drawing a lovely charcoal picture of his daughter in front of his shrine to the family I didn't know he had, and he's not speaking to me."

"Jesus, Emily, I hope you've got your therapist on speed dial."

"I can't afford one, thanks to Rich."

"And here you are back in Amarillo."

"Where everybody is a little too interested in my business. 'There goes poor Emily who wasn't enough woman to hold onto her man.'"

He shook his head. "Honey, it doesn't sound like any woman was woman enough for your man."

"Ironic, isn't it?"

He reached over and patted my knee. "Don't worry. I'm sure you'll be old news by Christmas."

I snorted.

"And Emily? I think the term you're looking for about Stormy is transvestite."

"Good to know for when I tell the police why I slapped the bitch." I clapped my hand over my mouth. "Sorry."

He whooped. "Don't be sorry. That's the spirit." He smacked me a high five. "Okay, you're allowed one more hour to pout and be the center of attention. After that it's my turn."

"Deal."

"In the meantime, take me back to the part about Jack and half-naked."

The conversation lightened. It felt good to get all of it out, and my mood improved. I turned into Maria's neighborhood and decided to swing around the block first.

"I don't think she can park in back, but let's take a look," I said.

All we saw on the next street was more houses, and there was no alley between the two streets.

"Yeah, and she doesn't have a front garage either," Wallace said. "She's going to have to park on the street."

"I wish we knew what she drove."

"Or if she has a car at all."

"True. I didn't find anything registered to her."

I parked the Mustang three houses down. We walked to her door. I heard a giggle, and the sound of feet. I rang the front bell, then knocked. No answer. No lights. No more sounds.

"Someone doesn't want us to know they're here," I said. "But the laugh sounded like a child." I chewed my top lip. "Valentina?"

"It sounded more like a little boy to me."

"You're right. Let's watch the house for a while. Unless you can think of something else?"

"No, sounds good."

We hadn't been in the car five minutes when I pointed out a slight Hispanic woman in jeans and a black jack-o'-lantern sweatshirt headed toward us, from beyond Maria's house. She carried white plastic grocery bags with a red and blue logo on them looped over her arms.

Wallace leaned in her direction. "That could be her."

"She looks about the right age."

We knew to expect a fifty-ish woman from the information I'd found on her.

I tucked my handbag under my arm and put my hand on the door latch. The woman cut across the yard of the house next door at an angle toward Maria's. Wallace and I looked at each other and nodded, and we slipped out of the car. We walked toward Maria's house, moving quickly. The woman noticed us, and she started running, groceries spilling all across the grass. Oranges, avocados, a quart carton of milk, tortillas.

I shouted but my words were punctuated by gasping breaths as I ran to intercept her. "Maria, wait, someone kidnapped Valentina Perez. We're not with INS, we just want to help the little girl."

She didn't slow down. Wallace surprised me with a burst of speed and he made it to the door before she did. She stopped short, and I hit the front steps full tilt.

Crack! My foot exploded through the old wood and my momentum threw the rest of me forward into the steps: knees first, then gut and hands. All of the air came out of my lungs in a "woof." And then I yelled bloody murder, rattling the windows.

"Mother Goose!"

"Emily!" Wallace had a panicked look on his face.

The woman looked at me, then at her front door and moved toward it.

"No! I'm fine." I pushed myself up with my right hand, and I waved my left at her. "Don't let her get past you."

Wallace stayed put. "Maria, please. We don't care what you're doing, or who the little boy is inside that house."

She drew a shaky breath.

Wallace continued. "Some white guy, big, with a shaved head, took Valentina. You know who Valentina is, right? Sofia's daughter? Sofia, the one who used your ID to get a job, the one on the news who killed a guy at a hotel last week?"

I had meanwhile gingerly pulled my foot out of the splintery hole in the bottom step. My navy shoe stayed behind, so I reached in and got it. I sighed and put it back on. The wood had torn my knit pants, but the pants had protected my skin. I'd have an ugly bruise and I had splinters in both hands, but I wasn't really hurt that badly. I rubbed my stomach. The cramps that I'd endured off and on the last few days were still there, but no worse than before. *Sorry, baby.*

Maria took a step back, shaking her head.

I stood up. "I'm Emily and we talked about all of that on the phone last Friday. You're Maria, aren't you?"

She shook her head again.

"A six-year-old little girl. And you could help her, couldn't you?" She didn't react at all. I softened my voice, pleading. "Please. The man had a tattoo, an ESL, a weird E, here, on his arm." I pointed to the inside of my left upper arm.

Finally she spoke. "You not cops?"

I definitely recognized her voice from our phone conversation. "No, we're not."

"Not INS?"

"No."

"Then go. You trespass, and I defend myself."

"What?"

She pulled a handgun out of her purse. I raised my eyebrows and Wallace put his hands in front of him, palms forward, and said, "We were just leaving."

***

Back at the office, I took Snowflake out to do her business and then settled in at my desk. I was disappointed—and sore—from the visit to Maria's. I felt virtuous for the Johnson report I'd left Jack in his chair that morning and it didn't appear he'd been back to the office while I was gone. That meant my brownie points were already in the bank, so I allotted myself fifteen more minutes to sleuth online. I'd still have two hours left in the day to work on the new client projects afterward.

A text came in, Nadine answering mine from earlier: *I'm working tonight. Coffee tomorrow?*

I could go before my OB appointment at eleven. I texted back: *9:30 at Roasters on Georgia?*

She agreed. I had a girlfriend date. I typed it into my calendar, then started Googling ESL and ΣSL. ESL had common usage as "English as a second language," resulting in a crushing load of hits about adult education programs. No way would some thug tattoo English as a second language on his arm. ΣSL brought up concepts only an engineer or mathematician could understand. I added Mexico to each term, but that didn't help.

The door in front of me opened, and I rapidly closed my browser. I swallowed and looked up to try to make amends with my boss, but it wasn't him.

"Hello, Emily."

It was Rich.

The Colombian man standing in front of my desk didn't look much older than he had when I'd met him in my freshman English class at Tech. He was slight of frame in his skinny jeans, thin black sweater, and overly stylish ankle boots. Dark and sexy in an Enrique Iglesias sort of way. But I didn't feel the rush I used to with his intense, beautiful eyes locked on me—just a sadness, a regret that made my shoulders sag, a panic that stole my breath. What the heck was he doing here?

"How did you know where to find me?" Like I didn't know. But I wanted to hear him say it.

"Your mother. We must talk."

"I'm at work." I stomped toward the kitchen, away from him, but he followed.

"I understand, and I promise we will converse in a civil manner."

"Speak for yourself." I moved around to the far side of the kitchen table.

He stood in the doorway. "Emily, I'm so sorry. I do not deserve your forgiveness, but I'm asking for it."

I rolled my eyes. Three weeks without his private school South American English made it foreign to me again, and irritating.

"Yeah, but not so sorry that you can't cheat on me and leave me broke. Give me a break, Rich. This isn't about me. You're here because of the baby, so just get on with it."

"Come back to Dallas. I want us to be a family and raise this baby together."

I cackled like a deranged hen. "That's priceless. You, me, baby, and Stormy. We'll have to get a California King. I call dibs on the side of the bed closest to the bathroom."

"If you come back, I give you my word I will not continue with Stormy. I will take the reparative therapy classes your mother has suggested I sign up for. The conversion."

"No."

"No, you don't want me to take the conversion?"

"No, I won't come back to Dallas; I won't stay married to you. You are the baby's father, and we can work out what that will look like, and I won't try to keep you out of the baby's life. But I don't want you in my town, or in my office, or in my house. I will not see you anymore while you're here. And if you show up again, I will call the police and tell them you're harassing me."

"You don't mean these things, surely?"

I stood up, put both hands on the table and yelled louder than I had when I fell through Maria's porch step earlier. "Get out. Get out, get out, get out!"

Rich stood for several moments, his mouth working but no sound coming out. I crossed my arms, but then a horrible pain tore through my abdomen. I grimaced and put my hands back on the table. Rich didn't notice, or if he did, he must have thought it was about him, because he put his hands up in defeat, took two steps back, and then turned, stopping at the door. "As you wish. Goodbye, Emily." Then he left.

As soon as he disappeared from sight, I gasped and clutched my stomach. I half-turned and put my hip on the table, then stood up again. Blood. Blood on the table. Panic gripped me. I heard the office door open and shut.

"Are you okay?"

Jack's voice. He was standing in the kitchen doorway, and his warm, golden eyes looked concerned, not angry. Had he heard everything? Probably. But that was the least of my problems now.

I shook my head no. "I think I need to go to the emergency room."

Chapter Seventeen

The Southwest ER nurse squeaked away on white hospital shoes. He'd taken my blood, my temperature, and my pulse and pressure. Now the waiting for a doctor began. The light pink and white curtained space didn't give much privacy, and not only could I hear the moaning woman to my right, but I could see skinny ankles and bare feet under the curtain to my left. Liquid dripped to the floor by the bare feet and I averted my eyes, adjusting myself on the absorbent pad the nurse had placed under me. Jack sat in an armchair with a pleather seat, to the right of the bed.

I trained my eyes on my cold bluish toes. "You don't have to stay," I said.

"I'm not leaving you alone." He folded his arms across his chest and leaned against his seat back.

For the last hour, I'd tried to stay calm and keep my fears at bay. I didn't really want him here. At the same time, I did. I didn't know what I wanted about a lot of things. But one thing was for sure: I wanted to think about something other than why I was here.

Work. We could talk about work. "I left you a report on Johnson."

"Thanks. Did you get started on Freeman?"

Words fizzed behind my lips, then died. Did I get started on Freeman? *Of course not,* I wanted to shout. *I was looking for that little girl you don't care about.* But I didn't have the moral high ground here. I had been a giant horse's rear end to him.

"No. I'm sorry." I took a sip of water through a straw and felt calmer. "Johnson may have atrocious manners and business deals on the fringe of polite society, but he hosts the biggest annual charity event in Las Cruces."

"Really?"

"Yep. It's a whole weekend of activities anchored by a three-day golf tournament that raises money for after-school shelters and programs. A keep 'em off the streets initiative."

"Huh."

"He's never done time, although most people suspect he gets away with breaking the barrier before the flag is tripped, if you know what I mean." He didn't answer, so I quickly added, "You know, when a horse starts early, before the steer breaks the barrier—"

"No, no. I know what you mean. I was just thinking."

I nodded, but he didn't elaborate, so I continued. "I can't make up my mind about him. He has a bad reputation with women, but I read that he's a good father. I met his daughter at your office last weekend, and she doesn't seem to like him, but it could just be a teenager thing."

Jack nodded.

"People hint that he's shady with his businesses," I continued, "but he raises money for kids. He may just be someone rough around the edges who's risen above his past."

Jack rubbed his forehead. "Which could make him a great client. He sent us our first case this week. An assault and battery charge against one of his employees."

"That's good." He didn't respond, so I added, "Right?"

He ignored my question. "This weekend he's having a housewarming party. Out at his ranch. We're all invited, and I think we should go. I mean, if you're feeling up to it and you don't have other plans."

I thought of spending time with my mother giving me the silent treatment, versus out at Wrong Turn Ranch with Jarhead, where I could possibly sneak over to Roswell and see what I could find out about Spike and Harvey.

"Okay," I said. "Sounds good."

He cleared his throat and looked down. "About this morning."

Oh, spit. I closed my eyes. I didn't want to think about it. I shouldn't have to deal with something that big and humiliating while I lay bleeding in an ER, should I? I could change the subject. Yet I didn't want it to linger on.

"Yes?"

He took a pen out of his pocket and thumped it on his leg, one time. "It's okay."

I swallowed hard, and then tears came. I tried to speak, failed, then tried again. "No, it's not, and I know it. You asked me to give you privacy, and I violated your space, and your, your—"

He sighed, cutting me off. "Memories. But it's not like you took them from me. I still have them."

His words sunk in, and I realized that my earlier suspicion had been right. His wife and kids were gone. It was sad, but a tiny place in me felt a flicker of hope.

"I'm so sorry."

He rubbed his chin, and I saw he hadn't shaved today. "Hey, guess what? I bunk in my office."

"Yeah, I kinda saw that."

He laughed, and I gave him a watery smile, but inside I hurt for him, and, I admit it, I wondered what had happened. The wife must've left him for someone else, I decided, because he sure didn't act like a guy who'd quit her of his own accord. I'll bet they were the reason he'd come to Amarillo, maybe following them here. I wondered about the little girl and her pony in the charcoal drawing. About her brother. I hoped his kids knew how much he missed them.

"So don't sneak back there outside of work hours—you might catch me snoring."

"I'll ring the bell."

He smiled. My heart did a crazy flip and I cursed it. How could I go from so frustrated to feeling like this, while I was working for this man and pregnant with someone else's baby? Meanwhile he was hung up on his ex-wife and kept a shrine to her in his office, or apartment, or whatever it was when you lived where you worked.

Just then, the curtains to our space parted, and a tall, thin woman with pale skin, freckles, and light auburn hair stepped in. She looked a little like Katie, only not as pretty. She read from the notebook in her hand. "Mr. and Mrs. Bernal?"

Jack stood up. "No, we're not married. I'm Mr. Holden and she's Ms. Bernal."

The doctor looked up. "Okay, no judgment here. I'm Dr. Marshall."

I jumped in. "He's not the father."

My mother's voice shredded the uncomfortable silence following my words. "Oh, my baby, I'm here."

Jack put his hand on my mother's shoulder and said, "Agatha, I'm leaving her in your good hands. And Dr. Marshall's, of course."

I shot a frantic glance at him. He started backing up and nodded at me. "Emily."

My mother grabbed my hand and wrung it in hers.

***

"I'm sorry to have to tell you this, but you've lost the baby."

Dr. Marshall's cool voice an hour later made the words sound innocuous. But they weren't. I'd expected them, but still they gouged a black, empty hole inside me. She turned to include my mother.

"I'm not sure if you know the stats, but one in five pregnancies end in miscarriage, so this is fairly common."

"Oh my God," I said. "I had cramps for a few days. I spotted. I should have come in sooner."

I felt sick with guilt, certain that my baby would have lived if I'd come in the first time I'd spotted, if I hadn't been running around all over Amarillo trying to find Valentina, if I hadn't fallen through Maria's steps, if Rich hadn't cornered me, if I hadn't galloped Jarhead at top speed across the New Mexico highland desert last weekend. So many ifs. So many possibilities, all pointing back at me. I hadn't kept my baby safe. I hadn't protected the life entrusted to me.

I had let my child down.

Mother wailed. "Oh no. I did this. I did. I'm responsible." Her words sounded hollow to me. She couldn't be. I was.

The doctor shook her head. "Really, miscarriages around the eighth week aren't unusual, and—"

"But emotional distress . . . and upsetting her . . ."

"No, no. Our ultrasound shows bleeding from her right Fallopian tube. She had a tubal pregnancy. It was never viable."

Dr. Marshall's words rang in my ears: Never viable. Never viable. *Never* viable.

So I hadn't done this to myself, to the baby. Instead of making me feel better, it made me feel worse in an incredibly empty way. The prospect of this baby was never viable. Never *real*. I stared at the speckled white ceiling tiles over my bed. Square after square marched across the room in a military-style cadence, chanting, "Never real. Never real. Never real." Like being a man's beloved daughter. Or wife. Never real. Never real.

"Oh, my poor darling girl!" Mother pushed my hair back from my forehead.

Dr. Marshall touched my mother's arm. "She's doing great, Mom. Pregnant ladies are tougher than you'd think." She turned to me. "We need to get you into your regular obstetrician as soon as possible for follow-up. They'll decide whether you need surgery."

Surgery. Well, who cared? If the baby wasn't real, nothing was at risk, and surgery was just a bother, a nuisance. "I have an OB appointment tomorrow," I said.

My mother grabbed my hand in a grip as strong as a man's. "What kind of surgery?"

"In a low percentage of the cases after a tubal pregnancy hemorrhages, part or all of the Fallopian tube has to be removed. But it's a very low percentage."

The blood drained from my face. I know this because I could feel every drop.

"But I only have the one Fallopian tube," I said. "On the right. I had the other removed years ago. Tumors. Noncancerous. But they were bad, and, well, I can't lose the right tube or I can't ever have children."

My mother pulled my hand to her chest.

"We saw that on the ultrasound, and it's something to discuss with your obstetrician, of course. But, again, removal isn't required very often, and even then it's usually only partial. You can still get pregnant with only part of one tube."

My free hand pressed into my mouth, holding in my heart.

"I'm surprised your doctor didn't see this earlier, actually. While it wasn't viable, a tubal pregnancy can be ended before it causes damage to you."

One time, when I'd been coming to get Jib from the pasture, she'd startled and ran into me headfirst. The crack of our skulls had knocked me out, and I still remembered the impact. I felt that skull crashing again now from Dr. Marshall's words against my brain.

"I just moved here. I was between doctors."

"Ah, I understand. That's too bad. But your chances of losing that tube are so slim. You have to try not to worry about it. Now, I'm going to release you because we were able to stop the bleeding. But I'd like you to stay off your feet until you get to the doctor. Come right back here if you start bleeding again before then."

Dr. Marshall rattled off some more instructions, and I saw Mother nodding, but I just stared at the doctor's bouncing lips.

Oh God, I thought. *Please forgive me for being a careless, selfish, vain woman.*

Numbness spread over me, everywhere but my chest where a heavy weight crushed down on my heart. My baby had never been real. And now I might never get another chance to have one.

Chapter Eighteen

Two Tylenol PMs and a few large glasses of Mother's boxed white zinfandel had silenced the voices in my head last night, but I'd awoken three times, screaming. Each time, it was Valentina's face I saw. Once, the girl was calling my name. She was dressed in an odd skirt with white markings on her face and a funny hat that stuck up around her head like the rays from the sun—the way a child would draw them. Once, she was bloody and lifeless. The last time, around six a.m., she lay in a coffin.

I knew further sleep was futile. The scent of coffee already filled the house, so I rose.

I padded on bare feet to the kitchen. "Mother?"

She looked like a ghost in her long white gown, standing at the sink. She turned to me. "You should be in bed."

"I couldn't sleep." I poured myself coffee into an extra-large, blue ceramic mug and added some powdered hazelnut creamer. Stirring, I said, "Nightmares. No cramping or bleeding, though. I think the worst has passed."

She turned back to the sink, and I saw that she was staring out the window into the predawn darkness. Her coffee cup sat full beside her on the counter.

"I'm sorry, you know," she said.

"About what?" I asked.

"Being rough on you. Pushing you about Rich."

I absorbed her apology. My response didn't come easily to my lips. "Thank you," I said, finally. "And I'm sorry I didn't tell you sooner. I'm sorry that you won't be having a grandbaby yet."

At my words, her shoulders heaved. I went to her, put my hand on her shoulder as she sobbed, "I've been so lonely for so long."

I pulled her into a hug and rubbed between her shoulder blades, hushing her. "Shhh. It's going to be okay."

"After you, I had miscarriages, you know. Tubal pregnancies."

My stomach twisted, hurting for us both. "I didn't know."

"Finally, I just gave up. And your father . . ." She took a few deep breaths and pulled back until she held my eyes with her own, wounded. "I don't want to drive you away, too, Emily."

I stood frozen in her gaze, immobilized in the minefield of our shattered memories, losses, and fears. When I spoke, I tiptoed through them, half-expecting an explosion with every syllable. "You are my mother, and I am your daughter. That's forever."

She tightened her hold on me, her hug fierce and desperate, and I hugged her back just as hard. Behind me, the kitchen clock tick-tocked its witness to my promise. Then she released me.

She didn't bother to wipe her tears, just grabbed her coffee and asked, "Toast?"

"That would be perfect."

We ate together in silence, taking turns with the sections of the newspaper. My hands shook as I held the sports section, and I laid it on the table to read.

After breakfast I showered and retreated to my room. I closed the door and leaned back against it, exhaling slowly. Long minutes passed while I just breathed. When my shaking stopped, I stood and tried to figure out what to do with myself. Not long term, just for the next few hours. All I had to do was figure out right now, nothing else.

My coffee with Nadine was at nine thirty and my doctor's appointment wasn't until eleven, so I had an hour and a half to fill; I didn't want to spend it thinking about a legacy of never-to-be-real babies. I booted up the desktop computer Mother kept in there on a little table. I checked my personal email. I had responses from both of the jobs I'd inquired about yesterday. I drummed three fingers on my desk and decided that I didn't want to pursue them. Not now anyway. But I didn't want to close any doors either, just in case. I moved them to my "saved" folder.

I texted Jack: *I'll be out today.*

I figured he could guess why. I started to type more, but I couldn't decide what to say, so I stopped and hit send.

Then I wrote a quick email to Rich, whom I prayed had flown home last night: *Went straight to ER after your visit. Lost baby. I'm sorry. Appreciate no further correspondence.*

I hit send, and then a new email appeared in my inbox. I didn't recognize the address: AmarilloMama@gmail.com. I opened it.

Sofia mentioned a man she called Antonio.

That was it, and there was no name at the bottom.

Antonio. The same first name as the man who had rented the apartment Sofia and Valentina lived in, per Wallace. Could this Antonio be the same person? It seemed highly unlikely he wouldn't be. I hit reply.

Thank you for contacting me. Who are you? Can we talk?

I clicked on send.

I sat stock-still, hand on the mouse, thinking. Who could have sent the email? It had to be someone who was involved with Sofia or Valentina and knew that I was, too. Maria Delgado. Michael Q. Scott. Victoria. The employees I'd interviewed at the hotel. For that matter, Wallace, Melinda, Jack, or someone from the jail. Any of them could have sent it.

Who would have my personal email, though? Or who could have found it? But then I remembered something. I pulled up Google and typed in my own name. Several entries came up. My LinkedIn profile. My Facebook profile. And my old blog, *Just Emily*. I hadn't posted on it in over a year. I clicked through to the "About" page. I read my bio:

Wife, daughter, legal professional, and rodeo enthusiast. I'm many things to many people, but underneath it all, I'm really just me, just Emily.

Wow, that needed an update. Beneath the bio, my email address. The one I'd just heard from AmarilloMama on. So it could be anyone. Truly, anyone.

My insides churned. For twelve hours, I'd thought of nothing but myself, and nothing of Valentina, while she was out there somewhere, captive, or, God forbid, victim. If nothing else in my life had been real,

I knew this little girl and her plight were. My heart pounded a call to action. Someone had contacted me, because they believed I was the right person for this information. That I was the one Valentina could count on. Not the police. Not CPS. Me.

If I'd wanted to find Valentina before, now I was consumed by the need—like a terrible thirst. Well, I wasn't at work today. Jack couldn't tell me no. I pulled a piece of paper out of the printer and started making two lists: 1) Facts and 2) Questions. The list of my questions was twice as long as the facts.

It was past time to get serious about finding this girl.

***

I was hard at work when Nadine spotted me, making up for lost time on volume consumption of caffeine. The round Roasters logo haloed her head as she walked up to my table, and she neatly blocked out its picture of a bright red mug. It made her look a little angelic, except for her facial piercings and dark arm tattoos. Well, those, the Harley outside, the pack of Pall Malls in her shirt pocket and her biker boots and chains. But, still, more angelic than it probably sounds. She was right on time, and I was early. I'd camped out in Roasters Coffee two hours ago, sitting with my back facing the window and my front toward the counter service and its blonde wood veneers, and a great view from my seat of the trophy pronghorn antelope mounted on the wall.

"Emily?"

"Hi, Nadine."

"Hey," she said. "I'm just going to grab a coffee and be right back."

"Sounds good."

She joined the long line at the counter. I looked for a stopping place on my research and made a few quick notes. I'd spent the last two hours trying to find Antonio Rosa and Harvey Dulles. So far, I didn't have much to show for my effort, especially with Antonio. Sure, I'd found some people with the name, but no mention of any in Amarillo in the last ten years—except from the mouth of Michael Q. Scott and the email of AmarilloMama. There was no reason the Antonio I was looking for couldn't be from elsewhere, though. I found one in Lubbock: deceased. One in prison in Oklahoma: not promising. One in Houston: long shot. One in Billings, Montana: also deceased. I tried looking for an Antonio in conjunction with the names Sofia and Valentina, and that didn't add a single thing to my results. I even tried him with ESL and ΣSL. Zero, zip, nada.

I did a little better with Harvey. All I had to do was call the probation department for Potter County and ask to be connected with his probation officer. Two transfers later, I verified Harvey's address and employment. Only I knew he wasn't living at the address the crotchety old male voice had barked at me, which I wasn't able to share with him because he hung up on me so fast. But I hadn't known Harvey worked road maintenance for the Texas Department of Transportation, so the call had been worth it.

So I phoned TxDOT and learned that Mr. Dulles no longer worked there, a fact over which I expressed deep dismay, because poor Mr. Dulles's father had died and I couldn't find him to let him know. The very young-sounding woman with the high-pitched voice on the other end of the line told me that that I should try the Polo Club, because that's where his supervisor had found him when he hadn't shown up for work.

"Leering at strippers," she added. "And drinking al-co-hol."

I had years of practice adapting to this line of conversation, in my own home, no less. "Oh no. It seems Mr. Dulles has strayed from the path."

She dropped her voice. "I don't mean to sound un-Christian, ma'am, but I'm not sure he was ever on it."

We ended our call, and I pulled the Polo Club up online.

The interesting thing (to me) about this fine entertainment and libation establishment—besides that a strip club called themselves a Polo Club—was that they were mere blocks from my old high school, in a nice area of town, right next to the city Girl Scouts of America offices. Anyway, they didn't open until four-thirty, but I would definitely be checking them out later.

A text came in from Jack, and it made me happy to see his name on my phone: *Take care. Let me know how you are.*

I wondered if it was a good idea that I was developing a crush on my impossible boss who was still hung up on his ex-wife. Probably not. And probably a rebound crush anyway. I needed to get over my divorce before I started thinking about other men. And then I needed to focus on something—someone—real.

I thumb-typed quickly: *Headed to doctor now. I'll let you know if I need to be out after today. Thanks for rescuing me yesterday.*

Nadine set a foamy mug down on the table, the clack of the cup pulling me out of my work. She bounced into the seat at my three o'clock, bobbing and wriggling a few times to get comfortable. The small chairs weren't quite enough for her ample curves, and her thighs and bottom spilled over the sides.

I slid my papers aside. "I am so glad you could come. I've kind of had a poopy last day or two, and this is a high spot."

She peered across the table at me, a serious look on her face. "Whoa, if coffee with me is the high spot, then we need to get you laid or something, fast."

If I'd had coffee in my mouth, she'd've been wearing it. "I think I need to hold off on that until we get my female medical issues straightened out."

"Girly problems? Yuck." She pulled the cigarettes out of her pocket and started rotating the packet in her fingers.

"Miscarriage. Headed to the doctor after this."

"Mary, mother of Jesus!" she said. "I'm so sorry. And, of course, ignore me on the getting laid part. Nadine opens mouth and inserts her big, fat freakin' foot."

"Nah, you're fine," I said.

She put the cigarette pack on the table. "I had a miscarriage before I had my first son." She inhaled, nodded, exhaled, like she was toking weed or something, which I had never done, but had witnessed Rich do repeatedly enough back at Tech. Maybe I had tried it, courtesy of secondhand smoke. "It happens. It's awful. But I'm sure you'll be pregnant again in no time."

I hoped not soon, but someday. I changed the subject. "So, you worked at My Thai last night?"

"No, My Thai is my part-time day job. I take some late shifts as a bartender now and then."

"I'll bet there's more money in bartending."

"Especially where I work. I have to put up with a high douche-baggery-to-IQ ratio, but other than that it's fine."

Again she would have made me spew out my drink in shock. "Sounds interesting. Which bar?"

She grinned. "It is. The Polo Club. And no, I don't dance. I just push the booze."

My mouth dropped.

She saw my expression and said, "I know, I know. Objectification of women. Exploitation via the sex industry. Even working there perpetuates it. I've heard it before. But I prefer to think of it as a smart woman taking advantage of the weakness of men."

I grinned. "No, I was thinking I had planned to go to there this afternoon, to track down a witness in a case."

"Are you a cop?"

"Legal assistant. My boss is a criminal defense attorney."

"You should give me a stack of his business cards. I could keep him busy from here to eternity."

Business cards—something I should probably get ahold of. If I was going to stick with this job, I needed cards of my own, too.

"I'll bring you some," I said. Then I reached into my bag and shuffled through papers for the picture of Harvey Dulles. I held it up and asked, "Does he look familiar?"

"Harvey? He lives there. Literally, for the last few weeks, he's there every time I am. Sits at the bar and drinks Crown and Coke, slow and easy. Drinks and stares."

I half-jumped to my feet in excitement. My abdomen chided me, and I sat back down very gently. "That's who I'm looking for!"

She smiled, and it pulled one corner of her mouth up, like Jack, but without the dimple, and plus one nose ring. "Fun. Can I be of any help?"

I grabbed Spike's picture and slapped it in front of her. "Have you ever seen him with this guy?"

A man's voice spoke before Nadine could answer. "Emily?"

Inwardly, I shouted, *Can't you see we're having a conversation here?* Outwardly, I hit the tape mark on the stage, tilted my head, and flashed my pearly whites. Which reminded me that I really needed to pick up a pack of whitening strips at the store. Coffee, tea, and soda were not a friend to sparkly teeth. I greeted my mother's boss.

"Pastor Robb. How are you?"

"Good, although worried about you. Your mother sent around a prayer request for you again last night." He pulled at the collar of his sweater. His face was so florid I wanted to fan him with Spike's picture.

"She must get a volume discount. Pastor Robb, this is my friend Nadine. Nadine, Pastor Robb."

Nadine beamed. "Oh, we've met. Great seeing you, Eugene."

His tomato-red face drained of all color in an instant. "Nadine, you said? Um, hello, yes, well—" he pulled up his sleeve and looked at his watch, "—so sorry, church business, and I'm running late." He scrambled like a dog on a tile floor toward the exit.

Nadine turned to me. "Eugene is a big fan of dancing." She winked. "Now, where were we?"

I laughed and slid the picture of Spike an inch closer to her. "I love your job. Have you seen Harvey with this guy?"

She tapped the picture four times with her middle finger. "That's the guy that got blasted off the balcony at the Ambassador, or whatever they're calling it now. He came in with Harvey the day before it happened. Freaked me out when I saw him on the news."

"Has Harvey talked about it?"

"No, but I asked him. And he said he didn't know the guy. I wasn't sure why he lied, but most of the slimeballs in the Polo Club do."

"Did you hear Harvey and this guy, or Harvey and anyone, talking about a woman named Sofia, or hear of a little girl named Valentina?"

I handed her a printout of Victoria's picture of Sofia and Valentina.

"I've seen the woman," Nadine said. "But only on the news. She's the one that popped Spike, right?"

"Right," I said.

"No one mentioned their names around me." She handed the photo back.

"Okay, how about someone named Maria?"

"There's a dancer named Maria. Harvey talks to her sometimes."

My Maria was definitely not a Polo Club dancer. "What about a tall white guy, shaved head, a tattoo like this?" I fished Victoria's drawing from the papers and placed it over Spike's picture. "On his arm, maybe the upper arm, or the inside of his arm."

She moved closer to the table, which started her bobbing and wriggling again. "You mean other than Harvey?"

I couldn't believe my ears. "Really? Harvey has this tattoo? Are you sure?"

"Not a hundred percent, because he's been wearing long sleeves now that it's getting colder. But he came in a few times this summer, and I saw a tattoo like this. I'm ninety-five percent sure, and I know I haven't seen anyone else with it. As for tall white guys with shaved heads, I see a lot of them, in addition to Harvey."

My pulse accelerated and I wanted to get up and break into the Cotton-Eyed Joe, my equivalent of a touchdown dance. My instincts had been right all along. Harvey was involved. And now I had an inside source.

Hold on, Valentina, hold on.

"How about you text me whenever he comes in, and I'll come check him out myself?" Maybe I could find out where he lived. And who was keeping him in Crown and Coke.

"Yeah, sure. I'm working again tonight. He's always there."

"Awesome. Either I'll come in, or my friend will. He's a CPS investigator, Wallace—"

"Oh, I know Wallace. I volunteer for the Rainbow Room. He's my favorite investigator."

I should have expected she'd know him, in a town where everyone knew everybody. "Yeah, he's great. And you—two jobs, kids, *and* a volunteer gig? You're like Wonder Woman."

"You know it." She flexed an arm, then leaned toward me. "Seriously, the Rainbow Room helped me, once upon a time. I owe 'em."

I stood up. "I'm going to refill my coffee. Need anything?"

"I'm good."

I filled my cup, dumped in a packet of yellow stuff and a splash of Half & Half, and returned to the table.

After I sat down, Nadine spoke in a soft voice. "Um, Emily, I think you're bleeding."

"Oh my, where?"

"It's on your pants. And a little on your chair. I saw it when you walked over to the coffee. It's not like really bad or anything. But, with the miscarriage and all, I figure it's not your monthly visitor."

No, please God, no. I didn't need more of this stuff now, not when the trail to Valentina was getting hot. I stood up and craned my neck to see the back of my pants, but all I saw was stars as I slumped back into my chair.

Chapter Nineteen

Nadine's discovery put an abrupt end to our coffee. She insisted on helping me to the bathroom, even though I was sure I'd only gotten lightheaded because I stood up too fast. I assessed my bleeding problem from the stall and found that I'd forgotten to put a maxi pad on before I left home. Not smart. Definitely, I was bleeding, but I was also only an hour away from seeing my doctor, and I wasn't bleeding *profusely*. Not enough to run to the emergency room. I'd just go to the doctor's office a little early and maybe they could work me in.

We exited Roasters into a twenty-five mile per hour grit-filled wind—double the speed I'd found unpleasant earlier. Nadine mother-henned me all the way to my car. I opened the door to the Mustang and the wind caught it, pushing it to its furthest point. I got in and had to use both arms to pull it closed again, even with Nadine pushing from the outside. The sky had turned to the color of dust, and trash tumbled across the parking lot—not just the paper and bags of a normal windy day, but cardboard boxes and glass bottles. I waved goodbye to Nadine and headed quickly toward my obstetrician's office, careful to dodge the projectiles that whirled past one of Stanley Marsh's signs (Road Does Not End) across the street in front of me. It seemed all the Marsh signs I saw followed a similar, creepy theme. Gusts pushed my car in and out of my lane.

While driving, I realized that it wasn't too terribly out of the way to drive past Maria's again. I tried to assume the best of people and, right now, that theory told me that there was always a chance Maria had softened. That if I could just look her in the eye as I held up a picture of Harvey and ran the name Antonio Rosa past her, I'd at least see a flicker that would tell me whether she knew something—anything at all. Heck, I could show her Valentina's drawing. Yeah, it was a long shot, but something about it seemed right. Plus, I didn't feel bad and I wasn't really bleeding very much and it was way too early to show up at my doctor.

Thinking of Valentina's drawing reminded me of something I'd dreamed. I tried to pull it back into my consciousness, but all I could remember was that I'd seen Valentina over and over, not where or when or what she was doing and with whom. But there was a similarity between my dream and her drawing, just out of sight, just out of reach, like the fireflies that I would try to catch each summer when they'd light up, only to grasp at nothing as they darkened and buzzed away.

I didn't bother hiding my Mustang down the street this time. I parked in front of Maria's house and opened the door only to have it ripped from my hands by the wind. It had gotten even stronger in the last ten minutes. The sky around me was in full-blown brownout. I strode to the door, leaning so far against the wind that if it had died suddenly, I would have fallen face-first to the ground. I used one hand for my purse and the other to hold my hair out of my mucous membranes. That left none to cover my mouth and protect it from grit, so I breathed through my nose with my head tucked down, trying not to suck too much dirt down my windpipe, and feeling really glad I hadn't worn a full skirt or flimsy blouse. When I got close to the house, its bulk somewhat blocked the gale. I straightened up and pulled errant hairs away from my eyes and mouth. Nothing like a windstorm to strip a woman of her dignity and professionalism.

I walked the outside edge of the steps where I knew the treads had maximum structural support, giving the unrepaired hole I'd left the day before a wide berth. I rapped smartly on the door, and it fell away under my knuckles.

I tightened my grip on my handbag. An unlocked door didn't seem very Maria-like.

"Maria? Are you home?"

No answer.

"Is anyone here?" I called.

I hesitated. If the door was open, I was invited in, which seemed to be a trend for me lately. I glanced at my watch. I had fifteen minutes before I needed to leave for my doctor's appointment. Plenty of time to run through and scan for information. Or to find and question the little boy and possibly other people that didn't like to answer Maria's door. I just wouldn't touch anything, I'd be silent as Sacajawea, and I'd hurry.

I stepped into the first room, remembering my father's lessons from long ago. I imagined leaves and twigs and rocks under my feet, and I placed each foot down light as air, and did it again. And again. And again. If I was less than silent, the sound of the wind muffled my indiscretions. I tiptoed around the living room. It was a dump, with ratty, dirty furniture that smelled as bad as it looked. The walls were bare except for stains and pockmarks.

My silent feet moved on to the kitchen. White linoleum, white counters, white cabinets, white sink, white refrigerator, white microwave, black oven, and a silver range top crowded the box-like space. Dirty dishes teetered in the sink, far too many for one woman, or even a woman with a family. These were dishes for a party of ten. The trash bulged up on its lid as well.

I stepped out of the kitchen. The little house couldn't have many more rooms. Two bedrooms and a bathroom, I'd guess. Suddenly a loud thrumming interrupted the silence, and I reached in my handbag, groping for my Glock. Frantically I searched the small purse then remembered. I'd left it in the glove compartment of Wallace's car, and wherever it was now, it didn't do me a lick of good. I listened more carefully to the thumping thrum, and then almost laughed aloud. The sound wasn't coming from the house. I was frightened of my heartbeat and a ringing in my own ears.

I moved quietly to the back of the house and stepped into the left bedroom. Sleeping bags were rolled and stashed against the walls. One, two, three, four, *five* of them in a rainbow of colors. A double bed sat in the middle of the room, but it was stripped bare, its sheets nowhere to be seen. The only other furniture was a desktop and a funny little machine in the back corner, like a printer, sort of, but smaller. I walked closer to it. It said Zebra ZXP Series 3 on top. Some ID cards lay by the desktop—Hispanic faces and names—and I compared the output hole in the Zebra thingy to the cards. They matched.

I scanned the room again. The closet accordion door was closed. I opened it. It was crammed full of clothes arranged by men's, women's, and children's wear in descending sizes. Holy crap, was Maria helping out the entire undocumented community? Food, bedrolls, clothes, IDs? Excited now, I resumed my search, but the dense silence was shattered with a terrifying ringing noise. Not my ears this time. Spit. My phone. I fumbled in my handbag. My display read Wallace. I pressed accept.

"Wallace," I whispered, "Meet me at Maria's ASAP. She left her house open, and I've found—"

Something incredibly, unpleasantly hard cracked into the back of my head. I felt myself crumpling, my phone tumbling, and my cheek landing on the carpet as the lights went out.

***

I returned to the conscious world with another loud ringing in my ears and two blurry faces peering down at me in front of a white background that hurt my eyes. "Where am I? What happened?"

The two faces turned to my left. A third face appeared, this one above a police-blue uniform. It said, "Emily Bernal?" It sounded like a he.

"Yes?" Each word, his and mine, was an anvil strike on the wedge that was cracking open my skull.

"I'm Officer Wilson. Do you know a Maria Delgado?"

A light brown mustache floated above his upper lip, bobbing up and down like a prairie dog from its hole. My eyes locked onto it.

I spoke carefully, trying not to hammer the wedge. "Sort of."

Talking hurt so much. I lowered my voice, and he leaned the mustache further toward me. It smelled like garlic and onions.

"This is her house," I said. "I, um, I was meeting her here." I hoped he could see how painful this was for me and would stop.

But the mustache kept bobbing. "Did you see her?"

"No." Ouch.

"How'd you get inside?" The mustache did a hippety-hop. It almost made me giggle, but even the thought of giggling hurt.

"Door was open. I called her name and came in. And, sir, my head really hurts."

"Sorry." The mustache didn't stop, though. "What happened next?"

"My phone rang. Something hit my head." I gestured at him and behind him at the other faces. "Then, this." My voice faded on the last word.

His eyes narrowed into slits that further emphasized the furry creature on his upper lip. Maybe not a prairie dog. A mole? No. Possibly a rat? Yes, I'd seen plenty of rats in the barn behind our house, and they jumped around like this thing did.

"Did you ever see Ms. Delgado?"

"No."

I winced. I reached up to touch my head but missed and got nothing but air. I put my hand back on my leg.

The rat loomed over my face, blocking out the glare behind his head. "Did you see anyone else?"

"No." I closed my eyes. No more rat.

"So Ms. Delgado was alive last time you saw her?"

"Yeah, yesterday. What, she isn't now?"

"Ms. Delgado is dead."

My eyes flew back open. "What happened? Where is she?"

"Blunt force trauma to the head, like you, but apparently you got lucky. She's across the hall." He wrote something on a notepad he had in his left hand. "I'll let the paramedics get back to you." And he and the rat disappeared.

I felt a little irritated. I was a victim, but he had pumped me for information as if I were a suspect. But then my bleary brain got smarter. I *was* a suspect. I'd never been one before. How weird, in a not-good way.

The two faces I'd first seen moved back into the tunnel of my vision, a white man with longish brown hair and a black woman with short dark hair. Behind them, a third face appeared. Things darkened and took shape. A popcorn-textured ceiling with water stains. The open closet full of clothes. The edge of a mattress. Floppy sand-colored hair streaked with highlights.

"Wallace . . ." I reached a hand toward him.

He couldn't get past the paramedics, and I let my hand drop.

"Way to scare me to death, Emily," he said. "I nearly had a heart attack trying to get here, worried about you, only to find Maria dead and you *looking* dead."

"You called the ambulance?"

"911 the second I saw you."

I tried to smile. "Thank you."

The woman spoke. "Excuse me, ma'am, we need to ask you some questions, and then we can let you speak to your friend." Her voice flowed like warm honey. Alabama? Mississippi?

Wallace shot me a thumbs up.

The woman resumed. "You appear to have been struck in the head with a heavy blunt object. You lost consciousness, and you have a concussion, which is why your head hurts. You probably feel a little foggy and nauseous, too?"

"Yes."

"You'll feel like that for a while. Anyway, we just got here right before you woke up, and, because your vitals were steady, we let the officer go first, before we could do a complete exam on you. There's a fair amount of blood around your torso." She put her palms on my abdomen and probed gently in a search pattern. "Do you recall why?"

I looked at her blankly.

"Do you remember being shot, or stabbed, or sexually assaulted?"

Oh God. My girly parts. "I was about to go to my doctor's. I had a tubal pregnancy and hemorrhaged and lost the baby yesterday. I'd just started bleeding again, right when I got here, before I got knocked out." To my dismay, I started to cry, which made my head hurt worse.

"And they said if this happened they might have to remove my tube and I can't lose this tube or I can never have a baby because this is the only tube I've got."

Wallace crouched beside me, and a shocked expression flitted across his face. He grabbed my hand. "I didn't know you'd lost the baby. Why didn't I know? You poor thing." He turned to glare at the woman. "She needs to be in the ER, not laying here with her reproductive organs spilling out. Or do you want to be responsible for the babies this gorgeous creature will never have?" He jumped to his feet, clapping. "Come on, people!"

And unbelievably, the paramedics snapped to attention. Wallace hovered nearby. I beckoned him closer. He put his ear near my mouth, and I spoke in a rush.

"Harvey Dulles has the tattoo Victoria described and my friend Nadine says he's at the Polo Club daily. I got an anonymous email telling me Sofia talked about a man named Antonio. I couldn't find anything on him, but that must be critical. And, of course, I'm sure you noticed Maria is running some kind of underground house here and—"

"Shh. I've got it, and I'll fill in the police. You've done good. Worry about you for a change." He kissed my cheek. "I'll be right behind the ambulance."

A swell of emotion surged up through my chest and lodged in my throat. "Don't tell anyone else about me though, okay?"

He saluted me crisply.

Five minutes later, I was in the ambulance, speeding toward the ER with the sound of a siren battering my skull.

Chapter Twenty

I awoke to a familiar, white-tiled ceiling and pink curtains around my bed. Even as my eyes opened and took in the room, vivid images remained in my mind, and their resonance shot white-hot panic through me. A slim, short Native American in a clunky headdress and tall buckskin moccasins stood pointing after a bald man running with Valentina under his tattooed arm. Tall evergreen trees loomed behind them.

"Go after her," the Indian said, the words a little cloud of fog in the air.

I stopped to look at the Indian again. I couldn't help it. It was just so odd. The Indian's body was painted white and he wore a mask that looked like it was made of real animal hide, down to the animal ears protruding in front of the headdress.

"Go," the Indian shouted, and this time I ran, but it was too late. A bull thundered between us and barreled straight at me.

"Valentina!" My voice came out hoarse and thin. I tried to sit up.

A hand pushed my shoulder down. "Emily, you're in the recovery room, at the hospital. It's okay." I knew the voice, but its words made things worse.

"Wallace, the Indian tried to send me after Valentina, but now I can't see her. Where is she? Where did she go?"

"You're dreaming. You need to be still so you don't hurt yourself."

I rolled my head to face him, pleading. "But it was real. She was here. She was . . ."

My voice trailed off as I tried to explain to Wallace where I'd seen her, but the images had slipped away. I didn't know where she was anymore. Valentina was gone. I dropped my head to the pillow.

He lifted my hand and squeezed it, then held on. "It was a night-mare," he said. "It's okay. You've just woken up in the hospital from surgery."

I didn't want to be in a hospital. I didn't want surgery. I nodded and tried not to cry. It had been so real. I wanted it to be real.

A very short man with coarse salt and pepper hair on either side of a smooth cranium and face appeared behind Wallace. He looked Indian, as in from-the-country-of, and he had just the slightest hint of curry on him, like he'd lunched at My Thai. It cleared some of my haze.

"Ms. Bernal, you're awake," he said. "Good. I'm Dr. Patel, and I performed your surgery today."

His cheerful voice and distinctly Indian accent seemed surreal in Southwest Hospital in Amarillo. "Thank you."

"Well, I am pleased to report the operation was a complete success. Your hemorrhaging was getting much worse, quite dangerous to you, actually, and we were able to stop the bleeding."

"My tube?"

His head bobbled right to left to right almost imperceptibly. "Yes, well, unfortunately we had to take out most of the tube to secure your recovery. There's still a bit left, possibly enough that you might be able to become pregnant later, possibly not. I wish I could provide you with a more precise prognosis, but I can't. There is reason for optimism, however, and I urge you to embrace it."

Wallace squeezed my hand again. "This is good news, Emily," he said. "The most important thing is that you will be fine." He repeated himself, emphasizing the words: "The most important thing."

I nodded, and I thought I heard myself say "Thank you" to the perky-voiced doctor as I stared at his blue scrubs. But, inside, I saw myself standing with my back to the edge of a swimming pool in a hotel where I'd seen a dead man sinking. I felt my body fall backward and hit the water. It was so soft and warm slipping over my skin. I sank below the surface and realized I couldn't breathe, but I wasn't scared.

As I sank, I whispered, "My baby and Valentina, both lost. And now I can never have another one. Just like my mother. Everything, lost."

Dr. Patel's singsong voice pulled me up, up, and out of the water. "Ms. Bernal, I need to verify that you understand what I just told you?"

I wanted to slip back under, and it irritated me that he interrupted. I spoke in a short voice. "Yes, yes, I understand."

"You'll need to see your own obstetrician in two weeks. The name was in your file, so we alerted her office about your situation and told them to expect your call."

"Thank you."

"You should stay here perhaps another half hour, then our staff will check you out to whoever will be driving you home."

Wallace raised his hand. "That's me."

Heaven, I thought. *Home is Heaven. Do you hear that, God? I'm going to Heaven.*

"Very good. I'll be sending you with a prescription for pain medication, if you need it. Please rest for twenty-four hours. After that, you may resume your normal activities, but please refrain from strenuous ones, including sexual intercourse, for several days." He perched a pair of wire spectacles low on his nose and lifted an electronic tablet, his finger poised above it. "Do you have any other questions for me, Ms. Bernal?"

Water lapped against my chin again.

"No," I whispered, before I let myself sink to the bottom.

***

I sat in the front seat of Wallace's Altima and counted the Vicodin he'd picked up for me at the Target Pharmacy on Soncy Road. Six pills. I had enough to stay zonked for two days if I wanted to. Which I did. I looked at the clock on the dash: Five p.m.

Wallace buckled his seat belt. "It's too soon for one now."

"I know." My phone dinged, so I checked my texts.

Nadine: *Harvey is here. Thought you should know.*

Spit! And I was basically an invalid, unable to do anything about it. But not without a friend, one who was completely mobile.

"Wallace," I said, "remember how I told you that my friend Nadine said Harvey Dulles is a regular at the Polo Club?"

"Vaguely. There's been a lot going on."

I watched him watch me out of my peripheral vision. Had I only met this amazing human a few days ago? Here he sat with his best Salvage jeans covered in my blood, driving me to Heaven through a brownout, halfway to New Mexico. And with me about to ask him for another favor.

A knock on the window startled me. I turned and saw the person craning for a clear view into the car.

"Gah," I yelped. Out of the corner of my mouth, I gave Wallace the scoop. "ADA Melinda Stafford, who's been a burr under my blanket since we were kids." My voice dripped pique.

"Oh God, I hate that bitch," Wallace said.

"Well, put on your happy face, because I know from excruciating experience that she's not going anywhere." I pressed the button to lower the window. Nothing happened.

"Let me turn the key."

He did, and I tried again. The window slipped into the door.

Melinda wrapped her French manicured claws around the door-frame and leaned so far in she was almost in my lap. The wind and dirt followed her.

"Emily, I thought that was you," she said. "How are you?"

"Fine. How are you Melinda?"

"I'm fantastic. I heard about you on the news just now. You're fa-mous."

"I guess." I conceded.

The Maria Delgado murder would be topping the hour tonight on the local stations. Jack had texted me that a camera crew and reporter had shown up at the offices. He hadn't asked any questions other than if I was all right, for which I was grateful. And thank God I'd missed the reporters. Wallace and I had heard some coverage on the radio when we'd driven from the hospital to Target. They'd pronounced my name wrong—then again, everyone around here said BUR-nal instead of Bare-NAHL.

"So, that's interesting that you're working with Jack Holden."

My headache was coming back. "Yep."

She flicked lint I couldn't see from the sleeve of her charcoal gray suit jacket. "Is he dating anyone? I've got this campaign fundraiser for my boss, black tie, and I need a date. I'll bet Jack looks yummy in a tux."

I heard a noise like a strangled cat from the driver's seat. Melinda did, too, and she finally seemed to notice Wallace.

"Oh. Hello, Wallace." She gestured back and forth between us. "I guess it makes sense that the two of you are friends."

He put his hand over mine and pinched it, hard. "Hello, Melinda. And why is that?"

"Well, you know, Emily's ex-husband, and, um, stuff."

I lightly smacked Wallace's hand and tried to block out her last words. Before I could think of a way to redirect her, she went on. "My goodness, Wallace, you are just covered in blood." Her eyes gleamed with excitement, and she turned an eye for crime scenes on the inside of his car. "And you are, too, Emily. "

She reached in and snatched my prescription bottle from my hand. I wrested it back from her, but not quick enough to keep her from grasping the essentials.

"Yes, Dr. Patel, the surgeon, I've used him as an expert witness. Are you okay, Emily? Vicodin, that's heavy stuff. What was it, were you injured at the scene where that woman was murdered? Or was it a car wreck?" She stood back and worked the car over with her eyes, looking for evidence.

I stuffed the pills in my handbag. "Female problems."

Melinda put her hands back on the door, arms straight, shoulders high, face leaning in. She studied me like a chemistry experiment gone awry.

"You didn't, Emily, surely you didn't—I mean, I can hardly bear to say it, but you didn't abort your baby, did you?"

My lips moved, but nothing came out. My hands flexed and closed into fists.

Wallace grabbed both of my wrists and leaned over me to yell at Melinda. "What in the world would make you think it's okay to ask that question? Emily had a miscarriage yesterday and emergency surgery today. She could have died, and you march up here like the Morality Police? Who do you think you are?"

Melinda didn't appear to realize she was getting her rear chewed, or at least she didn't care if she did. She put a hand over her chest.

"Oh, I am so glad to hear you didn't do that, Emily." She patted my shoulder. "A miscarriage, huh? It's for the best, I'm sure."

I jerked my wrists away from Wallace, and with a quick twist to my right, I made room to draw my arm back. Then, in one diving lunge, I punched Melinda in the jaw, landing halfway out the window, with my sore gut across the door. It hurt my hand, my head, and my abdomen, but it made the rest of me feel so much better. I pulled myself back in, wincing.

Melinda squealed like a stuck pig and covered the side of her face.

Wallace banged the steering wheel with both hands. "Holy shit, holy shit, holy shit."

Over her histrionics and Wallace's hysteria, I said, "It's my legal right to choose, but I wanted this baby, and I'm heartbroken to have lost it."

Melinda's words came out muffled by her hand. "I think you broke my jaw!"

"Impossible. I had a terrible angle."

She pointed at me. "I'm going to call the cops and have you charged for assault."

I gave her my mother's address. "Be sure you tell them how much Vicodin I'm on. I've only been in criminal law for a week, but from what I've learned, I'm pretty sure they'll find I lacked the capacity to know right from wrong at the time my fist met your face." I rolled up the window.

Wallace put the car in gear. "Holy shit," he said again. "You just punched an ADA in the face."

I smiled weakly. "I've wanted to do that since fourth grade."

***

Dr. Patel hadn't said a word about abstaining from alcohol, so I'd raided Mother's box of white zinfandel again that night. Really, I hated the stuff and could barely get the first glass down without gagging, but the second was easier. I heard the door open, close, and lock when Mother got home. Wednesday nights are big church nights, but she was home early.

"Emily?" She whispered from outside my door. "Pastor Robb said he ran into you today, with the wrong kind of person. And then I heard about you on the news." She increased her volume. "Emily? Are you okay, honey?"

Pastor Robb was one to talk. My light was out, so I stayed very still and didn't answer. I didn't have to tell her my news. If I did, she'd have it in the inbox of every member of Believers Church in seconds. I'd be mostly normal by tomorrow, anyway, so it wasn't something she needed to worry about. Or worry *me* over.

I made my voice sound half asleep, which wasn't hard. "Fine. Sleeping. Love you. Talk to you tomorrow."

Silence. She stood outside my door for a long time, then said. "Well, goodnight, then. I love you, too."

I listened to her footsteps down the hall. I waited through the sounds of water in her bathroom and the click of her bedroom door closing. Then I tiptoed to the kitchen for a wine refill. When I was safely back in bed, I turned on the lamp and got out my phone.

A text message had come in while I was in the kitchen.

Wallace: *I can't believe I skipped church tonight to come to The Polo Club.*

Wallace: *I bought a drink for Harvey, using my gaydar-blocking super powers. Got him to talk about Spike's death. Tried to bait him about Sofia. He didn't bite.*

Pffffft. I typed fast: *Keep me posted. Hate feeling helpless.*

Wallace: *Helpless? WTF, when I'm on the case? Go to sleep.*

Fat chance I'd sleep, not with Western décor assaulting me from the outside and the ravages of my messed up life assaulting me from the inside. I took a slug of white zin. Another text came in, but it wasn't Wallace. I swiped over to my Messages homepage.

It was Jack: *Worried about you.*

It was crazy, because I'd swung up and down and through every emotion in my repertoire in the last day and a half, but this was the moment that made me sob like a child. My shoulders heaved, but I muffled my cries, scared of attracting Mother. Tears overflowed my eyes. Why did Jack have to go and turn out to be so damn kind? As many people as I had run into here that reminded me of the things I didn't like about this place, I'd met that many more that gave me hope, like Jack, Wallace, and Nadine. The problem with hope, though, is that it sometimes reminds you of the reality that keeps you from feeling hopeful in the first place.

So here was my reality: I couldn't have a baby. I tilted my wine glass up and drained the last drops from it.

Sure, the doctor had said I had a slim chance. What that really meant was that I had barely any chance at all, almost none, which always ended up meaning none. No hope of a father coming back. No hope of my husband wanting me. No hope of babies. Tears pooled below my nose. I was thirty years old, alone, broke, and barren, a cautionary tale to every rodeo queen who'd ever worn the sash.

I pulled out my phone and hit a number in my favorites.

"Emily?" Katie's voice was a happy squeal.

I cut her off fast before she could congratulate me and said, "Something bad has happened."

A pause. The sound of a small child's laughter. "Hang on," Katie said. "Let me ask my mother-in-law to put Thomas in bed, and I'll go where I can hear you better."

"Okay."

I heard jostling and muted voices for thirty seconds or so. Then she came back on. "I'm here. Tell me."

I started talking, fast, trying to beat the blubbery tears I knew would come. I almost made it. "I lost the baby today. Miscarriage. And I lost Rich, I lost the condo and our savings, and I've lost the baby, too. And now, and now . . ."

"Shhh. It's okay, I'm so sorry. Shhh now." Her beautiful soothing voice harmonized with my sobs until I got myself under control.

"I may not be able to have a baby now."

Katie knew my background, so I filled her in only on the new development.

"I lost most of my only fallopian tube."

I downed the rest of my wine in one swallow.

"I'm sorry, honey. Very sorry." She paused. "You sound a little slurry."

I barked a laugh. "Yeah, I've been nipping at Mother's stash of box wine."

"Do they have you on pain meds?"

"Some."

"Go easy on the booze. Take it from a semi-pro. It's not going to make it better."

Maybe not later, but it would now. "You know what else?"

"What?"

"I'm working for a criminal attorney, and his client's little girl disappeared, and it's like I'm the only one who really, really cares. How messed up do you think that is?"

"I think what's messed up right now is my sweet friend Emily. I think you need to stop thinking and go to sleep. Things will look better in the morning. You can start working on all this then."

"I'm not sweet," I said. "I haven't been sweet since Stormy came to dinner."

Shows how little she knew. Why had I called her again? What I needed was another glass of wine.

"I gotta go, Katie."

"I love you, Emily," she said. "Call me tomorrow—or any time."

"Love you."

I ended the call and snuck to the kitchen for another refill. I left the lights off, opened the refrigerator and pulled the box out. It felt almost empty. I shook it and the meager remains sloshed around. I knew that this was at least my third glass, but certainly no more than my fourth. And they were very small glasses. It sure wasn't my mother who'd drained the box. She drank thimblefuls every Friday night and then apologized for it. If she were Catholic she'd probably even confess it— though, to her, Catholicism was a sin in and of itself. My head spun. Religion was just too dang confusing for me.

I lifted the hem of the red flannel nightgown I'd borrowed from Mother and wiped the tears from my face, then lost my balance just a little bit. I caught myself against the doorway to the kitchen. I sipped my wine. I couldn't end up like my mother. I didn't want to be a bitter church secretary living alone in a house as far past its prime as me, judging and begrudging everyone else. I loved her. She was my mother. But that didn't make these things untrue. I weaved down the hall, trying to be Sacajawea again and running headfirst into the door to my room instead.

"Ouch," I whispered.

"Is that you, Emily?" Mother called.

I shook my head and put a finger over my lips. "Just using the bathroom. G'night."

"Goodnight."

I opened my door. Maybe this was my fourth glass after all. I crawled back in bed, leaned against the wall, and pulled the cowgirl-covered bedspread up to my chin. So, yeah, I couldn't have hope, and that included about Jack. Still, I couldn't *not* answer the man's nice text. He was worried about me. I stared at my phone on the bedside table until my eyes closed. Opened them and stared at it some more. Thought about Jack's half smile and dimple and twinkling eyes and great boots. I really did love his boots. And his jeans. Yes, I loved those Wranglers. My eyes closed again.

The phone rang, waking me. I had listed over and drooled on my pillow. I reached for the phone and turned it to face me. Wallace.

Adrenaline coursed through my veins, and I sat up straight again. It could be about Valentina.

I answered. "Hello?"

"Hey, I'm driving Nadine home, so I decided to call instead of text and die."

"Good choice." Choice came out like "choyse." I touched my lips, but they felt okay.

"Your voice sounds funny. Did you take too many pain pills?"

I spoke carefully, enunciating brightly. "Nope. I only took one."

"Emily?"

"I've had a little . . . wine.'"

He sighed. "Stop it. You're going to make yourself sick mixing booze and painkillers. And I need you to sober up so I can tell you about Harvey. I'm putting you on speaker, okay?"

I stretched my jaw and eyelids, trying for sober. "I'm good. Tell me."

"Hi, Emily." Nadine's voice.

"Hi," I said. "Thanks for your help."

"No problem. This is fun."

Wallace took over. "Okay, so here's the scoop. We followed Harvey home, and—"

"Noooo, Wallace, that's dangerous." As hard as I'd tried, dangerous came out "dangerush."

"Look who's talking—or trying to," he said.

I nodded to myself. True on both counts. "Whaddya find?"

"We know where he's shacking up—with one of the Polo Club dancers. Not one of the better-looking ones, if you ask me, but my opinion may not count for much."

Nadine said, "You have a keen eye for beauty, Wallace."

"Thank you, Nadine."

I made a gagging sound. "Not important. What about Valentina?"

"I couldn't exactly barge in after him, or knock on the door in the middle of the night. But I can tell the cops about him now, and we can check it out, later."

I tried to sound like I was in charge. "Tomorrow morning."

"You're on bed rest through tomorrow," Wallace said. "And you're about to have a wicked hangover."

"But the cops won't do spit."

He laughed. Nadine did, too. She asked, "Did you just say spit?"

"What?" I asked. "What's wrong with spit?"

They both laughed harder, and Wallace clucked. "Go to sleep, Emily."

I hadn't said anything funny, at least I didn't think I had. Plus, I needed to know something. "Wallace, wait."

"What?"

"Do you think any man will ever want to marry me now that I'm thirty and barren?"

He yelled in my ear. "What? A) You're gorgeous. Maybe even more gorgeous than I am, thanks to that perfectly precious gap between your teeth, although it's still a very close contest. B) You're not barren, and no one uses that word anymore. C) Stop choosing gay men and you'll find plenty who want to marry you. Shit, you've almost got *me* wanting to propose."

Did I choose gay men? I counted back. Rich. That was one. Now Wallace. That was two. Hardly a trend. Then I remembered. Gordon, my rodeo team mentor, had come out his sophomore year. Okay, that made three.

Nadine chimed in. "I'd marry you."

This confused me. "I thought you were straight, Nadine? You have kids."

"I'm just jumping on the bandwagon."

I held my hand up in the stop gesture, then dropped it because I realized they couldn't see. "But even if some straight man does want to marry me," I said, "if I do turn out to be barren, he'll leave me then. Or he might even leave me anyway, regardless."

Both of them yelled "No" at the same time. Then Wallace said, "No shit, Emily, stop drinking right now. Pour the wine out. You've poisoned your brain."

"I'm serious."

"I know you are, but you're also wrong."

"So I should text Jack back?"

Wallace sort of shouted at me and I pulled the phone away from my ear, staring at it in surprise. I could still hear him, though. "What? Where did that come from? Oh my God, woman, you make no sense. Yes, if Jack texted you, answer him, after you sober up. Right now, pour out the wine, and when you're done with that, go to bed. And don't get up until tomorrow night. You hear me?"

I put the phone back to my ear. "I hear you." I started to hang up. "Wait!"

Wallace sighed. "I'm pulling up in front of Nadine's place. Make it snappy. I want to get home and go to bed."

"You said you skipped church. What church do you go to?"

"Unitarian."

Nadine said, "Agnostic here."

"I'm not sure what I am." I stopped, thinking hard. I wasn't one hundred percent sure what agnostic was either and how it was different from atheist, but now probably wasn't the time to ask. I knew, though, that the three of us, we were like refugees from the Island of Misfit Toys. Thinking that made me smile. "Wallace, I need a church. Can I visit with you?"

"Yes, you can. Now, goodnight."

"Goodnight."

I pressed end and stared at Jack's text again, trying to think of what to say to him, this time holding my phone by my head on the pillow. I typed: *Had minor procedure, I'm fine. Thanks for checking on me. I've been thinking about you all day, and I was really happy to get your text.*

That sounded ridiculous and schoolgirl-ish. I changed it to: *Had minor procedure, I'm fine. Thanks for checking on me. See you Friday.*

It still sucked, I knew, but I couldn't send the first one, and I couldn't come up with anything better than the second. I sent it, then stared at the ceiling, thinking about Jack in his boots and babies and lost little girls until I fell asleep.

***

When I walked into work Friday morning, I had the wicked two-day Vicodin and box wine hangover Wallace had predicted. I also had a bad case of the blues over my single remaining Fallopian tube—a sliver so tiny it was about as useful as teats on a boar hog. I thrust the door to the Williams & Associates office open. Lost in my own thoughts, I nearly ran over the man kneeling to lay tile in the lobby/my office. It was beautiful tile—a large, beigey-rusty-streaky tile. The brand new carpet that had been removed to make room for the tile was now in a roll leaning against the wall. If the lobby had needed remodeling, this tile would've been a great choice. But it hadn't, unless something drastic had happened since I'd last seen it on Tuesday.

Snowflake danced back and forth between the tile guy and me. I reached into my handbag and tossed her some toast crusts. She gobbled them and returned her full attention to the tile guy.

"Good morning," I said.

"Mornin'," he replied.

He didn't stop his work. He was kneeling on the concrete subfloor in dirty white kneepads over baggy blue jeans. He had just finished smoothing and cutting lines into gray grout, wielding his hand trowel like a paintbrush. Now he placed one of the tiles on the grout, perfectly aligned with the one beside it. When he'd finished securing it, he wiped his forehead with the sleeve of his New Orleans Saints sweatshirt, knocking his LSU Tigers cap loose and revealing his shaved black head.

I walked around him to my desk and sat down. It was going to be hard to concentrate with a construction project going on in my personal space, not to mention with the shrill whir of the tile saw and the chalky smell of fresh cut tile. I rested my head in my arms for a moment, trying to pull myself together. I'd slept until five p.m. yesterday, and my days and nights were all mashed and mixed up. I breathed in and out slowly. All I had to do was manage to get through today.

After that, I could take my last few Vicodin and put my brain to sleep for the weekend, with my door shut, and the world at bay.

"You okay?" The tile guy had stopped working and was staring at me with eyes of deep black ink.

"Oh, yes, sorry. I just need some coffee."

He grunted and went back to work. I grasped the bell on my desk and rang it, then walked down the hall, stopping by the door to the kitchen.

"Jack?"

He appeared at his office door and said, "Good morning." He pulled out his half smile-dimpled-raised eyebrow magic.

It made my heart sing, but today it was a sad song. "Teardrops on My Guitar."

I avoided eye contact and said. "Thank you for the flowers."

I'd discovered the arrangement on the porch when Wallace and Nadine woke me the previous afternoon to let me know the police had found no sign of Valentina at Harvey's. Mother had come home while they were there. Her discombobulation over my obviously gay and biker chick friends was the brightest part of my last few days, other than punching Melinda Stafford.

"You're welcome."

I ducked into the kitchen and took a seat.

"How are you?" He sat down, but at a sideways angle. Our knees were inches apart.

"Fine." Physically, anyway, but I kept the rest to myself. "What's going on in the lobby?"

"New tile."

"No, I mean *why*? Was there a water leak or something?"

He jerked his head toward the door, speaking softly as he did. "That's Freeman, our client. He does tile. So he's doing ours."

I clenched my fists. Five minutes after I got to work and Jack already had my eyes crossed. I just wanted to know why we were getting new tile. It didn't seem like a complex question. Could the man ever answer me straight? I opened my mouth to snap at him, but snapped it shut instead. Jack and Clyde had talked earlier in the week about the new carpet. A client that couldn't pay his bill. Services in kind. Okay, it took me a while, but I got it. My eyes grew moist and my hands relaxed. Something about crying most of the last few days had loosened my on-off switch. I swallowed the tears back.

Jack filled the silence. "I read your Johnson report. I think we're good to go there."

I gave him a leaky smile. "Thanks. And it appears he can afford to pay in cash."

Jack leaned back in his chair, which scooched his knees forward. They bumped mine, and I jerked my legs away by reflex. Jack didn't appear to notice.

"I had a very entertaining call from ADA Stafford yesterday," he said. "She claims to have suffered physical injury and mental anguish at the hands of one Emily Phelps Bernal."

I slouched back down, which bumped our knees again. "I'm sorry. I can explain."

He put his hands behind his head, his elbows out to the side and tipped his chair back just so far that the front legs lifted from the ground. He'd rolled his sleeves up this morning, enough that I could see the smooth, tan underside of his forearms. I'd assumed Jack had a suntan on his face and neck, but instead it appeared to be his natural skin tone.

"I can only imagine," he said.

"Seriously, she's evil. When we were eight she sat behind me in class and cut my ponytail off one day. Short."

His chair came down with a thunk, and he brought his hands back to his knees. "I messaged over a check to cover her doctor's bills."

"I'll pay you back."

"No need. I'd have paid more than that just to have seen it."

A horrible thought occurred to me. "Are you going to the fund-raiser with her?"

"She did ask."

"But are you going?"

After a long pause, he said, "Conflict of interest. And lack of."

I hadn't realized I'd held my breath until he answered and I started breathing again. He clasped his hands between his legs. Today he was wearing a pair of jeans so old the knees were white, with a flannel shirt. Flannel and faded jeans meant he didn't have court today.

"If you're up to it, I need you to help me on Freeman," Jack said. "We could be going to trial before Christmas, and I've got a long way to go with it."

I nodded. Maybe if I worked really, really hard on Freeman and Jack's other clients, he'd let me get started on a wrongful death survivor case, which would mean we would have to find Valentina.

"We'll leave for Tularosa after lunch."

My throat tightened. I'd forgotten about New Mexico this weekend. "I don't have my bag with me," I said.

And I'd planned to do my own reconnaissance at Harvey's stripper-girlfriend abode later that day. I'd lost twenty-four hours—more, really—on finding Valentina, and no one seemed to have made any progress in my absence.

"We can swing by Heaven on the way." He levered himself out of the chair and started walking out.

My emotions went to war, over Valentina, and wanting to stay here to look for her. My lost baby, and desire to hibernate. My job, and needing to keep it. Jack, and my attraction to him. New Mexico, and the possibility of a sleuthing side trip to Roswell.

"Jack, wait," I said. He stopped, and I continued. "I don't think I'm very good company right now. I might not be at my best for Johnson's housewarming. I'm . . . recovering."

At least the parts of me that could recover. The part of me that wanted to be a whole woman and a mother someday wasn't even near the path yet.

He puckered his lip up to the left, and I fell for it. With that one little expression my emotional resistance crumbled like dry sod. How could the left side of his face do such interesting things? He was right-handed, after all. I'd checked.

"Noted. Now, let's get to work," he said.

Chapter Twenty-one

The next eight hours passed in a blur and ended with the wheels of Jack's plane thudding to earth at Wrong Turn Ranch. I still wasn't a fan of small planes, but last time I'd puked my guts out in the little Skyhawk, and this week I didn't use a single barf bag. It wasn't lost on me that Jack had replenished the stash in the seat pocket to overflowing. Amazing what the absence of a fetus could do for a woman's queasy tummy. Even more amazing what its absence did to her heart. The rest of me didn't feel that bad, and I hoped I could put away everything sucky about my life for a weekend. Some things I couldn't change anyway, and I needed to learn not to dwell on my new reality. Mountains, horses, and green chiles might be just what I needed to try to get my head right.

As we bounced down the runway, I checked my phone. Jack had practically hog-tied me to his side the entire morning as we put together a work list and game plan for Freeman and Escalante and the new Johnson case. We'd barely finished in time to grab lunch at Taco Villa on the way to Heaven. A bean burrito with sour cream usually cheered me up, but it didn't today. Besides my sadness about the lost baby (babies?), I hadn't managed to sneak away to Harvey's crash pad, and I knew I had to entrust it to Wallace. I loved Wallace, and Lord knew he meant well, but he was a rule follower, at least in his professional life. I'd texted Nadine on my way to the airport, asking her to go with him. She was someone who knew that there was more than one way to skin a cat, and she'd texted back a *Yes* five seconds later.

That was over four hours ago, and it was six o'clock in Texas. I'd hoped to hear how it went from them by now. But I had no messages.

I sent them a group text: *Update?*

Jack pulled the plane to a stop in front of his little barn-hangar, then spun the Skyhawk. He turned off the engine and the propeller slowed gradually, *thwum, thwum, thwum,* until it stopped. The silence screeched in my ears, but I was getting used to it after several flights.

Jack leaned around his seat. "You okay back there?"

I nodded and pulled the corners of my mouth up. My face felt like it would crack.

He opened his door and pushed his seat forward. Brisk air hit me in the face—cold air, really. I noticed the sky for the first time. Black clouds to the west veiled the falling sun. I shivered and hopped out. Then something strange happened. The temperature and the dry scent of sage and pine acted like shock paddles to my emotional system. I drew in a full breath and let it out. I looked around me, and it was like someone had adjusted the focus on my lens. Emily lives on, even if just barely.

Jack's eyes sparkled. "Brr. Let's gas her up quick, then get her inside before we unload."

"Good idea."

This time there was no Judith to meet us, but I knew the drill. He opened the roll-up door and I moved the Suburban outside. When I returned, he had fastened the tow bar to the nose wheel. We maneuvered the small plane to the gas tank.

"Why do you gas it up when we land?" I asked as the fuel pumped.

He pointed at the sky. "Sometimes the weather or other circumstances dictate a rapid departure in less favorable conditions."

"Oh. Okay."

I rubbed my arms. When the plane was full, we pushed it inside. He chocked the wheels and chained the plane in place. Wind gusted into the hangar and rattled the walls and roof. We grabbed the dog and the bags and made it into the Suburban in one trip. By the time Jack started the engine, snow was falling and the sky all around us had turned dark gray.

I rolled down the window and let the flakes fall against my hand as we drove. "It's beautiful."

"Yeah, I love these early-season storms."

"Not great horseback weather." Not that I should ride anyway.

He took a left, toward the ranch house. I don't know why it surprised me, since it was after the workday, but it did. Something about heading straight to the house felt more like a date than a work weekend. But, of course, it wasn't a date. And if it had been, what a horrible date I'd be. The weather and high desert smells had helped rejuvenate me, but I had a long way to go before I was good company. I wanted to slap my cheeks to perk myself up and put some color back into my face, but held back.

Jack rolled his window down, too. "Yeah, but the weather will change five times this weekend."

The house appeared out of the dark skies, sudden and large, and no less impressive than last time. Jack swung the Suburban around to the far side and parked in a three-car garage. Even in there, the snow and cold wind followed. He closed the garage behind us.

Just before he opened the door to the house, Jack turned back to me. "Your friend Collin contacted me this week. I told him we'd be back tonight for a Saturday work function. He asked if he and Tamara could take us to dinner. And I . . . uh . . . I told them we needed an early start so that it would be better if they came out here."

Did I mind? I wasn't sure. "So you *didn't* tell them about my miscarriage?"

Jack opened the door and motioned me through. "They said they're bringing dinner. All we have to do is sit and eat."

I wanted to throttle Jack for forcing me into this. My mood had improved, but only enough for a soak in the claw-footed tub I'd discovered in the guest bath last weekend. I wasn't going to give that up.

"How long do I have?"

"They'll be here at six-thirty. Oh, and Mickey and his wife will be here, too."

Ten minutes from now. A regular dinner party. "No promises. I'm really not feeling all that well, but I'll try to come down."

He looked at his feet, then opened the door. "Yeah, I understand."

I escaped up the stairs, each step ponderous. How could walking up one flight make me this dizzy? I knew I was out of shape, but maybe the surgery had weakened me more than I'd realized. I dropped my handbag on the bed and my suitcase in the corner and headed straight for the bathroom. The white porcelain tub stood regally in the corner on its pewter feet. I turned both spigots on full blast and started opening cabinets and doors as fast as I could, searching for bath salts. I found cucumber bubble bath and dumped in half a cup. The water steamed, so I eased off on the hot, tested it with my hand, and eased it back further. I let my clothes fall to the floor. I took out my clip, twisted my hair high on my head, and refastened it.

Two bottles of water stood by the sinks, and I grabbed one, uncapped it, and slugged it down. Then I looked at the counter again: a bottle of Dancing Bull merlot, an old school corkscrew, and a plastic wine tumbler. This was a giant step up from boxed white zinfandel. Naked, I sunk the corkscrew deep in the cork, my hands shaking. I twisted, twisted, twisted, then flipped one end down to make purchase on the bottle's lip and depressed the other end, easing the cork out slowly until it made a soft popping noise. The velvety, red liquid splashed into the glass, *glug, glug, glug*. I filled it the proper two thirds, then, after a pause, I filled it to millimeters below the rim.

The aroma called to me and I buried my nose in the top of the glass, inhaled, then inhaled again, deeper. I sipped, holding it in my mouth, the liquid gliding over my tongue, the different notes of the wine playing out their symphony, and I closed my eyes while I savored the sweet music until it crescendoed, then I swallowed.

A deep sigh broke from my lips. I set the wine glass on the small wooden table at the head of the tub, dialed the timer to fifteen minutes, and sunk eyeball deep into the bubbles and water.

***

When I climbed out of the tub an hour later, waterlogged and wrinkly, I was a little unsteady on my feet. Only one glass had made me tipsy? Well, that little lunch burrito had been hours ago. I needed food, and the only place I could get it was downstairs. I didn't want to waste the wine, though. I poured another full glass emptying the bottle.

I padded to my suitcase and put on a mossy green velour dress with my boots. The fabric whispered over my skin. A chorus of laughter erupted below. Male and female voices. Happy, normal people. The scent of something tangy. My stomach growled, long and echo-y. I held my hand to my belly, feeling its emptiness, its deep pit of nothingness. Food wouldn't fill that void.

I applied burnt sienna lip-gloss and ran a brush through my hair, still undecided about whether to join the group. While I wavered between stay or go, I teased my bangs back into shape and sprayed them with Aqua Net. I opened the door without crossing the threshold, just to test the air outside my room. More laughter. Voices. Collin's. Tamara's. Jack's. Mickey's. Others I didn't recognize. I smelled that tangy aroma again, plus something spicy, and my stomach rumbled. Darn it, I had to go down there. My hand reached up of its own volition and did one last touch test on my bangs. They were fine. Vanity even in the depths of a blue funk. I ventured out, and down the stairs.

I entered the kitchen with my half-full glass in hand. Faces swam before me. At the kitchen table, Jack and Mickey sat with a woman I didn't recognize, who had her hand on Mickey's knee. To my surprise, Paul Johnson sat with them, too. What was he doing here? Tamara and Collin manned the business end of the kitchen, busily arranging a platter of pizza slices.

I waved. "Hello, all."

My name echoed in the air. *Hello Emily-ly-ly-ly-ly-ly*. I blinked. Snowflake bounded to me. I reached down and ruffled her ears.

The woman I hadn't met stood and grasped my hand. Hers was cold and tiny, but she had an iron grip. "Laura Begay," she said.

We shook. She was so short I could see the top of her head, the side part of her sleek, brown bob. She probably weighed half what I did, max.

"Emily."

She sat back down and patted Mickey's knee. "Wife of this charac-ter."

Mickey's eyes reflected her, and in them you could see how lovely she was. "She left out 'jockey of international reputation.'"

"Wow," I managed. Normally, I would have clung to her every word, dying to hear about such a fascinating job. Maybe she'd give me another chance some other time.

Paul did better than me. "Hey, I knew I'd heard of you."

She smiled at her husband and then at Paul. "It's a job."

Conversation resumed, and I sidled over to Jack and spoke under my breath. "What's Paul doing here?"

He tilted his head toward mine. "Paperwork."

Which explained why he'd come, but not why he'd stayed. I waited, but Jack didn't elaborate.

Collin removed the foil off some buffalo wings he'd pulled from the oven. "Voilà." He gestured his hand in the air with a flourish, throwing his hip as he did it.

Tamara golf clapped then went back to work uncorking a bottle of white wine on her hip—3 Blind Moose pinot grigio—while Jack set out glasses, seven of them.

"Fill 'em up, people. You can't eat anything Collin cooks sober, I promise," she said.

No one needed further prodding. I poured pinot grigio in a fresh glass, feeling conspicuous, but no one even glanced at me, which confirmed my suspicion that Jack had clued everyone in on the change in my maternity status. Somehow I'd become unable to keep anything about my life private, like I was a walking Match.com billboard, a constantly updating Facebook status. Maybe my blurting everything out last weekend had something to do with it, as did my mother and her friends. Even Collin.

Voices pulsed and throbbed around me. People teased and laughed. I stayed quiet. My wine buzz had me a little queasy, until I polished off two pieces of the chile-enhanced New Mexican pizza that

Tamara and Collin had made, after I picked off all the chicken, anyway, as best I could. The queasy went away, as long as I kept my eyes off the food in Paul's mouth. It gave way to mellow, and I watched Snowflake successfully beg for food from everyone assembled until she collapsed in a food coma on her pillow in the corner. I tried to follow the conversations around me, and more than once I felt my lips curve upward, until finally I laughed.

I glanced up into Jack's eyes. He looked away quickly, but the aftereffect remained, a wake lapping against my skin.

Laura shushed everyone. "I want to play a game."

Mickey splayed his hands around her waist and pulled her back onto his lap. "Me, too."

She slapped at one of his hands. "Not that game. I brought Boxers or Briefs."

"Which one are you wearing now?" Collin asked, his eyebrows peaked high.

Tamara punched his bicep. "It's the name of a game, dipshit."

"I should go," Paul said. "I've already overstayed my welcome after barging in on your party."

"Noooo," a chorus of voices shouted back at him, although I wasn't one of them.

"How would your life ever go on if you missed Boxers or Briefs?" Mickey asked, and Paul laughed.

He stayed. Five minutes later we sat at the large wooden kitchen table. I cast my eyes on its scarred wood surface. There was a purposeful scar in front of me, a crude, childlike etching. I leaned down. *Jackson.* I looked to my left. No others there. I looked to my right. *Julia.* A shiver ran through me. Were these the names of Jack's kids? I sipped my wine and caught Jack watching me again from across the table.

Laura explained the rules. "We're playing to six. Mickey, you're going first. Roll the die, baby."

He did. The die had statements on it instead of numbers. It landed on *I have.* "Now what?" he asked.

Laura said, "Everybody reads the 'I have' lines on their cards and picks the one that best fits Mickey, either because it's true, or because it's funny. Then we'll vote on the most funny and the most true, and each of the winners get a token." She pointed at the box, which held the round blue token disks. "Then we move on clockwise, so Jack will roll next."

We studied our cards. I picked, "I have fun in the dark," and slapped it down on the stack the others had piled in front of Mickey.

He cleared his throat and read the lines from each card in a serious tone. Soon we were all whooping and hollering, even me. I won for "true." Tamara won "funny" for "I have zits the size of Sweden."

Jack rolled the die, which landed on "I like." We all piled our cards and he read them. "I like mullets" won for true and for funniest.

Jack said, "I refuse to give a token to that one for truth."

"Whoa, cousin, is your Apache name Cheating Bull now?" Mickey said, straight-faced. "In high school he won a special award from the cheerleaders. 'The tight end with the tight ass and the nice hair.'"

This caused an uproar. Snowflake opened one eye, but closed it again quickly.

"It's nice to know my attorney has two advantages to use in my favor every time he enters the courtroom," Paul said.

Jack smiled and touched of the ends of his hair. Mickey leaned around Paul and patted Jack on the bottom, and we all just laughed harder.

Tamara set two fresh bottles of wine in front of us. "Now that everyone is drunk, we're breaking out the cheap shit."

I chose the Chateau Ste. Michelle Riesling. As I took a slow swallow, Jack's eyes again sought me out. When I pulled mine away, I stumbled across Collin's gaze.

He didn't pretend he wasn't looking. "You hanging in there, beautiful?"

A silence fell over the group. I lifted my glass in in the air. "Recovery by grape." As I set the glass down, I saw Tamara glare at Collin.

"Here, here," Paul said, and lifted his glass toward me.

I smiled, grateful to him.

"Your turn, Standing Hair," Mickey said.

I looked up and saw he was speaking to me. "Huh?"

Everyone laughed so hard they spewed wine. Jack pretended to pat his bangs. Snowflake stood up and turned around once before lying down again, but not without shooting us a disapproving glance first.

Oh. Standing Hair. I reached up to mine. My bangs felt all right to me. A little stiff, possibly, and fluffy, but standing? "Hardly," I said.

I rolled the die and got "I don't think." Five heads bent to their cards followed by five cards hitting the table in front of me. I picked them up and starting reading them aloud. When I got to, "I don't think those pictures on the Internet were of me," I felt heat in my face.

Collin rubbed his hand across his mouth, leaving a straight face behind. "Sure they were. I'd know that sweet ass anywhere."

The laughter from four people hurt my ears, and I pretended to laugh with them, but I couldn't. I was too conscious of the fact that Tamara wasn't laughing. I liked her, and Collin was going to make her hate me when I hadn't done a thing.

We voted, and Laura got her sixth token and won. Game over, thank goodness. I started to say I was headed up to bed, but Laura beat me to it.

She waved an almost empty wine glass in the air. "Girl time. Boys go smoke cigars and drink boy stuff."

"Yay!" Tamara shouted. She plunked another bottle of wine in front of us. My bleary eyes couldn't read the label. It was white, and I was drinking white, so I topped mine off.

Jack rose. "Let's take a walk, gentlemen."

Paul, Collin, and Mickey got up, grumbling but good-natured.

As he stood, Mickey asked, "Hey, Standing Hair, did you ever find that little girl you were looking for?"

Heavy silence fell. Everyone turned toward me.

I swallowed. "Not yet. Her mother was murdered in jail, so now the girl's an orphan. I will find her though, if only Jack Ass will let me look for her."

Howls around the table. "Jack *Ass?*" Mickey asked.

I sniffed. "I always assumed that was what Jack was short for."

More peals of laughter. I locked eyes with Jack, and his surprised me. They weren't angry, they were something like proud. Of me? He was laughing as hard as everyone else.

Mickey nodded. "It was supposed to be a family secret. Seriously, though, about that little girl, you'll find her, I believe it. Last week, I felt it. That you're the one."

Paul said, "So, do you have any leads?"

I looked over at him. I couldn't read his eyes, but I thought he looked amused. *Don't write me off as a piece of fluff,* I thought. Others have before, and they learned better.

"I do," I said.

"Oh?" Mickey raised his eyebrows.

The room around me seemed to shrink, wood-framed windows and backsplashes of rectangular slate moved toward me, butcher block island and Shaker-style cabinets loomed closer, and the waves of gold, rusty brown, blue-gray, and tan in the granite crashed forward. Everything blurred at the edges.

"Ask me when I've recovered from this hangover," I said.

Laura brandished her wine glass. "But we've only just started."

I shook my head and held up four fingers. "This is day three for me." I looked at my hand and pulled a finger down, amidst snorts and more raucous laughs.

Laura sat down at the head of the table. "Okay, enough of this serious stuff. Y'all go away." She waved her hand at the guys.

Snowflake followed them, trotting with head and tail up. Someone had her second wind, and believed she was a boy.

"So, Emily," Laura said. "Tell me more about you. Jack said you work for him?"

"I'm his paralegal in Amarillo."

"How long have you guys been dating?"

I shook my head vigorously, which was a mistake. The closed-in room listed a little. "Oh no, we're not together. I just started working for him a week or two ago. I'm here for a client event tomorrow. At Paul's house."

Tamara and Laura looked at each other, and Laura's eyebrow height told me she didn't believe me while the set of Tamara's lips suggested I'd answered wrong. Was the boy-girl grouping designed for Laura and Tamara to interrogate me?

"I swear. In fact, I pissed him off so bad earlier this week I thought he was going to fire me. The only reason he didn't is because he felt sorry for me about what happened, you know, my, um, miscarriage."

Both women made sympathetic big-eyed faces and tsking noises. Laura reached across the table and put both her hands on mine. "I'm so sorry, honey."

"Thank you." I needed a new subject. I blurted, "So, Laura, a jockey? What do you ride?"

"Quarter horses."

"Did you ride Jarhead?"

She grinned. "I sure did. He's my favorite."

This interested Tamara, and the conversation took off between her and Laura. I watched the two of them for a little while. They both had on silver and turquoise earrings, and it made me wish I'd worn mine. They would have looked great with my dress. I picked up a pencil from the center of the table and started doodling on a napkin.

Tamara snatched the napkin. "What are you drawing here, Standing Hair?"

My face burned. "Um, I don't really know. "

She held it up in front of her. "You like the bad boys?"

"What?"

"You're doodling the gang sign for the East Side Lobos."

I pointed at the ΣSL I'd drawn. "You know that symbol?"

"Sure, I grew up in Las Cruces, and they were big there."

"I've seen it around here, too," Laura said.

Tamara cocked her head at me. "How do you know them?"

"The man who took the little girl I'm looking for has a tattoo like this."

Tamara patted the inside of her left upper arm with her right hand.
"Here?"

"Yes."

"Then I'd be willing to bet he's a Lobo."

"You're the first people who've recognized it," I said. "Can I ask
you a few more questions?"

"Sure."

I stood up, unsteady on my feet. I held up my index finger and
tried to speak clearly. "One minute. Let me grab the file."

***

Five minutes later, after I'd finished visiting the potty in my room,
I pawed through my laptop bag in the dark, feeling for the Redrope file
that my fingers knew by heart. When I found it, I ripped it out, letting
the bag fall to the floor at the foot of the bed. I spun around, quick like
a cutting horse, in a hurry to get the file back to my new best source of
information, Tamara, but I bumped into something very solid in the
doorway. Big hands wrapped around my shoulders.

"Whoa there, Em, where're you off to in such a hurry?"

Collin, too close, blasting booze in my face. The lights in the hallway weren't on, so I couldn't see him well, but I'd know him anywhere.
He wasn't all that tall, five foot nine or so, but he made up for it in
muscle mass, which I couldn't miss, as close as he was to me. I wanted
to run, but he'd been a friend for years, and I couldn't duck him. It was
rude. I brandished my file.

"Taking this file downstairs to show Tamara," I said.

"Well, I was taking this upstairs," he said, slurring his words,
thumping his chest, and tilting his head back. The downstairs light was
just bright enough to illuminate that wide Collin grin. His eyes were
half-mast. "I was looking for you."

"Me? Why?"

"I can't quit thinking about how you went and got yourself un-hitched. You've known I've been in love with you since I met you, haven't you?"

I closed my eyes, mortified. "No, I mean, I kind of thought maybe, but not for sure, and not—"

He wrapped his hand around the back of my head and pulled my forehead against his. I pulled back, to no avail. "You knew. And here you are, and I'm engaged, and . . ." His words dwindled off and his lips landed on mine. I stumbled backwards. My mind was screaming, *No!* but my lips were trapped by his.

Before I could twist away from him, I heard a shriek from the stairway.

"*Pendejo!*" Tamara stood on the top stair, Paul one below her, but towering over her. She snarled, but Paul grinned.

Collin released me and jumped back. I fell on my bottom against the doorframe in the entrance to my room. As I did, I saw Jack from my peripheral vision at the opposite end of the hall. I turned. His lips were set in a hard line. I wanted to run to him.

"Hey, baby," Collin said.

"Don't 'hey baby' me. I saw you sneak up here after her. "She wrestled something off her left hand, then threw it at Collin. Metal hit the wall and I heard what I knew was her ring fall to the carpet. "I hope you've got a ride, asshole. And a place to stay."

She whirled and ran into Paul, who turned sideways to let her by. Collin took off after Tamara without looking back at me crumpled on the floor.

"Tamara, baby! Tamara, it's not what you think—" His protests echoed through the house.

Paul stood there, sipping from a cocktail glass, watching them go.

I sat where I'd fallen and put my head on my knees. The file lay on the floor beside me. I scooted it to me, protecting it from God knew what, and wrapped my arms around my legs. Jack's footsteps thudded in the hall as he walked toward me, and I didn't look up. I could feel the heat from my face on my thighs, even through my skirt. I sucked in a breath and held it until Jack passed.

Except he didn't. The boots stopped by my feet. He leaned against the wall and slid down the length of it until he was sitting on the ground beside me.

"You and Collin, are you . . . ?"

"No, never. That whole thing was quite . . . disturbing."

He grunted and I heard a slosh and a swallow. "So, you okay?" he asked. His voice sounded different than before, and not just because he slurred even worse than Collin. It was gentle. No fending me off. No teasing. Just caring. Warm.

I nodded then realized he couldn't see me in the dark. "Not really." I lifted my head just enough to wipe my nose, and when I rubbed my sleeve under it my hands brushed against wet cheeks. I hadn't even known I was crying again. I swallowed, determined not to let Jack know. "What were you guys drinking, anyway? Collin's wasted and you sound drunker than him. Not that I'm exactly sober."

"Mescal tequila shots." His arm went up and I heard the slosh again. "Mickey's downstairs puking."

"Nice."

Jack scooted his butt closer to mine and put his arm around me. I stiffened, nervous, but that was all he did and I relaxed into him.

I heard the slosh again. "Want some?" he asked.

I guffawed, half laugh, half sob. I lifted my head and reached out. My hand met a bottle. I leaned against the wall, arching my back slightly so I could tilt my head. It tasted like drinking a bottle of my face astringent, not that I had ever tried it, but what I imagined it would taste like. I gasped, and some of the tequila sprayed from my mouth. I giggled. My eyes had adjusted to the light and I looked at my boss's profile. He had nice lips. A perfect nose. I didn't know many men who had perfect noses.

"Good stuff," Jack said.

"Yeah." I tipped the bottle back again, and this time I did better. The liquid burned my throat and warmed my insides.

"Better stop." Jack reached for the bottle.

"One more." I tilted it back and managed another big swallow. Warmth settled over me, and I passed it back to Jack.

We sat side by side for a few minutes. From downstairs we heard the front door slam, heavy footsteps, then Collin's voice called up the stairs. "Jack?"

"Yeah?"

"Can I crash on your couch?"

Jack groaned softly. "All right."

"Thanks, man."

I giggled again, and Jack leaned his face toward mine. I drew a quick breath and held it, my heart hammering. Then I burst out with giggles again. "I think I'm drunk."

"I think I should tuck you in," Jack said.

He leaned forward and got up onto his knees with an *oomph*, then turned and used the wall to stand all the way up. He held a hand out to me and pulled me up. I fell into him, giggling again.

I whispered, "Tamara is so mad at Collin," and laughed more. "He tried to kiss me." I held up a finger and waggled it in the half-dark. "That was not a very smart move."

Jack gave a rumbly snort. "Not at all."

Movement caught my eye. The teenage girl I'd met last weekend at Jack's office appeared in the stairwell beside Paul, who had never left, it seemed. With the light behind them, the girl's hairdo was even more impressively large than last time.

"Come *on*, Dad." She grabbed his arm.

"Stella, you're such a good girl to give your old man a ride home," Paul said.

She muttered, but loud enough I could hear her. "Like I ever have a choice."

I watched the back of Paul's head as he descended the stairs. I shivered and threw both arms around Jack's neck. Then I laughed again, nestling there until my mirth tapered off. I kept one arm around his neck and removed the other, standing up straight. "Kay, where's my bed?" I whispered.

"Over here," Jack whispered back.

We lurched to it like two kids in a three-legged race, and fell face first into it.

I mumbled into the covers. "Jack?"

"Hmm?"

I turned to him. "Thank you for tucking me in."

He rolled to face me, and that's when it happened. I wasn't sure which one of us started it, but the next thing I knew we were wrestling in a ferocious lip lock that was just about the best kiss I'd ever had. Shoot, it probably was *the* best, but I was too drunk to be sure. His big, rough, cowboy hands grabbed both sides of my face and his mouth consumed me, like my lips were the only thing between him and certain death. He kissed me like I was the first place belt buckle at the county fair. Like I was the prize at the bottom of the Cracker Jacks box. Like it was the Olympics and I was the gold medal.

And I kissed him back, my hands tearing at his shirt and shimmying up his tight stomach and sculpted chest. His breath hissed at my touch, and I wriggled closer. My bare foot slid and hooked around the back of his knee, pulling him into me.

He groaned. "Emily."

I kissed him harder, panting. "Jack."

"Emily," he said again. "I have my boots on."

I rubbed my foot up and down his leg, definitely feeling boot. "You doooo."

He sat up on one elbow and stared down at me. He reached his free hand behind my neck and grasped me at the nape of it, pulling me up to him for one last kiss. My lips clung to his even as he released me. "Wait," he said.

I watched him as he stood and stumbled around, yanking at his boots, hopping, cussing, and finally falling on his rump. My eyelids fluttered. I let them close for just one second, and I murmured his name as I thought about how good his lips felt on mine. I sighed, smiling. The last thing I remembered before I fell asleep was the hard contours of his body pressed into me, and then nothing at all.

Chapter Twenty-two

When I woke up, I had a face full of warm skin, but the bed was spinning too fast for me to enjoy it. I mumbled, "Sorry," and rolled onto the floor with a thud, then ran into the bathroom. I splashed cold water on my face and swished it in my mouth and groaned. My clothes were mussed but all in place, and I sighed in relief. I had a vague memory of a make-out session, and that was mortifying enough without the horror of waking up naked. Jack was my boss, and I was a not-yet-divorced woman who had just lost a baby, for God's sake. One who didn't want to put herself in a position where she had to figure out how to tell a man she was probably not the one he wanted to take home to mama, because she was a bust as a baby-maker.

Oh God, that reminded me. What if I hadn't fallen asleep and had done . . . more? Dr. Patel had told me not to have intimate relations for some period of time, but I couldn't remember how long he'd said. I hadn't really listened because I didn't think there was even the tiniest of chances that it was relevant. Who knew?

I paced in a wavering line back and forth in the bathroom. What was the right thing to do? Should I go sleep somewhere else? No, that was even worse. I had to get back in my own bed, I just couldn't plaster myself all over my boss, that's all. A memory of his hands tangled in my hair, my body pretzeled around his washed over me in a haze of lust. It was undignified, somewhat slutty, even, no matter how good he felt.

The clock on the bedside table read five a.m. I crept back to the bed in the dark, tripping over my shoes. I held myself motionless, not breathing. The bulk in my bed shifted and the mattress creaked. I stole around to the other side and tried to alight with the weight of a feather, outside of the covers. Once in place, I held myself frozen, listening to be sure he was asleep.

His body flipped over, and I tensed.

"Good morning, Standing Hair."

I felt a giggle wave starting and I bit my lip, trapping it inside. "Good morning to you, Cheating Bull."

"You sure do fall asleep fast."

I moaned. "I know, I'm sorry."

"Me, too."

He reached for me, sliding his arm under me and around my waist with the covers still between us. He pulled me to him in a strong and possessive way that made my pulse pound in a place that was supposed to be recovering from its recent medical procedure.

"Jack," I said.

I'd intended my voice to sound like I was holding up a stop sign, but it came out more flashing green light, and then nothing came out at all because Jack had his mouth on mine. A knock on the door broke us apart, and Jack growled.

"Just a minute," I called.

Jack's hand around my waist drifted south. "If that's Collin, I'm going to beat his ass."

I grabbed his bottom lip between my teeth and sucked once, hard. "Just a second."

After cupping my bottom and pulling me into him once more, Jack released me. I crawled out of bed and walked to the door. "Who is it?"

"Mickey. I need Jack."

"I haven't seen him."

"Well, if you do, tell him that one of the hands just called in to tell me that he found a dead body in our southeastern pasture."

"I'll find him and tell—"

Behind me, Jack jumped to his feet and pulled the door open. Mickey stood outside, wearing last night's clothes, Snowflake at his feet. From the bags under his droopy, bloodshot eyes, and the yellow tint to his skin, it looked like he'd had a rough time.

Jack turned back to me and said, "I'm sorry." He pulled my face to his by the nape of my neck. I had a sense of déjà vu, then he kissed my socks off, almost literally, since when he grabbed me, the carpet dragged one of them down to my toes. He released me and reached back inside the door and grabbed his boots, Snowflake leaping at his face to steal a kiss as he did.

I stood open-mouthed, my lips burning, as the two men and the dog walked away. Then I gave myself a shake and scrambled after them.

Jack stopped long enough to step into one of his boots, and I caught up with them.

"Tell me everything you know," Jack said to Mickey.

"Kenny was doing rounds and he found a dead guy in the middle of the southeastern pasture, right off the highway. He said there was no identification on him, and he didn't recognize him, but the guy looked Mexican, really skinny, and like he'd been beaten pretty badly. No signs of anyone else out there, or any kind of altercation, either."

Jack hopped into the other boot. "Have you called the police?"

"Waiting on you, cousin-man."

They walked down the stairs, with me still hanging on their every word.

"Call 'em," Jack said. "I'll get coffee and we can drive out together when you're off the phone."

Mickey had his cell phone out by the time Jack finished speaking, and he walked over to the mountain-facing windows in the great room. I followed my boss into the kitchen and leaned forward against the breakfast bar. He put the dog out and poured her some food and water.

"I'll make coffee if you want to change or anything."

He smiled at me, and it was strange to see this new, open Jack in the full light of the kitchen.

"You should sleep," he said. "Save up your energy for Johnson's party later, and maybe a ride with me, if we can squeeze it in."

In light of our shenanigans last night, it seemed odd to think, but I probably shouldn't ride. I hadn't really told him anything about my surgery, but I would just have to deal with it later, if it came up.

"A dead body?" I said. "I can't sleep now. Is this a normal thing around here?"

Jack turned on his automatic coffee maker after filling it with grounds from a canister that smelled spicy and delicious.

"Nope," Jack said. He set out two travel mugs. "Want one?"

"Sure."

He placed a WTR porcelain mug beside the others. Snowflake yipped, and I walked to the door and let her in. She went straight for the food bowl.

Mickey joined us in the kitchen. "Tularosa is on the way, and it sounds like we should expect Alamogordo to show up, too. If they decide there's a chance he came from the reservation, they'll get the res police involved as well. Gonna be a long day."

Jack poured each of us black coffee while Mickey talked. Mickey claimed his mug and headed out the door to the garage. Jack hung back. He opened a cabinet by the refrigerator and retrieved keys, handing them to me.

"I'll be riding with Mickey," Jack said. "The Suburban is yours. Go into town, get yourself food, go shopping, whatever you want. We'll leave here for Johnson's at about four-thirty, so I'll see you sometime before then. Call if you need me."

He leaned in and kissed me hard, and a smile broke out across my face. He grinned back, his face an inch from mine. "What are you smiling about?" he asked.

I shook my head. "I can't help it."

I watched his Wrangler-clad butt as he walked out, and covered my mouth to keep my smile from coming out aloud.

***

Collin's voice behind me on the stairs broke me out of my trance some minutes later. "What's going on?" He yawned.

As I turned away from my view of the mountains, I caught sight of most of his midsection as his morning stretch lifted his shirt. I averted my eyes. I didn't feel ready to talk to him, but it seemed I didn't have a choice.

"Dead man down out in a pasture. Cops converging." I stifled a yawn. "Too early."

"Too early for me to comprehend a word you just said," Collin said. "Other than it sounded too much like my day job."

Motioning at the mug in my hand, Collin walked toward the kitchen. "Coffee?"

"Should be some left. Jack just made it."

I moved to the base of the stairs, halfway into the kitchen, halfway in the great room.

Collin tilted the carafe all the way over until the last few drops ran out. "My head tells me we partied like rock stars," he said.

"Something like that."

He dug in his pocket. "I crawled around in the hall last night for half an hour and finally found this." He held up Tamara's ring. "She didn't come back for me."

"Do you blame her?"

He sighed. "No."

"Have you checked on her? She shouldn't have been driving."

"Yeah. She called me when she got home, to chew my ass again."

I nodded. "Good."

Snowflake sidled up to me and rubbed against my ankles.

"Yeah, um, Em, about what happened between us—"

I crossed my arms. "Whoa, Collin. There was no us. There was you, wasted, and there was me, blindsided."

"Well, yeah, that. I'm sorry. I really messed things up."

"Yes, you did."

He sipped coffee. "But I spoke the truth, even if I shouldn't have. I fell in love with you the first time Katie brought you around. Life never works out like I expect it will. I always thought someday you'd dump that putz husband of yours for me and we'd be together. I didn't ever imagine you'd go through what you have, or that I'd find Tamara in the meantime."

"Thank you, I think."

"Don't be like that. You know I don't mean anything bad. I may be a dumbass, but I'm a dumbass that has been in love exactly twice. You're the first, Tamara's the second. I should have told you years ago, but my pride never let me. Which doesn't matter now, because I'm going to make up with Tamara, even if it takes me a decade after pulling an asshat stunt like I did last night."

I smiled. "Well, if I had to tell the truth, it would be that I was pretty convinced you'd be around if I ever needed you, and that I was disappointed when I found out you were engaged."

Collin strutted around the kitchen but then clutched his head, like the cock of the walk with a tequila headache that he was. "Ha. I knew it."

"For about two minutes."

"Don't ruin my moment."

"A minute and a half."

"Hey, let me take you to breakfast, make it up to you."

"Don't you need to make it up to Tamara instead?"

He shook his head. "She flew out this morning. Doesn't get back until tonight. Military shit. I'm stranded and starving."

I looked at the clock. Six a.m. I'd have to drive him home anyway, since I suspected we were a little outside of Yellow Cab's range, and I needed food. He was behaving, so, why not?

"Okay, but let's wait for a civilized hour. I'm going to shower. I'll be back down here at seven-thirty." I retreated up the stairs with Snowflake right behind me.

***

I shoveled in a bite of huevos rancheros, minus the huevos. *More like frijoles rancheros,* I thought. Refried beans stuck in a mass of heat to the roof of my mouth. I opened my lips a smidge to suck in air. After a few cooling breaths, I chewed happily. Our surly waiter had made no apologies for the forty-five minute wait for our food, but the chow was so good that I forgave him.

Collin had ordered steak and eggs, and he dug into his rib eye, extra rare. Blood oozed onto the plate, and he sopped it up with his tortilla in one hand and his meat on the tines of his fork in the other. He waved the beef bite as he talked, and its delicious aroma wafted toward me, teasing me. Sometimes I missed meat, especially now that I didn't live with Rich the vegan.

Collin talked while he chewed. "This place is an institution. Tamara introduced me to it the first time I came to visit her."

"This place" was the Old Road House in Mescalero, a joint so local it had no sign out front. The red adobe restaurant was one-story on the parking side, and two-story in back, with wooden rafters, red tile floors, and a casual crowd of locals who seemed to find us slightly repellant, if fascinating. Green and red chiles hung in bunches on the inside walls alongside an elaborate papoose board, a feathered headdress, and a magnificent Apache bow.

"You come down a lot?"

"I do. She can't get away as easily as me."

I half-listened as Collin continued talking. The other half of me concentrated on my food . . . and eavesdropping on the two guys at the table behind me. They'd come in after us, and, when I'd turned to look at them, it was clear they were from a branch of Mickey's family tree. From the sound of their hushed voices, something had them excited. Or maybe agitated was a better word for it. I resisted the urge to turn and watch them.

The first man's voice said, "Well, I heard somebody's been selling silver, a lot of it, and they found it near here. Sure wasn't you or me or anyone else we know working a claim."

A higher voice, still male, answered him. "Ain't nobody been spending money that I can see. It's probably just rumors, man. There's always rumors."

The first voice spoke again. "Yeah, probably. But still, keep your ear to the ground and your eyes wide open. I want in on it if it's real."

Collin snapped his fingers in front of my eyes. "Earth to Emily."

I jumped. "Sorry. I'm in a hungover daze." I cut another bite of frijoles rancheros and scooped it up. Delicious. It was the perfect eating temperature now.

"So, you said you were taking a file to show Tamara last night. Want to run it past me? I've been told I'm a fairly competent investigator."

"I can't believe you even remember." Last night was a blur, but I took myself back and recalled the conversation I'd had with Laura and Tamara. "Tamara identified a tattoo for me, one on the arm of a guy that kidnapped that little girl that's missing, Valentina. She's the daughter of our client, who died in Amarillo."

"Show me."

I drew the ΣSL on a napkin like I'd done the night before and slid it over to him.

"And what did Tamara say about it?"

"That it was the sign of the East Side Lobos, a gang that runs in Las Cruces."

"Interesting. And Jack?"

I sat, blinking, as I realized that I hadn't told Jack about the tattoo. My mind retread the day Valentina had been taken, rushing to PCCB, telling Jack the story but cutting it short to meet with Melinda, her news about Sofia, and then nothing. I'd never given him this piece of information. I felt like an idiot, a greenhorn.

"I don't know," I said.

Collin squinted at me, but I shook my head. He shrugged. "Okay, what else do you know about the guy?"

"White skinned. Bald head."

"Like a skinhead?"

"The witness didn't give me that impression. But maybe."

"I'd be surprised. Not many skinheads in the Las Cruces gang community. They're usually up northwest. I deal with gangs all over the state in my job, even though I'm based in Santa Fe. Them and every other low-life scumbag within five hundred miles."

"Well, honestly, I'd thought the kidnapper was an Amarillo-based scumbag, this guy who's a known pedophile with jailhouse ties to the man Valentina's mother murdered."

"Did he grow up in Las Cruces?"

"I guess he could have. He's done time in New Mexico."

"Yeah. So maybe this doesn't rule your guy out."

I pondered it for a moment, then shivered. "I've been focused on someone in Amarillo, but whoever has her could have taken her anywhere. Even here, I guess."

"It's easy to hide someone in this area."

A cold dread seeped through me. I'd seen how desolate it was around here. "I don't get it though. Why take Valentina in the first place? And there's more. Her mother was murdered in jail the same day Valentina was taken. The ADA said it was an accident, but how is Sofia the only one hurt in a jail fight? I don't buy it. It feels connected to Valentina's kidnapping, to me. And now we're talking about the kidnapping being potentially tied somehow to southern New Mexico. But how? Maybe if I could figure out the tie, I could find her."

"Didn't you say they were undocumented?"

"Yes. Why?"

"Lots of illegals come through here from Mexico. Their community is very tight, very closed. They help each other out. It's also big business, though, and some less scrupulous types traffic folks illegally across the border. Usually the same type of assholes smuggling drugs, so I'm involved with more of these immigrations gone wrong than you'd imagine."

"Well, even if she entered the U.S. here, I still think it's more likely we'll find her somewhere in West Texas. I mean, why would someone go out of their way to kidnap a six-year-old child in Amarillo and bring her all the way back to southern New Mexico?"

He took another bite of bloody steak and talked through it. "Not for anything good, I can promise you that."

His words put the exclamation point on my fears, and I felt nauseous. The events since last night had been distracting, to say the least, but the full weight of Valentina's disappearance was bearing down on me again.

"Emily?" a woman called from the side of me nearest the dining room.

I turned. It was Laura. "Hey, good morning." I pulled a chair out. "Would you like to join us?"

She looked from me to Collin and back to me again, and her voice grew chilly. "No, thank you. I saw Jack's Suburban outside. What a surprise to see you with Collin."

I felt my brow crease. What was the matter with her? "Um, Jack left with Mickey hours ago, and he told me to take the Suburban for breakfast."

"Yes, I'm picking up food to take out to them."

I realized that Laura had every patron in the restaurant hanging on her words. I asked, "Is everything okay?"

She shrugged. "About what you'd expect."

A male voice called out from the cash register. "To-go order's ready for you, Laura."

She looked at me again, then pointedly at Collin. "See you later, Emily."

"Bye," I called after her.

"Brrrr," Collin said. "Is it just me or is it freezing in here?"

I ignored him, my stomach churning. Laura hadn't liked seeing me here with Collin, and it was her version of the tale that was headed straight back to Jack.

Chapter Twenty-three

I dropped Collin off at Tamara's place in Alamogordo and navigated my way back to Wrong Turn Ranch by noon. I'd canned my hopes for a quick trip to Roswell to see what I could find out about Harvey and Spike. Laura's censorious face had worried me since she'd left the Old Road House. I'd all but jackhammered Collin out of his seat when he'd wanted to linger over coffee and reminisce about the old days in Dallas. I tried not to panic. I hadn't done anything wrong, even if, apparently, it had looked bad to Laura. It was still okay to feel hopeful. I parked the Suburban out front and hurried into the house.

Sucking in a deep breath for courage, I opened the tall, wooden front door. "Hello? Anyone home?"

No answer except the sprinting feet and jingling tags of a little white dog.

I stepped inside and pulled the door shut behind me. Snowflake appeared, acting as excited to see me as if we'd been parted for years. I knelt and rubbed her ears, then straightened. Since Jack wasn't there, I decided to snag some apples or carrots or whatever I could find and head down to the stables. I was in the kitchen filling a brown paper bag with horse treats when I heard someone on the stairs. My heart pounded, and I watched the foot until a man appeared. He was a dark-haired man, but darker than Jack. Mickey, not looking any fresher than when I'd seen him that morning.

"Hello," I said to let him know I was there.

He looked at me in a way that said Laura had given him an earful. Mouth set, eyes flat and cold. His voice matched. "Emily. You've had a busy time since you got here."

His words cut me like razor wire, and I wanted to lash out. He didn't have to be so presumptuous. But Jack was his cousin; I was just some woman Mickey hardly knew.

I nodded. "Yes, it's been a busy morning. I had to run Collin home, and we grabbed breakfast on the way."

As I spoke, the apples started rolling off the cabinet and dropping to the floor, one by one. Bounce, thud, roll. Bounce, thud, roll. I crouched and grabbed one in each hand, but still they kept rolling away in all directions.

"Mickey, Collin is my best friend's brother, and—"

He held up a hand. "I don't need the details. There's only one thing I need, and that's for you not to fuck with Jack. He's had a really bad time of it, and you're the first smile I've seen on his face in five years."

I stood up in the middle of the green mess at my feet. "I promise, I didn't. I'm not. I won't." I spluttered in my protestations.

Before I could ask Mickey to enlighten me, he grunted and broke in.

"Make sure it stays that way."

He continued on the path I'd interrupted—his exit. The door to the garage slammed behind him, and the kitchen windows in the kitchen rattled with the force.

"Hey," I yelled after him, remembering too late that I had no idea what had happened with the dead man they'd found, or where Jack was. But Mickey was gone.

I crawled around on the kitchen floor, picking up the rest of the apples. I finished filling my bag with produce and started toward the barn. It felt crisp and clean outside. Jack had been right about the weather changes over the weekend. Last night's snow had already melted, and the temperature had soared. The sun shone directly overhead, warming me even more than the air did.

I needed that sun, I needed to overcome the cold water lapping waist-high around me again. Laura's and Mickey's reactions to me had knocked me back, and that precarious hold I had on a hope for happiness seemed to be slipping from my grasp. As the water rose, I felt vulnerable, to thoughts of losing my baby, of losing my chance at any babies, ever, of losing Valentina. A drowning Emily was no good to anyone, not to Valentina, who was still out there (I hoped) and not to

Jack, who—it appeared—faced his own troubles, ones I knew little to nothing about. Which was a problem, too. He knew my problems, or most of them, and I knew none of his. So I turned my face up to the sun and soaked it in, greedy and desperate for its warmth.

It was a short walk to the horse barn. The huge doors on either end stood wide open, creating a tunnel down the center. A strong breeze bordering on a wind whisked through it. It blew much of the sweet odor of bedding, feed, and horse away, but I still got a whiff, and it comforted me some. I walked from stall to stall, stroking necks and scratching heads. I wanted to find Jarhead, to see if he remembered me, and let him have first dibs at the treats, as was the due of a champion. He was near the end on the left, as he'd been the weekend before.

Just past his stall I noticed something I hadn't last time. A half glass interior door. I walked past Jarhead to take a look. A sign on the door read Mickey Begay, Ranch Manager. Inside was a large, modern office. What I wouldn't give for an office in a barn full of horses. I admired it for a few moments, then walked back to Jarhead.

"Hi, boy." I held my hand out, palm up, to let him get a good sniff of me. He did, and he snorted and tossed his head. "Hey." I rubbed his neck, giving his muscles a quick massage. He nuzzled my arm roughly, as if asking me to take him out to play. I laughed and dug into my bag for a carrot.

"What do you think you're doing?" Jack snapped.

His voice jolted me like an electric cattle prod, and I jumped back, the bag dropping to the ground, the same apples rolling around the barn as had rolled across the kitchen floor. There was no sign of a dimple on Jack's glowering face; I ignored the spilled fruit.

I bumbled my words. "Carrot . . . Jarhead . . . looking for you . . ."

"We have him off food and water. He has colic." He had his hands on his hips, but he was looking at the horse, not me.

"I'm sorry. I didn't know. I could walk him for you, if you'd like."

"I've got him." Jack snapped a lead line onto Jarhead's halter.

"Okay." My eyes strayed to the apples, some of them still rolling. "How did it go with the police and the dead guy this morning?"

"We're done." His voice clipped the word.

"Thank you for letting me borrow your car. I took Collin home. We stopped for breakfast first and I saw Laura."

"I heard." He led Jarhead from the stall and shut it.

"Jack, whatever you heard, whatever is making you act this way toward me, I just want you to know I didn't do anything, and nothing has changed. About me, I mean about me and you. How I feel about you, about last night."

"Good to know." He started walking Jarhead away from me.

"Jack."

He kept walking.

I'd tried as hard as I could. I didn't know what else to do, so I raised my voice. "JACK ASS. Listen to me, please."

He stopped, shook his head, and looked back at me. "Too much, too soon, for both of us. Let's rewind. Start over where we were yesterday, before last night."

I stood there, slack-jawed.

Jack and Jarhead walked out of the barn into the sunshine together. I sank onto a bale of hay, apples at my feet in the half-light of the barn, by myself.

***

My black skirt for the Johnson housewarming cut into my waist, giving me a muffin top where I'd tucked in my red silk blouse. I'd packed without considering the lingering impact of my former pregnancy on my midsection. I'd only gained a few pounds, but apparently they were all around my middle. Luckily I'd brought a black fleecy vest, so I put it on, and checked in the bathroom mirror. It hid the bulge, but did nothing for the bags under my eyes. A crying binge in the bathtub had seemed like a good idea two hours ago. Now, not so much. Good grief, my moods these days were as up and down as the Dallas Cowboys. I did one more pass under my eyes with concealer.

"Get it together," I told the woman in the mirror, then headed downstairs.

Jack and Snowflake waited for me in the great room. He was staring out the picture window and didn't seem to notice that I'd entered. It gave me a chance to study him.

When Mickey told me that Jack was part Apache, I hadn't seen it. But with him standing in the natural light beside a wall of family photographs, I did. His Apache grandmother wasn't hard to identify, not just because she looked Apache, but because in one black and white picture she was dressed traditionally, in a flowing hide skirt, a blouse with metal work at the neckline, and beads around her neck. Her features foreshadowed those on Jack's face: the stony set of his jaw, his thick dark hair, the intensity of his expression. All of these he got from her. But where did his tawny eyes come from?

My own eyes skipped from face to face in the photographs until I found the source. A tall, blonde woman whose light eyes glowed like a cat's, holding the hand of a light-eyed young Jack on one side and the hand of a Jack-lookalike husband with dark eyes on the other, a man with Jack's same lopsided grin punctuated by the same killer dimple. My eyes traveled further, to a picture of Jack with his wife and kids on horseback—Lena on Hopper, it looked like, and his daughter on the spotted pony—and further still to his daughter holding a tiny Snowflake with a giant red bow around the puppy's neck. I stood silently and breathed until I had myself under control.

"I'm ready when you are," I said.

He faced me, and it took a few seconds for his eyes to refocus from wherever they'd been. "Let's go then." He sent Snowflake to her bed, and she snorted and huffed to show her displeasure at being left, but settled into it anyway.

In the car, I broke the long, tense silence first. "Are things all finished up with the dead guy?"

Jack turned onto the highway and the tires hummed against the pavement as pine trees rushed past us on both sides. "The police haven't been able to identify him."

"Do they know how he died?"

"He looked Mexican."

Asking Jack questions was like a game of tetherball, with only one person hitting it. Me. I tried one last time. "No tattoos, nothing at all to identify him?"

"Brown from Alamogordo PD told me they're going to run prints." He added in a mutter, "After he made himself at home in my living room and drank a pot of my coffee."

I wanted to scream, "Give a straight answer to just one goddamned question, Jack Ass," but it wouldn't do any good. Plus, I'd go to Hell for taking the Lord's name in vain. If Jack was trying to irritate me into being happy that he'd dumped me before we'd ever gotten started, his non-answers were a good way to do it.

I stared out the window for a while until I had calmed down. Without turning back to Jack, I said, "He's like a ghost."

"He's like an illegal."

How had I lived so isolated from the desperate world of undocumented immigrants for so long? I'd known that people of Mexican heritage came from Mexico, that there were immigration laws and that employers had to follow them. I watched the news and the vitriolic debate on the issue. I heard my mother's complaints about it from time to time. Yet, somehow, it had existed separate and apart from my real life. I hadn't known the people that risked their lives to get here. I hadn't imagined what was worse than living here, poor, on the fringes. I'd never bothered to think past how awful I believed it was to be the teenage daughter of a sad, penniless mother and a runaway cowboy.

We drove in silence, and my thoughts focused not on the irritatingly sexy man beside me, but on the dead man with no identity and maybe no country, about Sofia and what she had done—why she might have done it—and Valentina alone, or worse. It put my troubles in perspective. I had lost a baby that was never born and a percentage of a chance of a future baby that God might never have intended for me anyway. Sofia and Valentina were together for six years, and had lost each other. Valentina hadn't just lost her mama—she was without a father, too. What would happen if no one found her? Would she die? Would she be sold by Harvey—or whoever had her—to the highest bidder? Or simply used up by whoever was around? Hell, what would happen if she *was* found? She could be sent back to Mexico where she didn't know a soul—something her mother had gambled and lost her own life to prevent.

I chuffed and put my hand to my mouth. Jack glanced at me, then back at the road. My mind zeroed in on those huge brown eyes and pigtails, the threadbare jammies with pink pills of fabric and a giant Barbie smile across a tummy. The blue-shirted doll with the lace shawl, just one more thing the girl had lost. It was time for me to quit feeling sorry for me. I was letting myself get jammed up with an emotionally unavailable man that I didn't need, risking a job I did, and focusing on things that I couldn't have, while forgetting about what was real and right in front of me. Suddenly, I felt the scratch of flint deep inside, once, twice, three times, and then a flame that spread like wildfire.

I didn't know how, but I knew that I had to find her, that we were each other's second chance. Here I was giving up on myself, like some nag ready for the glue factory when Valentina needed me. I had more than enough clues pointing me to information in southern New Mexico, and I was here. I would figure out what those clues meant, one way or the other.

A sick feeling came over me, and I realized I had to speak to Jack.

"I forgot to tell you something important," I said.

His jaw flexed. "What?"

"When I was looking for information about Sofia, and I found Valentina, only I didn't know it, and then she was taken by the bald guy, there was something I learned about the kidnapper from Victoria, something I forgot to tell you because we were cut short by Melinda telling us Sofia had died."

He shot a glance at me. "Go on."

I searched my handbag for paper and a pen. No paper, but I found a pen, so I drew the ΣSL on my hand.

"He had a tattoo on the inside of his upper arm. His left arm. Like this one." I held my hand out beside the steering wheel. "Victoria saw it. Harvey has one. Last night Tamara told me it stands for East Side Lobos in Las Cruces. Have you seen it before?"

He turned his eyes to it, and they widened. He looked back at the road, then again at my hand. "Yes. Yesterday. On Spike Howard's autopsy photos."

Chapter Twenty-four

"You look beautiful, as always." Paul kissed my hand and then tugged me through the front door into a hug. His sheer size made me feel Lilliputian. "And how's my attorney?" He released me and clasped Jack's hand in a bro shake to his chest, clapping him on the back at the same time. "Can't tell you how glad I am to have the two of you here. The bar's out on the back patio." He winked. "A little hair of the dog."

"Thanks, Paul," I said.

I moved far enough away to keep him out of my personal space. His effusive greeting was just too familiar for me, especially after the weird last twenty-four hours.

Galvanized by the newly rekindled fire to find Valentina, I decided I was done feeling guilty. I saw Jack's stern jaw from the corner of my eye. He looked like a man who'd eaten a mess of bad eggs. Well, good. He deserved to feel bad. He'd overreacted and shut me out when I'd tried to explain. I ignored him and turned for the bar.

The entry hall emptied into a room with an amazing ceiling that pulled my eyes upward, and I marveled at the octagonal cupola lined with rafters across intricate tongue-in-groove boarding. Inset windows alternated levels on each of the cupola's sides. Below it was a sitting area of oversized leather and cowhide couches and armchairs. An enormous rug in caramel brown and white spots with darker brown sections every few feet anchored the furniture. It was one of the most uniquely beautiful floor coverings I had ever seen. The chandelier of two metal hoops, one suspended three feet above and within the circumference of the other, hung from fifteen-foot chains. An immense stone fireplace dominated one wall and its opposite wall opened onto a bustling kitchen. Huge wood-framed glass doors and windows covered the back wall and opened onto a patio. The doors were propped open, and a brisk breeze coursed through the space carrying the dry smell of pine and sage.

I wanted to find a quiet place where Jack and I could continue our conversation about Spike's tattoo. I walked ahead of Jack through the room toward the back patio, where a few on-time guests like us milled about. When I got outside, I stopped, mesmerized by the view. Paul's backyard ended in a high, rock-faced hillside with trees hugging the edge of its summit, their coniferous branches bouncing and swaying in the wind. It was pure, rugged drama, and I stared at it for long seconds before I turned back to Jack, but he'd disappeared.

I started to look for him, but was interrupted by a teenage boy.

"Drink, ma'am?"

A tattoo of a snake wound around his neck, but his real attention grabber was a nose ring. Where I came from, you used those things to clip a lead to an animal that needed a little extra motivation to behave. And the tattoo? I wanted to tell him that he didn't need to brand himself like a steer, but I held my tongue.

I almost ordered wine, but last night had left me tired and dehydrated, which more alcohol would only make worse. "Sparkling water with lime, please."

"No problem."

Round metal tables and chairs dotted the patio with centerpieces of stone and cactus weighting down each table. Movement to my right caught my eye, and I saw Paul's daughter Stella leaning against the far back edge of the house smoking a cigarette. She looked angry, and incredibly alone.

"Thanks for your note," a woman's voice said, from my left.

I followed the voice and saw Jack's secretary, Judith. With makeup on, she was strikingly beautiful. Jack had told me all of his employees were invited, and I'd hoped she'd be here, that I'd get another chance with her.

"Hi, Judith," I said. "Isn't this house amazing?"

"Yes. Big. And very expensive," she said. "Lots of people from the reservation have worked on it."

Something about Judith whispered to me of ancient things, of traditions that lived on in more than photographs. She looked timeless in turquoise and silver dangling earrings and a matching neck cuff that looked as old as the land around us. Her low, thick ponytail was fastened with a large clip, and it, too, was silver, with round pieces of turquoise set within etched scrolls.

"Did you know Paul before he became a client?" I asked her.

"No, he's not from around here—the Mescalero reservation, I mean, or Tularosa. But my brother worked construction here. At this house."

"Oh really? What does your brother do?"

"He's an electrician."

The teenage cocktail waiter returned with my drink. "Here you go, one club soda with lime. And for you, ma'am?"

My phone chimed. While Judith gave her order, I checked the text. Wallace, in a group text to Nadine and me: *Nadine and I visited Harvey today.*

I typed a quick reply: *Any sign of Valentina?*

Wallace: *No. He swears he's never met Sofia or her, and that he lost track of Spike when they got out of prison.*

Me: *Impossible. He was seen running away from the hotel the night Sofia shot Spike.*

Harvey's denial made me want to dig deeper with Wallace. What did you ask him? What did you see? How did he explain that tattoo? But I reminded myself that I could count on Wallace and Nadine to handle it. I had to.

Wallace: *We'll take another pass at him.*

Me: *Thank you, guys.*

I needed to stay off the phone at a work function. I slipped it in my pocket and returned my attention to Judith, who stood gazing up at the rock face. Without turning toward me, she started talking again.

"I used to come out here with my friends when I was a girl," she said. "There were fences, but we didn't care." The wind blew a wisp of hair from her clip and it fluttered to the side of her sharp cheekbones. She pointed to the top of the rocks. "When we first came out here, we convinced ourselves we'd seen Mountain Spirits dancing up there. Who knows, maybe we did."

She tucked the hair behind her ear. The sun reflected off her earring. "It became our place. We started to dance when we came here, like them, facing the Sacred Mountain." She pointed north to the white-capped Sierra Blanca Peak in the distance. She turned to me and smiled for the first time since I'd met her, then returned her gaze to the rocks.

You know of the Mountain Spirit dancers?" Judith asked.

"Yes. Mickey told me about them," I said.

She nodded. "I was always the clown, painting myself white, wearing the nose and the ears. I liked scaring the little ones."

How to say this nicely? "I'll bet you were good at it."

"I was."

"I was a clown, too. A rodeo clown."

As I looked at her profile, images ran through my head, of my recent dreams of the Clown Dancer, and of something else. A crude drawing in Crayola, a man in a skirt, an oversized crown of sticks on his head, his skin crayoned white. Animal ears and nose. Was Valentina's drawing of the Mountain Spirit Dancer's clown? If she had come to the U.S. through southern New Mexico, it could be. That brought up interesting possibilities. But maybe I was just projecting my thoughts onto her picture.

"We have that in common." She sighed. "I worked for Jack when he was with the DA in Las Cruces, did you know that?"

"I didn't."

"Yeah. I moved to the city when I was younger, but I always wanted to come back here."

"I can see why. It's magical, spectacular."

"That day when the bomb went off, I was there. Before it happened, I saw the Dancers, I saw the Clown. They were in front of the building, by the flags."

She'd lost me, lost me in a way so profound I didn't know how to ask what she was talking about. She wasn't making sense. Was she crazy, or was I missing something? It felt important, game-changing even, so I didn't dare interrupt.

"The Clown took the Dancers to the parking lot, to Jack's car," Judith said. "And I followed them. Then he cried, the Clown did. I didn't know what he meant, so I looked around, to ask someone else, but I was the only one there."

I held my breath, literally. Judith's eyes had teared up, and I didn't think it was from the wind. I stayed silent.

"Nobody else saw them. And later, when it happened, I knew they had been real, and what the Clown had been trying to tell me."

She turned to me again, tears now streaming down her face. "Being here, it forces me to remember. I still feel guilty—I didn't understand what the Clown meant, and I should have. I could have saved Mrs. Holden and the children from the bomb. I could have kept them out of Jack's car. They would be alive today."

A chill ran through me, and my mouth hung open uselessly. Jack's wife hadn't left him and taken the kids. They were dead. *Dead.* Judith looked into my eyes, and I realized that she needed me to respond.

"I'm so sorry," I said.

She backed away. "Please tell Jack I was here," she said. "I just don't think I can stay. Because of the memories."

***

In the wake of Judith's revelations, I couldn't stay either. My mind reeled, sifting through her words for the facts. A car bomb at the courthouse? Jack's wife and kids *dead?* It was so much worse than anything I'd imagined about Jack's past. Losing your whole family to a car bomb—one I had to assume was meant for him since it was in his car at his workplace—how did you ever recover from that? I choked on a sob and took off from the patio toward some outbuildings in the distance. I needed a place to hide, a place to think, a place to mourn Jack's family. My rapid walk morphed into a slow, blind jog.

Loss was everywhere. My loss. Sofia's. Valentina's. And now Jack's loss—his loss swallowing mine up whole in its immensity. Mickey had mentioned Jack not smiling for five years. I wondered if Jack fled to Amarillo after the bomb, had lived in his office shrine for this whole time, hiding from everything but his memories, only for me to come along and defile his sanctuary. My jog sped into a blind run, until I planted my booted foot on a rock, stumbled, and went down on my hands and knees.

"Oomph."

I lifted my palms. Dirt and rocks and blood. I rose and lifted my skirt. More rocks, dirt, and blood. There was a gaping hole in my black stockings on my right knee, but my long, black skirt would cover it. I brushed off my knees and let go of the fabric. Hair fell around my face, and I probed for the bobby pins that held my back-teased strands in place. I pulled one out and re-secured it. That would have to do. The fall had sobered me a little, and I started walking again, aimless but still generally toward the three green metal buildings now only a hundred feet away.

When I reached them, I walked to the back of the first one, out of sight of Paul's party. I crouched with my back against it. *Breathe. You can't make sense of this unless you breathe, and think.* Maybe it was time to ask for help, too. Like from the Big Guy. But I was really rusty. Sure, I muttered pithy little prayers now and then, but when was the last time I'd truly meant it? I didn't really need to ask myself that, though. I knew exactly when. My senior year at Tech. When Christmas and my birthday passed without hearing from my father, I quit religion cold turkey. In retrospect, I could admit that God probably wasn't the one to blame, but it was easier at the time. In the ensuing years, my problem was more organized religion than Him, but the result was the same either way.

Ever since then—and especially lately—I'd done a little too much of the *why me* and the *not fair* instead of just being thankful for what I did have. I probably didn't deserve to ask for help now, but I was going to give it my best shot anyway. I pressed my hands together and closed my eyes, but all that came out of me was *why me, why this, why anyone, you have to make it better.* I tried again, softly, under my breath.

"God, I don't understand all this."

Long moments passed, silent except for my deliberate breaths. In. Out. In. Out. The rhythm hypnotized me, and underneath my closed lids, my eyes fluttered. Just as I faded out, I realized with a sudden clarity, a certainty, that things in my life were as they should be, that I was where I should be. I closed my eyes again.

"Thank you for bringing me home and to a new career and new friends, and a chance to help make a difference in things that really matter. And I promise I am going to find a church, just not that Believers one or any church that Melinda Stafford would consider attending. Amen."

Men's voices interrupted me, close and moving my way. I looked harder at the outside of the building where I'd taken refuge. It appeared to be a warehouse of sorts. To my right was a huge roll-up door, open about halfway. The voices came from inside the building. Instinct took over; I stood and crept to the edge of the door, craning to hear.

A deep voice spoke. "Mr. Johnson said the police don't have a clue that's Alejandro they found dead at Wrong Turn Ranch. And I haven't heard any talk about the stupid bastard taking his silver mine story to the Apaches. You may have dodged a bullet, this time. But we need to make an example out of him to the others, because this can't ever happen again. Or next time we'll be making an example of you."

A higher, thinner voice answered. "Alejandro was our only problem. The rest of 'em are scared shitless. Once they see we got the girl back—and what we do to the little brat—they'll be back down in that mine diggin' Apache silver for all they're worth—with their mouths shut."

Their words had frozen me in place, once again forcing me to decipher the truth from half the story. While I didn't have enough to get the full picture, I got the gist. Making examples out of people, problems with a terrorized labor force, silver belonging to the Apaches, a recovered little girl, them knowing who the dead guy was at Jack's place: trouble that all added up to bad, bad stuff here on Paul's ranch.

I had to get out of there, and I had to get to Jack. I gathered my skirt in one hand and placed my feet one in front of the other gently and carefully, but quickly. As I crested the side of the building back toward the house, I broke into a run. An arm snaked out and grabbed mine, jerking me to a stop.

"Whoa, whoa, whoa now," the higher-pitched man said.

I yelped and clawed at the hand cuffed around my arm, at the fingers biting into my flesh. I couldn't get the hand to budge, so I turned to face the body at the end of the arm.

Two white men stood beside an open side entrance that I hadn't noticed on my blind flight out here. They both grinned, but not in a friendly way. The man holding my arm was tall and thin, with dusty clothes and limp hair that bore the imprint of a hat brim.

The other man—the man with the deeper voice—was thicker and paler and he had a shaved head. He wore pressed jeans and a checkered shirt and spoke first. "Sorry, miss. You scared us. We aren't used to strangers out here where they aren't invited. You here for the party?"

I swallowed hard and nodded. "Yes."

Tall guy loosened his grip on me some but didn't let go.

"Didn't you see the 'no trespassing' signs?" He pointed back toward the house. A metal pole with a rectangular sign jutted up from the ground. It did say No Trespassing in black letters against a white background.

My heart galloped in my ears. I struggled for composure, for the bravado that had always sustained me, like when I faced down a drunken two-hundred-pound Neanderthal from the Tarleton rodeo team who had mistaken my decision not to knee him in the balls the first time he'd groped me as weakness. He didn't get a third chance.

I straightened my shoulders. "No, I didn't. I'm so sorry. I was looking for a private place to make a call." I held up my phone.

Tall guy snatched it from me. "Let's see." After a few swipes and taps, he said, "Huh. Nothing here."

I had to convince them I was harmless. "I know. I've got man troubles. I got out here and lost my nerve." I lifted my shoulders in a "silly little me" gesture.

"What's your name?" tall guy asked.

"Emily. I'm a friend of Paul's."

"Ah, shit, Tanner, she's that nosey Texas woman he told us about. The one that works for the lawyer."

Tanner, the thicker, paler man, narrowed his eyes.

I forced out a hollow laugh. "That's me! See, I'm his friend. I'm sorry I came out here, guys, really. I won't do it again."

Inside, my heart twisted. Paul was dirty, and he was talking about me to his henchman—and not in a nice way.

Tanner thwacked my phone against his palm a couple of times. And then I heard a child's scream, high-pitched, soul wrenching. My face reacted before I could steel my features, and I knew how I looked. Scared. Horrified. Concerned.

Dangerous.

"Fuck," Tanner said.

He ripped off his snap front shirt, revealing a plain white T underneath it. He whipped the shirt over my mouth, muffling me, as he reached into his pocket and pulled something oblong out and jammed a sharp point at one end of it into my arm, all in a series of deft motions.

"Whaaa—"

I felt myself crumpling to the ground, but not before my eyes locked on Tanner's left arm. At his tattoo.

"East Side . . ." I whispered. But before I finished my thought, the world went black.

Chapter Twenty-five

I opened my eyes but saw nothing. The smell of dust filled my nose. My eyes adjusted to the darkness, but still I could barely see. Everything looked so indistinct. I shook my head, trying to fix my vision, but all it did was make me nauseous and create blurry after-images of the things I couldn't make out anyway. Where was I?

"Lady?"

A little girl's voice, clear and close. I turned my face toward the sound and saw a darker blob near what seemed to be the floor.

"Yes, hello."

"You okay?"

I tried to reach toward her, but couldn't move my hands. I pulled harder and realized they were fastened together with something rough. "I'm okay, but I can't see you very well. And I'm tied up." I closed my eyes again.

"I see you, but the mans tie my hands. When I first here, I no can see. The bad man stick me. It make me sleepy and sick."

Her voice was heavily accented with the sounds of Mexican Spanish.

"Yeah, me, too."

I closed my eyes for a moment and focused on calming down. I needed to be in the moment, be aware. To think things through. Like, how does a blind idiot who's gotten herself knocked out for the second time in a week free herself and a little girl out of hand bindings? I shifted my feet and groaned. And foot bindings.

"Sweetie? Are you okay?" I asked.

"Yes." She stopped speaking then said, "I'm scared."

"Me, too, but that's okay. My name is Emily. What's yours?"

There was a long pause.

"Sweetie, are you there?"

"I call myself Betsy."

Her English grammar came out as a literal translation of the way it would be said in Spanish. How formal, how cute, how painfully sincere. My heart leaned toward her and I wished I could hug her. Heck, I wished she could hug me.

"Betsy. Okay, well I'm starting to feel a little bit better, and I'm going to need your help getting us out of here. Can you help me?"

"I try. How?"

"I'm figuring that out right now. Are your feet tied up?"

"Yes."

"Can you roll over to me long ways?"

"Roll like log?"

"Exactly, like a log."

"I can!"

I heard the sound of a little body rolling across the floor to me, and I smiled, despite our circumstances. The kid was charming. I opened my eyes again and realized my vision was clearing. I saw her small body and long black hair.

"I'm here!"

"Very good. I want to untie your hands. Can you roll behind me and put your hands against mine, so I can feel the knot in the rope they tied yours with?"

"I try."

Her bright little voice sounded so can-do. I smiled. She pushed the rope around her wrists into my hands.

My fingers worked it as I talked to her. "So, Betsy, tell me about how you got here and where you're from."

I found the end of the tough twine and worked my fingers to the knot. I needed to loosen the piece across the top into a loop, then push the stiff twine back through.

"From Mexico with Mama and Papa. We hide in a truck with chickens and lizards."

The twine was so tight that I couldn't get it to budge, and I had no leverage. I pushed and pushed and was finally able to wedge my thumbnail between the strands. I wiggled my thumb back and forth, up and down, back and forth, up and down. The twine strands gripped each other as if with pinchers. Was it loosening? I couldn't tell. Back and forth, up and down. Finally, I felt the tiniest of gives and gave a little gasp.

"What?"

"Hold really still. I think I'm getting it."

Back and forth, up and down. Another tiny slip. Back and forth, up and down.

"How you get here?"

"By being really dumb."

Back and forth, up and down. I now had the whole tip of my thumb in the loop, thank God, because I couldn't keep doing this much longer. My thumbnail was about to come off. I put my wrist into the movement as I answered her.

Now I worked the end of the twine through my hard-won loop. I felt the knot. At least two more. I ignored the pain in my thumbnail and started wedging my nail in again.

"You pretty, Miss."

I grunted. "Thank you, sweetie. I can't wait to see you once we are both untied. My eyes have started working again."

And were adjusting to the dark of the room, lit only by waning light from two high windows, too high, I saw, for me to reach.

Five minutes later I got my thumb tip through, and gritted my teeth in agony. I didn't want to see my poor thumb. I could feel the shredded skin on either side of my nail with my forefinger. It felt like hamburger. After another three minutes, I had one loop left to go. I switched to my left hand. It was slower, but at least I had the hang of it.

"Done."

"You did it!" Betsy said. I heard rustling behind me. "My hands hurt."

"I'll bet they do. Can you undo mine now, please?" Urgency strained my voice. The process had taken far longer than I'd hoped, and now that I could see the door, I expected it to burst open any moment with Tanner and Skinny Guy. All this would be for nothing.

I felt her fingers go to work. "Too tight. I can't."

Of course. Her little fingers weren't as strong as mine. I scanned the empty room, looking for some kind of tool. But it was just us, four walls, and a concrete floor. I frowned, concentrating as I took inventory, then I smiled. I did have something. Saved by my own vanity and how oblivious men are to all it takes to make a woman a goddess.

"Reach up into my hair and pull out one of my bobby pins. You can slide one into the knot to help you loosen it."

"Bobby pins?"

"Hair pins. Pins in my hair."

Small hands picked through my hair. Even in these circumstances, it was a lovely feeling. I felt a pin pull free.

"Got it."

"Great. See if you can stick the whole thing between the edges of the top knot."

She made little grunts and I felt pressure, this way and that. "I did it! I got it!"

"Good girl. Okay, wiggle it and move it around to make the knot looser. You can keep doing it until it's big enough to pull open."

More pressure. I listened for footsteps outside our door, my mouth dry as wood shavings. The pressure on my wrists changed and I felt grating as one strand of twine slid its way out of the first knot.

"I do it again."

"You're awesome. Thank you." The tension of listening was making it hard to breath. Faster, I prayed. Faster.

"One more."

Dear Heavenly Father, thank you for bringing Betsy and me together. Help me to help her. Amen.

The rough twine abraded my wrist as Betsy pulled it off altogether.

"You did it! Now I'm going to have to give you a big hug."

I wheeled around and saw for the first time the girl I'd been working with and talking to. Pink Barbie pj's, big black eyes, and long black hair. One of the three little girls I had watched giggle on a couch in Amarillo, the one who had shown me her favorite doll, a child whose picture Victoria sent me and I kept on my phone. Valentina Perez, who it seemed was calling herself Betsy. My heart roared.

She threw her arms around me. "You the lady who knows my mommy, right?"

There was no time for questions now. I hugged her tightly for a brief second, my emotions raw and swollen, then let her go. "I am, and I've been looking for you. I'm so glad to see you! Now, we need to hurry, so let's untie our own feet."

I grabbed one of my bobby pins to help me with the knots this time, because, as I had suspected, my thumb was pulp. I made fast work of them.

Valentina aka Betsy had made good progress on her own knots. "Want me to finish that?"

She nodded and I quickly freed her legs.

"Okay, now, stay close behind me, and don't make a sound."

I palmed the bobby pins and dropped them in my skirt pocket for later, just in case. We stood and faced the door. I held my breath as I tried the handle. Locked. Time for the bobby pin after all? I eyed the door handle but there was no lock in it. I looked closely at the jamb and just made out the dark presence of a thrown deadbolt, from the other side. No bobby pin was going to solve this problem. I stood staring, thinking, despairing, when the lock snapped back and the handle turned. I clapped one hand over my mouth to stifle my scream and threw the other in front of Betsy as the door opened slowly toward us.

***

A ghostly figure stood in the doorway, light behind it, a finger across its lips. Male or female, I couldn't tell, but it was slight and tall for a woman or short for a man, with some kind of enormous thing on its head. Its body was clad in a white mesh suit, with a black skirt nearly to the top of knee-high buckskin moccasins. Its face was ghostly white with an animal hide mask over the nose. The drawing, I realized. It was like the figure from Valentina's—or Betsy's—crayon drawing in the apartment back in Amarillo.

Behind me, Betsy clung to my skirt, her head against my hip. My arm slipped around her shoulders like I'd been protecting her all her life.

"It's okay," Betsy said. She stepped around me. "She's my friend."

The figure nodded. It pointed down the hall and whispered in a low voice, "Go, quickly, out and left to the stable. There's a horse ready for you there."

"Thank you," I whispered.

"My backpack?" Betsy asked.

"Do you know where it is?"

She shook her head.

"We'll look for it later. Now, we have to go."

Betsy ran to the figure and hugged it hard. "Bye, friend."

I snatched her hand before she'd removed her arms from the apparition. "Let's run."

But as I stood close to the figure, I suddenly realized I knew her, and as our eyes met she knew it, too. Stella. Paul's daughter. I didn't have time to analyze the hows and whys. I nodded at her, and we ran.

I pulled Betsy behind me so hard that she was practically aloft. I tried to run silently in my high-heeled cowboy boots on the concrete floor, but they clomped alarmingly. I fought through the cobwebs in my brain, trying to shake off the lethargy of Tanner's drug. It felt like I'd spent days as a captive in that room, but I realized only hours had passed. Lights still twinkled from the back patio of Paul's house, and party sounds floated toward us .We raced through the dark out of the office building and to our left.

"Hey! Stop right there!" a deep male voice yelled.

It sounded like Tanner, but I wasn't turning around to verify. My boots were so loud I couldn't hear his steps, but he had to be closing in on us. I couldn't go faster than Betsy was able. Suddenly, the stable loomed ahead, close, its opening a black cutout in green metal sides. We burst in, and a startled nicker to my right stopped me short. A saddled horse. I pulled the reins from a hitching post and jumped on. I held out my hand to Betsy.

"I'm scared," she cried.

"I've got you," I said. "I promise."

She grasped my hand and I pulled her up with strength I didn't know I had. The horse snorted and hopped as Betsy's small body landed belly first across the saddle horn in front of me. She cried out, and I pulled her upright and slung her leg across the horse. A figure grew larger in front of the backlights from the ranch house. I would have to rush him with the horse, but I knew he'd go for help after we got away. I scanned the barn frantically for a club or a whip or, or, or . . . but all I saw was a lasso hanging from a peg on the wall. Well, it would have to do. I wheeled the horse, grabbed the rope, wrapped its end around the saddle horn feverishly, whacking poor Betsy over and over in the process, but the brave little girl didn't make a sound. I gave the horse a sharp kick.

"Yah!"

The horse bolted from the barn, straight at Tanner. I held onto the reins and Betsy with my left arm and swung a loop around and around over my head with my right. I guided the horse with knee pressure and my body weight as I leaned to the left, and Tanner scrambled away from us. The horse responded, moving in unison with me. I could thank God later for a well-trained quarter horse, but for now we were nearly upon Tanner. He ducked, reaching for his hip.

Gun.

I let my loop fly, the hiss of rope gliding off my fingers. In slow motion, it sailed through the dark and over the unsuspecting Tanner. I gave it a jerk as it settled over him, and wrapped the lasso around the saddle horn.

"Back, back," I ordered, throwing my weight against the back of the saddle, pulling firmly with the reins.

The horse all but sat on its rump as it stopped, then began backing quickly. Tanner hit the dirt, his arms immobilized. He grunted, loudly, then cussed me at the top of his lungs as the horse dragged him through the dust and gravel.

"Betsy, sit here, and hold on to this horn. I have to tie him up so he won't follow us."

I could see the huge round whites of her eyes. She nodded, speechless. I ripped the tie-down rope from where it was fastened. Later, I'd have to thank God for well-outfitted tack. I ran to Tanner, who was still slowly being dragged by my new favorite horse.

"You bitch," he said.

I lashed his feet together, then dragged them up behind his rump and caught his hands in the same tie-down, rendering him helpless. When I'd finished, I jumped up and threw both hands in the air automatically, to signal I was done, but there was no official dropping the flag and timing my efforts, and this was no rodeo. I pulled my arms down and pretended I hadn't just done that.

I looked down at Tanner. "Looks like you're the bitch to me."

I searched the ground behind him for the gun I'd seen him draw. I caught a glint of light ten yards back. I trotted out and grabbed the six-shot pistol. 357 Magnum. I checked that the safety was on and then stuck it in the tight waistband of my skirt. I took the horse by the bridle and guided him as he dragged Tanner into the barn. That was better, but still, the man could squeal for help. I needed something to use to gag him. I took off a boot and hooked two fingers through the tear in the knee of my tights and ripped until I had the whole lower section off. I jammed my foot back into the boot then leaned over and pinched Tanner's nose shut until he had to open his mouth to breathe, and I shoved my stocking in, moving fast to avoid his teeth. Then I unfastened the lasso from the saddle horn, tied it to a post, and pulled the barn door shut as I led the horse out with Betsy astride him.

I remounted behind Betsy and gave her a squeeze. "Let's get out of here."

Chapter Twenty-six

It was getting out of there that presented the next problem. I couldn't go barging in on Paul's house party, since I no longer had any idea who was friend or foe. Except for Judith, who had long since left, and Jack, who might not be there anymore, either. I didn't have my phone so I couldn't call them. A really hideous possibility occurred to me: Paul knew about the Collin fiasco last night. Who was I kidding? He probably knew about this morning, too. All Paul had to do was tell Jack I'd left with Collin. When I didn't show up at Wrong Turn Ranch, Jack wouldn't worry about me. He'd make the natural assumption. *Spit.*

Well, I knew the way home, and I had a good horse and a gun that I wasn't afraid to use, so I'd just ride. The only problem with this plan was that when Tanner was discovered where I'd left him hog-tied and gagged, he'd tell them I'd fled via horseback, and they wouldn't have any trouble guessing which way I'd gone. Okay, so that meant I'd have to move quickly, and maybe even be a little bit sneakily.

I leaned down toward Betsy's ear and whispered, "You ready to go real fast?"

Betsy nodded, her silky hair rubbing under my chin. "What's the horse's name?"

"I don't know. Why don't you give him a name?"

Again the silky caress of her nod. "Thunder."

"Yah, Thunder," I shouted into the night as I smacked him lightly on his shoulder with the reins.

He responded by leaping forward in a quarter-mile sprint that would have earned Jarhead's approval, then settled into a ground-eating gallop. I steered us wide of the house, down the dark side of the entrance, the only way I knew to get off of Paul's land.

True to his name, our mount's hooves thundered on the ground beside the road. I caught sight of the highway ahead, but as we neared it, headlights swept across the pasture in front of us to our left. It was a vehicle, behind us, and it would catch us in its beams when the curves of the road aligned in its favor. There was nowhere to hide.

"Yah, Thunder, yah."

"Yah, Thunder," Betsy echoed.

The horse ran faster, panting but eager and fleet. The pavement ahead would be slick and treacherous under his hooves. I had to pull him up and let him trot across, but not too soon. I tried to judge the distance in the dark as the headlights swept across our backs and to our right. If they'd seen us, we were goners no matter what I did. We had almost reached the highway, and I pulled Thunder up short. He whinnied, but obeyed, and I urged him into a trot to cross the road at an angle away from Jack's place, trying to get far enough east that a vehicle turning toward Wrong Turn Ranch wouldn't see us. When we reached the grass on the other side of the highway, I guided Thunder to the right and gave him his head. He galloped easily. I turned back to look at the vehicle exiting Paul's ranch. Thunder's tail flew high behind him. *Turn left*, I willed the car. *Turn left*.

And it did. As soon as its taillights disappeared, I slowed Thunder and wheeled him back around.

"Where we go?" Betsy asked.

"To my friend Jack's house."

"How far?"

"A little far. We're looking for a gate so we can turn off this road onto his ranch. Can you help me look for a place on the fence where two posts are close together?"

She pointed ahead of us. "There?"

Her young eyes were far better in the dark than mine, and I strained to see two posts close together. I found them; she was right.

"Yes, good job. You hold onto the saddle horn and stay on Thunder while I open the gate."

Again, we were exposed to any vehicles leaving Paul's ranch. I hopped down and pulled on the tight wire with all my might. My arms shook, but I was able to get it just clear enough that I could slip the top loop off and pull the post out of the bottom loop. I threw the gate aside and led Betsy and Thunder through. I hated to take the time to close the gate behind us but, if I left it open, it would be an easy clue for anyone following us.

I pushed us faster again now, following the eastern fence line to the north, straight away from Paul's ranch and the highway traffic. I kept a hand on the saddle horn with Betsy's, fearful that Thunder would lodge his hoof in a prairie dog hole in the dark, but he ran on at a three-quarters pace without faltering.

Betsy shouted, "Fence."

Again, she was right. The quarter moon gave her just enough light to be our eyes. *Another thing to be thankful for*, I noted. We cut left along the fence and soon came upon a west-facing gate. I stopped, wavering. As much as I wanted to cut farther north, we could go west here, then north at our next opportunity. I wavered, then chose. West and north it would be. We hurried through and resumed our journey northward along the eastern fence. I slowed Thunder to a lope and his breathing settled with it. He nickered. His hooves drummed the ground rhythmically. We spooked some horses as we ran past their sleeping figures, and they jumped to their feet, snorts and whinnies following us. Betsy's head began to sag against my arm until she slumped in a dead weight. With my adrenaline ebbing, drowsiness sank over me, too. It wasn't so long ago I'd been unconscious and drugged. I shook my head vigorously. I had to stay alert.

As I rode I started thinking through all I'd learned and what might lie ahead. Assuming Paul and his buddies were looking for me, they'd go to Jack's. They could be there now, passing the mescal bottle around, waiting for me. That meant I needed to come from the direction opposite the entrance—north to south—and find a phone to call Jack from, to let him know what was up.

I came upon a north-facing gate. "Wake up, sleeping beauty," I said to Betsy.

She rubbed her eyes and grabbed the saddle horn. I opened the gate and let us through. We rode north again. I tried to think of where I could find a phone. I pictured the barn and fixed my mind's eye on the closed door at the end of the stalls. It had a sign on it. Mickey Begay, Ranch Manager. A business office. It had to have a phone, or a fax, or a computer. Well, it didn't *have* to. Everyone carried cell phones these days. But it might.

Thunder must have sensed the ranch headquarters with all its stabled horses before I did because he tossed his head and sped up again. A few minutes later, I saw the lights and the dark shadows of the Wrong Turn Ranch buildings on my left.

I bobbed my head. "Heck yeah."

We'd managed to end up on the north side, in the dark and everything. I patted Thunder's flank. He was sweaty and warm and magnificent. A final gate was just ahead— an iron one with a latch, which was far easier for me. I roused Betsy for the last time and told her our plan, then pointed Thunder toward the stock tank for some long overdue sips of water.

Once we were through the gate, I held Thunder to a walk and we picked our way to the back entrance to the barn. I hopped down, and this time I set Betsy on the ground beside me. "Hold Thunder's reins for me, okay?"

"Okay."

There were two doors: the big one to the center aisle between the stalls, and a small one into a room with a window. The one with the window was the office. I pulled at that door, but it didn't budge. Locked. I had tools though: bobby pins and a gun. The gun was too loud and too much tool for the job, so I pulled out the bobby pin and set to work. The lock didn't yield.

I put the bobby pin away. Guns were good for more than shooting bullets. I pulled it from my waistband and held it by its barrel. I gave the windowpane nearest the door a thwack with the butt of the handle. The glass emitted a high-pitched crack as it splintered inward. I stuck my hand through and tried to reach the doorknob. It was too far away, and the opening was too small for me to crawl through.

But I had one more tool at my disposal. A slim little girl. "Betsy, I'm going to help you crawl through that window, okay? When you get inside, you need to unlock the door. But don't turn on the light."

She nodded, her eyes silver dollars.

I used the gun handle to whack out the rest of the glass, the bits clinging to the window frame. Betsy gave me Thunder's reins, and I dropped them, securing them under my boot. I picked her up and boosted her through the window, shaking with strain as I held her in the center, away from any shards I might have missed.

"Is there somewhere for you to land? Just with your shoes, though. I don't want you to cut your hands."

"Yeah. A table."

I grunted as she swung her legs down, then her weight eased off of me as she stood up. I heard her knocking over God knew what as she climbed down. I stuck my face in after her.

"The door is right there." I pointed to my right.

She turned the knob and it stopped.

"Okay, is there a button you can turn in the door knob? Or is there a latch you can turn above it?"

She peered close. "In the knob." She twisted something.

"Okay, try the door again."

She did, and smiled so brightly it nearly lit up the darkness. The door swung open.

"Great job! Now, can you hold Thunder?"

While she held the horse, I went in the office. On the far side was the open door to the interior of the barn, and on the adjacent wall, a desk. I searched the small room for a phone. Buried under Friday's newspaper on the desk, I found one. I picked it up. It had a dial tone, thank goodness, but I realized I had no idea what Jack's number was. I had his cell phone number programmed into mine, but Tanner and his skinny sidekick had taken that hours ago. I lifted the phone's base and looked for speed dial buttons. Nothing. But there was one that held promise: Redial. I pushed it and held the receiver to my ear.

"Hello?" It was Jack.

I hadn't expected to cry, but a sob broke from my throat.

"Mickey? Is that you?"

"No, Jack, it's Emily, but don't say my name. Say, hey, okay, Mickey."

There was a pause. "Hey, okay, Mickey."

"I'm in the barn office. Some of Paul's men drugged me and locked me in one of their outbuildings, with a little girl. Jack, it's Valentina. I have her. We escaped, and I have so much to tell you, later. But I was scared that they would be there with you."

"Yeah, that's great, but you're right about that," Jack said.

"I can't let them find us. I'm going to take Valentina to the hangar and we'll hide there until you can come for us." I heard voices in the background, voices I recognized. Paul. Tanner. The tall, skinny guy. My hands trembled around the receiver.

"Sounds like the only thing you can do about it," he said.

"Are you okay? Should I call for help?" I asked.

"Yeah, but I'll call the vet myself in the morning. Meet me there?"

"Yes, thank you, Jack, thank you!"

"Be sure to keep an eye on the other horses though. It might be catching."

A breath caught in my throat. "I will."

"See you then."

"Yes, see you then."

As I hung up the phone, I heard the sound of the stall entrance opening in the far end of the barn. I tiptoed out of the office and shut the exterior door as quietly as I could. I sure didn't feel groggy anymore.

"Someone's coming. We have to go." I put my finger to my lips.

Betsy put her finger to hers.

I lifted her onto Thunder's saddle, and heard a noise right behind me. Glass crunching underfoot in the office. I looked from Betsy to the exterior door and grimaced, hesitating, then got the gun from my waistband again and stood by the door with it raised over my head in both hands. When the door opened, a man's head poked out, and I lowered the butt of the pistol with all my strength on the base of his skull.

"Ugh phuh." He landed on his face in the dirt.

"Good enough." I said.

I slipped the pistol home in my skirt and hoisted myself up quickly behind Betsy. So much for avoiding strenuous physical activity for a few days after my surgery. Between riding, roping, and whatever you'd call what I'd just done, I'd be lucky if my uterus didn't fall out on the desert floor before the night was over.

"Is he dead?" Betsy whispered.

"No, sweetie, he'll just sleep for a while," I said into her ear, my voice barely more than a vibration.

I squeezed my heels into Thunder's flanks, and turned him north again. Behind me, I heard the bolt throw in the near end center stall entrance and the doors creak open. There was more than one of them. Spit. I dug my heels into Thunder's flanks and he flew over the ground in the dark.

"Son of a bitch," I heard a voice say. But if he said anything else, we were too far away by then to hear.

***

The echoes of the gunshot shattered the silence of the night, and the cry of an owl followed them. I'd hated to use the gun, but it was the only way I could think of to get past the padlock on the hangar door. I'd just have to count on the wind to cover—or at least disguise—the location of the sound. Luckily, Thunder appeared to be used to guns, because he hadn't even flinched. I slipped the lock off. I pantomimed for Betsy to take her fingers out of her ears, and she did.

"In here, sleepy girl." I pulled the door up and motioned Betsy in-side.

Betsy hesitated. "It's dark."

"Yes, but Thunder and I will be with you. Here, you hold his reins. I have to get the airplane outside, all right?"

I'd decided that if we needed to make a run for it, I'd have the plane ready. If all was well, putting it back in the hangar was no big deal for an old hand like me. And I was sure all would be well, and that we'd just sit here and wait in the dark for a little while, because, by now, Jack would have called the cops and Mickey and who knew whom else. The cavalry would be on the way.

Giving Betsy the job of holding Thunder's reins seemed to help her. The calming impact the horse had on her was amazing, and I sensed a budding horsewoman. She led Thunder in and his hooves clopped on the concrete floor. I heard her whisper to him. "It's okay, Thunder. I'm not scared of the dark, are you?"

I nudged along the base of the wall with my foot looking for the tow bar. My boot clanked metal. I reached down and lifted it. The darn thing wasn't as light as Jack had made it look. I remembered that he'd somehow attached it to one of the plane's three legs. After a few false starts I clamped it around the front one. I crouched down, leaned back, and heaved on the bar. The plane crept forward, inches at a time, but gathered speed. I did it again, over and over, until I had it clear of the building, where I removed the bar and tossed it into the brush.

In the distance, a pair of headlights bounced. Jack. My heart seized. At least I hoped it was Jack. I had no way of knowing if it wasn't. I needed to act fast now, but I didn't know what to do. My thoughts tumbled for slow, agonizing moments, then I pulled them together.

"Okay, Betsy, can you bring Thunder back out? We're going to take one more ride."

Girl and horse appeared in seconds. She was solemn, seeming proud to be in charge of the gorgeous creature.

Now two sets of headlights shot through the darkness toward us, bouncing up and down as both vehicles hit the bumps on the one-lane dirt road out to the airstrip. Two wasn't necessarily bad news. If the first car hadn't been Jack, then the second one surely was. A girl could hope, anyway.

"We're going to ride out to the runway so we can have a good view of my friend Jack as he drives up." I threw Betsy up onto the saddle and checked my waistband for the gun. It was still there. I jammed my foot in the stirrup and threw my leg over. "One more time, Thunder. Yah!"

The powerful hindquarters bunched and Thunder shot forward, down the worn grass leading to the airstrip. I wanted out of gun range in case one of those vehicles or both were the bad guys, but close enough to see what happened at the hangar. I had to gamble that the bad guys were packing shotguns or pistols— there was no way I could get out of range if they'd brought rifles with scopes. I shivered at the thought of night vision capability. However, even if they *did* bring the long-range guns, I had a really quick ride. I patted the horse's neck as he ran.

I pulled Thunder up halfway down the runway and turned us back around. A Suburban was lurching to a stop at the hangar. Jack. Thank God. He looked around, not finding us, so I pulled the pistol out and shot it in the air. He turned toward the sound.

"Jack! Meet me here!" I yelled, as loud as I could.

He must have heard me or sensed me or just flat out guessed right, because he jumped into the plane in three strides. I heard the engine and propeller roar to life. The vehicle on the dirt road was only a few hundred yards away from the hangar. The Skyhawk started out to the runway, and I urged Thunder toward it at full gallop, his hooves pounding faster than the racing heartbeat crashing in my ears. When we were ten yards from the plane, I pulled back on the reins.

"Whoa, boy." I jumped off, pulling Betsy with me, and slapped the horse on the rump. That's when I noticed the brand on his flank: ΣSL. "Get, yah, get."

He took off toward the ranch house at a dead sprint, the stirrups bouncing on his sides. As he ran from the runway, he passed a tall Indian in a gigantic headdress made of wooden stakes, his whole white-painted body naked except for his tall moccasins and black skirt. This was not Stella, no mere girl playing dress-up. A chill ran through me, and the Indian raised a hand in the air. "Mountain Spirit Dancer," I whispered. I closed my eyes and reopened them, and he was gone.

I scooped Betsy into my arms, shaking off the ghostly vision. "You've been very brave, and I need you to do it one more time. Okay? Can you trust me?"

"Yes," she yelled, over the roar of the propeller.

I stood off to the side of the runway. The plane lurched to a stop beside us. Jack threw the door open and I approached it from the rear of the plane—his warning before about the propeller in my mind—and handed Betsy to him, scrambling in after her. I strained to see back the way Jack had come. The chase vehicle careened into the hangar area and barely slowed down as it turned toward the runway. I slammed the door.

"Hold on, this will get rough," Jack said.

I put Betsy in my lap and pulled the seat belt over us both as the little plane gathered speed and leaped and bucked down the runway.

"Do we have enough runway left for takeoff?" I shouted over the engine noise.

Jack didn't answer. He pulled back on the yoke, hard, as I heard shots ping off the skin of the plane.

"Spit!" I screamed.

The front wheels of the plane lifted, dropped back to the sod, and lifted again as headlights bore down on the wing outside my window.

With a final jolting lunge, the Skyhawk lifted off the ground, perilously low, wings dipping from side to side. Betsy turned in my lap and buried her face in my chest with both her arms tight around my neck. She made a noise like an inward scream. I hugged her hard, my face buried in her hair. Three more bullets shook the plane in rapid succession. I held my breath—*please God, please God, please*—and the Skyhawk shucked them off and climbed, up, up, up into the night sky.

Jack leveled the plane off and leaned toward me. "Did you really just scream 'spit?'"

Chapter Twenty-seven

"But I not understand. Why I can't stay with Miss Emily?"

The words came from the sweet voice I'd grown to love like no other in one short day. We were sitting around the kitchen table at my mother's house: Betsy, Jack, Nadine, Wallace, and me. I looked at my mother standing by the refrigerator, and she walked over to Betsy, crouched before the child, and reached for one of her hands before I even knew what she was doing.

"We wish you could, Betsy. You are welcome in our house any-time." She looked at my friends one by one. "All of you are."

I nearly dropped my eyeteeth over that one, and I reached out and grabbed my mother's hand for a squeeze, then said to Betsy, "Wallace is going to find you a family with a mommy and a daddy. A really nice family, maybe with brothers and sisters for you to play with."

So much had come to light in the last twenty-four hours. Not just that this little girl's real name was Elizabet, changed to Valentina when her father had broken the girl and her mother free from Paul's human trafficking operation. Not just that he'd put them on a bus to Amarillo via an Underground Railroad of sorts for illegal immigrants. Not just that this child with no country had Americanized her name to Betsy all by herself. But also that the man who died on Wrong Turn Ranch was her father, Alejandro, beaten by Paul's men.

The police had pieced that together when they rescued the small army of immigrants that Paul had smuggled over the border with his import business. Paul had put the illegals straight to work in the tunnels from his property to a lucrative vein of silver he'd discovered under Mescalero Apache land. At least it was lucrative if the labor was free. Some of the immigrants—the kids and the young women—had a higher value when sold to the kind of people that liked their sex toys untraceable and disposable. A task force was at work now, hunting for the ones they knew about. All we could do for the others was pray.

By the time we figured out that Antonio Rosa was just a pseudo-nym for Alejandro, we weren't even surprised anymore. How the man had scraped together the money to get his wife and daughter to safety, no one quite knew. We did know the ending though: Spike Howard—Paul's private bounty hunter—floating face up in a hotel swimming pool in Amarillo. Sofia's arrest and murder contracted by Paul. Tanner, suspected (at least by me) of murdering Maria Delgado, who police confirmed to be the person who sent me the AmarilloMama email with information that she might have learned while helping Sofia and her daughter. Paul, it seemed, had hired Jack so he could keep tabs on what we were learning. And then there was Betsy, now an orphan in a country that wouldn't claim her as one of their own.

And it was that last part that I was leaving out in explaining things to her. That the U.S. government would have to decide whether Betsy stayed here or went back to Mexico. That I was no shoo-in to keep her, even if the INS let her remain in the U.S.: single, no kids, living with my mother, and months away at best from being approved by the foster care much less the adoption system. I kept my face smooth and smiling, though, because Betsy didn't need to know any of this yet. And she might never know.

She stared at the tabletop. "Will you come see me?"

"Of course I will!" I said. I ignored the pain shooting through my abdomen from overdoing things so dramatically in the previous twenty-four hours and scooted my chair nearer to hers. She launched herself into my arms. I breathed in her sweet smell and let her hair dry my tears.

After a few minutes, Wallace stood and cleared his throat. "Okay, Betsy. Time to go."

"I'm taking you to the Rainbow Room so you can pick out some clothes and a toy. Would you like that?" Nadine took Betsy's hands and pulled her up.

"But I have clothes." I had bought her a new set of Barbie pj's at Walmart on our way here.

Nadine smiled. "So you do. But this will be fun."

I stood up, too, and patted Betsy on the shoulder. "A girl can never have too many clothes."

Betsy turned to me. "But I lost my backpack."

I squatted, eye level to her. "I'm so sorry."

"Mama said never lose it."

"You can get a new one, honey."

She shook her head. "I can't."

"Would you like me to see if I can find it for you?"

She nodded at me, round-eyed. "Yes, please."

I stood up and let Wallace and Nadine lead her away.

Jack and I waved goodbye to them from the front door, not stopping until the Altima taking Betsy away had disappeared from sight. When it had, I broke down completely. Sobs tore through me, and I buried my face in my hands. How could I lose another child in less than a week? I couldn't be thankful that she might go to someone else, maybe even someone in Mexico. Everything in me screamed that she was meant for me, and me for her. God meant this to be, didn't he? Wasn't that why he'd thrown us together, her when she'd lost both her parents, and me when I'd lost everything else? Wasn't it?

Jack put his hand on my shoulder, guiding me down the sidewalk toward his Jeep. I didn't resist, but my body stiffened at his touch. Besides pushing me away, he kept secrets so large that they crowded all the air out of a room, and I had kept one of my own from him, too, that my procedure hadn't been minor, and that it had serious consequences. I could go along with him now, but I knew better than to let him in.

"Come on," he said.

He turned and raised his hand to my mother, who was watching from the living room window.

Mother gave him a thumbs up through the glass.

"Where are we going?"

"You'll see."

We drove in silence from Bushland to downtown Amarillo. He parked on the street outside the Maxor Building.

"You're taking me to work?"

"To the office."

We got out, and I followed him to the elevators. We rode up together in silence and got off on the fifth floor. He unlocked the office and motioned me inside first. The silence bothered me. Something was missing. My heart lurched. Snowflake. In our frenzied escape, we'd left her in New Mexico.

"Snowflake—"

He smiled. "Is just fine. She's having a fun vacation with Uncle Mickey and Aunt Laura."

I nodded, relieved, but then asked the important question. "Why are we here?"

He took me by the arm. "Come on."

We walked back to his office. He positioned me facing the wall of diplomas and pictures.

"What?"

He pointed to the photograph of Geronimo. "Read that."

I stepped forward. He did, too, and put a hand on my shoulder. At first I shrugged and tried to move away from him. He was part of my loss, after all, by his own choice. But he just held on. I quit fighting him.

Then I read the engraved quote aloud. "There is one God looking down on us all. We are all the children of one God."

I couldn't breathe. I had told Jack of the Mountain Spirit Dancer on the runway, of Stella's impersonating one to help the people her dad had enslaved, of Judith's childhood story, of my dreams, and of Betsy's drawing. He hadn't said much at the time, but I realized now that this was his response, and it was, well, the most perfect answer ever, secrets or no secrets between us.

"Jack—"

He pulled me around to face him and wrapped both his arms around me, my arms and hands the only barrier between us. Tears slid down my face again. Faster and faster they came until I gave in to the sobs and let the anguish pour out of me.

They slowed and I found my voice. "They have to let her stay. She doesn't have anyone." I hiccupped and wiped my face with one of my hands. "I want her. I want to adopt her. What do you think, Jack? Do you think I'd be a good mother to her?"

Jack leaned back and held me in front of him with one hand on each of my shoulders. That dangerous dimple pulled the left corner of his mouth into his even more dangerous half smile, and his eyebrow lifted along with them. "Why wouldn't they let you give a little Heaven to Betsy when you're represented by the best family and immigration lawyer in a two-state area?"

For once, I didn't mind that Jack hadn't really answered my question.

I smiled and lifted my chin three degrees, forcing the river of tears into a new tributary across my face. "With the best criminal law practice manager on the fifth floor of the Maxor Building."

He lifted the picture from the wall and handed it to me, and something like hope flickered in my chest.

The End

Now that you've finished *Heaven to Betsy*, won't you please consider writing an honest review and leaving it on the online sales site of your choice and/or Goodreads? Reviews are the best way readers discover great new books. I would truly appreciate it. Be sure to watch for *Earth to Emily*, the second book in the *Emily* series, and *Hell to Pay*, the third, coming soon. — Pamela

Acknowledgments

Once upon a time a bright-eyed Amarillo girl took a course on persuasive speaking at Texas A&M University. She wrote and delivered an assigned speech in support of the Immigration Reform and Control Act of 1986. A class member of Mexican descent argued passionately against IRCA and the girl's points, using personal, family examples and pointing out, correctly, that all Americans descend from immigrants, except Native Americans. The girl, appearing calm and cool on the outside, debated with her classmate and walked out with an A+ as her grade. But the girl never forgot that exchange and the shame she covered up in that moment, as she was confronted with the ease and privilege in her own life. And for failing to see the perspective of her classmate's family, even though she never knew their names. The girl—me— grew the heck up, and eventually she wrote this book.

Thank you to my classmate at Texas A&M, for your passion, courage, and eloquence in speaking your truth.

Thanks to my husband, Eric, for brainstorming the *Emily* books with me over many miles hiked in Pedernales Falls State Park and on our property in Nowheresville, and during 11,000+ miles logged in the Bookmobile. Eric gets an extra helping of thanks for plotting, critiquing, editing, listening, holding, encouraging, supporting, browbeating, and playing miscellaneous other roles, some of which aren't appropriate for publication.

To each and every blessed one of you who have read, reviewed, rated, and emailed/Facebooked/Tweeted/commented about the *Katie & Annalise* and *Michele* books, I appreciate you more than I can say. It is the readers who move mountains for me, and for other authors, and I humbly ask for the honor of your honest reviews and recommendations.

Blessings and hugs to my friends Stephanie, Betsy, and Walt, who inspired me to write about my own hometown.

Editing credits go to Rhonda Erb, Sara Kocek, and Emily Kristin Anderson. The beta readers and critique partners who enthusiastically devote their time—gratis—to help us rid my books of flaws blow me away. The special love this time goes to Patty, Gay, Melissa, Nandita, Dina, Stephanie, Ginger, Ridgely, Melissa, Terry, Rebecca, Susie, and Ken. Thanks to Walt for expert assistance, as well.

Kisses to princess of the universe, Heidi Dorey, for fantastic cover art. Thanks for evolving with us as we evolve with the world of publishing. Credit for the photo on the cover goes to Beau and Shirlene Baer. Isn't it amazing?

Finally, my eternal gratitude to Eric and our kids for teaching me the ways of blended household love.

About the Author

Pamela Fagan Hutchins holds nothing back and writes award-winning and best-selling mysteries and hilarious nonfiction from Nowheresville, Texas, where she lives with her household hunks—husband, Eric, and their one-eyed Boston terrier, Petey—plus three rescue dogs, a herd of goats, a coupla cows, a flock of turkeys, and a peacock. She is the author of many books, including *Saving Grace, Leaving Annalise, Finding Harmony, Going for Kona, Heaven to Betsy, Earth to Emily, How To Screw Up Your Kids, Hot Flashes and Half Ironmans,* and *What Kind of Loser Indie Publishes?* to name just a few. In 2014, just two years after publication of her first book, the *Houston Press* named her as one of the Top 10 Houston Authors.

Pamela spends her non-writing time as the Chair of the Board of the Houston Writers Guild, a writing coach, a workplace investigator, and as an employment attorney and human resources professional, and she is the co-founder of a human resources consulting company. You can often find her with her husband—and a few grown kids from their blended brood of five—hiking, running, bicycling, and enjoying the great outdoors.

If you'd like Pamela to speak to your book club, women's club, or writers group, by Skype or in person, shoot her an email. She's very likely to say yes.

You can buy Pamela's e-books, audiobooks, and paperbacks at most online retailers. You can also get her paperbacks from "brick and mortar" stores. If you want a signed copy, contact SkipJack Publishing: http://SkipJackPublishing.com. If your bookstore or library doesn't carry a book you want, by Pamela or any other author, ask them to order it for you.

You can connect with Pamela all over creation, and you should:
Website http://pamelahutchins.com
Email pamela@pamelahutchins.com
New releases newsletter http://eepurl.com/iITR
Facebook http://facebook.com/pamela.fagan.hutchins.author
Twitter http://twitter.com/pameloth
Goodreads http://goodreads.com/pamelafaganhutchins
LinkedIn http://linkedin.com/in/pamelahutchins

Books by the Author

Fiction from SkipJack Publishing:
Saving Grace (Katie & Annalis, #1)
Leaving Annalise (Katie & Annalise #2)
Finding Harmony (Katie & Annalise #3)
The Jumbie House (Katie & Annalise Outtake)
Going for Kona (Michele #1)
Heaven to Betsy (Emily #1)
Earth to Emily (Emily #2)
Hell to Pay (Emily #3), coming 2016

Nonfiction from SkipJack Publishing:
The Clark Kent Chronicles: A Mother's Tale Of Life
With Her ADHD/Asperger's Son
Hot Flashes and Half Ironmans: Middle-Aged Endurance
Athletics Meets the Hormonally Challenged
How to Screw Up Your Kids: Blended Families, Blendered Style
How to Screw Up Your Marriage: Do-Over Tips for First-Time Failures
Puppalicious and Beyond: Life Outside The Center Of The Universe
What Kind of Loser Indie Publishes, and How Can I Be One, Too?

Other Books by the Author:
Eve's Requiem (anthology), Spider Road Press
OMG - That Woman! (anthology), Aakenbaaken & Kent
Ghosts (anthology), Aakenbaaken & Kent
Easy to Love, But Hard to Raise (2012) and *Easy to Love, But Hard to Teach* (coming soon) (anthologies), DRT Press, edited by Kay Marner & Adrienne Ehlert Bashista

Audiobook versions of the author's books are available on Audible, iTunes, and Amazon.

Other Books from SkipJack Publishing

The Closing, by Ken Oder
Old Wounds to the Heart, by Ken Oder
Deadly Thyme, by R. L. Nolen
The Dry, by Rebecca Nolen
Tides of Possibility, edited by K.J. Russell
Tides of Impossibility,
edited by K.J. Russell and C. Stuart Hardwick
My Dream of Freedom: From Holocaust to My Beloved America,
by Helen Colin

9 781939 889256